THE

SEVEN MOONS OF

MAALI ALMEIDA

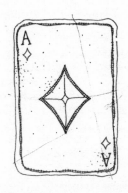

First published in Great Britain in 2022 by
Sort Of Books
PO Box 18678, London NW3 2FL
www.sortof.co.uk

Distributed by
Profile Books, 29 Cloth Fair, Barbican, London EC1A 7JQ.

7 9 10 8 6

Typeset in Minion Pro to a design by Henry Iles.

A CIP catalogue record for this book is available from the
British Library.

ISBN 978-1908745903 (HB)
ISBN 978-1914502064 (PB)
eIBSN 978-1908745910

Printed and bound in Great Britain by Clays Ltd, Elcograf S.p.A.

THE
SEVEN MOONS OF
MAALI ALMEIDA

Shehan Karunatilaka

Sort Of
BOOKS

Acknowledgements

Aadhil Aziz, Aftab Aziz, Amrit Dayananda, Andi Schubert,
ARL Wijesekera, Arosha Perera, Arun Welandawe-Prematileke,
ASH Smyth, Chanaka de Silva, Chiki Sarkar, Chula Karunatilaka,
Cormac McCarthy, David Blacker, Daya Pathirana,
Deshan Tennekoon, Diresh Thevanayagam, Diya Kar,
Douglas Adams, Erid Perera, Ernest Ley, Faiza Sultan Khan,
George Saunders, Haw Par Villa, Imal Desa, Jeet Thayil,
Jehan Mendis, Kurt Vonnegut, Lakshman Nadaraja, Ledig House,
Mark Ellingham, Marissa Jansz, Meru Gokhole, Michael Meyler,
Nandadeva Wijesekera, Natasha Ginwala, Naresh Ratwatte,
Nigel de Zilwa, Pakiasothy Sarvanamuttu, Patsy de Silva,
Philips Hue, Piers Eccleston, Prasad Pereira, Rajan Hoole,
Rajeeve Bernard, Rajini Thiranagama, Ramya Chamalie Jirasinghe,
Ravin Fernando, Richard de Zoysa, Rohan Gunaratna,
Rohitha Perera, Roshan de Silva, Russell Tennekoon,
Shanaka Amarasinghe, Smriti Daniel, Stanley Greene,
Stefan Andre Joachim, Steve de la Zilwa, Stephen Champion,
Sunitha Tennekoon, Tracy Holsinger, Victor Ivan,
William McGowan, www.existentialcomics.com,
www.iam.lk, www.pinterest.com.

Special thanks: Natania Jansz, Eranga Tennekoon,
Lalith Karunatilaka, Kanishka Gupta, Manasi Subramaniam,
David Godwin. Andrew Fidel Fernando, Govind Dhar,
Wendy Holsinger, Jan Ramesh de Schoning, Mohammed Hanif.

Drawings by Lalith Karunatilaka.

For Chula,
Eranga
and Luca

THE
SEVEN MOONS OF
MAALI ALMEIDA

There are only two gods worth worshipping.
Chance and electricity.

FIRST MOON

Father, forgive them,
for I will never.

Richard de Zoysa
'Good Friday 1975'

Answers

You wake up with the answer to the question that everyone asks. The answer is Yes, and the answer is Just Like Here But Worse. That's all the insight you'll ever get. So you might as well go back to sleep.

You were born without a heartbeat and kept alive in an incubator. And, even as a foetus out of water, you knew what the Buddha sat under trees to discover. It is better to not be reborn. Better to never bother. Should have followed your gut and croaked in the box you were born into. But you didn't.

So you quit each game they made you play. Two weeks of chess, a month in Cub Scouts, three minutes in rugger. You left school with a hatred of teams and games and morons who valued them. You quit art class and insurance-selling and masters' degrees. Each a game that you couldn't be arsed playing. You dumped everyone who ever saw you naked. Abandoned every cause you ever fought for. And did many things you can't tell anyone about.

If you had a business card, this is what it would say.

Maali Almeida
Photographer. Gambler. Slut.

If you had a gravestone, it would say:

Malinda Albert Kabalana
1955–1990

But you have neither. And you have no more chips left at this table. And you now know what others do not. You have the answer to the following questions. Is there life after death? What's it like?

SOON YOU WILL WAKE

It started ages ago, a thousand centuries ago, but let's skip all those yesterdays and begin last Tuesday. It is a day you wake up hungover and empty of thought, which is true of most days. You wake up in an endless waiting room. You look around and it's a dream and, for once, you know it's a dream and you're happy to wait it out. All things pass, especially dreams.

You are wearing a safari jacket and faded jeans and cannot remember how you got here. You wear one shoe and have three chains and a camera around your neck. The camera is your trusty Nikon 3ST, though its lens is smashed and its casing is cracked. You look through the viewfinder and all you see is mud. Time to wake up, Maali boy. You pinch yourself and it hurts, less like a short stab and more like the hollow ache of an insult.

You know what it's like to not trust your own mind. That LSD trip at the Smoking Rock Circus in 1973, hugging an araliya tree in Viharamahadevi Park for three hours. The ninety-hour poker marathon, where you won seventeen lakhs and then lost fifteen of them. Your first shelling in Mullaitivu 1984, stuffed in a bunker of terrified parents and screaming children. Waking in hospital, aged nineteen, not remembering your Amma's face or how much you loathed it.

You are in a queue, shouting at a woman in a white sari seated behind a fibreglass counter. Who hasn't been furious at women behind counters before? Certainly not you. Most Lankans are silent seethers, but you like to complain at the top of your lungs.

'Not saying your fault. Not saying my fault. But mistakes happen, no? Especially in government offices. What to do?'

'This is not a government office.'

'I don't care, Aunty. I'm just saying, I can't be here, I have photos to share. I'm in a committed relationship.'

'I am not your Aunty.'

You look around. Behind you, a queue weaves around pillars and snakes along the walls. The air is foggy, though no one appears to be exhaling smoke or carbon dioxide. It looks like a car park with no cars, or a market space with nothing to sell. The ceiling is high and held by concrete pylons placed at irregular intervals across a sprawling yard. What appear to be large lift doors mark the far end and human shapes crowd in and out of them.

Even close up, the figures look blurry-edged with talcum skin and have eyes that blaze in colours not customary for brown folk. Some are dressed in hospital smocks; some have dried blood on their clothes; some are missing limbs. All are shouting at the woman in white. She seems to be having conversations with each of you at the same time. Maybe everyone is asking the same questions. If you were a betting man (which you are), you'd take 5/8 on this being a hallucination, most likely induced by Jaki's silly pills.

The woman opens a large register. She looks you up and down with neither interest nor scorn. 'First must confirm details. Name?'

'Malinda Albert Kabalana.'

'One syllable, please.'

'Maali.'

'You know what a syllable is?'

'Maal.'

'Thank you. Religion?'

'None.'

'How silly. Cause of death?'

'Don't remember.'

'Time since death?'

'Don't know.'

'Aiyo.'

The swarm of souls presses closer, berating and badgering the woman in white. You gaze upon the pallid faces, sunken eyes in broken heads, squinted in rage and pain and confusion. The pupils are in shades of bruises and scabs. Scrambled browns, blues and greens – all of which disregard you. You have lived in refugee camps, visited street markets at noon, and fallen asleep at packed casinos. The heave of humanity is never picturesque. This heave throngs towards you and heaves you away from the counter.

Lankans can't queue. Unless you define a queue as an amorphous curve with multiple entry points. This appears to be a gathering point for those with questions about their death. There are multiple counters and irate customers clamour over grills to shout abuse at the few behind the bars. The afterlife is a tax office and everyone wants their rebate.

You are pushed to one side by an Amma with a young child on her hip. The child stares at you as if you have smashed its favourite toy. The mother's hair is caked in blood which stains her dress and smears her face. 'What about our Madura? What has happened to him? He was in the back seat with us. He saw the bus before the driver did."

'How many times to tell madam? Your son is still living. Don't worry, be happy.'

This comes from the man from the other counter, who wears a white smock and an Afro and looks like Moses from the big book. His voice rumbles like the ocean and his eyes are the pale yellow of beaten eggs. He repeats the title of last year's most annoying song and then opens a ledger book of his own.

You take another picture, which is what you do when you don't know what else to. You attempt to capture this car park of chaos, but all you see are cracks in the lens.

It is easy to tell who is staff and who isn't. The former carry register books and stand around smiling; the latter look unhinged. They pace, then stop, then stare into space. Some roll their heads and wail. The staff do not look directly at anything, especially the souls they are counselling.

Now would be an excellent time to wake up and forget. You rarely remember your dreams and, whatever this is, the chance of it sticking is less than a flush or a full house. You won't remember being here any more than you remember learning to walk. You've taken Jaki's silly pills and this is just a trippy dream. What else could it be?

And then you notice a figure leaning against a sign in the corner, dressed in what seems to be a black garbage bag, who looks to be neither staff nor customer. The figure surveys the crowd and its green eyes shine like a cat's under headlights. They fall upon you and linger for longer than they should. The head nods and the eyes do not break gaze.

Above the figure, a sign reads:

DO NOT VISIT CEMETERIES
Next to it is a notice with an arrow:

→ EAR CHECKS AT LEVEL FORTY-TWO
You turn back to the woman behind the counter and you try again. 'This is a mistake. I don't eat meat. I only smoke five a day.' The woman seems familiar to you, as perhaps your lies are to her. For a moment, the jostling seems to stop. For a moment, it feels like you are all there is.

'Aiyo! Every excuse I have heard. No one wants to go, not even the suicides. You think I wanted to die? My daughters were eight and ten when they shot me. What to do? Complaining won't help. Be patient and wait your turn. Forgive what you can. We are short-staffed and looking for volunteers.'

She looks up and raises her voice at the queue.

'You all have seven moons.'

'What's a moon?' asks a girl with a snapped neck. She holds the hand of a boy with a cracked skull.

'Seven moons is seven nights. Seven sunsets. A week. More than enough time.'

'Thought a moon was a month?'

'The moon is always up there, even when you can't see it. You think it stops circling the earth, just because your breath stops?'

You understand none of this. So you try another approach. 'Look at this crowd. Must be all the killing up north. Tigers and Army killing civilians. Indian peacekeepers starting wars.'

You look around to see no one listening to you. The eyes continue to ignore you and glisten in their blue-green hues. You look around for the figure in black, but it has vanished. 'Not just up north. Down here also. Government is fighting the JVP and bodies are piling high. I fully get it. You must be busy these days. I understand.'

'These days?' The woman in white scowls and shakes her head. 'There's a corpse every second. Sometimes two. Did you get your ears checked?'

'My hearing is fine. I take photos. I bear witness to crimes that no one else sees. I am needed.'

'That woman has children to feed. That man has hospitals to run. You have photos? Sha! How impressive.'

'These are not holiday snaps. These are photos that will bring down governments. Photos that could stop wars.'

She makes a face at you. The chain around her neck is an Egyptian cross, once worn by a boy who loved you more than you loved him. She fiddles with it and screws up her nose.

It is only then that you recognise her. Her toothpaste ad smile had been all over the newspapers for much of 1989. The university lecturer slain by Tamil extremists for the crime of being a Tamil moderate.

'I know you. You are Dr Ranee Sridharan. Couldn't make you out without your loudspeaker. Your articles on the Tamil Tigers were superb. But you used my photos without asking.'

The thing that makes you most Sri Lankan is not your father's surname or the holy place where you kneel, nor the smile you plaster on your face to hide your fears. It is the knowing of other Lankans and the knowing of those Lankans' Lankans. There are aunties, if given a surname and a school, who can pinpoint any Lankan to the nearest cousin. You have moved in circles that overlapped and many that stayed shut. You were cursed with the gift of never forgetting a name, a face, or a sequence of cards.

'I was sad when they got you. Truly. When was it? '87? You know, I met a Tiger with the Mahatiya faction. Said he organised your hit.'

Dr Ranee looks up from her book, she gives a weary smile, and then shrugs. Her pupils are clouded white, as if stuffed with milky cataracts.

'You need to get your ears checked. Your ears have patterns as personal as your fingerprints. The folds show past traumas, the lobes reveal sins, the cartilage hides guilt. All things that prevent you from entering The Light.'

'What's The Light?'

'The short answer is Whatever You Need It To Be. The long answer is, I don't have time for the long answer.'

She passes you an ola leaf. A dried palm leaf, said to have been used by seven rishis three thousand years ago to write the fortunes of everyone who would ever live. Angular incisions would rip the grainy texture, so South Asian scribes developed sensuous curves on lettering to stop the leaf from tearing.

'Did you take photos of 1983?'

'I did indeed. What's this?'

The ola leaf has the same words written in all three languages. Circular Sinhala, angular Tamil, scribbled English and not a rip in sight.

EARS———————————————

DEATH———————————————

SINS————————————————

MOONS ——————————————

STAMPED BY—————————————

'Get your ears checked, your deaths counted, your sins coded and your moons registered at Level Forty-Two. And get it stamped by a Helper. She closes her book and, with that, the conversation. You are replaced at the front of the queue by a man in bandages who will not stop coughing.

You turn and face the people behind you. You raise your hands like a prophet. Always the show off, you were. Always loud, except when you weren't.

'None of you ghouls exist! You are phantoms from my snoring brain. I have swallowed Jaki's silly pills. This is hallucination. There is no damn life after death. If I close my eyes, you will vanish like farts!'

They pay as much attention to you as Mr Reagan does to The Maldives. Neither the car crash victims, the abductees, the old folk in hospital gowns, nor the late lamented Dr Ranee Sridharan, notice your outburst.

The chances of finding a pearl in an oyster are 1 in 12,000. The chances of being hit by lightning are 1 in 700,000. The odds of the soul surviving the body's death are one in nothing, one in nada, one in zilch. You must be asleep, of this you are certain. Soon you will wake.

And then you have this terrible thought. More terrible than this savage isle, this godless planet, this dying sun, and this snoring galaxy. What if, all this while, asleep is what you have been? And what if, from this moment forth, you, Malinda Almeida, photographer, gambler, slut, never get to close your eyes ever again?

You follow a throng stumbling through the corridor. A man walks on broken legs, a lady hides a face of bruises. Many seem dressed for a wedding, because that's how undertakers decorate corpses. But many others are dressed in rags and confusion. You look down and all you see is a pair of hands that do not belong to you. You wish to inspect the colour of your eyes and the face you are wearing. You wonder if the lifts have mirrors. It turns out, they barely have walls. One by one, the souls enter the empty shaft and fly up like bubbles in water.

This is absurd. Even the Bank of Ceylon doesn't have Forty-Two floors.

'What's on the other floors?' you ask anyone with ears, checked or otherwise.

'Rooms, corridors, windows, doors, the usual,' says a particularly helpful Helper.

'Accounting and Finance,' says a broken old man leaning on a walking stick. 'A racket like this won't fund itself.'

'It's all the same,' wails the dead woman with the dead baby. 'Every universe. Every life. Same old. Same old scene.'

You rarely dream, let alone have nightmares. You float along the edge of the shaft and something pushes you. You scream like a horror movie damsel as the wind takes you skywards. You are startled by the figure in black floating behind you. Its cloak of black garbage bags fluttering in a feral wind. He watches as you ascend the shaft and bows as you float away.

You try another question and ask what The Light is. But all you get are shrugs and insults. A frightened child calls you a ponnaya, an insult which alleges both homosexuality and impotence, and you will plead guilty to only one of these charges. You ask the staff about The Light and get a different answer each time. Some say heaven, some say rebirth, some say oblivion. Some, like Dr Ranee, say whatever. The options hold little appeal for you, aside from maybe the latter.

At Level Forty-Two is a sign with one word on it.

CLOSED

Figures float through this vast corridor, not noticing the walls until they bump into them. There is a reception with no one in it. And a line of red doors, each one obeying the sign by staying shut.

At the centre of the hall stands the figure in black, uninterested in the aimless wanderers who collide around him. He stares at you and beckons you over. His eyes track you as you float away; this time they glint in yellow.

The universe yawns in the time it takes for you to get back to Dr Ranee's counter. Outside, the night fills with winds and whispers. In this place, there are only counters and confusions.

Dr Ranee notices you and shakes her head. 'We need more Helpers. Less complainers. Everyone is doing their best.'

She looks at you. 'Except for those who aren't.'

You wait for her to finish her thought, but it appears she already has. She pulls a megaphone from under her desk. Now this is the Dr Ranee you remember, shouting at campuses when TV cameras were around.

'Please do not get lost. If you haven't had an Ear Check, don't come here. Level Forty-Two will be open tomorrow. Come back then. Remember you have seven moons. You must reach The Light before your last one rises.'

You are about to launch a rant of expletives when you notice it once more, the figure wrapped in black garbage, beckoning with both hands. Its eyes flicker like candles and it is holding what looks like your missing sandal. Dr Ranee follows your gaze and drops her smile.

'Get that thing out of here. Maal, where are you going?'

Two men in white leap over their counters and sprint towards the figure in black. The man with the Afro who looks like Moses raises his arms and bellows in a language you have never heard spoken. Next to him is a muscleman in a white robe who sprints towards you.

You fade back into the crowd, drift between the broken people with blood on their breath and reach the figure holding your footwear.

You float towards it, this garbage bag grim reaper, like you floated towards many things you shouldn't have. Casinos, war zones and beautiful men. You hear Dr Ranee screeching but you ignore her like you did your Amma right after Dada left.

The figure smirks with teeth as yellow as its eyes.

'Sir, let us get out of this place. It is a brainwashing bureaucracy. Like every other building in this oppressive state.'

The hooded figure stands with its face to yours. Though the face is in the shadow, you see it is a boy, younger than you once were. One eye is yellow and the other looks green, and you are unsure what silly pills could bring on a hallucination like this. The voice appears to be nursing a sore throat.

'I know your name is Maali-Sir. Don't waste your time here. And please stay away from The Light.'

You follow him to the lift shaft, but this time you descend. The angry falsetto of Dr Ranee and the baritone bellows of Moses and He-Man become distant echoes.

'Even the afterlife is designed to keep the masses stupid,' says the boy. 'They make you forget your life and push you towards some light. All bourgeois tools of the oppressor. They tell you that injustice is part of some grand plan. And that's what keeps you from rising against it.'

When you reach the bottom and exit the building, the wind hits you from all sides. Outside the trees groan, the rubbish dumps belch and the buses secrete black smoke. Shadows crawl across the streets and Colombo at dawn turns its face away.

'Where did you find my sandal?'

'Same place I saw your body. You want it back?'

'Not really.'

'I meant your life. Not the sandal.'

'I know.'

The words come easily to you even though you have not had time to consider them. Do you want to see your body? Do you want your life back? Or the real question which you really should be pondering. How the hell did you get here?

You remember nothing, not pain, not surprise, not the last breath, nor where you took it. And, even though you have no desire to be hurt again or to breathe once more, you choose to follow the figure in black.

THE BOX UNDER THE BED

You were born before Elvis had his first hit. And died before Freddie had his last. In the interim, you have shot thousands. You have photos of the government Minister who looked on while the savages of '83 torched Tamil homes and slaughtered the occupants. You have portraits of disappeared journalists and vanished activists, bound and gagged and dead in custody. You have grainy yet identifiable snaps of an army major, a Tiger colonel, and a British arms dealer at the same table, sharing a jug of king coconut.

You have the killers of actor and heartthrob Vijaya and the wreckage of Upali's plane on film. You have these images in a white shoe box hidden with old records by Elvis and Freddie, the King and Queen. Under a bed that your Amma's cook shares with your Dada's driver. If you could, you would make a thousand copies of each photo and paste them all over Colombo. Perhaps you still can.

CHAT WITH DEAD ATHEIST (1986)

You have seen dead bodies, more than your fair share, and you always knew where the souls had gone. The same place the flame goes when you snuff it, the same place a word goes when you say it. The mother and daughter buried under bricks in Kilinochchi, the ten students burned on tyres in Malabe, the planter tied to a tree with his entrails. None of them went anywhere. They were, and then they were not. Just like all of us won't be when our candles run out of wick.

The wind takes you and the world swings by at the speed of a rickshaw, faces and figures flutter past, some less terrified than others, most with feet that don't touch the ground. You have one response for those who believe Colombo to be overcrowded: wait till you see it with ghosts.

'Are you following that thing?'

It is an old man with a hook for a nose and marbles for eyes, who appears to be travelling the same wind. His head is not between his shoulders as heads prefer to be. It is held with both hands in front of his stomach like a rugger ball.

'I wouldn't, son. Unless you want to be stuck here.'

As you pass the heads of trees and the cheeks of buildings, he tells you he has been in the In Between for over a thousand moons.

'What's the In Between?' you ask.

He says he was a teacher at Carey College who used to cycle from Kotahena to Borella every day. His clothing is tattered and stained with blood.

'Were you in a car crash?' you say.

'No need to be rude.'

He says all ghosts wear clothing from previous lives and that it is better than being naked.

'Those leaflets at the counter say you wear your sins or your traumas or your guilt. One thing I've learned in a thousand moons: if it smells like bullshit, don't swallow it.'

He recognises you from political rallies and you say you did not attend political rallies and he calls you a liar. He says that you photographed his headless corpse, but didn't include his name in the caption. That the papers called it a political murder when it wasn't. 'Most political murders have nothing to do with politics,' he says.

The thing with the hood stands on a rooftop and watches you chatting. You do not see it jump the wind, though it always appears to be a few steps before you.

'If you follow that thing, you're a bloody fool.'

You look at the blood on his shirt and fail to think of a wisecrack.

'It will make you promises and it will not keep them.'

Sounds like every boy I ever kissed, you think, but do not say.

'That thing promised to hunt down my killer for me. My killer just bought a house with my money. That's another story.'

Down There are people who look like ants, if ants were clumsy and unresourceful. You hang onto the wind as dead Colombo air blows at your feet.

The head smirks at you from the crook of the elbow.

'Were you a believer?'

'Only in stupid things.'

'Like heaven?'

'Sometimes.'

'I don't believe you.'

You shrug.

'I bet you thought the afterlife was like an Air Lanka commercial? With golden beaches and elephants in costumes and tea pluckers grinning for the camera.'

He is right to think you a liar:

a) You weren't a believer.

b) You do remember him.

The school teacher that ran for provincial council, whose gangster brother had him shot and won the election in his stead. There wasn't much left of his face when you photographed him, but recognise him you do.

'Did you believe in an afterlife of milk and kithul honey and virgins sucking you off? Or an afterlife of mysteries and riddles and questions that shouldn't be asked.'

'Do you know why deluded men crave virgins?' You repeat one of DD's stupid theories and rush to the punchline. 'Because a virgin can't know how bad in the bed you are.'

The wind carries you in swirls over parapets and bus tops. The world has fuzzy edges, colours where there shouldn't be any, and spirits wherever you look. Up ahead, the figure in the hood skims over the face of the Beira and lands like a crow on the headstone at the temple's entrance. It depicts an elephant chasing a cow chasing a peacock across the circle of time. His garbage bags flap like wings against the concrete carving. He stands with arms folded and eyes squarely upon you. He is making a gesture that you cannot read.

Your travel companion watches you watch the figure. He places his head on his collarbone. The hooded figure turns its back on you and drops towards the shores of the Beira Lake. Amber flecks of sunrise turn the surface into a mirror. The bending branches and office buildings check their reflections in the ripples.

The old man sighs. 'Or maybe you pictured a torture chamber of an afterlife? A civilian-caught-between-government-bombs-and-Tiger-mines afterlife? A picked-up-and-beaten-with-sticks-because-of-your-surname afterlife? Hell is all around us and is in session as we speak.'

He places his head on his shoulder and swivels it like a periscope. 'I, of course, believed in nothing. In an afterlife that never was, in an afterlife that wasn't in a service area. Why should there be anything? Why not nothing? Oblivion made more sense than heaven or rebirth or living the same sad shit over and over.' He tilts the head towards you. 'What I didn't expect was this bloody mess.'

'Who's the hoodlum?'

'JVP communist scum. Dead and still talking revolution. Another killer that got killed. You shouldn't be talking to it. You should go and find your Light and get out of here while you can. It's what I should've done.'

The Dead Atheist looks out to the Beira Lake as if pondering afterlives and things undone.

'What have you done for a thousand moons?'

'I've gone to every holy house to watch people pray.'

'Why?'

'I enjoy how stupid they look.'

'That doesn't sound bad.'

'Seven moons is shorter than you think,' he says. 'If you stop following that thing, then it will stop following you. If you stay here, you will run out of things to do.'

You line up the headless man with your camera and take a snap of him with the lake and the rising sun at his back. His voice evaporates like good intentions do. You look around and see neither him nor the thing in the hood. All you see are three bodies lying on the banks of that muddy lake.

BEIRA LAKE

On Tuesday 4 December 1989, a few minutes after 4 a.m., two men in sarongs dump four bodies in the Beira Lake. It is not the first time either of them have done this, or done it drunk, or done it at this hour.

On this day, the Beira Lake smells like a powerful deity has squatted over it, emptied its bowels in its waters, and forgotten to flush. The men get plastered on stolen arrack, not because years of dumping bodies have broken their nerve or grieved their conscience, but because breathing the stench sober feels like inhaling a public urinal.

The first body is wrapped in rubbish bags. It wears a safari jacket with five large pockets filled with bricks. Stylishly accessorised with one sandal, three chains and a camera around the neck. The men use coir rope to tie bricks to the battered torso. They think they know knots, despite being neither sailors nor Cub Scouts.

They hurl the body with the grace of shotputters, and it lands with a splash that barely clears the distance of a schoolyard jump. The first bottle of arrack robs them of disgust; the second takes away their motor skills. The knots give way as soon as the body hits the warmth of the Beira and the bricks sink into the black waters.

They try the same with the other corpses. One sinks and one floats. Columns of stone Buddhas from the floating temple stare down at the buoyant dead with neither interest nor alarm. Monitor lizards slither past the corpses during their morning dip. River birds argue over who gets to eat the eyes.

The Beira Lake used to be three times this size and was used to hide all manners of vice. Much lies buried in the centuries since the Portuguese merchant Lopo de Brito diverted the Kelani river to thwart a marauding King Vijayabahu. It used to stretch through Panadura, out by Colombo's backside, to join Bolgoda Lake. The Dutch seized it and squeezed it into canals. The English purloined it and put it to work. Corpses of traders, sailors, prostitutes, gangsters and innocents lie rotting in its belly. And every decade it lets out a belch that covers Slave Island in its rancid breath.

'You fool,' burps Balal Ajith. 'You didn't put tape?'

'I tied only. You said hurry. What time for tape?' says Kottu Nihal.

'Those knots were looser than your Amma's redda.'

'What you say?'

'Just there. Navam Mawatha, that hardware store sells masking tape. Would've taken five minutes.'

'It's not open.'

'So go open it.'

'Aiyo I can't. The abhithiyas are waking. Can't be punching priests early morning.'

Balal Ajith takes off his T-shirt and tucks the front of his sarong between his legs and over his arse crack. He lets out another burp. Curried cow stomach exits Balal Ajith's gut and then his throat. He relives the taste of babath marinated in old arrack.

'This is why, Kottu Aiya, you and me need to put a swim.'

The body has also become shirtless, its ribs cave-in like a broken coconut. You try not to look at the battered bones, the flesh in the beard, or the chunks missing from the face.

But you do. You know these animals. They work at the casino and are paid to beat those who beat the house and collect from those the house has beaten. You didn't know that they worked as garbage men. 'Kunu kaaraya' is a euphemism for those who dispose of bodies that can't get death certificates. A garbage man is cheaper to hire than a dirty magistrate.

Since Lanka's 1987 peace accord with India, garbage men have been in high demand. The government forces, the eastern separatists, the southern anarchists and the northern peacekeepers are all prolific producers of corpses.

Kottu Nihal and Balal Ajith got their nicknames from Welikada Prison, both owing to the culinary arts. Kottu Nihal worked in the kitchen, where he specialised in shredding roti to make kottu. The cooking utensils he smuggled into the compound effectively made him the prison arms dealer. He earned his stripes by pointing the sharp ends of two kottu plates at a prison bully's throat. Balal Ajith was known to boil cats or balalas and serve them as curry in exchange for cigarettes.

You stand on the corpse as if it were a surfboard. Did you ever surf in your former life? Looks like you had the build for it. What a fabulous-looking man you were. What a stupid waste. You sob like you never did when Dada left your Amma, and then you stop.

You don't disagree with the Headless Atheist. For thirty-four years, you passionately believed in nothing. Not the best explanation for the pandemonium, just the only plausible one. You thought you were smarter than the sheep that flocked to temples and mosques and churches, and now it appears that the sheep made the smarter bet.

Over a short and useless existence, you examined evidence and drew conclusions. We are a flicker of light between two long sleeps. Forget the fairy tales of gods and hells and previous births. Believe in odds and in fairness and in stacking decks that are already stacked, in playing your hand as best you can for as long as you can. You were led to believe that death was sweet oblivion and you were wrong on both counts.

The only god you ever believed in was a low-caste yaka called Narada. Narada yaka's peculiar job description was to think up problems for humanity. If he failed, his head exploded. He received a standard immortality package and an omniscience allowance. Though you suspect his main motivation was keeping his skull intact.

Evil is not what we should fear. Creatures with power acting in their own interest: that is what should make us shudder.

How else to explain the world's madness? If there's a heavenly father, he must be like your father: absent, lazy and possibly evil. For atheists there are only moral choices. Accept that we are alone and strive to create heaven on earth. Or accept that no one's watching and do whatever the hell you like. The latter is by far easier.

So here you are, watching men who burned Tamil homes in 1983 trying to drown your corpse. So much for sweet oblivion and dreamless sleep. You are doomed to stay awake. Doomed to look but never touch, to witness but never record. To be the impotent homo, the ponnaya, as the dead kid at the counter just called you.

The figure in the hood emerges from the shadow. It floats on wind and perches cross-legged next to the stone Buddhas. It does not move its lips when it speaks, but sits on a shadow and plants words in your head; its voice is a serpent clearing its throat. 'Sorry for your loss, Maali-Sir. Must be a great shock. You must meditate on your body.'

'Does that help?'

'Not really.'

Who hasn't seen a photo of themselves and realised how much chubbier and uglier they actually are. Mirrors lie as much as memories do. Why lie: you were a gorgeous creature. Trim, neat, with good hair and decent skin. And now you are a carcass on a slab sucked clear of breath and colour. Above you, a butcher of cats raises his cleaver.

'Are you my Helper?' you ask and receive no reply. The figure has vanished and you wait for it to creep up on you once more.

'No, sir. Forget Helpers. All bullshit. Those morons in white are bureaucrats and prison guards. They have turned the In Between into an asylum. Pathetic.'

The World Bank and the Dutch government once donated money towards rebuilding these canals. A bulk of it ended up in well-stitched pockets. A feasibility study was rejected and filed next to plans for unbuilt highways and skyscrapers. In Sri Lanka, everything is built by the lowest bidder or, most profitably, not at all.

Kottu holds down your body, hoping liquid will seep through the holes in the skull. The water baptises the brain, but the corpse still floats. Kottu swears and spits. Balal paddles towards the corpse, cleaver balanced over his head, like a frog playing a waiter. The cleaver is big and brown, dulled, no doubt, by the blood of a thousand cats.

You have studied these men, you have avoided them in streets and in jungles, you know who they are and that there are too many to count. They too think that no one is watching, unaware that you are spitting in their hair. The goons work for the goon-master, who is hired by the cops on the instruction of the task force, which is funded by the ministry, that answers to the Cabinet, that lives in the house that JR built.

1988 was about JVP Marxists holding the nation by the throat, and the following year was about the government crackdown. If you were politically inclined, the goons picked you up and handed you to an interrogator and, depending on your session with him, to an executioner. These are usually ex-army sadists and most of them wear black hoods with holes in them, like the Ku Klux Klan, except for the black bit obviously.

Follow any turd upstream and it leads to a member of parliament. Dr Ranee Sridharan of Jaffna University famously mapped out the ecosystem of a Tigers terror cell and of a government death squad. Those with dirty hands are unconnected to those in power, so those in power could blame whoever they chose. The good doctor used your photos in her book without permission. She was shot while cycling to a lecture. Probably more for speaking out against the Tigers than for stealing your snaps.

Besides, there are more serious things happening before you. Your body has been chopped at the spinal cord, as has that of the other corpse whose face you cannot see. You are used to seeing blood and guts but this you cannot stomach.

You watch as the other corpse is beheaded and relieved of its hands and feet. Balal chops while Kottu runs a hose from a tap by the temple. The blood disappears into the black of the Beira. The figure in the hood leads you away as the goon approaches your bisected corpse. He takes off his hood and you see his face. It is young and not unpleasant to look at, despite the scars and the peeled-off scabs.

'Are you OK, hamu?' he asks.

'Not really,' you reply.

He frowns and shakes his head.

'Sir does not remember me.'

You look down on the bruises on his neck and the burns on his shoulders.

'Can you stop calling me "sir"?'

He reminds you of railway tracks that connect Dehiwela with Wellawatte, he reminds you of a fight at a Wennappuwa Communist Rally, of a dark beach in Negombo. You don't recall his chocolate skin, his slender frame, or his thin lips, nor do you know his name.

Meanwhile, the buffaloes are squabbling about the rising sun, the blood not washing and the body parts not sinking. You see a head that once belonged to you placed in a siri-siri bag and hurled into the lake. You see limbs you once owned packed into boxes. You wonder why your head remains on your shoulders unlike the Dead Atheist's.

'I was Sena Pathirana. I was the chief JVP organiser for Gampaha. My body was dumped in this filthy lake many moons ago. We have met.'

You slide over to where other body parts are being wrapped. Limbs and heads in plastic bags as if parcelled for the freezer. 'I don't...'

'You tried to kiss me at a rally in Wennappuwa. Don't expect sir to remember sir.'

You watch the body parts float on the edge of the Beira and you hear the garbage men swear and you wait, with fading hope, for memories to return.

ABBREVIATIONS

You once made a cheatsheet for Andrew McGowan, a young American journo confused by Lanka's abbreviations. You recycled it many times for many visitors over many years.

Dear Andy

To an outsider, the Sri Lankan tragedy will appear confusing and irreparable. It needn't be either. Here are the main players.

LTTE – The Liberation Tigers of Tamil Eelam

* Want a separate Tamil state.

* Prepared to slaughter Tamil civilians and moderates to achieve this.

JVP – The Janatha Vimukthi Peramuna

* Want to overthrow the capitalist state.

* Are willing to murder the working class while they liberate them.

UNP – The United National Party

* Known as the Uncle Nephew Party.

* In power since the late '70s and embroiled in the above two wars.

STF – The Special Task Force

* On behalf of the Govt, will abduct and torture anyone suspected of being or abetting the LTTE or the JVP.

The nation divides into races, the races divide into factions and the factions turn on each other. Whoever is in the opposition will preach multiculturalism and then enforce Sinhala Buddhist dominance in exchange for power.

You are not the only outsider here, Andy. There are many others as confused as you are.

IPKF – The Indian Peace Keeping Force

* Sent by our neighbour to preserve peace.

* Are willing to burn villages to fulfil their mission.

UN – United Nations

* Have offices in Colombo.

* Are arseholes to work with.

RAW – Research and Analysis Wing

* Indian secret service, here to broker dodgy deals.

* Are best avoided.

CIA – Central Intelligence Agency

* Sits on the shores of the Diego Garcia islands, holding very powerful binoculars.

* Is this true, Andy? Say it ain't so.

It's not that complicated, my friend. Don't try and look for the good guys 'cause there ain't none. Everyone is proud and greedy and no one can resolve things without money changing hands or fists being raised.

Things have escalated beyond what anyone imagined and they keep getting worse and worse. Stay safe, Andy. These wars aren't worth dying over. None of them are.

Malin

CHAT WITH DEAD REVOLUTIONARY (1989)

You realised you liked boys very early on. When your Dada told you that all poofs should be tied up and raped with knives, you looked down at your slippers and never looked him in the face again.

There may come a time when homosexuals can kiss on the street, get mortgages together and die in each other's arms. Not in your lifetime. In your lifetime, you meet a stranger in a dark place and never see them again. Or you have secret affairs that end with no time for heartache. Or you do something radical, like have a girlfriend, live with her, and sleep in the spare room with the landlord's son.

'You came to a JVP rally. You asked me to pose with a banner. Then, you tried to smooch me. A week later, the first batch of my comrades were disappeared. A month later, they disappeared me.'

The details come to you in itches and aches. In the Sri Lanka of the '80s, 'disappeared' was a passive verb, something the government or JVP anarchists or Tiger separatists or Indian Peace Keepers could do to you depending on which province you were in and who you looked like.

'Let's follow these rats.' Sena leads you to the roof of the white van. The black garbage bags that form his hood and his cape are taped, unlike the ones swaddling his actual corpse, parts of which are swimming in the Beira, parts of which sit in this van. You cannot say for sure what made the marks on his ankles, but you can guess. You look down and see you are wearing one shoe, a chappal imported from Madras and sold in Jaffna.

The black Delica van starts to move. In the back seat are Kottu and Balal, who have hosed off and changed into banians. At the back of the van are boxes of meat that have begun to smell. Steaks, chops and offcuts that once belonged to you, and two others. Some seem to have come out of the freezer.

The driver is a young soldier who hunches over the wheel and mutters to himself.

'Someone is talking to me and it's not those two and it's not me. Who is it?'

He wears the uniform of a corporal but has the befuddled expression of an agitating student. He has a prosthetic leg that he keeps on the passenger seats, while his hand hovers over the steering wheel clutch. Sena whispers into the boy's ear and turns towards you, smiling. 'I can teach you how to whisper to the living if you help me,' he says putting his hood on and leaning back.

'Thought you were telling me how I died,' you say, still not sure if you want to know. The boy driving looks around nervously as if he hears something that you do not. He grabs at the clutch and the van jerks twice.

'Sir was picked up from the Arts Centre Club or wherever rich ponnayas go. Sir was put in the van, beaten with a pipe. Chained in a room filled with dead people's shit.'

He holds up his hand and you see bloody scabs where fingernails once were. 'Maybe you woke to a man in a mask asking you questions. "Are you JVP?" or "Are you Tiger?" Maybe, "Are you foreign NGO?" or "Are you Indian spy?" They'd ask why you were taking photos and who you were selling them to.'

The driver calls out to his passengers.

'These extra bodies, from where, ah?'

'Drivermalli! Shut your gob and drive.' Balal looks down at the stains on his hands.

'Mr Balal, I don't like this disgusting work.'

'Thank you for feedback. I will put in my report. Now drive.'

Meanwhile, Kottu taps Balal on the shoulder and lowers his voice. He combs his handlebar moustache with his finger while he speaks. 'Balal malli, I'm going to complain to boss.'

'Which boss?'

'Big boss.'

'The *big*, big boss?'

'I'll tell even him. I'm not scared. Very unprofessional how we are asked to work.'

Sena is now floating before you and shouting at your face. You hold your broken camera to your eye and line him against the moving trees.

'Maybe you wanted to spit in their faces and curse their children. But all you did was cry and shiver and plead. Maybe, they used nails on your fingernails. Maybe, you told them what they wanted to hear. Maybe, they made you eat a gun.'

He has tears in his eyes that he does not bother wiping.

'That's how they took you?'

'That's how they took us all. 20,000 in the last year. Innocent fools, mainly. There weren't that many in the whole JVP.'

'I wasn't JVP.'

'Minister Cyril Wijeratne said, "Twelve of yours for one of ours." He wasn't joking. Bugger just got the sums wrong.'

'Twenty thousand disappeared? You got the sums wrong.'

'I've seen the bodies.'

'So have I. Five thousand, max.'

'The JVP killed less than three hundred. To crush us, the government killed more than twenty thousand. Maybe twice that. These are facts, sir.'

'The government has killed over twenty thousand,' says Drivermalli, overhearing a conversation beyond his ears. 'Why keep killing? The JVP is crushed. The LTTE are silent.'

'Shut up and drive,' says Balal.

'If there is an afterlife, we will all pay for this,' says Drivermalli.

'Fool. There is no afterlife,' says Kottu. 'Only this shit.'

'Where are we going?' asks Drivermalli.

'Turn left at that junction,' says Balal. 'And stop talking.'

'Not a bad idea. To eat a gun,' says Drivermalli as he turns the wheel.

..

'So what are the rules, Comrade Pathirana?' you ask Sena from the rooftop of the white van.

'No rules, sir. Like Down There. You make your own.'

'I mean with travel. Can I go wherever the wind blows?'

'Not really, hamu. You can travel wherever your body has been.'

'That's all?'

'You can go where your name is spoken. But you can't fly to Paris or the Maldives. Unless your corpse is taken there.'

'Why the Maldives?'

'Ghosts mistake that place for paradise. There are more spirits than stingrays in those shallows.'

'But you can ride winds?'

'Like public transport for dead people, sir. I will show.'

With that, he disappears through the roof of the van. He calls out to you and you look around. The dawn has broken and the buses have filled with office slaves and schoolkids training to become them. Each vehicle has a creature like you hanging off it. You look down the line of traffic and see a ghoul on every car roof.

'Maali-Sir. Come. Dive in.'

You pinch yourself and feel nothing. Which could mean you're dreaming. Or that you no longer have a body. Or that you're dreaming of no longer having a body. It may also mean that you could safely attempt diving into a metal roof of a moving white van. In you go. It is like jumping into a swimming pool, if the water tasted like rust and wasn't wet.

'How can we travel in a van and not fall through the bottom.'

'Sir is not listening. We're attached to our bodies. Can ride any wind that passes where our corpse has been.'

'That's it?'

'If you kick the bucket in Kandana and are driven to Kadugannawa for burial, you can get off anywhere on the Kandy Road.'

'Yes, but if stabbed in a kitchen in Kurunegala and buried in the garden, options are limited no?'

He pushes you back to where the meat is and where the stench is. He stands between Balal and Kottu and waits. It is not beyond the realms of possibility that you tried it on with this skinny lad. In the last decade, you screwed anything that moved and many things that preferred not to. That's a quote from your roommate DD, shared over a martini. A taunt, disguised as a joke.

The van hits a bump near Bishop's College. Sena inhales something that isn't air and slaps both Balal and Kottu at the same time. The momentum of the van makes their heads bang together. Sena lets out a laugh and you do, too. Even the dead enjoy a bit of slapstick.

'What the hell?' shouts Kottu, holding his scalp.

'Sorry, boss,' monotones Drivermalli. 'Just a small bump.'

'I'll give you a small bump.'

'These roads are shit. Time for this government to go.'

'No one cares about your politics, Drivermalli,' says Kottu, rubbing the bump on his head.

You ask Sena how he did this and he says there are skills that disembodied spirits have access to. But only once you have decided.

Decided what, you ask.

'Whether you're joining us.'

'Us?'

'Ones like you and me.'

'Who wear garbage bags?'

'Who will give justice for all those killed. To allow those without graves to find vengeance.'

'How?'

'By destroying these fuckers. Their bosses. And their bosses' bosses. The scum who killed us. We will get them all, hamu. Sir doesn't believe me? That is your first mistake.'

'Aiyo, putha. I have made more mistakes than you have had screws.'

'My body was kept in a freezer with seventeen others. Before they finally got around to throwing me in that lake,' says Sena, wrapping the bags around him.

The van jerks and the goons grumble. Drivermalli seems to have clamped on the brakes while dozing. It is then you notice the lines on his face and the shadows that fall on his ears. His eyes hold a despair not unusual in one who navigates Colombo's traffic while transporting human meat. Sena whispers in the boy's ear as the van starts moving again.

'I will help you find what you have lost,' he says.

There is no indication that Drivermalli can hear him, other than a twitch in his brow.

'Those who have wronged will be punished. Those who are wronged will be soothed.'

'Can he hear you?'

'Oh yes.'

'We can talk to the living?'

'This is a teachable skill.'

The van comes unstuck at a Mirihana roundabout and makes its way past the suburbs into factory lands.

'Where we going, Sena?'

'Aren't you curious about the other two bodies in the back?'

You look at the flies circling the meat in the bags at the back of the van. You wonder if flies get reborn as us.

'Who are they?'

'You'll find out soon.'

'Now I'm curious. Where are we going, Comrade Sena?'

'I don't know, boss. Looks like we might be getting graves.'

'Is there much left to bury?'

'It is just meat, hamu. The beautiful part of you is still here.'

Not many have called you beautiful, though that's what you were. You think of your beautiful body being sliced by a cleaver. How ugly we all are when reduced to meat. How ugly this beautiful land is, and how ugly you were to your Amma, to Jaki and to DD.

EGGPLANTS

DD called it the ugliest thing in the universe and you told him there was plenty of ugly in the world and this wouldn't even make the top ten. The box under the bed contained five envelopes and each of them contained its own share of ugly. Each envelope housed black-and-white photographs and had the name of a playing card scrawled on its cover in felt pen. You lived in a room with no furniture and threw away everything in your life except for your photos and your boxes.

DD said he'd only seen three eggplants in his life: yours, his father's and his own.

'Such a privileged existence,' you said. 'They don't all look like eggplants. Most look like chicken necks, some like mushrooms, a few like baby's fists.'

'You've seen plenty, no?' asked DD, a question more loaded than the armoured car manned by children that carried you once in Kilinochchi.

'A few,' you said. 'They were all beautiful.'

'I bet you'd kiss anything,' said DD. 'Anything that moves. Anything that won't.'

'In the case of eggplants, they always tend to move when you least need them to.'

You told him your grand theories of the penis. How Asians do more screwing despite having the smallest ones. How the average member is both muscular and fleshy, moist and dry, hard and soft, smooth and wrinkled. It is the only part of your meat suit that can shape-shift. Imagine a nose growing inches whenever you lied. Or your little toe turning into a thumb.

'How many?' said DD with his chin over your knees. You were doing sit-ups and he was coaching. 'Twenty? Fifty?'

You once attempted counting and stopped when you had passed three figures.

'Less than ten? Bullshit. Twice that, must be. I knew it. More than that? More than twenty? That's disgusting.'

'We all like eggplant, what's the issue?'

'I only like yours.'

You told him how circumcision at birth instils rage in the subconscious and makes men violent.

'That's both stupid and bigoted,' he said. 'I'm cut, you're not. Who's more violent?'

'Hmm.'

'You think I'm violent?'

'You have passion.' You cradled the barbell over his pretty neck and watched him lift. 'When you're excited, it's terrifying. I can't imagine rage.'

He grins as the weight obeys gravity and his chest fills with blood.

'You've never seen me excited.'

'Untrue.'

'And your theories are horseshit.'

'Then how come Americans and Jews and Muslims are always waging wars? It's the rage in their subconscious from losing their foreskins as infants. A baby howls when it bumps its head. Imagine the agony of...'

'That's the most ignorant thing you've said. And you've said some really dumb shit.'

'I read it in a WHO report. All warmongering nations are circumcised. Israel, Lebanon, Iran, Iraq, USA. Congo...'

'The Soviets, the Germans, the Brits, the Chinese? Also cut?'

'No theory is perfect.'

'Ha.'

He smirked as he handed you the weights.

'What about Sinhalese and Tamils?' he said. 'Neither are cut.'

He raised his eyebrows and flexed his dimples. DD had the annoying habit of occasionally making a valid point.

After that, you would wrestle and then you would roll on the floor. Then DD asked about the largest and smallest you'd ever seen and you told him of the simple farmer in the Vanni and a burly rocker in Berlin. You omitted that the farmer, hung like a horse, was a corpse when you'd met him. Or that the guitarist beat you up in a sidestreet, despite being uncut and tiny – or, maybe, because of it.

You tell him the pecker is proof that man has no free will. There is a pause and, then, DD snorts: 'That is the lamest excuse ever.'

'We do not control what sends blood to our pricks. It is like there are devils whispering in our ears and placing blinkers on our eyes.'

'For you, maybe.'

That night you removed an envelope from the box. You had not given the envelope a title, but if you had it might well have been 'Eggplant'. In it was an assorted array of male genitalia, taken with and without the knowledge of their owners. You saved the very best of them, put them in the envelope marked 'Jack' and destroyed the rest. DD had taken to rifling though your photo boxes and this would be too much a sight for his pretty little eyes.

The box had five envelopes, each named after a playing card. Ace had pictures sold to the British Embassy. King had photos commisioned by the Sinhalese Army. Queen were snaps bought by a Tamil NGO. But Jack was just for you.

The fifth envelope was titled Ten, and had pictures taken of DD, and of Sri Lanka at its prettiest.

'You're the perfect ten,' you once told him. 'On a scale of one to thirteen.'

TRAINED BUTCHERS

The van starts to move. Kottu lights another Gold Leaf and scratches his belly. The interior is humid and smells of rust and ashtrays and rotting meat.

'I'll tell you what makes me fully angry?' says Balal.

'The big boss?' says Kottu.

'The whole unprofessionalism.'

'Of the big boss?'

'Everything with you is "big boss". Is he cupping you?'

'I am a small man doing a dirty job,' says Kottu. 'If I can get a proper job, I would. But who will hire a thief?'

Kottu strokes his moustache with sorrow, while Balal cracks his knuckles. Balal's arms are toned from years of chopping. Kottu's cheeks sag from decades of betel chewing.

'That's what I'm also saying,' says Balal. 'Do a proper job. Can't do a mad rush like this. Have to saw the fingers, smash the teeth, pulp the face. Then can't identify also. After that can dump anywhere.'

'This is not a proper job,' says Drivermalli to himself in the front seat.

'You said you had a plan?' says Kottu, patting his paunch. 'The fridge at the fourth floor is fully full. Can't take this back there.'

'Shall we chop them to pieces and bury them somewhere?'

'How many holes do you want to dig? Cannot solve everything with a cleaver.'

'I'm a trained butcher. But this work pays better than the chicken farms.'

Drivermalli calls out. 'Mr Balal. Mr Kottu. I'm very tired. When can we go home?'

The garbage men ignore him.

'Aiya, I'm saying we do it right,' says Balal. 'We gut, we drain, we chop, we bury. Different place every time.'

'Why not dump the garbage in the jungle and light a match?'

'What jungle here, Aiya? Sathutu Uyana kid's park?'

'So what's the big plan? They float in the Beira. They wash up in the Diyawanna. Beach is fully guarded. You need a permit for bonfires.'

'At Crow Island, there is a rubbish dump.'

'Too many human crows there.'

'I have eaten crow,' Drivermalli smiles with his mouth but not his eyes. 'Tastes like goat.'

'There's the Labugama forest reserve. They say STF and the IPKF are dumping bodies left, right and centre,' says Kottu.

'Can't just go there. Need permit for sure,' says Balal.

'I will talk to the big boss,' says Kottu. 'Must follow the law even when killing, no?'

'OK, so I have a plan,' says Balal as the van strands itself in traffic.

'This should be good,' says Kottu.

'We feed them to my cats.'

'Huh?'

Balal laughs, the giggle is mirthless and shrill. Drivermalli mutters to himself while Sena in the passenger seat whispers in his ear. You shiver by the bags of meat and put your camera to your eyes.

'Joking, joking. But I have enough and more cats at home. One is a fishing cat I found in the sewer. It's always hungry.'

'Fishing cat? Really?' says Kottu. 'Not a swamp crocodile? Or a zoo panther?'

Kottu is taking liberties with his tone and Balal is beginning to notice.

'Why do you have cats?' asks Drivermalli, who has stopped laughing and begun tooting his horn.

'It's good side business. The Chinese buy from me.'

'The Chinese Embassy? Don't lie.'

'No, Aiya. Chinese restaurants in Grandpass. Chinese never ask questions.'

They laugh like witches as they pass around the last cigarette.

'Balal, you're a filthy fucker. Drivermalli, let's go back to the hotel. We'll have to somehow find room in those fridges.'

'Any more pickups today?' Drivermalli neither smiles nor frowns, as if any answer would please him.

'No, malli. Let's get some sleep, no?'

'I never sleep,' says the driver as he kills the engine.

LIGHT THE CORNERS OF YOUR MIND

You don't remember learning to walk or talk or being taught to shit in a pot. Who does? You don't remember being in a womb, coming out of one, or being in an incubator. Or where you were before that.

Memory comes to you in bodily ailments. In sneezes, in aches, in scratches and in itches. Strange, as you no longer have a body, though maybe the hypnotists are right; maybe pain and pleasure reside only in the mind. Memories come to you in gasps and chokes and loose motions.

They happen each time you pull the camera to your eyes. In its glass peephole, you catch glimpses of light falling on faces, shadows spreading over hills, of pictures you took, and lenses you cracked. You remember bits and you retrieve pieces.

You feel the stab in the appendix as you see Albert Kabalana and Lakshmi Almeida at Pasikuda Beach holding hands on the eve of their boy's tenth birthday. Back when they still played mixed doubles badminton. Bertie is a few years from leaving; Lucky, a few years from drinking in the afternoons.

He is unaware of the disease already inside, she is unaware of Aunty Dalreen.

You click the silent Nikon and see a man stripped and beaten while a laughing mob gathers sticks for a bonfire. That's the picture that made the dark lady with the big lips call you. The Queen of Spades whose name does not arrive no matter how much you wince or groan.

You press down on the cracked button and see an unexploded suicide bomber jacket, whose owner was killed while 'trying to escape', filmed using candlelight. You didn't need any lights at the Sooriyakanda mass grave where the sunrise turned the paddy fields golden. You squint and stare at skeletons stretched to the horizon, dead children as far as the eyes could see. Young boys made to write suicide notes to their families before being executed. For the crime of taunting the son of the school principal who knew a colonel in the STF.

You don't remember how many times you cheated on DD, only that you felt guilt only once. You don't remember voting for JR or losing thirteen lakhs in three minutes or telling your father the thing that broke him. But you know you did all three.

You do not remember Sena. Neither meeting him, nor attending rallies, nor trying to smooch him. You do not remember dying. How it happened or who was around. And why you'd rather not know.

Maybe you were taken for doing your job too well, like all those journos and activists over the last decade. Maybe you were snuffed for taunting someone whose father knew someone. Maybe you did it yourself, not like you hadn't tried before. All scenarios are plausible.

Though, as every gambler knows, the biggest killer in this godless universe is the random roll of the dice. Plain stinking jungle variety bad luck. The thing that gets us all.

The camera fills with mud. You shake it like you're not supposed to and pull at the things around your neck. You hold the Nikon to your face and it is no longer brown. There is broken glass and blurred colours. You see the dead after the shelling at Kilinochchi. You see a broken dog, a bleeding man, a mother and child. You took this photo from the top of a crumbling building, and as you watch a hole grows larger in your stomach, until you feel it pushing at your throat. It is not the most gruesome photo in your box by a long stretch, but for some reason for you it is the saddest.

You switch back to the last thing you remember. Being in a casino and putting everything you had on something black.

Do Not Visit Cemeteries

'Oi! Where you going?'

The van stalls in traffic by the Borella cemetery. The garbage thugs have dozed off and Drivermalli is humming to himself. It is a tuneless version of the Lambada theme tune. So, exactly like the original.

'I have work,' says Sena. 'And I get the feeling, sir is wasting my time.'

'And what am I supposed to be doing?'

You'd rather not spend your seven moons in a van full of human meat. The garbage bags in the back rustle in the wind.

'No one can make anyone do anything. That's the problem.'

Sena jumps from the hood of a trishaw to the side of a bus and leaps onto the railings of the Borella Kanatte. You wonder if you are capable of leaping from a semi-moving vehicle. Sounds like the sort of thing that gets you killed. He calls out from the pavement. 'If you don't care why you died, why should I?'

You hear a rumble behind Balal and Kottu, who are snoring and drooling, respectively. Two apparitions rise from the bags of meat. Their clothing is torn, their eyes are empty, they both have mullets, they are familiar and you know why. You have seen their bodies on the banks on the Beira, chopped into eighths, placed next to yours and Sena's. They look like young men who have been beaten senseless. Their eyes roll in their sockets as they lurch towards you.

You leap like a triple-jumping ballerina and end up at the cemetery gates next to a laughing Sena. You look back and see the two ghosts following you. You shriek and Sena laughs some more.

They float behind you, looking deader than most and not speaking. Their fingernails gone; always a sign. As is the bruising under the feet, and the I've-just-swallowed-my-brain stare. You've seen a few in your time, strung upside down from telephone poles, baking on roadsides, nailed to trees. All with the same expression as these two. Except those corpses didn't move.

'Innocent buggers. Sin men,' says Sena. 'The fat one is an Engineering student from Moratuwa. The other is an agriculture student from Jaffna. Rounded up, tortured and killed.'

'For what?'

'The big question. Because they were Sinhala or Tamil? Or because they were poor?'

'Bullets can also find the middle class. The journalist Richard de Zoysa, the activist Dr Ranee Sridharan,' you say. 'Me, as you've pointed out. Though I don't remember being shot.'

You don't remember being dragged from your bed like Richard while his mother pleaded for his life. You don't remember getting death threats from boys you'd taught like Dr Ranee.

'These are innocent fellows. That's the point. At least you and me were involved.'

'I wasn't involved.'

'Keep saying that.'

'I wasn't JVP. How was I involved? I wasn't LTTE.'

You raise your voice, though the zombie engineers don't seem to notice.

'You said you worked for the British?'

'Did I?'

The mistakenly killed engineers let out gasps and you see the shadow before you see its source. The thing is large and ambles on four legs like a hound. It leaps along the roofs of cars, but all you see is a mass of hair, teeth and eyes.

It is what you hear that terrifies. Voices caked in fear, imprisoned in flesh, like souls beyond help. A cacophony of mewling, like duelling synthesisers played badly. As if synthesisers could be played any other way.

The thing has a head of a bull on the body of a bear and it lumbers towards you at a quickening pace. It has a necklace of skulls and faces trapped beneath its skin. Faces that you cannot draw your eyes away from.

'Move slowly,' says Sena. 'And move now.'

'What is it?'

'A naraka. A hell-being. Something worse than a yaka.'

Sena drags you onto a wind as you hear the growl. It projects to the space between your ears. The sound of a thousand voices shrieking off-key. The creature stands on a moving truck and watches you. It is more shadow than form and emits static like an old TV playing every channel at once, the dead souls in its belly screaming at clashing frequencies. You follow Sena's wind as it whistles through the cemetery.

..

The Borella Kanatte is a picturesque collection of trees and serpents and gravestones. You've stopped here many times for a peaceful walk. Today it is anything but. The cemetery teems with cripples and ghosts and horned figures, and it is difficult to know where to look and where not to. They are perched on graves, they hover behind mourners, they occupy the trees and the railings. They lurch like the damned, with eyes of every shade and a talcum hue to their peeling skin. The mistakenly killed Engineering students halt at the gate. Sena looks back and scoffs.

'What are you scared of? You're already dead! The worst has already happened.'

That's a Sinhala phrase you hear a lot, especially around war zones. You've heard it uttered by aid workers, soldiers, terrorists and villagers. All bad things have happened already. It cannot get worse than this.

'Aren't we supposed to avoid cemeteries?' you ask Sena as he floats down the pathway.

'The Mahakali can't enter here,' he replies.

'The what?'

'It has many names,' whispers Sena. 'Maruwa, Maha Sona, Kalu Balla, Kuveni. I know it as the Mahakali, the swallower of souls. It's the most powerful thing roaming these winds. It is a deity whom demons and yakas kneel before. Not a humble ghost like you or me. But, remember, demons or yakas, or those who command them, cannot go where they're not invited.'

'How do I find out?'

'About yakas?'

'About how I died.'

'Thought you weren't interested.'

'Thought you said you knew.'

Sena fiddles with his garbage bag cloak.

'I'm not your Helper, sir. I only help those who help me. If you don't want my help, I can leave.'

'You sound like the UN.'

The morning sun is completing its ascent. The road has filled with cars and folk wandering towards lunch. You look down at the blood on your clothes. Doesn't look like you died in your sleep. The LTTE took out Dr Ranee Sridharan, the government took out Richard de Zoysa, the JVP took out movie heart-throb Vijaya Kumaratunga. So who took you?

The trees are lined with eyes and the pathway is blocked by ghouls. There are three funerals in session and each is attended by a throng of spirits. Sena tells you that ghosts love funerals more than humans love weddings.

You have to push through the wind and are blown across graves of Colombo's dead. Here lie hero soldiers, slain politicos, journos with big mouths. You look for familiar faces, celebrities like Dr Ranee or Prince Vijaya perhaps. All you see are spirits as anonymous and as forgotten as they were in life. And among the bombed, the burned and disappeared is you, cause of death as yet undetermined.

'How come ghosts stay here?' you ask.

'It's where their bodies are,' says Sena.

'What about the ones who don't have graves?'

'Keep your eyes down. Do not talk to anything.'

The heat does nothing to deter the ghosts who cavort along the pathway. Two funerals are in procession and are well attended by ghouls and pretas, the hungriest of all ghosts, both looking for people to confuse and steal from.

Sena leads you to the crematorium building which is less crowded than the pathways through the graves. The two Engineering students stand by the crematorium wall next to a barrel of charcoal. Sena reaches into the barrel and rubs his hands. He then floats to the wall and starts marking out letters on it. He fills it with six names written in charcoal. The Engineering students look on in awe.

DRIVERMALLI
BALAL
KOTTU
THE MASK
MAJOR RAJA
MINISTER CYRIL

He lets the hood fall from his face. He looks at the students and then you.

'This is the death squad that killed me months ago. It killed you two last week. And it killed Maali-Sir last night.'

'Has this been confirmed by a reliable source?'

'I will make them all suffer. Each one. Will you help me?'

The Engineering students bow their heads and Sena smiles.

'How will you make them suffer?'

'I have a plan.'

. .

You are used to having people you don't trust talk you into things you don't want to do. Not this time.

'Sorry, Comrade Sena. I'd love to learn how to write on walls. But I need to go.'

'Don't call me comrade, Maali hamu. You are just a champagne socialist.'

'Why call me hamu? I'm not your master.'

'From a young age, we are brainwashed into calling mediocre people "hamu" and "sir". It is part of growing up poor. I have worked as a servant boy. I sold vegetables on the street even after I got my degree. The only way we can enter parts of this city is by calling the rich "sir".'

You listen at the wind and think of all the things you never understood. 'My friends. My mother. I have to see them.'

'Why?'

'To tell DD I'm sorry. To tell Jaki about the box. To tell Amma that I blame Dada.'

'That's touching, sir, but we have work.'

'I need to see them.'

'I didn't rescue you to talk baila.'

'I didn't ask you to rescue me.'

'No one asks for anything. No one asks to be born poor, no one asks for disease, no one asks to be born queer.'

'I am not queer,' you say, as you have said many times before.

'Did hamu lose his mind when they threw him off the roof? Or did you lose it at some Colombo 7 drug party?'

'I live in Colombo 2. Who says I was thrown off a roof?'

'Look at your broken body. Maybe your mind broke too.'

You look down and see only the absence of a slipper. Like Cinderella, except your half-sisters in Missouri weren't as wicked as you were.

'Every godaya envies Colombo 7. I needed a lot of silly pills to get through those parties.'

'You don't remember joining the JVP, do you?'

'I don't remember dying. I don't remember a death squad. I don't remember being thrown off roofs.'

'So you're only interested in photographing the poor. Not in helping them.'

'OK, OK. If I help you, will you stop preaching?'

'Of course.'

'And will you help me?'

'Why not?'

You are getting the hang of riding winds, though you struggle to explain it to yourself. Like gravity is a bus that lets you hang on its footboards. Like holding your breath until your breath holds you. Like a magic carpet without the carpet bit. You float like a particle must do when it's tipsy. But which wind will take you to DD?

'When they chop up your corpse, it doesn't matter if you're campus Marxist or café Marxist. Grass-roots socialist or champagne socialist. The flies will shit on you and the maggots will munch.'

Sena's garbage bag cape flutters behind him. He looks less like a superman and more like a broken umbrella.

'Where we going?' you ask.

'The mara tree at the edge of the kanatte.'

'What for?'

'I am helping you.'

'How?'

'I don't believe in many things. But I believe in mara trees.'

··

The mara tree stretches its limbs across shaggy grass and toppled rock. On every branch is a creature hanging by its claws. Rats, snakes and polecats hide among tombstones. There are many shadows to disappear into, though no one present appears to cast one. Sena climbs to a vacant branch and you follow. 'Why are we sitting here?' you ask.

'Mara trees catch winds. Like radios catch frequencies. So do bo trees, banyan trees and probably any other big tree that blows wind.'

'I thought the wind blows the trees.'

'Your grandfather thought the world was flat. Do you want to be a ghost or a ghoul?'

'What's the difference?'

'A ghost blows with the wind. A ghoul directs the wind.'

'What are we doing here?'

'If you quiet your mind, you may hear your name spoken. If you hear your name, you can go there. Do it while your corpse is fresh, so to speak. After ninety moons, no one will care about your Colombo 7 arse.'

'I liked it better when you were calling me "sir".'

You snort and look around at meditating spirits. Everyone on the tree mutters while rocking back and forth. It is tough to know who is in meditation and who is catatonic.

'Silence your mind and listen,' he says.

'I haven't meditated since the '70s,' you reply.

'Meditation is only for those who have breath.'

'What am I listening for?'

'Your name. Have you forgotten that also? Hear your name spoken, share in its shame.'

'Where did you learn poetry?'

'Because I went to Sri Bodhi College, I can't know poetry?'

'How many chips does that shoulder carry?'

'Listen!'

The sun is beginning its descent and the light has begun to play its tricks. The funeral processions scatter, while more hearses roll towards more graves. You remain still and listen for a song in your head. There is none. Not even Elvis or Freddie.

Every time you look around, the tree has changed texture. The bark is a different shade of coffee, the leaves are flecked with gold, the foliage veers between rainforest and moss. It could be the light, your imagination, or neither.

The hot air fills with the groans of traffic, the yawns of dogs and the slither of spirits. You empty yourself of thoughts and let the faces come to you, faces you recognise and cannot name. Among them is a large white man, a man with a crown, a dark lady with ruby lips and a boy with a moustache.

The faces turn to playing cards. A Diamond Ace, a Club King, a Queen of Spades and a Jack of Hearts flutter before you and that's when you start to hear. At first a whisper, then a word, then many, then millions. The whispers weave into one another, some create harmony, some static.

Then like ants with mics crawling over a carcass. Then like pebbles in plastic boxes shaken by horrid children. Then like Portuguese, Dutch and Tamil spoken at the same time. The airwaves are jammed with spirits cursing. Each voice hissing into the ether, screaming at the universe, bellowing into unused frequencies.

And then you hear the name. It is said once, then repeated, then shouted.

'His name is Malinda Almeida. He works for the British Consulate.'

'We don't know any Lorenzo Almeida.'

'You think this is a joke? Malinda Almeida. I have a letter from Minister Stanley Dharmendran. Will you kindly check?'

You know the voice and you have heard it angry on many occasions. You look around and the tree is reduced to brush strokes, an impressionist painting of greens and golds with nothing to focus on. Next to you, Comrade Sena Pathirana is smiling. He gives you a mock salute as you evaporate before his dead eyes.

TWENTY MOTHERS

'His full name is Malinda Almeida Kabalana,' says the young man with the spiky hair. 'This is a copy of his ID. Can you check, please?'

'It says here Malinda Albert Kabalana,' says the assistant superintendent of police. 'You don't know your friend's name?'

'Yes,' says the old lady in the corner. 'Bertie was the father's name. He changed it after the father left.'

'We'll use the name on his ID,' says the Detective at the desk.

For the past year, the city's police stations have entertained wailing parents inquiring after sons and daughters who never came home. On busy days, they round the worried and the frantic into poorly ventilated corridors and make them queue all the way to the cycle bay.

There are three mothers sweating in the hallway, their cries now silent. Inside, a beautiful boy leans across a desk and shows a photograph to the police. The young man, his spiky hair, the two women and their contrasting handbags have all managed to jump this endless queue.

'I'm Dilan Dharmendran. My father is Minister Stanley Dharmendran,' says the beautiful boy. 'This is Malinda's mother. This, his girlfriend. Yesterday morning since he missing.'

DD spoke Sinhala as well as Mahagama Sekara spoke Afrikaans. And, when he was nervous, he lost all syntax.

'Sorry, but nothing to be done,' says the ASP standing at the doorway. 'You must understand. Until seventy-two hours we can't call him missing.'

'Has he been arrested?' asks the girl in the red dress. 'Can you check on that, please?'

The young lady wears silver earrings, black lipstick and dark mascara that trickles down her cheek. She wraps herself in a jacket as a draught enters the room, despite all windows being closed. You float on it and perch on the sill.

'What are your names, please?' says the older woman, putting her hand on the girl's shoulder.

'I'm ASP Ranchagoda. That is Detective Cassim. He will note your complaint. But cannot file report for three days, very sorry.'

Dilan Dharmendran looks at both ladies. One in her seventies, one in her twenties, one scowling, one crying.

Detective Cassim is stocky and fidgety, like a chubby child in uniform. Ranchagoda's body looks made of coat hangers and his uniform drapes upon it. Cassim hands over a form and peers through the doorway as more mothers enter the lobby flanked by men in sarongs.

'Madam, please fill this. Mr Dharmendran. When you last see Malinda Albert Kabalana?'

'Almeida. He was away in Jaffna since last week. He called my office yesterday, said he was back in Colombo.' says DD. 'He said he had big news and he'd call me later that night.'

DD takes a deep breath and pulls at the chain around his neck. 'He didn't call.'

'Maybe he's still outstation.'

'His bags are back at the flat. His damp towel's hanging in the bathroom. He called my office from our flat. Said he had to meet some clients. Then he'd call me.'

'What clients?'

'He didn't say.'

'It's very dangerous these days in Jaffna. Why was he there?'

'He was on a work assignment.'

'What kind of work?'

'He is a photographer.'

'Weddings?'

'Newspapers.'

'For?'

'He does work for the army, the Associated Press, a few other news agencies,' says the little girl with the big hair, the only one who listened to you recount your day.

'Sri Lankan Army?'

'That was a few years ago. He's not with them now.'

'Then he might be doing another assignment for a newspaper, no?' ASP Ranchagoda has turned his attention from the corridor. His head wobbles as if it is unconnected to his shoulders.

'He tells us when he goes outstation. He calls us when he's back,' says DD. 'He was supposed to pick up Jaki this morning. Not a word.'

'I do the night show at SLBC,' says Jaki. 'Maali always picks me up.'

Detective Cassim looks up from the illegible things he is scrawling. He turns to the older woman. You know her as Amma.

'Madam, why don't you all go home and see if he comes back.'

'You think we're here for a joke?' snarls Amma. 'He called me yesterday. We haven't spoken in months. Said he wanted to meet for lunch. Which he never does. Something wasn't right. I knew it then.'

What? Lunch with Amma. The last time you did that, Elvis was still in the building. You shake your camera, hoping it will dislodge a memory that would make all of this make sense. But the lens stays muddy.

Detective Cassim and ASP Ranchagoda exchange a look that is noticed by everyone in the room. The former nods, while the latter shakes his head.

'You all have ID?'

DD extracts a card from the wallet you gave him two birthdays ago. Your Amma, who lost her ID to a washing machine, pulls a maroon Lankan passport from a leather bag. Jaki produces a blue British one from a cloth bag and rubs a hanky over her eyes.

Detective Cassim moves his lips as he transcribes. The ASP walks over to peer over his shoulder.

'Jacqueline Vairavanathan. Twenty-five. Tamil,' says ASP Ranchagoda. 'Lakshmi Almeida. Seventy-three. Burgher.' He looks to the older lady. 'Malinda Kabalana is a Sinhalese name, no?'

The lady looks up from the form she is filling. She speaks in a voice as cold as her stare. 'His father was Sinhalese. I am Burgher. We are Sri Lankan. Is there an issue?'

'No issue, madam. No issue.'

Ranchagoda makes a laugh so awkward it sounds like a snort.

Outside in the waiting room, there is wailing. Ranchagoda walks outside to console the weeping woman. He does so by pulling out his baton and asking a constable to remove her.

'You have checked the hospitals?'

'Yes. And the casinos,' says Jaki.

'He's gambling again?' asks DD.

'He's a gambler?' asks Detective Cassim.

DD says no and Jaki says yes, and mother dearest shakes her head and looks at her purse.

'You come back Thursday, ah,' says ASP Ranchagoda, nodding as the Detective pushes his pen across a paper no one will read. 'Nothing we can do till then. Nowadays, so many missing cases.'

He points to the waiting room outside, where someone's mother is shouting at someone else's. Jaki's eyes spit like they did in Nuwara Eliya when the boy she was flirting with started hitting on you. 'DD, why don't you call your father?'

DD fingers the bone carving below his Adam's apple, the cross with an oval head gifted by you, given with guilt after you played with the boy from the FujiKodak shop on DD's bed and DD never found out. Below it is a wooden pendant that contains your blood.

'DD. Call your fucking father.'

Jaki hisses, and the Detective and the ASP raise their eyebrows.

'I need you to calm down,' says DD. 'Aunty Lucky, are you done with that form?'

Your Amma sits in the corner, looks at the four pages of mostly Sinhala script, a language that is not her first, despite living her entire life in country that claims it is their only. She shakes her head. 'He could be anywhere.'

'We will check the airport and the train stations,' says Detective Cassim. 'There was trouble in Jaffna last week. He may be still there. Or staying with other friends. Did he have other friends?' He looks at Jaki. 'Girlfriends, maybe?'

'No girlfriends.'

'People have secrets, you know. In this job, we have seen everything there is to see.'

'Check if he's being held at another station? We will wait.'

DD remains polite and his syntax does not waver but you spy lava bubbling beneath the eyelids. He always plays with jewellery before he explodes. He is squeezing that ankh on his neck like it is bubble wrap.

'We'll get someone on it,' says ASP Ranchagoda. 'Department is busy.'

'Looks busy,' says DD, staring through the window at a huddle of cops drinking tea. The mothers in the queue curse DD and his tight, queue-jumping butt. Jaki dabs at her eyes and glares back.

'He's been picked up before. All misunderstandings. Can you find out please, officer?'

'Is he doing politics?'

Your Amma looks at DD, who looks to Jaki. They know nothing of anything of what you have done, and for this you are grateful. 'He is a photojournalist,' says Lucky Kabalana née Almeida, handing over the form. 'He takes photos for the news.'

'JVP?'

'Never,' she says.

Ranchagoda takes ten minutes to sign off on the form. Cassim takes another ten to find the official stamp. DD calls his father from the waiting room phone, while the mothers in the queue keep glaring. Jaki and your Amma take turns insisting that Maali Almeida was never connected to any political or terror group.

'He worked for the army, you say? Who was his CO?'

Jaki shakes her head at DD. The policemen swap looks. They do not know that you are sitting between them and cursing them in filth. You feel a wave of nausea and pictures flood your vision, images of blood and bodies and strapping corporals. If you could speak, you would've told them that the answer was the King of Clubs, Major Raja Udugampola.

Cassim arrives with the stamp and smiles. He points to the thing dangling from DD's choker.

'Did you get that from the Crow Uncle?'

'Excuse me?'

'The Crow Uncle. Kark Maama from Kotahena? Who gives out charms? Never mind.'

And then DD starts scolding the cops' names in raw filth mixed with bad Sinhalese. 'Sperm dog... Your Amma screw! I will sue you in court both.'

It is a rage from nowhere that you have seen on multiple occasions. Amidst expletives and insults he unveils a very logical set of grievances like he did when you asked to go to Vanni for three months. Jaki pulls him out into the waiting room and sits him next to the waiting mothers, who all look tickled to see the rich boy lose it.

Inside the room there is a beat of silence. Your Amma looks at Ranchagoda and then at Cassim.

'You will find my boy,' she says.

'Madam,' says Ranchagoda, closing the file. 'You know how it is, no?'

'I will cover your expenses. Go find my boy.'

Your Amma's negotiation skills made up for her complete lack of empathy, sympathy and decency. She could bargain an insolvent fruit seller into giving away free mangoes.

'The army and STF are arresting revolutionaries around the country. Police are only called to clean the mess. If the Forces are involved, our hands are tied. There are no guarantees, madam, especially if your boy is political.'

Your Amma leans forward while Ranchagoda holds his skeleton still. 'I don't expect any.'

'You must know, madam. Some bodies are never found. Every day, I speak to twenty, thirty mothers like you.'

'Then you must be rich. Take this. If you return my boy, there will be more.'

'Rich and poor are all equal before the law.'

'That's a good joke.'

Your Amma smiles without dropping her glare, her resolve steeled by years of marriage to a narcissist.

'You will find my boy. Or we will have your badge and your uniform. No need for courts. Do you understand?'

Ranchagoda raises an eyebrow and shakes his head. Cassim has been silent all through the negotiation. He adjusts his belt, tucks in his belly and stares at the freshly stamped report.

'Madam, Cinnamon Gardens Police Station don't take bribes. We don't run errands for politicians. Even for big men like Stanley Dharmendran. We don't bend laws. Not all police are thugs, Mrs Kabalana.'

'I am Mrs Almeida. I may be Burgher, but I also have connections. Stanley Dharmendran is a Cabinet Minister. He will bring the Minister of Justice to talk to your boss.'

'Madam. The Minister of Justice is our boss,' chuckles Ranchagoda. 'What is Dharmendran? Youth Affairs Minister?'

'I thought Women's Affairs,' mutters Cassim.

DD and Jaki storm back in and there is more heated discussion, which you do not quite follow, owing to the choppy Sinhala and the shouting. More mothers enter the waiting room before the constables blockade them with forms and questions and unsheathed batons. The mothers threaten to storm the office room, pointing at DD, Jaki and your Amma, and ask why they did not queue. Detective Cassim gives ASP Ranchagoda a nod and receives an eye roll in response.

'We are told to wait seventy-two hours,' says Ranchagoda.

'But, as a personal favour to Minister Stanley, we will begin investigate,' says Cassim. 'You say he was meeting a client last night?'

'He was working for a human rights NGO. Something to do with 1983,' says Jaki, the only one in the room who listens more than she speaks.

'He didn't tell me that,' says DD.

Jaki turns to the Detective. 'He had clients. Not just army or AP. BBC, Pravda, Reuters. He had private clients. But he wasn't political. He didn't believe in sides.'

'Everyone has a side, madam. Especially in these times. You have any names or numbers? At least for his Commanding Officer?'

You stand behind her and whisper the name 'Major Raja Udugampola' over and over as if you are planting a melody in her brain. It doesn't appear to be a catchy one.

'We don't know.'

'How do you expect us to work? What about his Pravda or Reuters or *Dinamina* contacts? Give us something.'

Jaki takes a breath and speaks slowly. 'He met his clients at the Hotel Leo.'

DD and Lucky look at her in surprise.

'The casino?' asks DD.

'Hotel Leo is a shady place. Why there?' asks Cassim.

'I don't know. He liked it there.' Jaki frowns and then turns to DD. 'You thought he gave up gambling?'

'You are missing the point.' Your Amma doesn't need to raise her voice to command the room. 'My boy is missing and you need to find him. We are wasting time.'

Ranchagoda remains at the door, swivelling his neck like a giraffe. One eye on the commotion in the waiting room, one on the negotiation in here. Cassim rolls back to his desk like a panda and runs over the missing persons form, two hours in the making and freshly stamped.

'I'll be honest, Mrs Almeida. These are not good times. We will do our level best.' He rises, and everyone else in the room gets to their feet.

'We will personally investigate,' says Ranchagoda. 'And we will be in touch. Madam, if you like, you may leave your form here.'

Lakshmi Almeida née Kabalana, mother of the fatherless Maali Almeida, places some currency atop the form and watches Ranchagoda's floating skull bob up and down while Cassim turns his chubby face and walks away.

DD, Jaki and your Amma walk through the oven that is the waiting room, past the mothers, reduced to simpering at guards, and the broken fathers, who glare and spit curses, both of whom your people pretend to not see. The snarls on their faces and the confusion in their eyes remind you of another waiting room from which you only recently escaped.

You should follow DD, Jaki and your Amma, and tell them the things you couldn't. Tell them where the photos are hidden. Tell two of them you love them. And one of them that you don't. It's what you want to do, what you should do. Though instead you follow the cops.

THE ODDS

The memories come to you with pain. The pain has many shades. Sometimes, it arrives with sweat and itches and rashes. At other times, it comes with nausea and headaches. Perhaps like amputees feeling absent limbs, you still hold the illusion of your decaying corpse. One minute you are retching, the next you are reeling, the next you are remembering.

You met Jaki five years ago in the Casino at Hotel Leo. She was twenty, just out of school, and losing pathetically at baccarat. You were back from a torrid tour of the Vanni, unhinged by the slaughter, breaking bread with shady people, seeing the bad wherever you looked, and wearing your notorious red bandanna. You had sold the photos to Jonny at the Associated Press and cashed a welcome six-figure cheque. Even in Lankan rupees, six figures are better than five.

You had outplayed the house at blackjack, whacked the crab at the buffet and washed it down with some free gin. A regular day at the office.

'Don't bet on ties, sister,' you said to the strange girl with frizzy hair and black make-up. She looked at you and rolled her eyes, which you found strange. Women usually like the look of you, not knowing that you prefer cock to cooch. A trimmed beard, an ironed shirt and a bit of deodorant will elevate you above a herd of sweaty Lankan hetero males.

'I just won twenty thousand rupees,' she said.

You noticed she was alone and that no one was hitting on her, both unusual for women in casinos in Colombo.

'And the chances of you winning that again are nine per cent. And this house only pays out seven-to-one, minus commission. Which means, follow that strategy a hundred times and you will lose, even when you win.'

'A man who knows everything. What a surprise.'

The croupier stared you down. You shrugged and placed her chips on the banker. She half smiled and half frowned, but let you commandeer her bet.

'You better pay if I lose that.'

'If you can't think in numbers, this place will eat you up, sweetheart. The universe is all mathematics and probabilities.'

'I come to get mellow. Not to do sums,' she said.

When the bet came in, she let you place another, and then another.

'It's no fun when someone else does it for you.'

'That's not true at all,' you said.

You took her to the buffet and had chocolate biscuit pudding and smoked Gold Leafs while an ageing diva sang 'Tarzan Boy' to a Yamaha keyboard. Jaki complained in a

London accent about how she hated Sri Lanka, living with her Aunty, and working mornings at the Sri Lanka Broadcasting Corporation. How her aunt's new husband came into her room without knocking and how it creeped her out.

Your father, absent since you were fifteen, paid for many of your failed careers. In your twenties, you studied finance for a summer and worked insurance for a winter. You left with a loathing of both games, but knowing everything you needed about the rudiments of gambling. Investment vs Yield. What you put in vs What you earn. The likelihood of something happening vs What it costs.

You've never placed a bet you couldn't win. Which is not the same as not losing. You went in eyes open, knowing all the angles and most of the odds. The odds of winning the lottery are one in eight million. The odds of dying in a car are one in four thousand. And, according to Mr Kinsey, the odds of being born homo are one in ten.

What are the odds of being born in a war-torn shithole? Considering most of the planet lives on nothing, and considering there's never been an era of peace in all of recorded history, you'd say pretty high.

You told Jaki to stop thinking red vs black, and to start thinking odds. What are the chances the guy next to you has a Jack or that the dealer will draw a Five or that everyone believes your hand is better than theirs?

She got drunk and passed out at the roulette table. When you volunteered to put her in a taxi, the bouncers gave you a wink. She couldn't tell you her address so you took her home. When she woke on your couch, you gave her a lecture about going out alone and getting drunk. She was too busy staring at your photographs to listen.

'These photographs could get you killed,' she said.

'So could getting drunk at casinos,' you replied.

She went home with you for many nights after. While your Amma snored down the hallway, you sat up drinking wine, listening to *Top of the Pops* on your shortwave and talking ends and odds. What are the chances that the slaughter will end, that you'd be caught in a bomb, that the voices in your head can survive your death? What are the chances that a woman could walk down a Colombo street without being called 'nangi', 'darling' or 'slut'? What are the chances that Colombo would get a nightclub that opened past 2 a.m.?

Usually, when you brought women home, which was about as frequent as a free and fair election, the women – usually drunk – expected you to paw them and rub lips against them and got offended when you didn't. This one didn't seem to care.

'You have a girlfriend?' she asked, her eyes giving you a squint.

'No one that matters,' you said.

'But plenty that don't?' She did a strange laugh.

There was something brazen about her, something odd. Something beyond the make-up and the hair and the ill-fitting dress. She spoke with the squeak of a child but with the authority of a tyrant.

'If you want me to come back, you need to stop calling me 'girl' or 'sister' or 'sweetheart'.'

'You have a boyfriend?'

'I'm saving myself for my wedding night. So don't get any ideas.'

'That's fine with me, girl.'

First, you became her gambling buddy, then her agony aunt, then her clubbing partner. You told her how to handle the creeps at work and the aunts at home and her new uncle visiting her room without knocking.

'Always be cheerful. But never put up with shit. And put a lock on that door.'

In exchange, she kept you from thinking of the things you'd photographed in the war zone. She got you into parties at embassies and hotels thrown by rich Colombo International School classmates, among whom were confused boys with perfect skin. Jaki didn't mind that you disappeared from parties, Jaki didn't mind if you talked to boys, though she hated you talking to girls. And Jaki didn't care if you didn't touch her.

On some evenings, Jaki would inflict her music on you, off-key singers mewling over tedious rhythms. She'd drown you in Chardonnay and suggest zany schemes like moving to a hippie colony in Arugam Bay or staging an exhibition of all the photos under your bed. It was she who came up with the genius plan of becoming flatmates.

The beauty of studying odds is knowing which cards are worth betting on. And knowing that freak occurrences happen every day while no one watches. You can shuffle a pack this minute and deal a sequence that has never occurred in the history of all humanity. By your estimation, you have more chance of dying in a bomb blast in cosmopolitan Colombo than in deepest darkest Jaffna. Because, at least in the war zone, you knew which direction the bombs were flying and who was dropping them.

There was surprisingly little scandal for an unwed twenty-two-year-old sharing a flat with two unwed males in their thirties. Her aunties were happy to relinquish the burden, and your own Amma, as usual, did not give a flying toss. As far as Jaki's parents in London were concerned, she was sharing with her cousin and his friend, and Uncle Stanley would overlook proceedings. Her friends thought you and Jaki were dating, a rumour that neither wished to confirm nor quell. Being a couple gave you a chaperone and a shield, whichever room you chose to enter.

'You may not like my cousin,' she said. 'The guy's super-posh.'

'Is he fun?'

'We don't talk,' she said. 'You don't have to talk to him. He's a lawyer who plays rugby and dates bimbettes. He's shallow and dull. Will make a great politician.'

For the first month, you were hardly at home. You were photographing captured arsenals for Major Raja Udugampola, covering the Anuradhapura bomb blast with Andy McGowan from *Newsweek*, and beating your losing streak at Pegasus Casino.

You didn't meet the cousin until your second month and when you did there was little more than small talk. You recognised him from school, though he had no idea who you were. Then you noticed how he smelled after returning from a swim, the rhythm of his walk, how his shorts clung to his hips and how he looked at you from the corner of his eye. You sat in the lounge with windows that overlooked Galle Face Green, watched crows and daydreamed of the landlord's son.

The flat belonged to Stanley Dharmendran, Minister for Youth Affairs, MP for Kalkuda, lone Tamil in Cabinet, ower of numerous favours. His son, of course, was Dilan Dharmendran, former swimmer, athlete and ruggerite, old boy of St Joseph's College, and love of your short sad life.

CHAT WITH DEAD LAWYER (1983)

You try to follow the cops, but the wind dissipates and blows you above the trees. Every corrugated roof has a cat or a mongoose or a spirit slithering along its curves. You glide across the Beira, skim past the railway lines, and lose direction at the Pettah bus stand as you collide with other breezes.

Perched aboard the bus stop is a creature you recognise. A woman in a pink sari with rolls of tied-up hair. A woman you once saw burn alive. You took a photo of her that *Newsweek* paid for and never published. You hope she doesn't recognise you.

She glares at you with reddening eyes. Her sari has been singed and clings to her like cellophane. Her skin has the wrinkle of crackling pork, the only dish that DD could make better than your Amma's cook Kamala, under whose bed your life's work gathers dust.

'It happened too fast' – your excuse and that of those around you. 'She must've been a terrorist,' said no one that day and no one since. Because, in 1983, we had yet to consider all Tamils as the enemy. That would soon change.

You were on your way to photograph a punk band named Coffin Nail at their Green Path residence. They asked you to do it because you had a decent camera, one of those guilt-laden gifts that your Dada had sent you in lieu of love.

It was the same Nikon 3ST that you see around your neck now, but that one worked. You could do nothing but shoot and that made you feel like you weren't doing nothing. You clicked her being dragged by the hair and doused in petrol. And, right when the match was lit, the Nikon jammed.

'I know you were there,' she says. 'I remember every face. The Minister was there, watching from his car. You were there, taking my picture, like it was some fucking wedding.'

'I wasn't part of the mob, I swear. I just had the camera.'

'If you were part of the mob, I would feed you to the Mahakali.'

'I was in the wrong place holding a camera.'

'Is that your slogan?'

Her eyes are red and brown. Her voice is black.

'I'm sorry for what happened. I wish we could've stopped it.'

'Thank you. That means less than nothing.'

She heard that victims of the 1987 Pettah bomb blast have tracked down the bombers responsible and are holding them in a cave nearby. They are waiting for all 113 victims to arrive, so they can dispense justice. She is here to help them decide on a suitable punishment.

'If suicide bombers knew they end up in the same waiting room with all their victims,' says the ghoul in her slithery voice, 'they may think twice.'

The ghoul tells you she was a lawyer who had chambers in Maradana, until on 21 July 1983 she walked past the bus stand to buy cigarettes and encountered a Sinhalese mob with torches. 'I always knew smoking would kill me,' she deadpans.

She wears a sari and a pottu which may have been more to blame, you think but do not say.

She tells you that she wandered for a thousand moons before she found peace. That many of the victims of the 1983 riots are still roaming the In Between.

'Some walked into The Light. Some became demons. The Light makes you forget. We should never forget.'

In the flickering moonlight her skin looks made from snake. Her arms weave like cobras, her hair writhes like a nest of serpents and the burns on her skin glow like embers. Once again you lift your broken camera and take the photo without asking.

'In '83, we didn't think to get organised. We were too stunned. These days, people are angrier. Especially when they die. Did I say you could photograph?'

'There's mud in the aperture. The lens is cracked.'

'So, why carry it with you?'

'The photos I don't take are the best ones,' you say.

She says that all 113 victims of the '87 Pettah bus stand bomb have refused to have ears checked or be coaxed towards The Light. They want to see the suicide bombers punished and demand to speak to whoever is in charge.

According to the Dead Lawyer, the Helpers in white are volunteers. Souls who have visited The Light and opted to come back here. They claim to represent whoever is in charge, though they can't agree on who that could be.

'What's in it for them?'

'Who knows? Even do-gooders have their agendas.'

The ghoul says she was saved by a Naga yaka or snake demon and given back her skin. 'And my dignity. And my self-respect,' she says. 'Lord Naga helped me discard the pain and remember what was me. I am not my skin.'

You decide against mentioning that her skin resembles that of a garden snake and she hisses back at you as if reading your thoughts.

'As if I was a great beauty before.'

'If The Light helps you forget, is that bad?'

'I see they have got to you already.'

'Malinda... Almeida...'

You hear your name blow in from Pettah's streets and you scramble towards it. You look back. The Dead Lawyer in the pink salwar does not notice your departure. You climb to the top of the tree and listen, and you hear it again.

Below, at the bus stop, the ghoul in pink looks up and sees you fleeing. She hisses at you and bares her teeth.

'Come back here, camera man.'

You do not want to stay. So, you silence your mind and listen for the winds. You hear your name spoken. And, once more, you share in its shame.

HOTEL LEO

'No Malinda, no Kabalana, no Albert, no Almeida.'

ASP Ranchagoda and Detective Cassim take the blue Datsun instead of the squad car. Ranchagoda turns on the ignition and a Sinhala song that you don't know and cannot hum comes on. Cassim uses his rice belly as a desk and writes down all three of your names in his notebook.

'You checked all police stations?' he asks.

'You think I'm a computer?' says Ranchagoda. 'I called the big five.'

Cassim circles four names and sticks a question mark next to each one. 'We go to the hotel.'

'Now?'

'You took money from the mother.'

'So what?'

'Maali Almeida was meeting someone there.'

'Can't we go tomorrow?' asks Ranchagoda, as the Datsun turns into office traffic. It is evening and you have missed the first sunset since your death.

'Four bags of garbage went into storage at Hotel Leo last night,' says Cassim, looking at a Cyclostyled report. 'Only three were on the list.'

'When have the lists ever been accurate?'

'If you're taking money, we need to investigate.'

'So there's an extra garbage bag at Leo. Not the first time.'

'Let's find out.'

'I'm tired, boss. Not one day's leave in three months.'

'We can claim overtime.'

'Really?'

'That shut you up.'

'Can we claim for double?'

'Ado! Watch out!'

The car swerves to avoid a tilting bus and Cassim swears into his palm. They have entered Slave Island via the back of the Beira Lake. The streets are narrow and paved with garbage. In a box under a bed, you have a photo of this road at dawn, featuring a urinating dog and a cat eating a crow. You submitted it for many competitions that you didn't win.

The Leo was a cheap inn for migrant workers in the nineteenth century. The structure had been razed after the Second Big Euro war, bought by a businessman called Sabaratnam and opened as a cinema in 1965 by Prime Minister Dudley himself. It famously played *The Sound of Music* for nine months in 1967, and less famously *Hard Ticket to Hawaii* for two months in 1989.

Sabaratnam was friends with the ruling party of the '70s and leased the top floors to the Ministry of Justice. Floor eight housed interrogation rooms during the '71 JVP purge and the '77 Tamil riots. The mob in 1983 knew none of this when it set fire to the ground floor. The owner, a fortunate Tamil with wealth to protect him, watched in dismay from the safety of the Galadari Hotel. Old man Sabaratnam died of a broken heart, his family moved to Canada, the building went into decline, and the ghosts moved in.

In 1988, the Pegasus Casino moved to the sixth floor and began painting the walls, tiling over burned bricks and moving in furniture. Within a year, there was a nightclub and a massage parlour on the fifth floor and rooms to rent on the seventh. The fourth floor was leased to a company called Asian International Fisheries who packed, refrigerated and transported unsold seafood from across the west coast to three countries in Asia. The bottom three floors were home to a mall that no one went to.

How you know all this and how much money you have lost here may never be recalled. Nor the reason why you keep seeing the face of a lady whose name you do not know. The Queen of Spades. The lady with dark skin, darker eyes, red lipstick and a redder pottu. Sitting across from you, buying you beer, asking you that one question, 'Tell me, kolla, which side are you on?'

You follow the cops as they trample parquet floors and enter through a rusted door. The third floor smells like something between kerosene and mothballs. There are photocopy shops, job agencies and tailors. You follow the cops as they swagger down the hallway and turn into a shop called Pegasus Finance.

Cassim looks at his partner. 'Can you talk to these fools?'

'What's wrong with your mouth?'

'You want the overtime or not?'

'OK, but you file the claim, then? Deal?'

'I'm not here to do deals with you,' says Cassim.

'Are you sure?' says Ranchagoda.

'When my transfer comes through, you'll have to do this alone.'

'Where did you apply for transfer?'

'Somewhere with no corpses.'

'Where is that? Maldives?'

'Everywhere can't be like this.'

'Everywhere has corpses, my friend. You think the transfer will come?'

'Any year now.'

The shop has the same logo of the winged horse as the casino two floors above it. The cops enter it and you do, too. Seated behind the desk surrounded by file covers and a fax machine are two short men whom you wish you didn't recognise. They see the police officers and smile with their teeth while frowning with their eyes.

Ranchagoda puts his hands on the desk and slaps down a photo of you given to them by your Amma. You are wearing the red bandanna and have chains around your neck. It was taken by DD in Yala beneath a darkening sky.

'Kottu Aiya. Balal malli. Have you seen this fellow?'

· ·

Strange for a man of his hobbies, Balal cannot stand the smell of dead fish. Asian International Fisheries owns the fourth floor of Hotel Leo but only has keys to the front door. This is the wholesale room, where supermarkets and hotel chains bargain for frozen marine creatures. Men in sarongs drag mops across the floor. It is as effective against this stench as a stick of jasmine against a charging elephant.

Further in are the fridge rooms. AIF have keys to these and so does the Ministry that owns the building. Balal and Kottu are making nervous chatter about a cricket match with Pakistan that no one saw or cared about. They lead the way through the labyrinth, its walls smell of unwashed bodies, a smell you are not unfamiliar with.

The cops hold khaki hankies to their noses and muddle through narrowing corridors smeared with the russet brown of old blood. You didn't know that cops colour-coordinated their handkerchiefs with their uniforms. You used to always carry a hanky, the only lesson you kept from a month in Cub Scouts.

'Where did you find it?' asks Ranchagoda.

'Out back,' says Kottu. 'Wasn't in the usual spot.'

'And you can't call us?'

'Sir, if we call for every extra garbage bag, will have thumping bill.'

'Wasn't on any list?' says Cassim.

'Not on your list, not on big boss list.'

'Problem is you buggers have too many bosses.'

'Only sir's office gives list. Other police never give. Just leave us the mess to clean.'

'So, you recognise this face?'

'I never look at faces, sir,' says Kottu.

At the end of the corridor is a big door with a large padlock. The hallway is as brightly lit as a hospital. The ceiling contains shadows that only you can see. You hear whispers and dare not look up. Balal fumbles with the keys and the door opens to a room with more refrigeration units. These do not have the smell of fish but of high-grade chemicals.

On a metal gurney are three long slabs of meat. 'It's one of these?' asks Ranchagoda, removing the hanky from his mouth.

'No. That is today's garbage,' says Balal.

Ranchagoda frowns.

'Problem? Too much work?'

'No, sir. Nothing like that.'

'Then stop whining. Where's Almeida?'

Kottu points to a metal table with four parcels in a siri-siri bag. Two look like limbs, the others like pounds of flesh. Balal lets out a giggle and Cassim silences him with a hiss.

．．

The neighbourhood was called 'Kompanya Veediya' by the Sinhalese and 'Komani Theru' by the Tamils, both meaning

'Company Street'. The British called it 'Slave Island'. These names persist today and provide unsubtle clues to how natives and colonisers viewed one another.

The back of Hotel Leo is an abandoned lot that serves as a rubbish dump for the neighbourhood. The surrounding streets are crumbling buildings and slums. The crenellated rooftops are occupied by worried cats and bored bats.

'Body was here?' Cassim points to the dent in the garbage bags with the splatters in red.

Kottu and Balal nod.

'You thought it was a drop-off?'

'Sir, this building is a drop-off point,' says Kottu.

'You didn't think there was too much blood?'

'Didn't think like that, sir.'

Cassim shines a torch up the walls of the hotel. It looked like red and brown paint had been thrown down its side.

'You didn't notice those stains?'

'Sir, when collecting garbage, no time to look at scenery.'

'Keep talking like that and see what happens,' snaps Ranchagoda. 'From today, you will give full paperwork.'

Balal and Kottu are silent. Cassim shines his torch around the rest of the dump. The night has been one of bad smells. A breeze whizzes past him and makes him shiver.

Cassim turns to Kottu. 'He was thrown from one of those balconies. Not by us. Right?'

Balal nods, Kottu coughs and looks away.

'So, where's rest of the body?'

Kottu looks at Balal, who looks at his feet. 'It's gone, sir.'

'I'm supposed to give his mother some limbs, a shoulder and... I don't know what that is? How do we prove it's Almeida?'

Ranchagoda speaks up. 'If he was taken in before, his prints will be on file.'

Cassim shakes his head. 'I trust our fingerprint department less than I trust you. Where's the head?'

'We threw it in the lake.'

'I don't want to hear it. Get me the head. I don't care if you have to drain the whole stinking Beira. We need it tonight.'

Kottu picks up the phone in the office and gets Drivermalli out of bed. Cassim lumbers towards the lift.

'What are we doing, detective?' asks Ranchagoda, once they are out of earshot.

'Better put in for overtime, putha.'

Ranchagoda pauses outside the lift and does not go in.

Cassim gets inside and holds it with his finger.

'What's the issue?'

'Lokka. First you say you are transferring away from corpses. Now you want to put in overtime.'

'We have our job to do.'

'What's our job?'

'We protect the innocent,' says Detective Cassim.

'I thought we protect the powerful.'

'Do we need to discuss this now?' Cassim takes his finger off the button, which causes the doors to close. He curses and sticks his arm out to block the lift's jaws.

'I'm confused about another thing.'

'Get in the lift now!'

'Are we investigating this? Or covering this up?'

. .

It is only when you're inside the hotel that you notice the shadows and the faces hiding in them. The eyes come in many colours, in blues and browns and yellows and greens. You no more wish to engage with them than you wish to lick a beehive, so you keep to yourself and follow the cops.

Kottu goes back to the office on the fourth floor, where he mans the phones and receives terse messages on corpses coming in.

'Six more bags? From where?'

Balal waits for Drivermalli's arrival to take him through some very precise instructions.

One floor up, Officers Cassim and Ranchagoda enter the Mango Massage House with a photograph. It was taken of you by DD in, as they say, happier times. You are wearing your signature safari jacket and less of a beard than usual.

The girls are clad in saris and look used to being paraded. They deny having seen the man in the photo. The cops walk down the hall to a karaoke lounge named The Den. There are only cleaning staff and a man in a miniskirt who flees at the sight of men in khaki. The place is empty aside from apparitions at the bar drinking imaginary booze and having arguments.

The cops are ushered through the back to see the boss, a burly type named Rohan Chang. His predecessor was the notorious Kalu Daniel, currently serving time for armed robbery. Chang also robs people for a living, though his weapons are card packs and spinning wheels. He sits behind his desk, orders fresh juice for the officers and calls in his floor manager, his pit boss and two croupiers.

Chang looks as Chinese as his father and sounds as Sinhalese as his mother. 'Here, if you're coming to my casino, don't come in bloody uniform,' says the boss man. 'I know the Minister. You can't just come like this.'

'Very sorry, Mr Chang. Very urgent case.'

'What urgent case?'

'Mr Maali. Card man,' says the dealer who once played you out of five lakhs.

'Regular? Spender? Drinker?'

'Smoker. Doesn't talk. Plays cards. Blackjack, baccarat, bit of poker,' says the pit boss who once fined you for spilling chips.

'Reported missing,' says Ranchagoda.

Eyebrows are raised and shoulders are shrugged.

'He's disappeared?' The croupier whom everyone ignores scratches his beard.

'When was he seen?' asks Cassim, pulling out a notepad with nothing written in it.

'Last night, I think,' says the pit boss. 'He won a few lakhs. Bought drinks for everyone. Drinks are free was his little joke, which he kept repeating. Then he vanished.'

'He didn't vanish,' says the croupier. 'He went upstairs. I saw him drinking with a foreigner.'

You do not recognise the croupier, nor remember doing what he said you did. Either the croupier is lying or, worse, he is telling the truth. You look through your camera and see only mud.

'What kind of foreigner?'

'A suddha. White man. German, I think. But could be English.'

The Balcony

The balcony is five floors up and overlooks the slum and the rubbish dump. There is a bar at the end of it and five tables with snack menus on them. A metal staircase vines upwards to the balcony of the sixth floor and curls down past the casino to the landing on the fourth.

The croupier leads the cops through the kitchen, preferring not to parade them through the casino. The balcony has wire mesh from its railing to its ceiling.

'We had a few of our clients jump from here. So we sealed it up.'

'Why would they jump from here?'

'Have you lost a year's salary on a hand of poker?'

'My year's salary isn't worth betting on,' says Ranchagoda.

'Where was Almeida and his suddha friend?'

'They were seated near the edge.'

'And?'

'They ordered three gins, three vodkas, two tonics and three plates of devilled prawns.'

'You memorised that?'

'No. This is their bill,' says the pit boss, grabbing a pink carbon slip from the strapping young bartender.

'That's a lot of prawn. Why is a pit boss hanging around the balcony waiting tables?'

'I was with a client, officer.'

'Who?'

'Just a business client.'

'Did you recognise the white man?'

'Not really.'

'Is that a no?'

'Every suddha looks the same to me.'

Cassim stands at the edge of the casino bar and looks down into the rubbish dump. He surveys the bloodstains down the wall. Then he looks up at the balcony on the sixth.

'But you recognised Almeida?'

'Mr Almeida is a local.'

'So you knew him?'

'I know the people who like to gamble.'

Here's what you remember from two nights ago: (a) visiting the Leo Casino, (b) drinking at the bar, (c) eating the buffet, (d) fooling around with the bartender. Here's what you don't remember: (a) sitting with a suddha, (b) being thrown to your death.

'And what time did they leave?'

'They were here when I left with my client.'

'What time?'

'Around 11 p.m.'

'Any other staff?'

'Just the bartender.'

'That guy?'

The pit boss calls out.

'Chaminda!'

The lad isn't good-looking. He is built like an ox and has a face like one. You never asked his name, and after a few encounters it would've been rude to inquire, so you settled for the universal 'malli'. He served you promptly, accepted generous tips, let you accompany him to the sixth floor balcony during smoke break, and didn't worry about where your hands went. He looks the cops straight in the eye like liars often do.

'Yes, I know that sir. He came last night.'

No pun intended, you think.

'That was about 11 p.m. He was smoking when I took my fag break.'

Ha-ha, you think.

'What did you talk about?'

'Nothing. He said he was going to San Francisco. He had a big win downstairs.'

'Did he give you any money?'

The ox stiffens, darts his eyes around the bar, does not see you, of course, and then recovers, hoping that no one notices, though everyone does.

'Chaminda?'

'He owed me a few thousand. He paid me back.'

'For what?'

'He borrowed when he was short of chips. A lot of our customers do.'

'When was he going to San Francisco?'

'Ado, Cassim!' Ranchagoda has peeled back the wire mesh and stuck his head through it. 'Come see this.'

At the sight of his mesh being wrenched from its fastenings, the pit boss drops his polite veneer.

'Yako! Don't break that!'

Ranchagoda peers through the wire and follows the trail of blood leading up to the heavens.

He climbs up the fire escape like a pole cat, ignoring protests from the casino staff. Corpulent Cassim contemplates the ascent and thinks better of it. The balcony is dusty and cobwebbed and its connecting door locked. It is open to the sky and empty, except for a table and two chairs.

'Where does that door lead?' Cassim points up at the padlock.

Ranchagoda leans over the railing and examines the wall. Unlike its better-maintained twin below, this balcony is not protected by mesh.

'No one comes here.' The pit boss fingers his walkie-talkie and stares at ASP Ranchagoda. Chaminda the bartender looks at his feet, knowing, as you do, that the statement isn't strictly true. People have been known to climb through that mesh, go up those stairs and fool around in the dark.

'This place has been swept recently. This is where he jumped.' Cassim returns to detective mode. 'Or was pushed off.'

'So, where's the body?' asks the pit boss.

'Good question,' says Ranchagoda.

The pit boss has kept his smile and his patience, but both vanish when the cops ask to see the seventh floor.

'Those are just rooms, sir.'

'Who stays in them?'

'Guests.'

'Whores?'

'Casino guests. And their guests.'

'Did Malinda Almeida stay here?'

'I don't know.'

ASP Ranchagoda looks at the croupier and then at the pit boss. He follows Detective Cassim to the lift and smiles. There is an awkward pause.

'Is it common for your customers to jump off balconies?'

'No one goes to that balcony, sir.'

'That's clearly untrue,' says Cassim.

'Sir. There used to be suicides. But not any more. After we put up the mesh and kept the windows from opening.'

'You know there are others using Hotel Leo. Who don't want this building to get a reputation.'

'Understood, sir.'

'How long has that bartender been working for you?'

'A few months only. Good worker.'

'We will take him in for questioning. He seems the last one to have seen Almeida.'

The cops climb the stairs amidst protests from the pit boss.

'Sir, our guests pay for privacy. You need to speak to Rohan boss first.'

The cops ignore him and exit the landing via an unlocked door. There is a security guard at the seventh floor lobby. He wears a tight black T-shirt over a tight black chest and he frowns at the pit boss and nods at the cops.

'Officer, can I help?'

'We'd like to speak to whoever's in there.'

Cassim stands toe to chin with the bouncer and attempts to intimidate him with his chubby face. Ranchagoda reaches in and rings the bell. It is a Casio version of the '50s tune 'Cherry Pink and Apple Blossom White'. You know this shrill sound, this floor and this guard.

You hear several latches unlock before the door opens. You feel an ache where your belly used to be. It claws at your insides, like a creature trapped in your ribcage.

'Yes?'

And there she is. The lady whose face you know, but whose name stalls on your tongue's tip. Charcoal skin, crimson lips, the dark queen.

'Excuse me, madam. We are from the CID. We're looking for this man. Have you seen him?'

She hesitates, looks from Ranchagoda to Cassim, then looks between them, right at where you are floating.

'That's Malin. What's happened?'

Her eyes rest where you are hovering, you stare back and try to remember. Cassim squares his shoulders and Ranchagoda clears his throat.

'May we speak inside, madam?'

Behind her is a hallway with a framed black-and-white picture of bodies burning on a pyre, while men with sticks dance around the flames. It was taken in 1983 on a Nikon 3ST by an amateur photographer named Malinda Almeida Kabalana.

Canada Norway Third World Relief

The walls have photographs that you recognise and paintings that you do not. The photographs are mostly from 1983 and taken without preparation or expertise or a decent lens. There is violence in them all. The paintings are expressionist landscapes of paddy fields and village huts, procured from street markets for the price of a fancy dinner. Dripping with brushstrokes, smears and flamboyant colours, they are signed illegibly by an exploited amateur.

The room is neat except for the table by the window with boxes and files and teacups on it. The woman invites the officers to take seats on the cane couch. You have been in this room before. Of this you have little doubt. But what is her name? You have a vision of a pet lion in a film at the Savoy that your father took you to before he left.

'You have visitors?' Detective Cassim lumbers to the table.

'My cousin-brother is on a call with Toronto. Would you like some tea?'

'Water, thank you,' says Cassim casting his eye around the room.

'I don't mind a plain tea with ginger,' says Ranchagoda, taking a seat by the window and receiving a look from his partner.

'Of course,' says the lady.

A bearded boy who looks more clerk than domestic comes in to take the drinks order.

'Your name, madam?'

'What's happened?'

'Your name?'

'Is Malin OK?'

'Please answer the question.'

'I'm Elsa Mathangi. My cousin-brother and I work for CNTR. This is our office. We raise funds for victims of the war. We have a charity office in the mall downstairs.'

'CNTR stands for?'

'Canada Norway Third World Relief. It's pronounced "Centre".'

'CNTR. Hmm. Working late?'

Cassim looks through the frosted window at the top of Slave Island's shanties. Then he peers into the boxes on the table.

'Sorry, those are confidential,' says the lady.

Cassim ignores her and nods to his partner. The boy returns with tea and water and suddenly you feel thirsty, a sensation you have forgotten, among other things.

'When was the last time you saw Malinda Almeida?'

'Yesterday. He does freelance for us. He came to take his cheque.'

'What kind of work?'

'We use his photos in our newsletters.'

'Are these his photos?' asks Cassim, pointing to the box on the table.

'Some of them.'

'What do you do, madam?'

'We help small businesses, provide education and counselling to the poor. We help orphans in the north and east. We collect donations, spread awareness, protect civilians.'

'This is funded by Tamils?' asks Ranchagoda.

'It is funded by people who want to help those who suffer.'

'What's going on?'

The voice comes from the doorway opposite the kitchen. The man is dark and stocky, with a moustache as thick as the Tiger Supremo's.

'This is my cousin-brother. They're asking about Malin.'

'Tell them he doesn't work for us.'

He resembles his cousin-sister as a polar bear resembles a peacock. She is angular and he is stocky. She has features and he has a snout. Her accent has a North American cadence: he has the croak of a Madrasi Tamil.

Cassim turns towards him.

'And you are?'

'Kugarajah. Director of CNTR. I work with the governments of Canada and Norway. I know the Inspector General of Police. What is your good name?'

'I am Detective Cassim. This is ASP Ranchagoda.'

'Malinda resigned yesterday. Took his cheque and left. He may be downstairs gambling it away.'

'Why did he resign?'

'You need to ask him that.'

'We're asking you.'

'Said he was tired of the assignments.'

'He's been reported missing.'

Elsa puts her hand to her mouth and stares at the floor. The man named Kugarajah takes the edge of a vacant couch.

'Has he been arrested?'

'Not to our knowledge. He was last seen on his way here for a meeting.'

'Not with us.'

'You said you saw him yesterday?'

Kugarajah looks at Elsa, who stares into space and shakes her head. Her eyes go foggy.

'He sells us photos. Showing how people are dying in the war zone. We use them in our work.'

Cassim holds a pamphlet of mothers holding photos of their missing sons. Each with a '©MA' along its side. 'Work or propaganda?'

'It's not propaganda if it's truth,' says Kugarajah.

You feel the uncomfortable sensation of drowning and sneezing at the same time. The liquid from your nose does not feel gooey like snot, it feels metallic like blood. 'Kugarajah' is not his real name and he knows exactly why you resigned.

'Did Malin Almeida have enemies?' asks Ranchagoda.

'We don't know of his personal life,' says Elsa.

'What else did he photograph for you?'

'Scenes from the war zone. Burned homes, dead children. You know, the usual.'

'And what do you do with these?'

'We use them to try and stop the war.'

'Is it working?'

'One day it will.'

'Was Almeida doing blackmailing?'

'Like cousin-sister said, we don't know him personally,' says Kugarajah, helping himself to Elsa Mathangi's glass of water. 'Is there a body?'

'We didn't say he was dead.'

'Who's paying you? Army or STF?'

'Who's paying you, Mr Kugarajah? India or LTTE?'

'Watch how you talk, officer,' says Elsa.

'We're doing our job, miss. That is all,' says Detective Cassim. 'May we see the photos?'

Elsa opens a folder of pamphlets written in various European languages. There are shots from Vavuniya, Batti and Trinco. Dead children displayed on mats. The charred carcass of a village hut. Women tied to poles with rags. Air-raid survivors trapped in camps staring back at camera. You feel nauseous. The wind swirls to the ceiling as if the building's spirits are rising to the roof.

'Does your organisation deal with the LTTE?'

'I'd be offended, Officer Ranchagoda, if we didn't get asked that every day,' says Elsa. 'We are sponsored by the US Fund for Peace and the Canadian and Norwegian governments. We are moderates. Most Tamils don't want to run around jungles with guns.'

'Did Almeida have foreign friends? A Caucasian middle-aged man, maybe.'

'He has lots of friends. Old and young, foreign and local,' says Kuga. 'You're talking like he's dead.'

'These days, when someone goes missing, that's how they end up,' says ASP Ranchagoda.

'We all know this,' says Kugarajah.

'We'll let you know if we see him,' says Elsa, getting to her feet.

'You will?'

'Of course,' she says, opening the door.

'May I take some pamphlets?' asks Cassim, helping himself.

'Take and go,' says Kugarajah.

Outside the window there is tapping that only you can hear. A wave of icy air passes the room as if the AC on the wall has let out a burp. The police take their leave while cousin-brother and cousin-sister exchange looks behind their backs. You hear whispers and feel shadows fall across you. You are getting used to this. The hum in the air that only the dead can feel.

Outside, a hooded figure and a lady in white tap at the window and frown at you. They are floating seven floors up and arguing. You wish you did not recognise them, but they are hard to ignore. Grim reaper in garbage bags and fairy godmother in a sari. They are transparent, as all spirits are, and they point to you and then at each other. They are arguing, and the subject of their argument appears to be you.

Sinhalese Killing Sinhalese

The cops take the lift down to the mall. They visit the CNTR charity office and find it closed with a fat padlock. Its glass doors are decorated with posters asking for clothing, foodstuffs and donations. One of them features a Teledrama actress holding a refugee child from the north.

'Ranchagoda, you will type the reports. I will file them.'

'Like I have no other work.'

'Do two reports.'

'Saying what?'

'One saying that there is no record of Almeida, aka Kabalana, being arrested or wanted for questioning. That he is most likely in hiding from gambling debts. Another saying that we have two suspects. The bartender Chaminda Samarakoon, the last person to see him. And his employers, these two Tamils. Elsa Mathangi and Kugarajah.' Cassim mispronounces the names on purpose, Americanising the first and Bollywoodising the second.

He holds up the leaflets.

'If the body turns up, we can offer the second one. If not, use the first.'

'Haven't time for one report. You want two?'

'I told you, no? Mark it as overtime.'

'We should've got more money from the mother. This is not worth our time.'

'What if she asks for the body?'

'Send her on the usual dance,' says Ranchagoda.

'I'm sick of doing that. What do we tell her?'

'The truth. Her son's body has not been found.'

'She'll want her money back.'

'Or she'll pay more.'

'And then?'

'We get Balal and Kottu to find something.'

'Those two can't find the ends of their pricks.'

'What do you think about these Tamils?' asks Ranchagoda.

'Doesn't make sense to me. If they murdered him, why do it next to their offices? Tamils are many things, but they are not fools.'

When they get to the car park, they are greeted by a familiar lady wearing a purple scarf and holding a matching umbrella.

'Where's your squad car?' asks Elsa Mathangi.

'How did you get down so fast?' asks Ranchagoda.

'Some talk fast, some walk slow. Some use the service lift.'

'How can we help you?'

'I am helping you.'

'Is that so?'

'Malin was a big talker. Mostly about things that didn't happen. And about a box of photos under his bed. He said they could topple the government. If you help me find them, I will share them with you.'

'Very generous. But it is late and our shift is ending.'

'Excellent. So you are free.'

'Why didn't you tell this upstairs?'

'Kuga doesn't like cops. But you look like professionals.'

'Mr Kuga is your husband or your cousin?'

'Cousin... My husband is in Toronto.'

'Of course. What's in the photos?'

'Things your bosses may be interested in. Things they'd be willing to buy off you. We are also happy to pay for your troubles.'

She places an envelope on the windshield of the blue Datsun.

Ranchagoda opens the driver's side. Cassim looks annoyed.

'It is late, madam. Anything we are doing, let's do in the morning.'

Ranchagoda picks up the envelope and looks inside.

'This won't cover our overtime.'

'Maybe it will close your case.'

'Maybe you should stick to the north and the east. Let us solve the Colombo crimes.'

'If you get me a warrant, I'll take you to the box. You decide how much it is worth.'

She opens the back door and gets in. Ranchagoda places the envelope on the dashboard. Cassim hunches his shoulders like the sloth bear that he is. Ranchagoda slides into the passenger seat and turns around.

'For the last time, what's in the box?'

'Malin told us he had an envelope marked "Queen". That's all I want.'

'Nothing to do with us.'

'There are photos from Batticaloa, as well.'

Ranchagoda scratches the back of his head and looks down at the gear.

'The East has nothing to do with us.'

'Batticaloa Police Station. Three months ago,' she says.

'The massacre?'

'Six hundred of your brothers executed by...'

'Brothers of yours,' says Ranchagoda with an eyebrow raised.

'If every Sinhala thinks every Tamil is LTTE, this war will never end. The Tigers don't respect Sinhalese cops. I have seen the photos. They didn't even bother wearing masks. How many arrested for that crime?'

Cassim starts the car.

'You're saying Malinda Almeida took photos of the Batticaloa police massacre. He was there?'

'He has a knack for being in the wrong place,' says Elsa, looking out the window. 'Why are we not moving?'

'Not tonight, madam,' says Cassim, his eyes darting across the dashboard. 'Come to the Cinnamon Gardens Police Station at 8 a.m. tomorrow. We will do the needful.'

Of course, she is wrong. If you have a camera, no place is the wrong place. Elsa checks her lipstick in the rear view and meets Ranchagoda's eye. 'You think no one knows what goes on at the fourth floor of Hotel Leo?'

'That's Asian International Fisheries, right. What goes on, miss? Tell us.'

'None of my business. Everyone's catching their own fish.'

She lights a cigarette without lowering the shutter. It is a Gold Leaf from a red pack, which came from a carton that you stole in Batticaloa. The week that you filmed the police station with a telephoto lens from the hill behind the road. It is funny and unfunny what your mind chooses to retain.

'Bodies of dead JVP-ers are not our problem, Detective,' says Elsa. 'If the Sinhalese are killing Sinhalese, why do we care?'

'I thought you care about innocent people dying,' says Ranchagoda.

'We have to look after our people first.'

'That's a bit racist.'

'Only when it is government policy.'

'And when LTTE dogs kill TULF rats? Tamils killing Tamils. That's OK?'

'At least Muslims don't kill Muslims,' says Cassim.

The other two stare at him.

'In Sri Lanka, I mean,' he clarifies.

'Give it time,' says Elsa. 'One day, Malays will be killing Moors. And Burghers will be butchering Chetties. Nothing in this country will surprise me.'

'Malinda Almeida was a Marxist? A JVP-er?' asks Ranchagoda.

'The photos in the box will tell you everything you need to know.'

'If he was a JVP-er, will be easier to get warrant.'

'Fine. I think he attended a few rallies.'

'That's good to know.'

'8 a.m., then. What to do?'

'Where is the location?'

'Galle Face Court, I believe. How much time to get a warrant?'

You cling to the roof of the car, thoughts prodding you like infected needles. The wind around you is polluted with memories that you do not trust. A fresh wave of aches starts at your feet and travel to your eyeballs. You avoid looking at your camera. The car speeds off and you do not travel with it. You race after the blue Datsun but your feet do not touch the tarmac. You try to float but you can move no longer.

The lady in the white sari and the figure in garbage bags stand at your sides shaking their heads. They have finished their argument and it is unclear who has won. The hood comes off to reveal a sheepish Sena. His skin is now as bloodshot as his eyes. 'Maal. You do not have to talk to this woman. She will not help you.'

'Dr Ranee Sridharan,' you say. 'Nice to see you again.'

The woman in the white sari places a thumb in her ledger book, adjusts her spectacles and smiles up at you. 'You may call me Ranee. Helping you is what I am assigned to do,' she says. 'You have seven moons. And you have already wasted one.'

SECOND MOON

☾

Everything happens to everybody
sooner or later if there is time enough

George Bernard Shaw

CHAT WITH DEAD DOCTOR (1989)

They take you to the rooftop of Hotel Leo. It overlooks a stinking city where deeds go unpunished and ghosts walk unseen. Shadows move across the asbestos and not all of them belong to the cats or the bats or the roaches or the rats. Do animals get an afterlife? Or is their punishment to be reborn as human?

A wind blows in from the east, bringing with it the aroma of rain on trees and dew on temple flowers. The breeze smothers the stink for just a little while, before floating seaward, carrying Colombo's fragrances with it.

'That Sena fellow confirms you have amnesia. Very common. Everyone blots out their death. Like they do their births. Both memories return eventually. A good Ear Check will sort you.' Dr Ranee wears a cream sari and a cardigan; her hair quivers in its bun. She speaks into her ledger book and peers at you through her glasses, showing more interest than she did at the counter. 'Very sorry. This last moon has been busy. New systems are coming in, lots of meetings, don't you know? Anyway. Much better to do a face-to-face like this. What do you say?'

You think of all the pictures you have seen of this woman, plastered across the newspapers as saccharine tributes rolled in for the young mother of two and dedicated teacher, struck down in her prime. She was more photogenic than most Tamil moderates that ended up dead.

'Dr Ranee, you remember stealing from me? You used my photos in your articles without permission. I should've sued.'

'Aiyo, child. Now enough. Just leave it, will you? I've had seventy-four previous births. Each of them had tragedy and farce and mistakes. Just like everyone's. Just like yours.'

Activists, like politicians, are skilled in the art of dodging accusations.

'Your book, *Anatomy of a Death Squad*, used three of my photos. Vijaya's killers, Rohana getting beaten, and the burning salwar lady in '83. No permission, no acknowledgement. Definitely no payment.'

'I am not my previous birth. Neither are you.'

'Wanted to come to Peradeniya and blast you. I got sent on assignment to Kilinochchi. And you got... um...'

'Blasted. Yes, Mr Maal. We have a new fast-track system. Only three steps. First, you meditate on your bones, which you seem to have done. Then you receive your Ear Check. Then you bathe in the River of Births. All within seven moons.'

'Your book got banned in Sri Lanka. Does it mean you got killed for nothing?'

'Nothing is for nothing, putha. You can have that lesson for free.'

'Did you see your killer's face? Do you think he feels guilt?'

'This is the In Between. Not a place to loaf about, thinking of useless questions.'

'The Tiger who said he arranged it was part of the Mahatiya faction. I photographed him in Kilinochchi. He might have been just showing off. Lot of big talkers on both sides.'

The good doctor ignores the bait and consults the clipboard. 'The Ear Check will reveal if you're ready for The Light. The River of Births shows you your past. Shall we go?'

'Do you wish you'd written more books? Or less?'

'Nothing is ever enough Down There.'

'Why do you care if I go to The Light?'

'We help spirits that are stuck to their last birth. The In Between is overcrowded.'

'So?'

'This space has become dangerous. And there is nothing you can change. Your life is over. Anyone who tells you otherwise is taking you for a ride.'

Sena stands to the edge of the ledge, pretending not to eavesdrop. His hood resembles a cobra and his cloak flaps like crow's wings. From this distance, under this moonlight, it is no longer clear if his outfit is made from garbage bags or human skin.

'So, when do I meet God?'

'I hear you have seen the Mahakali.'

'Is God unable to stop evil? Or unwilling?'

'Aiyo. Grow up, will you?'

'My dad paid for my uni in Berlin. He didn't believe in God. Or in the University of Peradeniya.'

'The Mahakali feeds on lost souls. Lately, it has grown fat.'

'Who pays for the white saris?'

'If you stay In Between, you become a yaka or a preta or a ghoul or a slave to one of them.'

'Do they teach the trolley problem at Peradeniya?'

'You are not my only case.'

'If the murder of one can save a hundred, should we sharpen a machete?'

'Putha. You think each of the trillion bacteria who live and die on your carcass gets to meet you and question you about their purpose?'

'You're confusing me.'

'This is the In Between. It is no place for you.'

'I need the world to see what I saw.'

'That is ego. That is all illusion.'

At the other end of the roof, a crew of suicides stumble along the ledge like toddlers falling off tricycles. A girl in a tie with a puzzled expression walks to the edge and steps off. A woman with pigtails follows and does what looks like a Fosbury Flop, which you did not think possible in a sari. A hunched figure that looks like it has stewed in the ocean since the days of King Buvenekabahu III, totters at the edge before keeling over.

It is all done slowly, silently and solemnly. More silhouettes walk to the edge of the roof to stare down seven floors, like galley slaves made to walk the plank.

'Suicides love tall buildings. You're not scared of other ghosts?' she asks. 'I was terrified when I first got here.'

'They don't seem to notice me.'

'Because they don't. Shall we proceed with the procedure?'

'Look. I don't want to go back. Don't want to be reborn. Don't want to be anything. Can't I just be nothing?'

'You can't stay here.'

Sena is hovering above the ledge, whispering to the suicides as they stare into the abyss. His cloak and hood look regal. He appears to be making speeches and it is unclear if they are listening. When you fantasised about heaven, you thought you'd be greeted by Elvis or Oscar Wilde. Not by a dead professor with a ledger book. Or a murdered Marxist in a cloak.

'If you could tally up all the good things and all the bad things in the world, would your ledger book balance?'

She folds her arms and nods her head.

'Eventually everything balances.'

'Where's the evidence?'

'I have no time for this, child. Neither do you.'

She closes her book and looks along the ledge at dead suicides trying to kill themselves again. She drops the tour guide routine. You cock your camera and photograph her with the suicides in the background, her silhouette holding a book.

'I was obsessed with justice, with protecting the powerless, with my students, with the plight of Tamils. I didn't see my daughters grow up. I squandered my marriage. All for what?'

'Why are you championing The Light?'

'The In Between is congested. It is polluting minds Down There. Too many ghouls are running around whispering bad thoughts into the wrong ears.'

'So, if everyone went into The Light, the Tigers would stop fighting and the government would stop abducting. Is that what you're selling?'

'The In Between is filled with creatures who feed on despair.'

'So, if the In Between were empty, the rich would stop stealing and the poor will stop starving?'

'You stay here, you become one of them. Perhaps that has already begun.'

'I need to warn my friends. Whoever killed me will steal my photos. I need to watch and see who does.'

'No one cares, putha. No one cares. You have six moons to get this done. Shall we?'

'Who's we?'

'We have to check your ears. Just that.'

'We don't have to do anything. Any more. Ever.'

'Madam doctor, I think now enough, no?' Sena has his hood back on and a red-and-white scarf around his neck. He rests his head where your shoulder would have been.

You shudder and Dr Ranee snaps. 'We agreed you would not speak.'

'Always trying to shut us up, no. Typical middle-class intelligentsia.'

'You cannot touch him for seven moons. Neither can your boss.'

'I have no boss. I am Sena Pathirana, JVP organiser for Gampaha district. And this is Maali Almeida. Super photographer par excellence. Buggerer of everything south of Jaffna. Thrown off a roof by a death squad. Maali hamu. Please do not get your ears checked. Or your mind erased in that river.'

Dr Ranee advances like a schoolteacher with a ruler. Behind her, two men in white smocks burst from the shadows. They are both sprinting on air. It is Afro Uncle, whom you remember from the counter and who reminds you of Moses. Heavily bearded, a crown of brambles and eyes just an insult away from parting someone's sea. The other is tall and muscular, like He-Man from the cartoon, had He-Man been born in Avissawella.

They grab Sena and pin him to the floor. Dr Ranee hovers above him shaking her head. Sena looks up at her, eyes flashing.

'You've had your say. It is my turn now.'

BAD SAMARITANS

While boxes sleep under beds and the wicked dream of things they will steal, it is decided, in the interest of fair play and democracy – which are not always the same thing – that Sena be allowed to speak. He promptly adopts the posture of an orator at a JVP rally, stands on the ledge and takes slow steps. The suicides huddle in the shadows and listen like disciples.

'Sirs, madams, comrades, fellow travellers. I remember my last birth. I remember my last death. Didn't need to go to a counter for a number and have some Helper feed me garbage about The Light. It all came to me.'

There is a murmur among the suicides. Doc Ranee looks at you and shakes her head many times. She scribbles in her ledger book.

'I have been In Between for two hundred and fifty moons. There's no better place. I didn't win the birth lottery. I grew up in a quarry in Wellawaya. I worked as a servant boy in Gampaha. Down There, I was told that my poverty was my karma, my cross, my affliction. My fault. I joined the JVP not because it was fashionable, but because it was necessary. I have known poverty and I have known the poor. I have known struggles and I have known pain.'

He walks along the perimeter of his audience, stops where you are, squats and lowers his volume to a whisper.

'If The Light is heaven, as this madam doc tells, and if the In Between is purgatory filled with the Lost, then what does that make the Down Below?'

'Hell!' shouts someone in the crowd.

Sena chuckles. 'Every soul is allowed seven moons to wander the In Between. To recall past lives. And then, to forget. They want you to forget. Because, when you forget, nothing changes.

'The world will not correct itself. Revenge is your right. Do not listen to Bad Samaritans. Demand your justice. The system failed you. Karma failed you. God failed you. On earth as it is up here.'

The suicides' murmurings have risen a few decibels. They have now stopped throwing themselves off ledges. Dr Ranee hovers with Moses and He-Man and snorts.

'These are false words,' she shouts. 'Revenge is no justice. Revenge lessens you. Only karma grants what is yours. But you must be patient. It is the only thing you need to be.'

Sena screws up his face and spits out his words. 'Typical government office. Take a number and sit down until you forget why you came.'

Moses draws up to his full midget height. 'Show some respect, pig.'

'Many of you were killed. Many were driven to kill themselves,' says Sena. 'Maybe it is easier to forget. But forgetting cures nothing. Wrongs must be remembered. Or your murderers will roam free. And you will know no peace.'

This time, the pain swipes at your gullet, it chokes you as you remember things you had tried to forget. How scared you were on your first assignment for the army, how hurt you were when your father left, and how disappointed you were to wake up in hospital after overdosing. How much the twenty-nine-year-old you, the eleven-year-old you and the seventeen-year-old you would've hated each other. And how the dead you loathes them all.

Sena wipes the sweat from his neck with a red-and-white chequered scarf, the type popularised by oil sheikhs, terror groups and hippies. He floats towards you and grabs you by the ears. 'The death squad that killed me killed you, Maali. There are six men responsible for our murders. And, if you help me, I will make them suffer.'

'Chik!' says Dr Ranee. 'Just like your leaders. Cheap thugs. Selling fairy tales and false hopes,' says Dr Ranee. 'You're dead! You can't make anyone suffer.'

'The innocent have the right to avenge their deaths.'

'Revenge is not a right. This island does not need more corpses. You are being a child.'

'The powerful get away with murder. And all the gods in the sky look away. This changes now. We will change this.'

'How? You have no hand to hold a knife. You cannot be seen or heard by the living. How can you put revenge on anything?'

'I can whisper.'

A murmur ripples through the crowd.

'And I can teach you all to whisper.'

'That is black magic. It will make slaves of you all,' shouts Dr Ranee. 'Like your Crow Man. He is the Mahakali's slave.'

'Who cares what colour the magic? As long as it works,' says Sena, staring squarely at you.

'Do you hear that, Maal?' The good doctor appears agitated. 'Who cares, it seems?'

'Magic isn't evil or good. Or black or white. It is like the universe, like every missing God. Powerful and supremely indifferent.'

The suicides bang on the rooftops while the wretched applaud. Sena has found his audience and, despite the glares you get from Dr Ranee, you float down to join them. And that's when the Mahakali decides to crash the party.

BORU FACTS

The shadow takes the shape of a beast. It has the head of a bear and the body of a large woman. Its hair is serpents and its eyes are black from corner to corner. It bares its fangs and walks into the crowd as the Helpers in white back away. The creature growls and fills the roof with mist. You feel a chill that makes you retch. The Helpers unhand the suicides and pick up clubs.

It wears a necklace of skulls and a belt of severed fingers, but these are not what draw your gaze. It is the belly, bare and hanging over a belt of flesh. Human faces etched in them, the souls trapped within are screaming to be let out.

The creature raises its hand and lets out a wail, the sound of a thousand wails, the sound of animals feeding on their young, the sound of a universe being kicked in the groin.

Then the mist vanishes and, with it, the creature and the rabble of suicides. Is there a collective noun for suicides? An overdose of suicides? A hara-kiri of suicides?

Dr Ranee barks at her crew in white. 'That was him?'

Moses looks at He-Man, who looks at Sena, who looks at you. 'Was that *her*?'

The Helpers look around the roof for suicides who are no longer there.

'That was the Mahakali,' says Sena. 'You should all be worried.'

Sena is drawing a large rectangle on the wall that overlooks the city. He uses the same charcoal he used to write those names. He fills it with numbers and letters, which he prints out of sequence. It looks like a self-solving crossword puzzle.

'Are you working for her?' asks Dr Ranee.

'I am working against The Light. Against the forgetting. We must never forget. We must help the forgotten. We must destroy the lies and the boru.'

The letters on the wall begin to form words, which give way to sentences.

BORU FACT *1: THIS LAND BELONGS
        TO ITS CITIZENS.

BORU FACT #2: ALL CITIZENS ARE EQUAL BEFORE THE LAW.

Sena's writing is a mixture of Sinhala, Tamil and kindergarten English. It reminds you of street signs in Jaffna before they were tarred by angry activists.

BORU FACT #3: GOVERNMENTS DON'T TARGET CIVILIANS.

BORU FACT #4: PRESIDENTS WON'T NEGOTIATE WITH TERRORISTS.

'Enough now, Mr Sena.' Dr Ranee hovers above you, an angel with a ledger book. She swoops down to grab the charcoal from Sena but he dodges and a paragraph materialises on the black wall.

BORU FACT #5: THE COUNTRY BELONGS NEITHER TO THE VEDDHAS HERE FIRST, NOR TO THE TAMILS, MUSLIMS, BURGHERS HERE FOR CENTURIES. ONLY TO THE SINHALESE WHO FILLED IT WITH PEOPLE. AND THEIR PRIESTS WHO WROTE BIG BOOKS ABOUT IT.

You are unsure how you can read and process something written in three languages, but you can. Sena throws his head back and laughs.

'Maali-Sir. Dinner party activist. Photographer for all sides. Read this carefully. No one Down There is trying to expose these lies or right these wrongs. But we can.'

'OK, that's enough.'

Dr Ranee closes her book and floats towards him. Moses and He-Man grab Sena and pull him to the ledge where the Mahakali had stood. He does not stop laughing, and even though it is a fake laugh there is defiance in it.

'Let Mr Malinda make his decision,' says Dr Ranee. 'But first, we must do the Ear Check.'

She looks around, only to find that you are no longer there.

GALLE FACE COURT

You are not interested in following the creature with the head of a bear. You are interested in hitting the mara tree at the junction. Right when everyone's staring at Sena's stupid list, you hop on the creature's tailwind and come crashing down at the traffic lights.

It takes until morning to empty your skull of thoughts and to keep memories from invading your head. The world is noisy and voices slink along the branches. I believe in mara trees, you tell yourself. As the hour grows late, the whispers multiply. You hover above the tree and see yourself with closed eyes.

You wear a red bandanna, a safari jacket, one sandal and around your neck, three chains and a camera. Then you hover above that and see yourself watching yourself, though you wear a sarong and a T-shirt and have blistered hands. You see four bodies baking in Jaffna's dust. A dog, a man, a mother and child. They have their eyes open and they are all breathing. They are staring at you and asking you the same question and you are pretending not to understand. You pull the camera to your face and watch the bodies crumble to sand.

In the distance, you hear an argument. The shouts of Dr Ranee mixed with the laughs of Sena. You ignore these as best you can and listen to what the wind brings. Hear thy name spoken, share in its shame.

'Chief occupant: Dilan Dharmendran. Leaseholder: Stanley Dharmendran. Other occupants: Malinda Almeida and Jacqueline Vairavanathan.'

You follow the breeze and you find yourself drifting towards a blue Datsun crawling down Duplication Road, its nose pointed towards Galle Face Green.

You are in the back seat with Elsa Mathangi. In the front, Ranchagoda is humming along to the radio while Cassim fills in a search warrant.

'You know exactly where it is, miss?'

'He said under his bed. He may have been joking. He thought he was funny.'

'We can't waste time with jokes,' says Cassim, keeping his droopy eyes on the road. It is 9 a.m. and they look as well rested as you feel. A curfew has been declared for later that day and all of Colombo is racing to the shops in case the sugar runs out.

You were not joking. Though you hadn't expected your idle chatter to be scribbled down on a search warrant. You wonder if it is possible for a ghost to cause a car to break down. Perhaps that is where all car accidents originate. Bored spirits putting drivers to sleep, skidding their tyres and cutting their brakes.

'Praying to God is like asking a car why it had to crash,' said your Dada in one of his arguments with your Amma. 'Many of us will die in car crashes,' he said. 'And every fool believes it will happen to someone else.' These arguments ended up as soliloquies and happened on Sundays, right before your Amma dragged you to church.

'So, the plan is what?' asks Ranchagoda.

'You tell them that clues related to Malinda's disappearance could be in the house. If you like, I can do the talking. Actually, let's do that,' says Elsa, looking at a road laden with buses. Her gaze pans from the buildings to the coconut trees to the checkpoints along Galle Road.

'I am only doing this because it is related to a case under investigation,' says Cassim. 'I'm due for a transfer, anyway.'

'Whatever gets you through the night, officer,' says Elsa as they drive past Temple Trees, the heavily fortified Prime Minister's palace.

'And who will you say you are?'

'His employer,' says Elsa. 'You should always tell the truth, if you possibly can.'

'You know what?' says Cassim. 'I think I will stay in the car.'

They turn at the Galle Face roundabout where you and DD once made out at 3.33 a.m. They drive into the car park where you once kicked him out of his own flat. They enter a stairwell, where you were scolded for smoking by the Malay Aunty on the second floor. They enter a hallway as wide as Duplication Road, where many times you smuggled undesirables in from multiple exits when no one was home.

Ranchagoda thumps the door and rings the bell while Elsa practises her smile. The door is opened by little Jaki dressed in a kimono. Jaki does a double-take and then pretends that opening doors to cops is something she does every morning.

'What's happened?'

'Good morning, miss. May we come in?'

Jaki does not budge.

'Have you found him?'

'Not yet,' says Elsa putting on a smile. 'We need your help.'

'Who are you?'

'Detective Mathangi,' says Elsa. 'May we speak?'

Jaki doesn't see Ranchagoda roll his eyes. They enter through a hall lined with books that you and DD have gifted each other for misremembered birthdays. Neither of you have read the books received as presents, only the ones you bought for the other.

'Er, sorry. Didn't know Sri Lanka had women detectives. Or Tamil ones.' says Jaki. Her misshapen I-grew-up-in-South-London vowels come out more when she's nervous.

It's good to come home, which is what you have called this flat for the last three years. DD's dad, Stanley, renovated it for his only son as a reward for passing the London Bar exams and as a bribe for joining his civil practice in Mutwal. He didn't seem to mind when you and Jaki moved in, at least not at the beginning. The three of you occupied a bedroom each and let others speculate on who shared what with whom.

Stanley didn't kick up a fuss when DD painted the walls purple and started having parties for the Arts Centre crowd. He didn't disown DD when the son came home with piercings on both ears. Stanley only started charging DD rent when the son left Daddy's firm to work probono for Earth Watch Lanka.

Jaki leads them to the sitting room, though no one sits.

'That's true, not many women detectives in Colombo. And you are Miss...'

'Jacqueline Vairavanathan,' says Ranchagoda, opening Cassim's notebook to another blank page. 'How long is you and Almeida couple?'

'We aren't a couple,' says Jaki.

'But your cousin said...'

'My cousin doesn't know shit,' says Jaki.

'Do you know where Maali's box of photographs is?' asks Elsa.

'Photos of what?' says Jaki.

'He used to say it was under his bed.'

'Then it must be under his bed. He takes photos. He keeps boxes. He sleeps on beds, sometimes. What's your point?'

'May we see?'

'I don't understand.'

Ranchagoda walks to the window and gazes at the brown grass of Galle Face Green and the choppy ocean taking bites from the coast.

'Miss Jaki, we have warrant to search the premises.'

'Did you check if he's been arrested? If not police, then maybe army?'

'Which one is Maali's bedroom?'

Jaki does not answer, so Elsa blocks her way and smiles, as the ASP barges in. Jaki pushes her aside with a move learned from judo class, a move she once tried on you with a can of mace. She follows Ranchagoda into the wrong room. Elsa rubs her arm and swears.

You slink to the kitchen and let the smells swirl through you. Garlic and cardamom hang in the air, meaning that Kamala has come in to cook for the week and has made buriyani and Turkish rice at DD's request. This happens every Thursday, which means you have been dead for two days.

DD's room is a mess of sweatbands, racquets, sneakers and boxes marked 'Earth Watch Lanka'. This locker room fragrance is what kept you from spending too many nights here. The cops open the boxes and find case files for rubbish dumps, polluted rivers and bulldozed forests.

'Are these the photos?' asks ASP Ranchagoda.

Elsa joins in the search. She picks up a file on leopard extinction in Yala, followed by one on urban landfill in Kelaniya.

'This isn't his room,' she says. They wander through a corridor to Jaki's cave of teenage angst. The uninvited guests are unconcerned with the posters of Bauhaus and The Cure. The cops open the curtains while Elsa kneels down to peer under the bed. The dominant smells in this room are Chanel No 5 and sadness.

'Can I see this warrant?' says Jaki. 'Please don't touch my things.'

They ignore her and plough through the shared bathroom to the pentagon that you used to sleep in. In contrast to the others, this is barren and stark. There is a queen-sized bed, a desk with a lamp, a cupboard filled with cameras, and three framed prints on the wall. One of the Somalian famine by James Nachtwey, one from the last days of Beijing by Henri Cartier-Bresson, and one of the police massacre in Batticaloa by yours truly.

Ranchagoda gasps and Elsa nods. It shows a dozen policemen kneeling as if it is Friday at the mosque. This was cropped at the FujiKodak shop in Thimbirigasyaya, so you cannot see the edges of the window that you zoomed through. You did not crop the AK-47 muzzle on the top right corner, though from your hilltop vantage you did not have the angle to snap the person holding it.

Outside the almirah are framed X-rays. One of your chest when you had pneumonia, and one of your wisdom teeth hidden in your jaw like icebergs. You photographed the X-rays, turned up the opacity and framed them for an art project which, of course, you never completed.

Inside the almirah is one teddy bear and collections of safari jackets, Hawaiian shirts and chains. Under the teddy bear is an address book that no one is looking for. You hope things stay that way.

You liked to wear things around your neck that weren't ties. Wear a tie for the interview, your Dada used to say. You want me to put a noose around my neck every single day just like you do, you asked, but only in your head.

The chains are hung from the door, some are string and some are twine. These were your spares. A peace sign, a cross, a yin and yang, and an Om. Not present are the golden Panchayudha, the cyanide capsules stolen from dead Tigers or the wooden ankh containing DD's blood, from when you made that silly oath in Yala, back when every day felt like a holiday. Both were around your neck when your neck was finally snapped. Your neck was snapped? By whom? Who said that?

You look around to check if Sena or one of his disciples is whispering in your ear. But there is only the wind and your empty room.

The dominant smell here is from chemicals and cleaning products. Were you sitting here like a college hippie, cooking up LSD and hash and anarchy? Hardly. You were mixing developer, stop bath and fixer, taking canisters to the pantry, which you'd converted into a dark room without telling Uncle Stanley. If they bothered to look there, they would find reels of negatives from the past six years in carefully classified Tupperware boxes. But, at present, they are too busy crouching under your queen-sized bed.

This is a fair assessment of your skills. Gambling D−, Fixing C+, Screwing B−, Photography A+. You were a ham and a hack, but you knew how to frame a shot. You knew how to bathe paper in trays and extract light from darkened rooms. You could make monochrome shiver and sepia sparkle. You could give depth to the shallow, texture to the flat, and meaning to the banal.

All you needed in your palette were blacks and whites and greys − you never did colour. You started off photographing sunsets and elephants and ended up shooting closeted homos and butchered soldiers.

'He said that a shoebox under his bed contained his most dangerous photographs. He told us to publish them if something happened.' Elsa looks around the room to see if anyone catches her lie.

'So you knew him? asks Jaki.

'He worked for me.'

'As a detective?'

'Of sorts.'

'I thought he worked for an NGO?'

'He served many masters, my dear.' Elsa puts a hand on Jaki's shoulder and it is shrugged off. Jaki liked nobody touching her uninvited, not even men she had crushes on. It had to do with her stepfather and the hugs he used to inflict on her teenage self.

DD and Jaki were natural hoarders of useless things. They cluttered their rooms, their lives and their thoughts. They never trusted your minimalism, or how you kept throwing away what you didn't need. They both thought you had a secret room somewhere stuffed with all the things you never told them about. And they weren't far wrong. Though that room was the size of a box.

THE SEVEN MOONS OF MAALI ALMEIDA

'Are you sure he said *his* bed?' asks Ranchagoda.

'What the hell. Do you think. You are doing?'

It is a voice you have not heard in this house for many months. Stanley Dharmendran is known, both in his speeches to the parliament, and in his lectures to his son, for his overuse of the dramatic pause.

'Get the fuck out of my room, please.'

In contrast, DD's high-pitched upset voice has been heard many times within these walls and is known less for its pauses and more for its overuse of expletives.

'They say they have a search warrant,' says Jaki as she edges towards the doorway. Not like her to back away from drama.

'Let me see it,' bellows Stanley. DD wears a tracksuit and has wet hair. Which means his old man has taken him to Otters Aquatic Club and given him an early morning talking to. They are both tall men who consider themselves sportsmen.

'Kindly leave Maali's room, thank you.'

Elsa and the cops file into the sitting room while still conducting an illegal search with their eyes. Ranchagoda hands over the warrant, while DD and Jaki whisper in the corner.

'This has not. Been certified. By a judge,' says Stanley in an accent purchased from Cambridge in the early 1950s.

'Sir, we are investigating Almeida's disappearance. There are photos that provide clues to his whereabouts.'

DD and Jaki stop whispering and glare at Elsa.

'Madam, who may you be?'

'Lanka's only Tamil woman detective,' says Jaki.

'I work for CNTR, sir. Canada Norway Third World Relief. We believe Malinda has fled the country with photos belonging to us.'

'His passport was in the drawer you just checked,' says Jaki. 'Nice detective work.'

'We believe he was blackmailing using these photographs,' says Ranchagoda scrutinising the framed print of a pangolin taken at Yala. Elsa shakes her head at him.

Stanley calmly points out what a search warrant needs to have, which the one he is holding does not. The ASP nods as if these omissions were genuine oversights. Elsa tries to interrupt, but Uncle Stanley's pauses are impenetrable.

'Kindly. Leave this house. Now,' says Stanley, patting down his hair and his tie. 'Come back. With a properly certified warrant. Or not at all. Dilan, show them out please. Dilan? Jaki?'

Outside, they hear an engine rev and tyres biting into Galle Road. You recognise the sound as Jaki's Mitsubishi Lancer and you know exactly where they are both headed and you hope they get there fast.

A breeze carrying Elsa's perfume invades the air. It is lavender mixed with talcum powder and it sends spasms and smarts right through whatever's left of you. It is pleasant-smelling but it makes you want to retch. And reminds you of a man who hunted Nazis for a living.

WIESENTHAL

'Have you heard of Simon Wiesenthal?' was the first question Elsa asked you. It was at the Arts Centre Club where she ambushed you while you were pretending to listen to Coffin Nail playing Talking Heads. You were actually planning to seduce a boy with a French accent and she was cramping your style.

'He survived Auschwitz and spent three decades hunting Nazis with only photos to go by.'

Elsa had short hair then, but still wore ruby lipstick.

'I know who Simon Wiesenthal is and I don't know who you are and I'm here to watch this band.'

She paid for your drink and ordered another and you pretended not to notice. 'You're here because three casinos have banned you and you have a crush on that rich kid over there. He's not a homo, by the way. Even you know that.'

You considered neither 'faggot' nor 'homo' nor 'queer' as slurs because you were none of these things. You were simply a handsome man who enjoyed beautiful boys. Nothing more, nothing less and no one's business. You regarded her suit and her smarmy smile and sipped the drink she had bought you and said nothing.

'My employers will pay your debts at Bally's, Pegasus and Stardust, if you sell us your photos.'

You took her outside to the balcony where men and women embrace but not with each other. You sat in the shadow and let her talk.

'We understand you have reels of photos from the pogroms of '83.'

'Is that what they're calling them?'

'I prefer that word to riots. And people get testy when you say "genocide", especially Sinhalese.'

'I stopped calling myself Sinhalese after 1983,' you said, though it wasn't like you called yourself this before. You got more from Colombo's hippies in the '70s than just bad acid. You believed that we are all Sri Lankans, children of Kuveni, bastards of Vijaya. Kumbaya kumbaya.

'This is yours, yes?'

The photo of the woman in salwar being doused with petrol was never published by *Newsweek*. And this a 27x7 matte print from the original negative. Only two copies were ever made, one is in your box, the other in New Delhi.

'Who do you work for?'

'CNTR. Pronounced "centre".'

'Who?'

'We have funding and a legal team. And we're going after the murderers of 1983.' Your laughter startled the gays and lesbians necking in the shadows.

'We're told you have unpublished photographs.'

'Speaking of Wiesenthal,' you said, 'I met two Israelis in a casino last month.'

'Do you have more photographs from 1983?'

'They said they were movie producers. Until one of them got drunk and bragged about being in the armaments business. Said they sold heavy artillery to some heavy hitters.'

She did not get flustered, she did not drop her smile, she just sipped her orange and kept talking.

'I'm familiar with Yael-Menachem. They make shit action films and sell third-rate weapons to the government.'

'That's the problem with arms dealers. They make shit movies.'

'Mr Almeida. Do you have the photos from the '83 massacre of Tamils?'

'Do you work for the people who buy third-rate weapons from God's chosen people?'

'We are not LTTE. Though our goals are not incompatible.'

'You already sound like a politician.'

'1983 was an atrocity. eight thousand homes, five thousand shops, a hundred and fifty thousand homeless, no official body count. The Sri Lankan government has neither acknowledged nor apologised for it. Your photos will help change that. Tell me, kolla. Which side are you on?'

You took a deep sigh, as if you were about to throw a punch, and then you told her about the box. For the first time, she dropped her smile, raised her eyebrows and stopped interrupting.

..

At the beginning, it was fun. That was when it was just you and Elsa. You took your negatives to a nerdy lad called Viran at the FujiKodak shop, who helped you reprint your 1983 photographs, enlarging some, enhancing others. Viran was a skilled developer and a shy lover. At his house in Kelaniya, he had better equipment than the FujiKodak shop. He took your private work home, and sometimes you, though never Elsa.

'How on earth will you identify these faces?'

'There is a database of all ID photos. And there is computer software that can identify images. We can scan these close ups on the computer and match them.'

Elsa added cinnamon to her coffee until its colour matched her skin.

'You have technology like that?'

'Of course not, you fool. Maybe in fifty years,' smirks Elsa. 'But we do have contacts in Wella and Bamba who can name these faces.'

She gave you a cheque marked 'CNTR' and said she'd be interested in any photos you had depicting the plight of the Tamils. You went on a tour of the north with the army and then a tour of the east with reporters from Reuters. You came back with shots aplenty that met her brief.

When you heard again from Elsa, it was early '88. She invited you to Hotel Leo, except this time she wasn't alone. Kugarajah was seated on the couch. He was handsome and stout just the way you liked them, though you liked them many ways.

The suite at Hotel Leo had walls plastered with your photos from 1983 with Post-it notes on each face.

Sinhala men in sarong dancing outside a burning shops (4 faces).
Naked Tamil boy being kicked to death (3 faces).
Uniformed cops watching Tamil women being dragged out of buses (6 faces).

Kuga was introduced as Elsa's cousin-brother, but by the way he slid past her to sit down you suspected they were of the kissing variety.

He handed you a sheet of addresses and asked if you could take clandestine photos of the occupants.

'We have tracked down seven perpetrators of the 1983 pogroms. We need to confirm their identities.'

'And then?'

'We can prosecute.'

You laugh and Kuga gives you a sweet smile.

'Did I tell a joke?'

'No one will touch that case. Will CNTR be prosecuting?'

'There are many ways of dispensing justice.'

'I thought you weren't LTTE?'

Elsa puts her hand on her cousin's knee and he stops talking.

'Maali. Here's your cheque for the photos from the Vanni. And here's an advance for your next assignments.'

You looked at the cheques and thought of your Dada telling you that photographers don't make money unless they did weddings, and how a degree in Sociology would – at best – get you a teaching job. 'Do one thing and do it well,' said a man whose 'one thing' did not include being a father.

'There are more assignments?'

'Go to these addresses, say you are taking a government census. Photograph them. Offer them free ID photos. Sinhalas will take the Tamil newspaper if it's free.'

'Isn't that fraud?'

'Whose side are you on, kolla?'

'I am on the side that wants to stop Sri Lankans dying like this.'

'That's good. We want these monsters to suffer. And they will.'

'How?'

Kugarajah picked up a photograph taken from your tour of the Vanni. You had gone as only a fixer and therefore any shots you took could be sold to the highest bidder. CNTR got the photos that the Army and the Associated Press passed on.

'You know this man?'

You took it while pretending to clean your camera at the Tiger base. It was while you were ushering an obnoxious Reuters reporter to film an LTTE training camp.

'Colonel Gopallaswarmy,' you say.

'Also known as Mahatiya. What do you know about him?'

'He runs the only Tiger base that allows cameras. And he has the Supremo's ear.'

'They say he's plotting against the Tiger Supremo.'

'I don't listen to rumours. I only spread them.'

'Big joker, this fellow.' Kugarajah shifted his weight forward, which made you lie back in your chair and fold your arms. He had a look in his eye like he was about to crack a joke himself. Or a skull. You lit up without asking permission, because this brute terrified and excited you in equal measure.

'Whose side are you on, kolla?'

Elsa Mathangi follows your cue and lights up a Benson as instinctively as Pavlov's pooch.

'The side that pays me.'

They tell you that CNTR runs an orphanage in Vavuniya and a clinic in Medawachchiya and that the army refused to provide security. That Colonel Gopallaswarmy was in charge of the North-Central Province and could provide protection.

'We'd like you to fix a meeting with the Colonel for us.'

'I don't know him.'

'You know him enough to bring reporters to his camp.'

'It's a showpiece camp. Like a Hollywood set. The Colonel doesn't talk to outsiders.'

'We are not outsiders.'

'Isn't it risky for CNTR to deal with the LTTE?'

'Most of our projects are up north or out east. The LTTE are the government out there. You know this already.'

Maybe it was the size of the cheque, or the size of the shot Kuga poured, or the size of the forearms that passed you the drink, or the roughness of the palm that brushed against your back, but you found yourself warming to the company and the conversation.

They were excited by the '83 project, but you were fearful.

'You really think you can bring a mob of thousands to justice?'

Kuga gave you a wink that was either an expression of brotherly love or an indication that his thoughts were as pornographic as yours.

'With any mob, no matter how big, you hit the leaders first. That's basic.'

'That kind of talk means you're either serious or stupid.'

'Not everyone can be a joker,' said Elsa.

They discussed the so-called Mahatiya faction and the effect the LTTE splintering could have on the Tamil people. Elsa lamented that the LTTE had become a fascism, stifling other Tamil voices. And Kuga pounced on her.

'A unified Tamil voice is a luxury. It will not save the Tamils. A strong voice will.'

'Dr Ranee Sridharan had a strong voice.' says Elsa. 'And it got silenced.'

'Whose side are you on, Kuga?'

You put your hand on his shoulder and received a look that made you retract it. No more winks for you, Mr Maali.

'Your Amma is half-Burgher, half-Tamil, no?' he said. 'You are a mongrel like me. But you have the name "Kabalana" on your ID. You better thank your father. The best thing he gave you was your Sinhala surname.'

You wanted to get indignant and retort that he didn't know you or your father. But, of course, he was right. That, and a loathing for money and anyone who flaunted it.

'Most of Colombo's socialists don't love the poor. They just hate the rich,' your Dada would say, as if the phrase had sprung from his magnificent brain.

'I'll do this '83 project,' you said. 'Because you pay me. And because I was there. And because this government has a lot of answering to do.'

'Careful, kolla,' says Elsa. 'That kind of talk will get you put in a tyre.'

'And that's why I cannot spy on the Colonel for you.'

'We're not asking you to spy. Just set the meeting.'

'Is a burning tyre any worse than a Tiger jail?'

You used to make cracks about death when you considered it an unlikely event, as we all do, until we don't.

You took your cheques and exchanged them downstairs for chips, which you lost at the poker table, before winning them back at baccarat. You went to the railway tracks and found no one worth fondling. While staring at the rocks below the tracks, at that thin bulwark that kept nature from devouring the coast, you thought of Kuga's parting words to you.

'I hope you haven't told anyone about CNTR.'

'I'm not a talker.'

'Good. This country is full of big talkers. And small doers.'

'I haven't told anyone.'

'Good. We don't need publicity to do what's right.'

Kuga extended his hand. As you shook it, he pulled you in and squeezed your knuckles in his palm. You winced as he held it there and watched you writhe.

'No one wants to end up in a tyre, no?'

He gave you a wink before he let go.

HOME SOUR HOME

The house in Bambalapitiya was owned by your father's mother, left to your father's sister, and given to your father's first wife after the divorce. You, the first wife's son, grew up here amidst temple trees, sleeping dogs and warring parents. The arguments happened in the kitchen, on the veranda and the balcony. You arrive there on a friendly wind, to find that an argument has already spilled onto the streets.

Jaki's Lancer parks on the curve of the road three houses down, observing the commotion from a distance. Your Amma stands at the gate with Stanley Dharmendran and snarls at the cops and Elsa. Inside the car is a different type of argument.

'So maybe there's nothing in the box, maybe this is one of Maali's bullshit pranks?'

'You and your stupid shortcut,' says Jaki.

DD clenches his fist and cracks his knuckles. Which means he craves a cigarette. Nine months ago, you made a bet with him that he wouldn't last a year and DD hates losing more than he loves cigarettes or you. The memories arrive without pain this time.

Dilan Dharmendran was on every sports team at school. You hated rugby as much as you hated cricket, but you didn't mind watching him. He captained the St Joseph's water polo team and you were the prefect in charge who spent afternoons drinking in his glazed body and adjusting your white uniform.

When you met again, a decade after school was out, he didn't have the body, but he had the same grin, the same dark skin and the same slowness on the uptake. He was still the perfect ten, on a scale of one to thirteen. He had no idea that you had coveted him many years ago. When you moved into his father's flat with his cousin Jaki, he didn't recognise you and had little to say.

That all changed in increments over six patient months. By this time, you were visiting his room in the dead of the night and he would say this is the last time and you would end up talking about travelling together. When you went out together it was as old school chums and no one knew a thing, though perhaps everyone did. He thinks you are in a dungeon somewhere and that, if he uses his Earth Watch Lanka contacts to file the right complaint, he can free you. Your darling little idiot.

'Did he say he was leaving?'

'He told me nothing.'

'He said come to the Arts Centre or Hotel Leo. He had something to tell me. He said he'd call and confirm. As usual, he didn't.'

'He was gambling every day,' says Jaki, turning her head to her cousin and giving him a look that is equal parts pity and scorn.

'You think he's dead?' DD's voice breaks. He used to massage your shoulders and the bottom of your feet every time you came back from a tour and you'd tell him about the horrible things you'd seen.

He'd change the subject at your first pause to tell you of an American college that offered him a scholarship to study Third World environmental degradation or some such. You'd ask him what the greatest polluter on earth could possibly teach him about this natural paradise. Then, you'd argue the crimes and sins of the US of A and avoid arguing about having to live there.

'Maali said he was the only photographer to work for the army, the foreign press and the Tigers,' says Jaki. 'Thought he was just bragging, as usual.'

After you'd argued with DD, she'd take your massaged feet out on the town, give you the whose-husband's-been-sleeping-with-whose-wife report and tell you about the schoolgirls she'd been corrupting at theatre groups and the punk songs she'd been sneaking onto radio playlists.

After a few ales, you bitched about DD and she would give you one of her silly pills and you'd laugh like sillies and never get around to talking about the things you'd seen on the frontlines. About why you were broke even though you'd just got paid. Or about you and her and if you'd been faithful and if it mattered.

'What's the point of waiting in the car?' says DD, rubbing his perfect hand over his sweaty forehead.

'What's the point of getting out, genius? They can see us.'

'You know where the box is?'

'So do you. He told us at that after-party, when he was in one of his drama moods. You remember.'

'Maali used to make shit up all the time and then say, "Ha ha, so gullible!" like it was a big joke.'

'Yep, I know. And then get pissed if you didn't laugh.'

'He'd say he'd been hired as an assassin and sulk when you didn't believe him.'

'Or, that he'd saved a bunker full of kids. Or, that he'd seen a black panther in the jungle.'

'Or, that he had a box under his bed with photos that would shake the world.'

DD pauses. 'And you're sure he meant here?'

'He told me he'd moved it. Right after Richard de Zoysa got abducted. It'll be under Kamala's bed.'

She kills the ignition and they exit in a crouch and creep down Lauries Lane. You can see that they've both gained weight. He is a stallion with a cow's belly, she is a peahen with pangolin thighs. You wish your amnesia could choose to forget those San Francisco arguments, and the time wasted making them and countering them.

'I'm thinking of resigning at Earth Watch Lanka. Might go back to college. I've applied to some schools.'

The song he sang once a month. Usually, when you weren't giving him enough attention. Usually, when you were packing to go somewhere and didn't have time for a performance.

'If you are arrested for covering JVP rallies, I'm not getting Appa involved.'

You could've told him to go lick his Appa's left nut but that would've caused a big enough fight to make you miss your bus. You could've told him that the JVP rally was last week and now you were off to Trincomalee to cover a village massacre. That the risk of getting arrested was slim but the risk of being kidnapped by Tigers was high.

Instead, you told him that you loved him more than anything and you would talk about it when you returned. That usually shut him up.

You watch the stallion and the peahen disappear behind the mango tree. A breeze blows across you and you float like dust towards the gate where voices are raised.

'It is our property, we have paid for it,' says Elsa Mathangi, hand on hip, cigarette in mouth. She is the only one smiling.

'There is a thing. Called the law,' says Stanley, waving his finger. 'I have called the Minister of Justice. You can show him your warrant.'

'Who cares, Stanley? Let them search. We have nothing to hide,' says your Amma. You can tell from her quivering hand that she is on her third cup. Since your father left, she began pouring things into her teapot. First brandy, then whisky, finally gin. Kamala would always refer to the bottle of Gordons as 'Madam's medicine'.

'That is not the point, Lucky. They have no legal right.'

Your Amma stares at ASP Ranchagoda standing by the gate. Ranchagoda looks less embarrassed than Cassim, who sits in the car staring at his lap. 'You said you would find my boy? Have you found him? What is this?'

'To find him, we need your help, madam. This box has information,' says Ranchagoda. 'You are blocking our investigation.'

'You think my son is hiding here?'

Inside there is a crash. They stop talking. Then, your Amma scampers into the veranda shouting.

'Kamala? Omath?'

Her cook has not yet returned from the market and her lover is sweeping the garden, oblivious to the commotion. Both Kamala and Omath are Tamils who changed their names to find work in Colombo and then kept them changed after the '83 riots.

The house in Bamba was big enough for seven brothers and sisters to grow up in and for three servants to grow old in, but proved too small for Amma and Dada and you. An open-plan home, the kind they don't make any more, with courtyards of potted plants that got wet when it rained, with two verandas filled with cane chairs, and a back garden for Amma's dogs to poop in.

Your Amma shuffles through the front, flanked by Stanley, followed by Elsa and Ranchagoda. Omath, the gardener, rushes in from the side entrance into the lounge where no one ever sat unless there were visitors. Behind the kitchen there is the sound of thieves barking at each other, while Mother's pet dogs lie sleeping. You float through rooms where you have shouted and sulked, to arrive at the courtyard at the back.

Next to the garage and the back gate is the room that your Amma's driver shares with your Amma's cook. At the entrance is a cardboard box, or what was formerly a cardboard box. The box has lain there for over twelve months but has never been moved, certainly not in such a hurry.

Inside the box are old LP records exiled here by Jaki's tapes and DD's compact discs. And a shoebox containing five envelopes. After every tour, you added photos to the envelopes in the shoebox. And you buried the shoebox under the LPs.

Maybe the weevils and gullas under the bed had developed a taste for cardboard or maybe the dampness of the last monsoon had seeped in and stayed. The box's bottom had collapsed like the '87 Peace Accord. Below it is a mess of papers, records and a solitary white shoebox.

There are letters and aerogrammes, bearing your name and this address. Scattered love notes that could be used for blackmail were you so inclined, old water bills, mostly paid; and a letter from your father. There are also records – *Jesus Christ Superstar*, ABBA, Jim Reeves, Elvis's *Harum Scarum*, Queen's *Flash Gordon* soundtrack – none of them listened to very much and all of them scattered on the red terrazzo.

And, on their knees, rifling through the rubble, like children recovering fallen marbles, are DD and Jaki. She bypasses the letters and records and rescues the shoebox from the mess.

'Dilan! What are you doing?' barks his father, while your Amma hobbles over to the jumble and picks up *Twelve Songs of Christmas* by 'Gentleman' Jim and Connie Francis's *Who's Sorry Now?*, both hers. Behind them Elsa mutters something to the ASP. Ranchagoda steps towards Jaki, who is hugging the box and backing away.

'This belongs to Maali. He told me to keep it safe.' Jaki does her best stare.

'So, why are you taking it?' asks Elsa, moving towards the pile.

'Because it belongs to Maali. Not you.'

'Everyone must calm down. Let's go inside.' Stanley walks to DD and puts his arm around him. 'Omath, please clean this.'

You want to punch Stanley in his bald, fat skull, an urge you have had ever since you saw him speak in parliament with his affected Cambridge accent. He has been nothing if not polite to your face, though he has weaponised politeness as well as any Englishman. He sends Ranchagoda to stand outside while Elsa follows the home party into the lounge that no one sits in.

Normally, your Amma would offer everyone Ceylon tea and Elephant House soft drinks. But she looks in no mood for entertaining. She holds an envelope from your Dada in her hand, the only one you ever got to open. You do not want her to read it, but you do not know how to stop her.

DD and Jaki place the shoebox on the coffee table and everyone circles it as if browsing a display under glass in a museum. The box is white and has card names written on it in red and black felt pen. The titles form a royal straight: Ace of Diamonds, King of Clubs, Queen of Spades, Jack and Ten of Hearts.

'Whatever's in that box belongs to CNTR!' cries Elsa, pointing to the box that once contained a pair of brown chappals from Madras.

Jaki pulls it from the table and fiddles with its lid. You hover over it all, staring at the envelopes stacked inside, each marked with its own playing card. Images flooding the space behind eyes you don't have. Memories of photographs you don't remember taking and of things you cannot unsee. You don't want to pick up the camera around your neck because you fear what it might reveal.

'Don't. Open. Anything,' says Stanley D. 'This is not your property.'

'Sir, that's not true,' says Elsa. 'Maali told me he has our photos in a shoebox under a bed. That's the box, that's the bed. My cousin-brother commissioned photos from Maali. I paid for the master negatives. Those are ours.'

'And where did this scarecrow come from?' asks Stanley, pointing to Ranchagoda, who has just walked back in.

'Sir, Minister of Justice Cyril Wijeratne is my boss,' says Ranchagoda drawing his gangly limbs up to full height.

'Oh, really,' says DD's dad. 'Then why don't I ring him. Let him sort this out.'

ASP Ranchagoda does not flinch when Stanley calls his bluff. Elsa drops her smile and shakes her head.

'Till then, give the box to me,' says Stanley.

Jaki raises her eyebrows at him and gives the same look she did when she called her Aunty a foolish floozy. The same look she had when you convinced her to apologise to her boss and ask for her job back. The same look she had when she told you that she knew what you did with DD and she didn't care as long as you didn't get AIDS.

She turns her head from Stanley to Elsa and opens the box. She pours five envelopes onto the table and scatters the royal straight.

AFTER-PARTY

You told them about the box under your bed at one of the Arts Centre after-parties. You told it to DD and Jaki and to an uncle named Clarantha de Mel. All three were drunk at the time and you didn't expect them to remember.

DD hated the after-parties, where ashtrays filled and liquids spilled and the photos you took went into a box. He would crawl into his room in a sulk and pound on the walls when the decibels rose.

'You're not going to invite those morons to our home again, are you?'

'Jaki wants to.'

The after-parties happened on the terrace that looked onto Galle Face Green and the balcony overlooking the Taj car park. The living room was colossal and had enough soft surfaces to park inebriated bums belonging to the Colombo party set. Sena was right. Maali Almeida didn't just go to Colombo 7 parties, he hosted them.

Your flat was central to three of Colombo's nightclubs – 2000, Chapter and The Blue – so whoever Jaki had been dancing with ended up here. The guests, sprawled on cushions, got drunk on espresso from DD's coffee maker, on cassettes from DD's ghetto blaster, and on booze stolen from DD's dad. While DD lay in DD's bed and thought DD thoughts.

The recently graduated International School kids would sit there chugging vodka and moaning about having to run their parents' companies. The drama crowd would smoke dope and bitch about the drama crowd before hooking up with members of the drama crowd. The expat set would gaze out from the balcony at coconut trees silhouetted against ocean and wax poetic on the beauty of Lanka.

It was true. When the wind blew through the balcony and the smoke and the laughter filled the breeze, it was easy to forget that a horrible war was being fought a bus ride from here. Over here the stars and the lights of Colombo sang out in yellows and greens. The roads were quiet and the ocean purred. And Colombo wrapped itself in a safety blanket that we did not deserve.

The night you remember was the after-party following Miss Working Girl 1989. Your friend Clarantha de Mel, curator at the Lionel Wendt Gallery, was one of the judges and had treated his favourite misfits to free tickets, though not all were appreciative.

'Only Lanka will have beauty pageants and cricket matches while the country burns,' said Jaki, serving Stanley's vodka to the guests in our lounge.

On the balcony, a girl who inherited a café and a boy groomed to run a bank, both barely out of their teens, were making out. A tea broker was arguing politics with a radio DJ in the kitchen. On the cushions, joints were passed between strangers and pills were being turned into powder in a pestle used for grinding chilli.

A stout woman in a kaftan and a chubby boy wearing a feather boa plopped down next to you and Jaki. They sprinkled fun dust onto your drinks and addressed Clarantha as if speaking to the king.

'Uncle Clara, you look fabulous, as always,' said the boy, bowing like a butler. 'Great speech.'

'Hmm,' said the woman, eyeing Jaki's hitched-up skirt.

'You look very, very familiar.' Uncle Clarantha was sociable even when he was tired. And that parade of dolls in bikinis and business suits must have been as tedious to judge as it was to watch. Especially since Clarantha was twice as homo as you and ten times as closeted.

'I am Radika Fernando,' said the woman. 'I read the news on Rupavahini. This is my fiancé, Buveneka.'

'You are that Minister Cyril Wijeratne's son, no?'

The boy in the boa blushed. 'He is my uncle. I'm not into politics.'

He looked at you, as if requesting permission to smile. The fun dust curdled in your throat inducing a burp that tasted like you imagine poison would. You nodded.

'Look at this bubble. Partying after beauty contests while our soldiers die.' Radika Fernando had come over to give a speech and she was doing it in her news voice.

'Nothing wrong with bubbles, baby,' said Buveneka, raising a champagne glass. 'What else to do when you're trapped in curfew Colombo?'

Radika launched into a monologue which you struggled to follow. It began by criticising Clarantha's speech, which forecast a bright future for Sri Lankan working girls.

'Hard to imagine a bright future when over four thousand are raped in this country every year. Many by their own family.'

Clarantha slunk back, as he usually did from conflict. Jaki leaned in.

'And what are you doing, apart from reading about it on TV?' asked Jaki.

Radika blushes as if expecting the jab. 'I'm a hypocrite like you, sweetie. All our heads are colonised by Hollywood. We are brainwashed by rock and roll. The people dying up there aren't really our people, are they? What's your name, pretty?'

It is then you knew that this Radika woman was tripping balls, and when Buveneka's eyes started multiplying, you realised that you were too. Around the room the chatter and movement became blurry and distant. A note escaped from the record player and hung in the air and it was unclear whether it came from the throat of Freddie or Elvis or Shakin' Stevens. You settled back and stroked Jaki's hair as she told the newsreader her name.

Radika and Buveneka formed a Vaudeville double act. She did impassioned speeches, he did revolutionary soundbites.

She ranted about how evil doesn't know it is evil, like the mad don't know they're insane. That America doesn't think it has invaded too many democracies and killed too many innocents. That we shouldn't let them slaughter like the worst tyrants and drop bombs on children. That there's nothing exceptional about a country built on genocide and the backs of slaves.

'I thought like that in high school,' said Jaki. 'Who would you rather have in charge? The Soviets or the Japs?'

'If I'd grown up listening to Russian metal and watching Kurosawa, maybe it wouldn't sound ridiculous.'

'Russian metal sounds cool,' Jaki smiled.

'Napalm came from Harvard. The atom bomb came from Princeton. The H-bomb, from the Manhattan project.'

'You think the Tigers know they're evil?' you asked, and no one answered.

'Does our government?' muttered Buveneka Wijeratne, nephew of the Minister of Justice.

And then the music swelled and Radika was kissing Jaki and Buveneka was licking you. And suddenly you were in Jaki's room and all the lights were shining and the sound was gloomy and unmusical and Jaki was saying please stop.

'We're not like that, sorry. I think we had too much.'

Radika massaged her neck and Buveneka held your hand. You cannot believe you just kissed the nephew of Satan.

'Honey, we're all wasted,' said Radika.

'You two are engaged?' you asked.

'I'm his frock. He's my beard.' Radika stopped massaging and lay back on Jaki's bed. 'If that wasn't bloody obvious.'

'We have a group that meets every month. You two should come,' said Buveneka.

'We're not like that,' said Jaki.

'What are you like, then?' asks Radika, her toe drawing patterns on Jaki's spine.

Jaki looked at you and you looked at the Ouija board next to Jaki's cassettes.

'Are you guys up for a seance?' you asked.

Clarantha de Mel enters the room with one of the Miss Working Girl contestants, whose answer to the favourite author question was 'Enid Blyton'.

'Someone say seance?'

..

The event was a non-starter. People couldn't stop giggling, despite the candlelight and Clarantha channelling Olivier's Hamlet. Radika Fernando tried with her newsreader voice. She called for the ghosts of Queen Anula and Madame Blavatsky and the ghosts of the couple who had hung themselves from the Galle Face Court ceiling in the 1940s. But no spirits blew out our candles.

Jaki was about to turn on the lights, when Buveneka Wijeratne called out.

'I call out to the lost revolutionaries. Ranee Sridharan. Vijaya Kumaratunge. Richard de Zoysa. Sena Pathirana...'

A wind huffed in from Galle Face and rubbed out all the candles. Everyone shrieked and Jaki hit the lights and everyone laughed and then everyone was silent. Then, one by one, people started leaving. Jaki pointed to the newsreader and the Minister's nephew wrapped in a feather boa saying their goodbyes and said, 'Let's never do that again.'

Before he left, you asked Buveneka, 'What was the last name you said before the lights went?'

'Sena Pathirana, our driver's son. Was a campus communist who joined the JVP. One of the first to be taken out by my uncle's death squads. I'll never forget what our driver said to me when he resigned.

Buveneka straightens his hair and his shirt and stuffs the boa in his beard's handbag.

'"Baba,"' he said, "You are the only one in your bastard family that I will not curse. Even the Crow Man can't protect your uncle forever."'

. .

Only you, your flatmates and Clarantha de Mel are left at the after-party.

'Who's the Crow Man?' asks Jaki.

'It's all this local sorcery mumbo-jumbo crap. The Crow Man of Kotahena sells charms to protect rich ministers like Cyril Wijeratne. They say that's why the Minister of Justice has survived so many assassinations. People will believe anything except the truth.'

Over the last drink of the night, you told them about the box of photos and your decision to move it to your Amma's house. Jaki was half asleep and DD barely awake, but Clarantha listened and promised. 'If you ever go into exile, I will exhibit your pictures.'

Clarantha ran the bar at the Arts Centre, curated the art gallery at the Lionel Wendt and, as a homosexual grandfather of four, lived on plausible deniability. He said if Jaki and DD could get the photos to him, then he will hang them at the gallery until they are taken down. And then the four of you clasped hands like superheroes and toasted with stolen vodka and soon forgot.

The First Envelope

The box is flimsy, made of paper that wants to be cardboard when it grows up. It houses five envelopes. The box once contained chappals gifted by your Dada for passing your accounting exams. You wore those Madrasi slippers never and passed them to some boy at the Liberty Plaza toilets who fondled you after dark.

Jaki fans out the envelopes, like that flashy card dealer at Pegasus who got fired for dealing from the bottom. She displays them to all gathered and commands them with her stare. Jaki was fierce when she wanted to be, which was hardly ever.

'Jaki, let me see them first.' Stanley's tie is loose and his staccato is wavering.

'Those are our confidential projects,' says Elsa, getting up from her chair.

Jaki ignores her, opens the one marked 'Queen', and looks at each photo like it is a leech in her palm. She passes them to Stanley, who stares at each one, shaking his head yet unable to look away. The photos travel like a Chinese whisper from Amma to DD to Elsa to back in the envelope. You recognise each image, developed in Uncle Clarantha's short-lived studio.

At the beginning, they are just black-and-white shots of crowds, taken from a moving trishaw, taken with blurry eyes and unsteady fingers. Then of things burning: shops, cars, signs that end in consonants. Then people.

The lady in the pink salwar being doused with petrol. The naked boy surrounded by dancing devils. A house in Wellawatte aflame with faces pasted against the windows. These have been published and are familiar to many.

Then come those deemed too gory for international publication. The boy and his mother being beaten with sticks, the toddler with the broken arm, the fellow with the cleaver hacking at an old man's side.

Your Amma drops the last one in disgust. She gets up and pours more tea from her pot and takes a long gulp.

Then come the photos of faces, many enlarged in your Galle Face Court pantry. Close-ups of the men behind the clubs, unidentified animals, armed with petrol and electoral forms, unidentified bigots who hunted strangers and set fire to them. Unidentified, until now. The dancing devil, the man with the stick, the boy with the petrol can, the beast with the brown cleaver.

If Officers Cassim and Ranchagoda were there, they would've recognised the last picture. The trained butcher in a banyan, waving a cleaver dulled by the blood of chickens, pigs, hunted minorities and a thousand cats. Instead, they are in the car arguing. Cassim says they should leave, while Ranchagoda suggests they should steal the box. Cassim says he never agreed to work with death squads, and wishes he could quit.

They do not notice the approaching Pajero, spilling over with men who are neither army nor cops. Even if they did, they would not have seen the demon riding on its hood.

'We are building cases against the perpetrators of 1983,' says Elsa. 'We have put faces to the mob and names to the faces. We can track down the murderers.'

'Why have I not heard of your CNTR? Or of this project?' asks Stanley, taking off his glasses to scrutinise the photos.

He looks at one showing a pyre of bodies taken not far from where they are gathered.

'You have not heard of CNTR because we do not court publicity. We are not politicians.' Elsa scowls at the envelope marked 'Queen' in Jaki's hands like a starving crow eyeing a discarded lunch packet.

Your Amma holds the one envelope in the room that does not contain photos. A letter from your absent Dada that she hadn't managed to destroy like the many before.

'Maali told us about the box,' says Jaki. 'He didn't say anything about giving it away.'

'Keep your bloody box. Give us our envelope.' Elsa flicks her cigarette out the window.

DD is squinting at a photo of an Indian Peace Keeping soldier outside a hospital. 'This was last year. When Maali went to Jaffna. He asked me to go with him,' he says looking at his father.

You remember the argument. It was over condoms and why you insisted on wearing them. Were you sleeping with others when you went away, he asked. So you asked him to come to Jaffna with you. You told him you were fixing for an American journo named Andrew McGowan. You didn't tell him that you had accepted a commission from a lady with red lips and her handsome cousin-brother.

'Do you do things with Andrew McGowan?' asked DD as if it didn't matter to him.

'I don't do what I do with you with anyone,' you said, which was technically not a lie, as you didn't plan your future with anyone else after sex.

'The Indian Peace Keeping Force carried out two massacres of civilians this year. One was in a hospital. Malinda was in Jaffna on our commission when this happened. We have paid him for those. Can we have them back?'

DD screws up his nose and heaves a dry cough. He passes a photo to Jaki, who flinches. It is a picture of hospital beds piled with dead doctors and nurses, punished by the Indian Peace Keeping Force for the crime of treating wounded LTTE fighters. Stanley peers over Jaki's shoulder and mutters.

'These are foreign devils.' He looks over to Elsa. 'Invited by our own fools.'

'We are in agreement,' she says.

'Do you also commission photos. That show the atrocities. Of the LTTE?'

'As a Tamil organisation, we are bound by constraints,' says Elsa. 'You should know this, sir.'

'You're a Tamil organisation now?' asks Jaki. 'Not a woman detective?'

You look at the other four envelopes on the table. You only remember two things about their contents. That DD should not look in the one marked 'Jack of Hearts'. And that there is an even chance that one of these envelopes contains a picture of your killer.

DD grabs the envelope marked 'Queen' from Jaki and tries to scoop the photos on the table into it.

'What are you doing!' Elsa raises her voice and snatches the empty envelope from him, leaving DD in a conundrum on how to wrestle with a woman in front of his father. He drops the photos back on the table and Elsa reaches for them.

Jaki, less a slave to decorum, marches across the room. She once slapped the bouncer at My Kind of Place thrice for grazing her bum with his palm. She bites her lip, like she did that night, and Elsa backs away. You remember that Jaki knows judo and that Elsa has a knife in her handbag. They stand with the photos between them, eyeballing each other like spaghetti western cowboys.

Right on cue, there is an eruption outside. Elsa slides to the doorway as the commotion floods in through the veranda, and flows down the hall. The same passageway where you confronted Amma about those letters from Dada, the ones she destroyed without showing you.

Seven strapping lads, each wearing black and white, run in through the open doors. Your Amma's teacup bounces on the rug without breaking. Stanley gets to his feet.

'What. The. Hell.'

The men, who are neither cops nor army, station themselves at every door and window. In walks an old man in national dress. If you could spit on him, vomit on him, shit in his mouth, you would pay vast fortunes or sell whatever is left of your soul. It is the Minister of Justice, the Right Contemptible Cyril Wijeratne, stalwart of the government, credited with corrupting the judiciary, setting up the death squads and igniting the pogroms of 1983. The sixth name on Sena's list.

Stanley Dharmendran welcomes him in with bowed head, like the Tamil stooge that he is. Two men in black instruct Jaki and DD off the couch so the Minister can place his fat behind upon it. Neither looks thrilled. You remember DD writing an official letter to the president's office and refusing to use the term 'Your Excellency'. 'What was so excellent about staying mute during July '83?' asked DD rhetorically. He addressed the letter to 'Dear Sir' and did not get funding for his recycling project in Malabe.

Come to Jaffna, you told DD. You will see this country faces bigger issues than the loss of habitat of the native pangolin. I don't get off on photographing corpses, he said. If you saw what was happening to your people, you wouldn't be worried about smelly lakes, you retort. Don't be a sell-out like your dad, you say, upping the ante and winning the pot. If making the boy who loves you walk away in tears is a victory.

'What is this? Photo exhibition, ah?'

Cyril takes the envelope from Elsa and looks down at the table. He bends forward like a cricket umpire and surveys the jumble of photos. You hover above him, more like a mosquito than angel. The mosquitoes are said to have killed half of everyone who has ever lived. A lot more than angels have saved.

You notice the hum in the air, that rumble at the lowest frequencies, only heard by those who silence their minds and empty their ears of whispers. It could be the sound of the earth groaning or the screams of the thousands. It is a sound that you did not notice before and one that you cannot stop hearing. And then you notice the thing squatting behind the Minister.

The photos on the table reveal carnage and chaos, mostly caused directly by Cyril Wijeratne's government, of which Uncle Stanley is a pawn.

'Dharmendran. What is this nonsense?'

'My son's classmate, sir,' says Stanley. 'He is a talented photographer. An intelligent boy from a very good family. Old Josephian. He is missing and we are all worried.'

Aw shucks, Stan, didn't know you cared.

'This is what Old Joes do?' says Cyril holding up the shot of a burning house.

'The '83 riots, sir,' says DD, squeezing the wooden ankh around his neck.

'Ah,' says the Minister. 'When the sleeping lion was woken.'

'Sir. My son's flat was invaded by this lady and those police outside. No warrant, no approval. My son does not deserve this harassment.'

The Minister does not appear to be listening. He looks at Elsa as if he has seen a ghost. Even though the real ghost is crouching behind him. Its silhouette resembles a large ape with its arms shielding the ministerial shoulders. Two eyes go from charcoal to ember behind the Minister's ear, and you know that they see you.

The Minister is looking at the photo she is holding of the man in the Benz watching the mob. A man who wears his younger face. Elsa is gathering the bundle of black-and-whites and he extends his hand and nods for her to hand them over. She shakes her head.

'Sorry, sir. These are confidential.'

He looks up at Elsa and stares at her for the time it takes your Amma to pour another cup. You see the look she gives him and feel an ache where your head used to be. This time the pain is not accompanied with memory. Then you follow his eye to an enlargement of the previous photo. The man in the Benz wears sunglasses and a batik shirt and, though the image goes blurry when enlarged, you recognise who it is. It is a face the Minister sees in the mirror, whenever he bothers to look.

He nods at one of the bodyguards, who grabs Elsa's shoulders and relieves her of the photos. He passes them to the Minister, while Elsa rubs her collarbone. It is her second bruise of the day. The Minister looks at photos and you want to peek, but the shadow crouching behind Cyril Wijeratne gives you pause. Minister Cyril shakes his head and slips the photos into his coat pocket.

'Is this your work?'

'Sir, those are confidential,' repeats Elsa, as if the man who oversees death squads respects privacy.

'They most definitely are, my dear. Who took them?'

'His name is Malinda Almeida. He is an innocent boy,' stammers Stanley.

'Doesn't look innocent to me,' says the Minister.

'No, sir,' Elsa says. 'He is not.'

'I'm not a bloody Chinaman with a ponytail. This photographer must be brought in for questioning,' says Cyril. 'Where is he?'

'He hasn't been seen since yesterday,' says Stanley. 'We're afraid he's been taken, sir.'

'So what men, Dharmendran? You know whom to call. Am I your bloody secretary?'

'The Special Task Force reports to you, sir.'

'You are the mother?' The Minister asks Lakshmi Almeida who, after four cups, goes into silent mode.

'Please find my son. I used to go to school with your sister, sir. Tell her Lucky Almeida from choir. She will know,' she says.

'You are a Bridgeteen, ah? I am good friends with all the nuns.' The Minister pauses to consider his next statement.

'The nuns at Bridgets are very liberal. You know you can kiss a nun once.' He pauses and wags his finger. 'But don't get into the habit.'

He giggles and the lads laugh along with him. Even Stanley raises a smile. Your Amma is not amused.

'My son is not political.'

As usual, Amma knows nothing about nothing.

'Harmless? Then why is he photographing disgusting things?' says Cyril with the smile that molested a thousand interns. 'Thank you for calling me Dharmendran. This is very serious.'

Stanley points at Elsa. 'Sir. This woman does not have a warrant and she has brought police to my flat. I am a Cabinet member and this is harassment.'

It is curious how Stanley's pauses evaporate when he kneels before power. Even DD, with his ignorance of reality, can sense his dad's plans are crumbling. He places the envelopes back into the shoebox, thinking that no one notices even though everyone does.

'Dharmendran, I have enough and more on my plate. We are at war on two fronts now. Have to keep the JVP down and kick the Indians out. Police and Army and STF all coming to me, asking if they can bend the rules. How can you do this? I cannot bend the rules for anyone.'

Jaki picks up the box and shuffles towards the back doorway, not noticing the STF guard moving towards her.

And then your Amma gets teary, like she never has, not since the day you were born, never in your presence.

'Minister. Do they have my son? You sister Surangani taught him to sing. Ask her – she will remember.'

If Aunty Surangani can remember the tone deaf boy who quit her class after four lessons in 1966, you will march into The Light right away. You like making impossible wagers.

Like when you told DD you'd go to San Fran with him if Dukakis beat Bush.

'Madam, he has been missing less than two days. Maybe he is not missing. I am sure he will turn up. And, when he does, I would like to speak to him.' Minister Cyril turns to Jaki. 'Excuse me, sweetheart, where are you going?'

A burly lad in black obstructs her exit and relieves her of the box. She pushes at him and he grabs her arm. She winces and he lets go.

'Can we have the envelope marked 'Queen' please?' says Elsa.

'Next, you'll be asking for the north and east as well!' laughs Minister Cyril. His eyes dart from Stanley to Elsa. 'I will need to evaluate this evidence. May I examine these properly, Dharmendran? At my discretion, before I make a recommendation?'

'For fuck's sake,' mutters DD.

'Dilan, shut up. Sir, is that necessary?'

'Before I issue the warrant, I must know the facts. We can only find your boy with access to all the facts. Tell those cops outside I want to speak to them.'

'So, you're taking Maali's stuff without a search warrant, to see if you need a search warrant,' Jaki snorts.

It takes seven goons to pack up one box.

Elsa walks outside to where the cops stand, as useless as pedestrian crossings on Galle Road. She whispers to Ranchagoda in short sharp sentences while Cassim sinks into the passenger seat and covers his face. She asks them to refund her money and Ranchagoda ducks into the car as the Minister exits the gate of your once-home sour home. He pretends not to hear her.

The biggest goon carries the white shoebox containing your life's work. You watch the shadow beast flank His Excellency, the Right Horrible Bigot, out the door. It seems to have grown long arms which swing from the sumo wrestler body. The pointy face and blood eyes look at you.

DD glares at his father. Your Amma puts away the teacups and Jaki stares into space with that look she gave you that first time she said she was ready and you said you were not. You float to the ceiling and wish for pain. Because you know the box is as good as gone.

Which means you need to work harder at remembering. Memories may bring pain which you'd rather not endure, but there is one memory you wish for. And it should be how you died or who killed you, but it is neither. You wish to remember where you hid the negatives. And all you know is that it is somewhere obvious, and somewhere close by.

CHAT WITH DEAD BODYGUARD (1959)

The shadow smiles at you and nods as the goons pile into two Pajeros. It squats on the bonnet of the Minister's Benz and calls you over. You expect the bonnet to cave in under the weight, but the bonnet does not appear to notice.

'Come. Ride with me.'

'Enough people taking me for rides,' you shout back.

You are hovering on the veranda where your Amma used to read the papers and bitch about your father. Inside the home, familiar voices are making pointless arguments about you and the things you have done. You no more wish to eavesdrop than you wish to go back to living.

The thing on the Minister's car has maroon eyes, jagged teeth, overgrown nails, and is dressed in a white shirt and black trousers, standard uniform for waiters, bodyguards, thugs and goons. 'Those were your photos, yes? I managed to take a peek. Impressive work, ah. Super, super.'

'What kind of yaka are you?'

'I am the Minister's shadow. A shadow minister. Haha. Come, will you? As if you have anywhere else to be.'

Now that was a point you could not refute. It wouldn't be the first time you'd shared transport with unsavoury company. Like that time you boarded a bus to Kilinochchi with undercover Tigers and almost got shot at by the army.

You reach the roof of the car just as it is driving off. You notice that the creature's dress is ill matched. He wears a frilly shirt and slacks that look tailored by a blind man. He is barefoot, his toes are hairy and his nails protrude like talons.

'Your photos are gruesome.'

So is your face, you think. The motorcade passes a checkpoint where cars are lined up for inspection. The two Pajeros and this Benz are not detained.

'Then maybe people should stop doing gruesome things.'

'This land is cursed. No doubt about it,' says the creature, its eyes switching colour, from crimson to ebony, from mahogany to scarlet.

'How did you become a demon?'

You are ready to jump the car's tailwind if sudden moves are made. But this blob is lying on the bonnet, staring at the sky with its shadowy eyes. Moving seems not high on its agenda.

'Who says I became anything? Maybe, I always was.'

'What were you before?'

'Maybe, I was a leader like this one.' He points to the man in the back seat of the car, with his hand in a shoebox that belonged to you. 'Maybe, I was a tycoon who owned factories of people.'

'But you weren't.'

'I was a bodyguard. Though I never took a bullet for anyone. Unfortunately.'

'You wanted to take a bullet?'

'My last job was protecting Solomon Dias.'

'Who?'

'SWRD.'

You laugh properly for the first time since this whole bloody mess. 'Nice guy.'

'Say all you want. I have heard it all. Führer of Sinhala Only. Godfather of every shitstorm.'

'I've heard him called worse.'

'If he had lived, he would've repealed the act and promoted multiculturalism. He was a federalist at heart.'

'He was shot by a Sinhala Buddhist monk, the beast he was trying to tame, for not being bigoted enough,' you say. SWRD was the one thing you and your late father agreed on.

'How long have you been dead?' asks the demon.

'One moon, apparently. What was Solomon like?'

'It wasn't his fault. He meant well. This land is cursed.'

'I've heard that before. How so?'

'You took all those photos and you still have to ask me that?'

'Fair point.'

'Ceylon was a beautiful island before it filled up with savages.'

'True. Some countries import their savages. We breed ours.'

'You know there were people here long before the Sinhalese?'

'Kuveni's people?'

'They weren't considered people. We call them devils and snakes.'

'Were yakas and nagas before or after Ravana?'

'No one cares.'

'So, who were the indigenous Lankans?'

'Not Vijaya and his sea pirates. That's for sure.'

If the *Mahavamsa* is to be believed, the Sinhalese race was founded on kidnapping, rape, parricide and incest. This is not a fairy tale, but the story of our birth as given by the island's oldest chronicle, a chronicle used to codify laws crafted to suppress all that is not Sinhalese and Buddhist and male and wealthy.

Once upon a time in north India, a princess meets a lion. Lion kidnaps and forces self on princess. Princess gives birth to girl and boy. Boy grows up, kills lion-father, becomes king, marries sister. She gives birth to boy, who becomes troublemaker, who is banished with seven hundred flunkies, who arrive in ships on the shores of Ceylon.

Prince Vijaya and his band of bald thugs kick-start our history by slaughtering the native Naga people and seducing their queen, though perhaps not in that order. If the origin story is true, the mess we are in should be no surprise. Betrayed and ruined by the callous prince, Queen Kuveni of the Naga tribe curses the land before she kills herself and abandons her children to the forest. The curse sticks for a few millennia and, in 1990, shows no signs of lifting.

'Our ancestors have literally been demonised,' says the creature. 'I have heard that the Mahakali is a descendant of Kuveni. Some say she is Kuveni herself.'

The traffic bottlenecks on Galle Road. It starts to rain and neither of you get wet. You look around at people running with umbrellas and huddling under shopfronts. The only ones who keep walking are those who no longer have breath.

'The more I see, the more I am convinced,' says the creature. 'History is people with ships and weapons wiping out those who forgot to invent them. Every civilisation begins with a genocide. It is the rule of the universe. The immutable law of the jungle, even this one made of concrete. You can see it in the movement of the stars, and in the dance of every atom. The rich will enslave the penniless. The strong will crush the weak.'

It is now crawling up the windshield and is close enough to slap you. The Benz passes a shop that sells handcrafted souvenirs and flies a Sri Lankan flag on its roof.

'I always had a problem with that flag,' you say, while keeping an eye on his overgrown nails.

It looks through the window at the Minister, who has fallen asleep with your box on his lap. The traffic starts to move and the Minister's Demon smiles at you.

'The mighty lion flag?'

'When did we have bloody lions here? Or tigers?'

'Elephants might make more sense.'

'Or pangolins.'

Most flags have blocks of colour, not always belonging to the same palette: horizontal, vertical, sometimes diagonal, sometimes all three, like the Union Jack that ruled over us all. Some have friendly symbols like maple leaves, crescent moons, spinning wheels and suns with afros. In times more barbarous than these, houses carried sigils of wolves, lions, elephants, dragons, unicorns. Just to show off how bestial they could be if messed with. These days, the animal kingdom features on precious few flags. Mostly birds, stately and non-violent, with the exception of Mexico's snake-crushing eagle.

'Look at our flag. What an achcharu. It has everything. Horizonal lines, vertical lines, primary colours, secondary colours, animal symbols, nature symbols, weapons. Yellow, maroon, green and orange. Bo leaves, a sword and a beast. Like a fruit salad.'

'Seen the Eelam flag? No better.'

The lion holds the scimitar to the orange and green verticals that represent the Dravidian and Mohammedan, holding the minorities at knifepoint. As a retort, the separatist flag of Tamil Eelam has a tiger peeping Kilroy style between rifles. As if to say, I see your lion with sword, and raise you a tiger with two bayonets.

Both flags have a beast and a bad layout and are the colour of blood. Eelam has the tomato red of a flesh wound, Lanka has the plum maroon of an unhealed scar.

There is no evidence that either of these beasts ever roamed these lands, but here they sit on flags, waving weapons and swimming in blood. As if to acknowledge that Lanka was founded on bestiality and bloodshed.

The Benz drives past the harbour and you both squint at the horizon, far past the anchored ships. You daydream of distant gods and ageing suns. Of absent fathers and queer children.

'Wanna know why I think Lanka is cursed?'

'You just said. Kuveni.'

'Not just her. We were born in 1948. Do you believe in nakath?'

Any musician or sportsperson worth their sweat will tell you that timing is all. Aside from believing in yakas and curses, Lankans also believe in nakath, in the auspiciousness of time, extending Feng Shui to the passing of moments. On Sinhala and Tamil New Year, if you face west and light a lamp at 6.48 a.m., you will receive joy; if you face north and spark up at 7.03 a.m., the sky will fall.

'I don't believe in nakath.'

'How does 1948 sound to you? Auspicious or suspicious?'

'Do you whisper to the Minister?'

'When I need to.'

'Is it hard to learn?'

'Nothing is hard with the right teacher.'

'I need to get to the kanatte. So, I will get off here.'

'Why are you going to cemeteries? What funerals for you men? Only one moon old.'

'My teacher Sena might be there. He knows how to whisper.'

'Any so-called teacher who hangs out at the kanatte will want more than school fees from you.'

'What does that mean?'

The car pulls across Bullers Lane into the building that housed the Ministry of Justice.

'The Philippines also started in '48. Like us they are smiley, happy-go-lucky and vicious when they choose to be.'

'Were you really SWRD's bodyguard?'

'He was a powerful man. But not as powerful as Cyril will be. I will make sure.'

'Does every Minister have a demon?'

'Only the very best.'

You try and focus a shot of the demon riding the Benz, but all you see through the viewfinder is mud.

'Best? SWRD was rubbish. And Cyril is worse. You guard scum.'

The beast pounces at you but you are already reaching for the electric pylons on the roadside.

It takes a swipe and manages to flick one of your chains. You swing off the power line to the mango tree.

'You watch your mouth. Do you know which countries were born in 1948?'

The Benz halts in traffic, but there are winds in every direction. 'If this land is cursed, it is because of men like Wijeratne and Solomon Dias. And because of those who protect them,' you call out, emboldened by the distance between the creature and you.

The creature yells out the names of five countries. And the Benz disappears with the gargoyle on its hood. 'I'll be watching you,' it snarls and you see it no more. But the five names that it called out echo in your ears. 'Burma. Israel. North Korea. Apartheid South Africa. Sri Lanka. All born in '48.'

It doesn't matter if Maali Almeida believes in nakath or not. Because it appears that the universe most certainly does.

THE EARS

The Benz vanishes into traffic and you can no longer move. Invisible walls barricade you and all winds have ceased. You feel encased by padded glass, held by arms you cannot see.

You were never claustrophobic despite all that time spent in bunkers and narrow beds and lifelong closets. But, like any reasonable person, living or dead, you'd like to have the option of running away, especially when there is plenty to run from.

Instead you find yourself immobile and optionless, the involuntary detainee of figures in white smocks. Moses to your left and He-Man to your right. They look ahead and they do not smile. Before you is Dr Ranee: white sari, ledger book and schoolteacher scowl.

'Your Helpers will accompany you. They won't hurt you if you behave.'

'Why do angels need thugs?' you ask, as sweetly as you can.

'Who said we were angels?' says Dr Ranee. 'You're avoiding The Light because you're afraid of your sins.'

'Why force souls into The Light? Shouldn't we be free to go where we want?'

'Who told you this nonsense?'

'Comrade Sena.'

'You go where the voices in your head tell you,' she says. 'But the voices in your head aren't always you.'

The Helpers take you on a random route from Slave Island to Mattakuliya through what looks like an abandoned railway station to what you recognise as the place you once fled from. 'Aiyo. Not here again. Please.'

'This won't take long.'

You enter through the red doors and into the endless corridor. It is just as crowded as the first time you awoke here and just as organised. Helpers in white herding the unbalanced, the maimed and the diseased to counters of intertwining queues. Dr Ranee sends He-Man and Moses into the fray and floats with you at the edge of the chaos.

'First, shall we do the Ear Check?'

You watch freshly dead souls in varying states of grief bumping into one another like particles in flux. Some shiver, some struggle, some cling to the big fat nothing.

'Who's in charge? Who's your boss?'

Dr Ranee shakes her head.

'Let me rephrase. Is nobody in charge?'

'I'm just a Helper, Maal. We do what we can. Maybe there was a creator. Maybe he vomited the world like that African god Mbombo. Or handcrafted it in a week and slept on a Sunday like the fellow in the Bible.'

'So who do I get to meet? Yahweh or Zeus?'

THE SEVEN MOONS OF MAALI ALMEIDA

'We should know the soul of the Creator. Instead of arguing over Her name.'

'I have a superb name for God. Whoever.'

'Don't come to me on your seventh moon, begging to be set free. I've stopped doing last-minute cases.'

'Everyone should pray to Whoever. Then no one gets offended. "Dear Whoever, look after my family. And give us money and no pain. Love, Me."'

'I'm getting tired of your jokes.'

'That's the most serious thing I've ever said.'

She gives you a lecture about ears. Says the truth to everything you have ever been lies in their patterns. How cartilage, skin and flesh form shapes and shadows more unique than fingerprints. In them lie fossils of past lives and forgotten sins. It's a clue hiding just out of sight, as clues generally tend to.

'The fact that our ears are invisible to us is a sure sign of the Creator's genius,' says Doc Ranee.

'Or a sign that she hates us all,' says you.

Dr Ranee shakes her head. She tells you the ears are karmic fingerprints and that your 'meat-cloak' is littered with clues to previous lives. The suliya on your head, the ratios of your toes, the patterns on your skin, the angles of your teeth, the bounce of your gait. There are reasons even the most journeyman of charm makers include hair or nails or teeth or blood in their huniyam curses. You are dragged along towards the lift shaft. Moses holds his staff to the wind. He-Man glares as if daring you to run. The wind has grown to a gale and roars like a cornered beast. 'If you want answers,' shouts Dr Ranee over it. 'To find the "Whoever" behind it all. First find the "whoever" between your ears.'

You rise up through the shaft, amidst spirits floating in many directions. Floor after floor passes you by. If you were keeping track of levels, you would count Forty-Two.

'It is difficult to know God's face. When you do not even know your own,' she says.

Today, Level Forty-Two is open for business or whatever it is that takes place behind the line of red doors.

The spirits all look fresh, you can tell from their eyes and their gait and the figures in white who chaperone them. Your three guardians nod at their colleagues and lead you towards a red door. In your hand is an ola leaf with its carefully labelled sections. You recognise it, but you do not know how it got there.

The room inside looks like an opium den minus the smoke. Bodies lie supine and shirtless men and topless women with large bellies and purple eyes squat over each and peer into their ears.

You are asked to lie down while a village lass and what looks like a village drunk stare into your ears. Their skin is the purple of a mangosteen and their breath smells of fruit.

'Has lived thirty-nine lives,' says the nymph.

'Correct,' says the drunk.

The drunk stares into your left ear and the nymph looks into your right. They mutter to each other as they scribble on the ola leaf book.

'Was killed. Violent. Sudden.'

'Has loved incomplete.'

'Has stolen. And been robbed.'

The nymph and the drunk look at each other and then at you.

'Has killed?'

'Aiyo,' says Dr Ranee, holding a palm to her cheek.

'That's bullshit,' you say, before being pushed through a passageway with the other corpses, most of whose eyes change shade as you stare at them. At each stop, a pair of hands takes your ola leaf and scribbles on it. You are groped by different apparitions, some in dinner jackets, some in sarongs, and a few in gold finery and not much else. All with purple eyes and bellies.

'Pretas are hungry ghosts,' says Dr Ranee. 'They are also experts in reading ears.'

'They also said I killed someone. Small problem. I didn't.'

'Are you sure?'

And then you enter a room and it is just you and a mirror and you see nothing in the reflection and then you see your eyes on different faces, your face on different heads and your head on different bodies. Every feature changes as your focus falls on it. Your nose elongates then contracts. Your face grows bestial then beautiful. Your hair lengthens and vanishes. Your eyes go from green to blue to brown.

But your ears, they do not change.

Finally, you recognise the thing in the mirror. It wears a red bandanna, a safari jacket, one sandal and things around its neck – intertwining chains, the wooden ankh with DD's blood, the Panchayudha, and the locket hiding the capsules. You look closely at the tangled threads and realise how closely they resemble a noose. Your camera hangs like a millstone; you pull at it and look down its cracked lens.

You see a dog and an old man and a woman cradling a baby. They all sleep peacefully and the image punches you in the gut. For a third time, your eyes prickle with tears. When you look up, you are holding the ola leaf book but this time it has writing on it. The writing is pretty and precise, yet oddly bureaucratic.

Deaths – 39

Ears – Blocked

Sins – Many

Moons – 5

At the bottom of the leaf, it bears a stamp. Five white circles, each overlapping. The moons you have left.

..

You are at the reception of Level forty-two, He-Man and Moses have disappeared. No doubt to jostle some other unworthy sinner to The Light. It is just you and the good doctor and this noisy station and memories that lie at the edges of your thoughts, on your vision's periphery, at your tongue's tip. They wash against the windows of your mind but stay hidden in the storm.

Dr Ranee is giving you a lecture, but a kinder one this time.

'Your soul is not young, you have lived thirty-nine lives. You have guilt, you have sorrow, you have unpaid debts. They think your death was murder, not accident or suicide.'

'How can they know?'

'Maybe you caused deaths. You don't look like a killer to me. But neither did the boys who shot me.'

She waits with her head on one side to see how you react.

You are silent. If there is an answer, you can't remember it. Your brain secretes memories, but not the ones you seek. You remember your photos and where you stashed the negatives. It is not information Dr Ranee would appreciate, but someone might.

'I paid my debts.'

'Did you?'

'Except for my pictures. They need to be seen. And I have five more moons. Enough time.'

'They say your memory is blocked.'

You look down on the ola leaf. Do these scratches and squiggles really say all that?

You remember Jaki once telling you of a place in Kotahena filled with the horoscopes of everyone who ever lived. Jaki went through an astrology phase a week after her gambling phase and months before her drama phase.

The myth went as follows: three thousand years ago, seven Indian astrologers wrote down biographies for everyone yet to be born on vast collections of palm leaves. Each of which retailed for the price of a roll of fabric in Pettah.

If you gave them a time and date of birth, they imported your ola leaf from a cave in India and an astrologer in a starched shirt deciphered it for you here. Based on these etchings in Pali, Sanskrit and Tamil, the astrologer told young girls when they would marry and housemaids when they would depart these shores. He told old men that they had many years left and cripples that they may one day walk. Though, curiously, this astrologer never told anyone when they would die.

You remember telling Jaki it would take seven sages a million years to write biographies of 5.3 billion souls. That the paper trail alone would flatten all of Sinharaja Forest. And, in the end, it would be a pointless exercise.

All stories are recycled and all stories are unfair. Many get luck, and many get misery. Many are born to homes with books, many grow up in the swamps of war. In the end, all becomes dust. All stories conclude with a fade to black.

· ·

Dr Ranee's voice cuts through your black thoughts. 'It says you are damaged. It says you should not linger in the In Between.'

'Look, Aunty, I appreciate this.'

'I am not your Aunty. If you stay here, you will be taken.'

'By whom?'

'Your Comrade Sena works for the Mahakali. He is using you just as he is being used. The In Between is filled with ghouls and demons who draw power from your despair. Do not gift it to them. It helps no one.'

'Sena will help me whisper to the living. Can you give me that?'

You look at Dr Ranee and the angels with muscles. You look around the counter and do not see a hooded figure of Sena there, and for this you are grateful. You smell the air and know that the Mahakali is not far from here.

'I need to see Sena.'

'Are you mad?' says Dr Ranee.

'Everyone everywhere is working for some Mahakali. What do I care?'

'You are a fool. And a waste of my time.'

Dr Ranee goes quiet when she loses her temper, just like Jaki used to. Your father was the opposite. And, unlike your Dada, she knows when an argument is over.

'A demon cannot devour you unless you invite it. At least, not before your seven moons. And you only have five left.'

She is looking at you sternly, but you can tell that, despite it all, she still wants to help you. And those were usually the people you treated the worst.

'I'll come to you before then. Definitely.'

'I used to say that to my husband and daughters. Definitely. Always after I made a promise I couldn't keep.'

She floats away to a vacant counter and she does not look back. On the way she directs an old lady to the lift and a boy to a red door and she does not look back. She has not seen what you have seen, and she has not done what you have done. And she does not understand that if you step into The Light, it is not the forgetting that you fear, but the things that will step in there with you.

MYTHICAL CREATURE

You wait for a suitable breeze to take you to the cemetery, so that you may offer Sena whatever currency he requires in return for the power to whisper. As you wait for winds, you watch the souls float towards the bus stands of Maradana. You can now identify pretas by their purple skin and bellies, demons by their red eyes and claws, and ordinary ghosts by their looks of confusion.

'Watch out for those with black eyes. They will mess you up, my brother.'

You look down and spy a leopard. This is not a euphemism for armed humans hiding their violence behind the names of ferocious cats. This is an actual animal. Its coat is striped with slash marks and its eyes are pure white.

'I'm sorry, I don't follow.'

'Of course you don't.'

'I didn't know there were animal ghosts.'

'Then should I disappear, just to serve your ignorance?'

'Didn't mean to offend you.'

'And yet you did,' says the leopard as it scales the parapet. It disappears down an alleyway toward the canals of Panchikawatte.

Why would there not be animal ghosts? Why should only humans get souls? Does that mean every insect you ever stepped on gets to roam for seven moons and claim a refund at the counter? No wonder the Helpers look overworked.

You catch a wind and you look down on the souls on the rooftops gaping at the moon. You think of all the creatures you have seen, Down There and In Between. You pass a billboard for a dead politician and wonder why some humans get billboards and some don't even get graves. In all this madness, there is only one beast whose existence you doubt. And you are not thinking of God, also known as Whoever. You are thinking of that most impossible of all mythical creatures: the Honest Politician.

You have heard tales of only one. A gentleman who came to politics for neither greed nor profit. Don Wijeratne Joseph Michael Bandara, born in Kegalle in 1902, son of a cobbler, who won a scholarship to the Peradeniya Law Faculty in 1919. After years of fighting cases for plantation workers, he was elected on the Communist Party ticket and proceeded to work himself into an early grave. He worked for the downtrodden and the forgotten, argued for Tamil workers, Muslim traders, Burgher drivers and Chetty chefs. He built two libraries in the Kegalle district, taught a generation of children to read English, and banished all racketeers from the town hall. He never took a bribe, never philandered, never swore even after a drink. Yes, of course, he drank. Even mythical creatures get thirsty.

Don Wijeratne Joseph Michael Bandara died of a stroke in '67, caused by the Churchill cigars he supped on and the lawsuit that kept him awake at nights. Slapped on him by the local unions, the very ingrates he worked eighteen-hour days for. His youngest son, Don Wijeratne Buveneka Cyril Bandara, entered parliament in 1977 and remembered his father's masterclass in how to be unsuccessful.

Cyril Bandara's world view was coloured from driving his father to the labour courts every week for three years. Bandara Senior was sued for tender fraud by a timber company whose labour practices he had questioned. Bandara Junior watched the courts suck up his inheritance and defecate on his father's reputation – the likely reason for Junior to contest his first election as MP for Kalutara as Cyril Wijeratne.

When Cyril fixed construction tenders, he never got caught. Cyril used the excuse all married men use. If you are to be accused of the crime, you might as well commit it.

There are creatures for you to fear in this and every other tale. The Charred yaka who spreads rumours and cancers, the Riri yaka that rips babies from wombs, the Mohini, the Devil Bird, the ten-headed Ravana, the Mahakali.

Then there is the drunk bus driver, the dengue mosquito, the maniac monk, the crazed soldier, the torturer in the mask, the Minister's son. Men who are neither army nor police. Men who wear national dress to work.

Cyril Wijeratne had the ability to pacify pacifists like Rajapaksa, out-think ideologues like JR, outflank populists like Premadasa, impress foreign dignitaries with his borrowed accent and dupe the fools who voted for him by pretending to be his mythic father's son. And, if you asked him how he had survived five assassination attempts (three JVP, two LTTE), he would not have thought, 'I have the dead bodyguard of SWRD protecting this fortunate posterior.'

He would have thought, 'I am alive today because of the Crow Man.'

THE CROW MAN'S CAVE

You spy Sena at the cemetery car park. He is staring at the crematorium tower and handing out leaves to the freshly incinerated ghosts. He grins at you and calls you over.

'Afternoon, sir. Good to see you. Thought I lost you to the Helpers.'

'You never said your father was a driver for the Wijeratne family.'

'Sir never asked.'

'Did you know Buveneka Wijeratne?'

'Thathi never took me to his workplace. Why would he? He knew I thought he was a peasant.'

'Your father said he cursed the Wijeratne family.'

'A driver's curses are worth less than nothing. Is there something you need from me?'

'If I wanted to whisper to the living, is it possible?' you ask.

'It is possible to do all things, boss,' he says, pulling circular green things from his garbage bag satchel. 'But you need to commit. I don't see commitment from you, sir. I'm just saying.'

You notice that Sena only hands leaves to ghosts whose eyes are green or yellow, only to those who look stricken or confused. Like all purveyors of religion, Sena has wisely chosen to prey on the weak.

The cemetery air is still. Rats, snakes and polecats hide among tombstones. A banyan tree holds court over shaggy grass and toppled rock. There are many shadows to disappear into, though no one present appears to cast one.

'I assume the meeting with the Helpers went well,' sniggers Sena. He has an annoying habit of sticking his tongue between his teeth when attempting humour. There is something different about him. His teeth seem jagged, his lips fuller, his eyes more goggled, his hair spikier, his grin smarmier. He says the same thing to every poor ghoul he passes. 'We see you. We can make your killers pay,' he whispers as he forces a leaf into each withered hand. 'Justice will bring you peace. Your killers will beg for your mercy.'

'How many have you recruited?' you ask.

'I have those two Engineering students,' he says. 'And about seven others who might join. No one should be alone in this In Between. We are stronger together.'

'Yet, alone we all are. I need to contact my friend.'

'Why?'

'To help her rescue my negatives.'

'Why?'

'Because otherwise what I have seen will disappear. Like tears in rain.' A line from the first movie you saw with DD, which he snored through, while you held his hand and cried for Rutger Hauer.

'Hamu is a mara poet, no?'

'Can I appear before Jaki and speak to her?'

'Aiyo. Slow down, sir. If it's that easy, everyone will be seeing ghosts.'

'So, ghosts can't talk to people?'

'Only in horror films. But you can create moods and whisper thoughts.'

Sena hands the last of his leaves to a beast made from severed limbs. It is a bomb-blast victim who spits in your direction. You have seen plenty of them on your short sojourn.

'So, what can I do?'

'Malinda Almeida, sir. I believe it is time for you to meet the Crow Man.'

..

Under the bridge, below the steel staircase, closed at the mouth, an urban cave sits hidden from view. The fuse box on the pavement with the words 'Danger! High Voltage', camouflaged a sidedoor that you had to bend to access.

Sena pushes you through browned metal, shoves you between concrete and drags you across wood. What does it feel like to walk through a wall? It's like walking through a swimming pool that smells like dust and doesn't make you wet.

The cave has draughts coming from strange angles. You spy ventilation holes climbing the wall to the ceiling, allowing in sun and exhaust fumes.

Inside is not, as you would expect, a town hall for roaches or a urinal for bats, but instead a candlelit shrine to every god in every holy book. Laminated posters from the pavements of Maradana, hung with sellotape and nails. Jesus, Buddha and Osho. Shiva, Ganesh and Sai Baba. Marley, Kali and Bruce Lee. A cross, a crescent moon, a Tibetan proverb over the Dalai Lama's face, a Buddhist koan scrawled in Sinhalese on a pixelated bo leaf.

In the centre of the cave is a pot-bellied man in a T-shirt. His hair is combed and his beard has an orange henna hue. His spectacles are thick and shrink his eyes to beads. He sits at a desk littered with betel, flowers, incense ash and rupee notes. His eyes are closed and he is muttering in a made-up language.

Above him hang cages made of wood and wire, each without a door, some with nests, some with parrots, some with sparrows, most with crows. They fly in through the grill, nibble at the green gram in the bowl and leave no droppings.

In front of the fat man is a woman in a sari with a lot of make-up and not enough deodorant. She is clutching her maroon handbag and staring at the man. Sena hovers around the table while you take in the room and realise there are others here. Overlapping shadows huddle in corners watching the exchange in the middle and glaring at the two of you.

At first, it appears that the man is running a dodgy casino

(as if there were any other type), for she places hundred-rupee notes in the betel leaf after every statement he utters, like a drunk businessman placating a stripper. You drift closer and catch the conversation in snippets. She is asking after her father and he is delivering platitudes and she places more money and he delivers more platitudes.

'He says he loves you and is proud of you and is always watching over you.'

She dabs her eyes. 'Did he mention the jewellery?'

It is then you notice the bent old coot whispering in the fat man's ear. The apparition swivels around and spits on the table.

'This greedy pig cannot be a daughter of mine.'

'Mr Piyatilaka. Your daughter seeks her heirloom,' says the Crow Uncle, his eyelids flickering behind his glasses in a simulation of a trance state.

'Tell her I gave it to the bird I was screwing in '73. When her ungrateful mother stopped touching me.'

The Crow Uncle speaks to the daughter with his eyes closed. 'Your father loves you very much. He believes it has been stolen.'

'Who has stolen it?'

'Mr Piyatilaka, tell me where it is.'

The fat man removes his glasses and bobs and weaves his head like a soul singer. That's when you notice his eyes. They are white, but not quite like a Helper's. The pupil is grey with a black dot at its centre. It stares without seeing and sees things that aren't there.

The old man raises his head and his eyebrows. The daughter places more money on the betel leaf.

'You thieving shit. You think I'll tell you?' With that, the old man storms off into the shadows.

'Your father has to rest. The emotion of seeing you is too much.'

The daughter nods and closes her purse. 'Next time, can you find out about the jewellery?'

'I will try,' says the Crow Uncle.

He smiles and does not get up as she rises. He waits till he hears her heels clip-clopping on the staircase above before he turns your way.

'Who the hell is that!' he hisses. 'Who sent you?'

You are unsure whether his comments are directed at Sena or you. His grey pupils roll around their sockets without direction.

'You are this JVP fellow, no? Is that you, Sena Pathirana?'

'Yes, Swamini.'

'Don't call me that, you prick. What's that thing you've brought here?'

There are cackles in the shadows and you're not sure if you should retort or run.

'He wants the power to whisper.'

'Don't bloody come here when I'm working, ah!'

'Sorry, Swamini.'

'How long have you been coming here, Sena Pathirana?'

'About thirty-five moons.'

'And who gets to call me Swamini?'

'Your disciples, Sw—'

'And my disciples do what?'

'Visit you every three moons.'

'Correct. You promised me an army. Where?'

'I have spread the word. I will deliver what I said.'

'And all you can bring me is this? What is this? Another JVP?'

'He was killed for taking pictures of war. He needs to talk to his girlfriend.'

There are more sniggers in the shadow. You can make out shapes of figures that look too disproportionate to be human.

'Your good name?'

'Malinda Almeida.'

'Almeida, you seem troubled. And I don't care. I don't care about you or what you believe or what you have done. I only care about the transaction. If you help me, I will help you. That is all. Clear?'

You nod and watch a figure emerge from the shadow. It is a small boy with a missing hand. He sits at the desk with a piece of paper and feeds chickpeas to the sparrows. You are unsure if he is flesh or spirit, only that he appears to be neither.

'The Crow Uncle can't see a thing without his glasses,' Sena had explained on the way to the cave. 'Some say from the '88 bomb blast, some say from a landmine, some say from snakebite. In his cave, only he can crack the jokes. Do not get smart with him.'

'When he takes off his glasses, the world blurs and he cannot see the birds he feeds, the slum dwellers he makes shrines for, or the customers he lies to. But he can see spirits, he can hear ghosts, and they can hear him.'

The Sparrowboy's story also has many authors. He lost his hand on the rail tracks or in the '88 bomb blast or from an abusive uncle. He sits at the table holding a pen with his remaining hand. Along the ledges, you see crude dolls made of coconut leaf, a bowl filled with charcoal and a box with carvings on it.

'We must summon your girlfriend here first,' says the Crow Uncle.

'Through black magic?' you ask. 'Through huniyam?'

'No, fool. We will write her a postcard.'

Sena has disappeared to the shadows, where he chatters with the unseen. Sena told you that the boy does not speak, and to speak to him before the Crow Uncle is a grave disrespect.

'Your friend's name?'

'Jacqueline Vairavanathan.'

'Address?'

'4/11 Galle Face Court.'

'I will give her an appointment for tomorrow. Are you certain she will come?'

'I hope.'

'That is never good enough.' He uses two fingers to scoop some ointment from a shiny brass bowl and smear it on the card. 'Kolla, will you deliver this? Ah, yes. She must bring a personal belonging of yours. Something that is close to your heart. Tell me what it is and where it can be found.'

You think for a beat and playing cards flutter before your eyes. Aces and Kings and Queens and dead dogs. You tell him. The boy ambles through the door at the side, unlike most customers, he doesn't need to bend to leave.

'Malinda. This is how it works. I have a gift and a curse. I live in a blurry world, but I see all. The richest, the most powerful, all ask my help. Because I am humble. Because I am brilliant.'

There are shadows crouched behind him whispering in his ear. He nods and shakes his head.

'You are forbidden from questioning me. You will tell me what you need and, within my powers, I will provide it. If you want to talk to the living, I can help. You want to bless someone, it can be done. You want to curse, it will cost you more. But you will owe me favours. And you will deliver. Is that clear?'

The shadows huddle around his earlobes and Sena stands at the corner making gestures at you to bow before him. You do no such thing.

'I can give you the power to whisper in ears. I can even give you powers to possess the living. But you have to help me. Are you willing?'

You shrug your shoulders and Sena steps up.

'Yes, Swamini. We are willing.'

'Bring me this army you promised. Otherwise, shut up. I want to hear it from this fool.'

'I will not bow before you,' you say.

'Then why are you on your knees?' he asks.

You are astonished to find that, for neither the first nor last time in history or in mythology, a man with bad eyesight speaks the truth.

ROMAN-DUTCH LAW BOOKS

The Sparrowboy is waiting outside the lift when Jaki gets back from work. She has got through an early morning shift at the SLBC with a hangover. You can always tell when she's been drinking or gambling by the way she drags herself. The boy walks across the lobby and hands her a postcard. It is sticky to her touch and smells of lavender and gotu kola.

'What's this?'

The boy points to his mouth and opens and closes it soundlessly. He shows the address at the bottom, which Jaki reads while you lean on her shoulder and whisper in her ear. Her ear is pudgy and layered with curves. You wonder what lives are concealed in those folds of cartilage.

> Miss Jaki Vayranathan
> Almayda wish to speak you.
> He say bring address book. In almirah. Under bear.
> Come tomorrow morning to Kotahena Junction.
> The kolla will take you.

Who but Jaki would respond to such flimsy summons? She once turned up at Pegasus Casino with her mother's credit card and said nothing about the lecture she received over long-distance telephone. She once gave you her last happy pill when you told her of the smouldering remains of an infant you saw in Akkaraipattu.

'Why do you keep doing it?' she asked. 'Is the money that good?'

'No. I am.'

'OK.'

'I've been good at nothing. But I know how to get in close and get the shot. I'm not the best with a camera. But I always get to the place. Doesn't matter whose side it's on.'

You have carried Jaki drunk and rolled her out of taxis. You have protected her from many an unsavoury lad. She has covered your rent when you were on tour. She has lied to DD when you were on a card spree.

She took you to the clubs of Colombo 3, the salons of Colombo 4, the casinos of Colombo 5, the parties of Colombo 7. Spots that Sena would pay to peep into. You enjoyed the pills she got on prescription and shandied with gin. And you enjoyed solving her work dramas and relative issues, even though you'd never worked in an office or had an uncle you could name.

When she suggested you see her psychiatrist, who was effectively her happy pill dealer, to talk about your nightmares, you weren't offended.

'What nightmares?'

'The ones you have every night.'

'I don't dream,' you say.

'No. They don't sound like dreams.'

'How would you know? Have you been coming to my room?'

It was the touching that became a problem. It started out with held hands and rubbed shoulders and then one evening it was a hand on your thigh and fingers through your hair and each touch felt like a clown was tickling you. When she laid her lips on yours, you shuddered and let out a giggle. After that, things grew strange.

'You are the kolla, I suppose,' she says to the boy.

He nods and unfurls his fingers like a child learning to count.

'Have you eaten? Malu paan?'

He shakes his head.

She pulls two fish buns from her maroon handbag, the uneaten snack she'd always bring home.

'Take. Eat. Don't worry, I'm your friend.'

Sparrowboy stares at her while biting into the bun.

'We go tomorrow?'

He nods, crumbs spilling over his cheeks.

'Morning?'

He nods, savouring the feast and giving her the hint of a smile.

'You'll come here?'

He points with his stump to the words 'Kotahena Junction' which he himself penned on that very postcard a few hours previous. Jaki nods and enters the old lift.

She never argued with you, never played the drama queen or made scenes like DD did. Instead, she'd say, 'OK,' and say nothing for a while. But her eyes would get that glaze and she'd give you that half-smile and you'd know she was furious.

She said OK when you told her you couldn't meet her parents, when you told her you were visiting the Blue Elephant without her, and when you told her you were moving into the spare room. The room where she now enters, whose almirah she ransacks. She sees the framed photos of X-rays, the parade of jackets and shirts, and the chains with cyanide in them.

The jackets and shirts were autumn colours, selected to blend into the jungle and stand out in the city. The X-rays were of your mouth and chest, taken after a car accident, involving you, an older gentleman and an ill-advised blow job while driving. You tried to turn them into an art project, which got abandoned like most things did. And you got those vials from the bodies of dead Tigers you photographed in Kilinochchi for the army.

She also spies a teddy bear that your dad brought back from Colombo along with a sexually transmitted disease, which was his parting gift to your Amma. The disease was called despair. Your Dada died in a Missouri hospital, while you were stuck at LaGuardia Airport en route to his deathbed. You received whatever parting wisdom he had over the phone.

'Don't blame your Amma. She was a good woman. We were not suited. You should never be with someone who doesn't laugh at your jokes. Why are you here now? You never answered even one of my letters.'

He said he wrote to you every birthday, apologising for things and giving you his advice. He refuses to believe that you never saw them.

'What if your jokes aren't funny?' you asked.

'Are you still doing photography?' he asked.

'I photograph the war.'

'Thought you were doing your MBA?'

'That was ten years ago.'

'Such a pointless war. Now the Tamils want half the island. Don't know why you are wasting your time.'

'Are you feeling better?'

'I'm dying. That's my advice to you. Do whatever the hell you want, because we're all gonna be dead.'

'And what have you done?'

You were in a foreign airport, baking in heat, listening to the man you blamed for everything get the last word. No, Dada. Not this time. You grip the handle and put three more quarters in the payphone and imagined it was the slot machine at Pegasus.

'Excuse me?'

You pulled back the lever and let it rip.

'Your generation fucked this country. And then you ran away.'

'You are lecturing me about quitting?'

You heard a gasp on the end of the line and you paused before saying the lines you had scripted in teenage bedrooms all your life.

'You have done nothing. And now you never will. I have taken images that will outlast us all. The only good thing you ever did was spawn me.'

When you finally made it to Missouri, you found that your father had died of cardiac arrest while speaking to you and Aunty Dalreen commanded you to stay away from the funeral.

Your two half-sisters did not come to the door. Both Jenny and Tracy Kabalana refused your phone calls.

··

Jaki picks up the bear, sees your address book beneath it and says, 'OK.' You picked it up at a Goan giftshop and it had outlasted every book on your shelf. She frowns at the names she doesn't recognise and then sees a symbol that she does, the Queen of Spades and the number for the Hotel Leo.

'OK,' she says and takes it to her room. On her way out she spots a red bandanna hanging on the hook on your door. It has many stains on it and, if she would listen, you would tell her which ones came from mud, which came from petrol and which came from blood.

Her room curtains are drawn and her lights are low and some miserable British group is droning in the background. Next to her mirror is a wall of photographs, many of which were taken by you and feature the Awesome Threesome, as you called yourselves when you weren't bickering. DD, Jaki and Maali on holidays to Yala, Kandy and Vienna, boozing at the Arts Centre Club.

The names on the address book are scribbled in different-coloured pens at different stages of your many lives. It contains aunties, cousins, lovers, plumbers, gamblers, thieves, and a few very important men and women. Some names ring bells, some offer only silence, and those are the ones that you dread. Jaki will recognise but a fraction of these monikers though that will neither surprise nor perturb her. Unlike DD, Jaki grew to accept she had no jurisdiction over your life or your time or your affection.

She fingers through the pages from Alston Koch to Zarook Zavahir, and discovers more playing card symbols drawn in biro beside numbers with no names attached. They are the same symbols as the envelopes, the same royal straight. She places the book on her lap and stares into space.

Is she wondering whether you are alive and in hiding? Or is she remembering afternoons of happy pills, blackjack and the record player before it broke. The evenings spent playing Shakin' Stevens, Elvis Presley and Freddie Mercury – and not touching.

She opens it again and thumbs to a page with a number and an Ace of Diamonds drawn beside it in red biro. She holds it open as she walks towards the telephone.

.•.

Being a ghost isn't that different to being a war photographer. Long periods of boredom interspersed with short bursts of terror. As action-packed as your post-death party has been, most of it is spent watching people staring at things. People stare a lot, break wind all the time, and touch their genitals much too much.

Most folk think they are alone and, as usual, they are mistaken. At the very least, there are a hundred insects within spitting distance of you and a few trillion bacteria on everything you touch. And yes, some of them are watching you.

There will always be something hovering or passing through, though most things that hover and pass are as interested in you as you are in earthworms. There are at least five spirits wandering the space you're in now. One may be reading over your shoulder.

You watch Jaki sitting by the phone. She is munching on her own hair, an unseemly habit picked up at the gambling table. She pulled strands from behind her ear, placed them between her teeth and nibbled when unsure whether to bet or fold.

She shouldn't be opening the address book or calling those numbers. She should focus on getting those negatives, or she could end up like you.

You whisper in her ear, you stand in front of her and shout. You even try singing some Shakin' Stevens. And then, a head appears at the window, flushed and feverish, four storeys high.

Sena has puffed out like Elvis at Vegas, like his face has been munched by wasps. His flat nose looks Hawaiian, his curls look African, though his mouth remains all Gampaha.

'Ado hutto, come. We have a job.'

. .

Sena takes you north through Pettah and the winds move softly and drop without warning.

'Choppy night,' says Sena. 'Too many ghouls in the air.'

He is not wrong. At Dematagoda, Fanged Ghouls stare out at the traffic lights looking for three-wheelers to mangle. Pretas hang around the garbage bins that beggars rifle through, stealing the flavour and rotting the food.

He does not tell you where you are going; instead, he gives you a lesson in economics.

'The currency over here isn't rupees or roubles or bonds or coconuts. It is varam. The more varam you get, the more useful you become. To yourself. And to others.'

He tells you the best way to get varam is to have people pray to you, light candles, lay flowers and burn fragrant sticks and pungent powders just for you. Demons like Bahirawa, Mahasona, Kadawara and the Black Prince all source their powers from baskets of rotting fruit placed at their toes by those who kneel.

'Indeed. But we are not gods. We don't have shrines. How do nobodies like us get varam?'

He does not answer but floats down on the banks of the canal, to a pathway paved with broken brick, facing a neighbourhood of slums. The pathway weaves through washed-up rubbish and leads to a stone table below a mango tree.

According to Sena, the Crow Uncle has a congregation of the poor, the wretched and the maimed. Street folk, slum dwellers, and beggars who come to this flimsy shrine. It is a dilapidated arch raised from a broken shanty, furnished with a stone table and filled with figurines of gods and demon masks. Buddha, Ganesh and Mahasona are all surrounded by dead flowers, but they are not the main attraction.

In the middle of the shrine is a painting of a demon, crude and cartoon-like, in a Tibetan style of drawing, not usually seen in our line of Buddhism. You recognise the black eyes, the fangs and the serpent hair. You look from the necklace of skulls to the belt of fingers to the faces trapped in its flesh.

'They pray to the Mahakali,' you hiss and get a look from Sena.

Crow Uncle has ordered the Sparrowboy to place curios at the shrine, each representing a soul who seeks his counsel. Those who help the Crow Uncle receive the prayers of the myriad and build up enough varam to acquire skills.

'It's good to have power on your side.'

'Spoken like a true comrade.'

'If you want to speak to your friend, this is the easiest way.'

The kolla cannot see you; he does not have the gift or the curse of the Crow Uncle. But he feels the winds that you bring. You have seen him shudder and break out in gooseflesh whenever you are near. You watch him placing random objects onto the shrine – bits of clothing, books with names on them, teeth wrapped in hair.

'He needs a personal item. My Thathi brought my school uniform all the way from Gampaha.'

'What's Sparrowboy's problem?'

'Ask him yourself.'

The boy looks agitated. He has lit up a fistful of joss sticks and is hurling smoke and ash at the air, like a magician learning to use a wand.

'Find Mr Piyatilaka,' he says, whipping the air with his joss stick. 'Go find where he hides his gold.'

He does not see you, though he looks directly at you. He slaps the air with his stick and a wind from the east finds you. It knocks you sideways.

'Hang on,' says Sena. 'Your first assignment starts here.'

• •

The ghost formerly known as Mr Piyatilaka is not an impressive figure. He is a balding man who thinks he has hair, a hump-backed snaggle tooth who thinks his manicured moustache offsets the rest of his features. Which makes the palatial home that he haunts all the more impressive.

It is not far from the Borella cemetery and is decorated with fauna from everywhere in Sri Lanka except for Colombo 8. The main house is designed like an ancestral walauwa home and the garden has room for a second building and a garage filled with vintage cars. The plump woman from the Crow Man's cave, still wearing too much make-up and too little deodorant, is instructing a young man with big biceps to empty the boots and look under the seats in what looks like a Jaguar from the '60s.

Mr Piyatilaka watches with both anger and amusement. When he looks up to see you and Sena floating by the green Morris Minor, all the amusement disappears.

'Now the Crow Uncle is sending me sissies, is it? Very nice. Kindly piss off from my property.'

The young man is now under a Ford from the '70s and starts banging on the metal chassis.

'Smash it you buffoon. Why should I care? My harlot of a daughter is sick of you already. Let her try and sell those cars after you have mutilated them, you fool.'

Mr Piyatilaka floats out of the garage into the rain-forest garden. 'As if I'd hide the treasure in my cars!' He scoffs. 'These were heirlooms passed down to me from my grandfather's grandfather. Maybe my grandchildren will be worthy of them one day.'

At the foot of the garden is a building with a single room. Too small to be a cottage, too large to be called a shed. The old man sits on the balcony and smiles. 'You fools are wasting your time. Let me guess. Crow Man said you will get varam from selling me out. He is playing you!'

'Sir, this jewellery is of no use to you. Why hold onto it?'

You float inside a room that looks like legal chambers. There are law books filling the shelves on two walls. The rest is framed photos of degrees and diplomas and Mr Piyatilaka with his daughters.

'You know, I'm the only one in my family who studied. All my brothers sit in Polonnaruwa talking cock.'

'Are these your books?'

'My father was the attorney. I did business. But I know the law. And I know how varam works.'

Sena disappears into cupboards and almirahs. He ducks into the floorboards and climbs into the ceiling, to the further amusement of the room's former occupant.

'You won't find anything. My daughter already sent one of her boys Up There. Children should earn their inheritance. Someone should make that a law.'

Sena snaps at you to get to work, but from the host's demeanour you suspect there is no gold to be found here. You hear the daughter shrieking at her boyfriend in the garage. You hear the boyfriend take a spanner to the car and immediately halve its value.

'Go back to the Crow Man. There is nothing to see,' says Piyatilaka, gazing lovingly at his law books. 'Lawyers are arseholes. That's why I never became one. But laws are needed. Because made-up religions are not enough.'

'Another atheist,' you proclaim, sticking your head into the law books.

The afterlife appears to be the opposite of a foxhole. The books smell of mildew and must and you exit coughing and not finding a hollowed-out centre filled with jewellery. The books are volumes of the same title. *Commentaries on Roman-Dutch Law* by Simon van Leeuwen, 1652. Sri Lanka followed Roman-Dutch law long after the Romans and the Dutch had abandoned it.

'I wasn't religious, but I was a believer,' he says. 'Then, I got the cancer. Then, I read holy books and visited holy men and prayed at holy places. No one listened.'

'People in war zones pray every day,' you say. 'Soldiers, civilians, even the journalists. No one ever listens.'

'We need these law books, because religion doesn't even prohibit rape. Did you know that? The commandments punish the Lord's name in vain on a Sunday, but no "Thou shalt not rape".'

'That can't be true,' you say.

'Hindu disciplines mention brahmacharya and fidelity but no rape. Buddhism's *kaamesu michch charya* doesn't specify rape. Islam forbids bacon, foreskin and gambling. But no rape.'

'Laws are written by men,' you say. 'Who don't mind bad things happening to people who aren't them.' You think of DD and the selfishness learned at the London School of Economics. And of one of your recurring arguments.

'People have always suffered,' said DD. 'You can legislate against it, reduce it at a macro level. But you will never eliminate it. The best you hope for is that bad stuff doesn't happen to anyone you know.'

'We shouldn't congratulate ourselves for accidents of our birth.'

'No,' he replied. 'But we can enjoy them.'

'Let bad stuff happen to other people,' you murmured. 'Spoken like a Tory Republican.'

Sena has searched the room, the garage and the house and has come up short. 'Come, Maali. Must be buried in the garden.'

'My harlot daughter brought a guy with a metal detector!' laughs Mr Piyatilaka. 'That was funny. But not as funny as watching two sissy ghosts diving in my mud.'

You look at the volumes of Roman-Dutch law books, and the smug old man holding onto air and grudges. You wonder if your father is stuck in a Missouri In Between and if he ever thinks of you.

'Don't bother, Sena. You won't find any jewellery.'

'Exactly. Go back and tell the Crow Man to stop taking money from my daughter.'

'There is no jewellery.'

'I told you already! I gave it to my mistress in 1973.'

'If I tell you where his treasure is, will the Crow Man give me the power to whisper?'

'Of course, Maali hamu. Definitely.'

Sena looks at you in puzzlement and Mr Piyatilaka's eyes lose their twinkle.

'I think it is time you both left.'

'The law books. They are three-hundred-year-old first editions and there are forty-nine volumes. They are worth more than all those cars in the garage.'

Piyatilaka screams and charges at you. Sena pulls you out of the way and the angry son of a lawyer collides with the bookshelf, bringing with him a wind that slams the door. The wind causes volume 49, already teetering on a termite-nibbled shelf to topple onto volume 32 below. Volume 32 tips over volumes 33-38, which avalanche to the bottom shelf, that snaps on impact, bringing volumes 1-23 cascading to the floor like chunks of buildings during air raids.

Piyatilaka's daughter and her toy boy rush into it to find strange smells, frantic winds and a mass of law books lying on the floor.

THIRD MOON

*You forget what you want to remember
and you remember what you want to forget.*

Cormac McCarthy, *The Road*

THE VOICE

Now what? We hide in this tree from that Piyatilaka psycho?'

'Patience, hamu. We sit in this tree and wait for Crow Uncle's call. It will come.'

You climb to a higher branch on the mara tree's flailing limbs; its leaves feel alive in the wind, like fingers scratching at your face; its flowers are the colour of flesh wounds, of skin torn by shrapnel.

Sena is babbling about the skills that Crow Uncle can teach you. 'Sir, you can command insects, appear in dreams, you can even possess the living.'

You look at the people walking through the park. The everyday ordinary folk who see you not. Over half of them have spirits perched on their backs, running alongside them, whispering in their ears.

You've always thought the voice in your head belonged to someone else. Telling you the story of your life as if it had already happened. The omniscient narrator adding a voiceover to your day. The coach telling you to stop feeling sorry and to do what you were good at. Which was winning at blackjack, seducing young peasants and photographing scary places.

It was the voice that led you to tour the war zone on five occasions, each for a different master. It was the voice that led you to casinos and alleyways and strange boys in dark jungles. And yet you wonder about that voice. If you had a spirit on your back whispering in your ear, how would you possibly know? And, even if you did, how could you separate that voice from every other whisper?

You hear someone saying your name and then Sena's. It is the Crow Uncle and he sounds as annoyed as you feel. Once more you evaporate in a sensation that has become familiar and not all that displeasing. You are back in a cave filled with birds and fruit and myriad rows of candles singing in flame.

You hover by the circular window with a bar bisecting it, overlooking a shrine with many gods, the largest of whom has a necklace of skulls and technically isn't a deity, though neither was the Buddha. Milling around it, heads bowed, are families of homeless people, known more commonly in these parts as beggars. There is a lady who makes roti south of the canal, a lottery seller in a wheelchair and a cobbler who looks smart enough or dumb enough to run a blue-chip company had he been born to Colombo 7.

'Finally!' barks the Crow Uncle, his sightless eyes darting across the room and settling on the nook where you both cower. 'Good work with that Piyatilaka. I hope you keep that up, ah.' He then sneezes into a red hanky and empties his nose of gunk.

'When do I learn to whisper?' you shout. 'There's someone I need to talk to.'

'Crawl before you can jump, Mr Maali.'

Sena takes off his hood and smiles. 'Sorry, Swamini. We are only here to serve.'

'Is that so, Mr Sena? I too serve, but only those who are worthy. Come, Mr Maali. Meet your visitor.'

You notice the boy seated on a stool by the door, three fingers on his good hand scratching at his ear. You notice that the empty guest chair is empty no more. For in it sits your best friend and never-lover, Jaki Vairavanathan.

ADDRESS BOOK

Jaki has one hand propping up her chin and one in her cloth bag. You know that she is holding a can of mace, part of a carton of twelve sent by her cousin in Detroit, horrified that an unmarried girl in her twenties could walk alone on the mean streets of Colombo.

You wonder what she is thinking of as she scans the cave for movement. There is, of course, plenty of movement in this cave, none of which she can see.

The wind you bring snuffs out the candle and Jaki jumps.

'He is here, miss. Did you bring something that belongs to him?'

'Who gave you my address?'

The Crow Man catches a sneeze in a hanky with an Om sign on it. He blows snot all over the symbol for the infinity within and the infinity without. Then he coughs. 'I'm sorry, miss. But your friend has passed on. He is speaking to me now.'

'I will report you to the police,' says Jaki. 'You hear me?'

'Tell her to calculate the odds,' you say.

'Huh?'

'The odds. Ask her, "What are the odds?"'

'What odds? Sorry, miss, I have a cold today. It affects what I am hearing.'

Jaki pulls her head from her palm and raises her plucked eyebrows. 'What did you say?'

'Ask her what are the odds of someone knowing about the address book under the teddy.'

'The odds about the address what?'

'Tell her the odds are one in 23,955. Less than a straight flush. Tell her the universe is nothing but mathematics and probabilities. That we are nothing more than the accidents of our birth.'

Crow Uncle repeats this word for word and, when he reaches the end, a tear pops out of Jaki's aimless eyes.

'Do you know where he is?'

'He is here, miss. He tells to forget about the box under the bed.'

'There is no box any more. It was taken.'

'He knows. He says don't worry. Find the negatives, he says.'

Watching her, you begin to cry even though you have no eyes or tears or anything to sob with. And crying is something you do as often as you have sex with girls. You didn't cry when you stepped over dead bodies to photograph the retreating Tigers, or when you watched the eight-year-old cradling his dead sister, or when you heard your father had died while you were stuck in customs.

'I need an item. May I have the address book?'

'No.'

Jaki takes her hand from her bag and, instead of a spray can, she pulls out a red bandanna with multiple stains. She rubs her tears on it, takes in your smell and places it on the table. Your brain floods with images too numerous and grotesque to describe. Like someone else's life flashing before yours, someone who'd led a life filled with corpses and blood.

You shout and the Crow Uncle covers his ears and has another coughing fit.

'Calm down or we won't get anywhere. Miss, he wants you to hand over the address book.'

'Why?'

'He tells me something about the King. King of Elves? Or Queen. Or something.'

The Crow Uncle keeps sneezing and blowing his nose and you keep screaming at him.

'He says the negatives are with the King of Elves and Queen. Sena, are you there? Tell him I can't hear when he's shouting.'

You speak calmly and he still cannot decipher.

'I'm sorry, miss. I am not well. He says there are records of something negative. About Kings and Queens and DD and something. He wants you to hand over the address book. It will gain him varam.'

'I can't hand over any more of his things,' says Jaki. 'If he's dead, where is his body?'

Crow Uncle touches the bandanna and holds it out for the boy.

'Put this on the shrine, kolla. Miss, I am not well. Come in next week and we'll do this properly. I am sorry for your loss. Do not forget to make donation. For the poor.'

The boy takes the bandanna and steps towards Jaki. He grimaces as if attempting to mime a word. He opens his mouth slowly and then closes it. His silent word could be anything, but you suspect that it might be 'friend'. She stands up, pulls a strand of hair to her mouth, takes a nibble and then ducks into the side-exit. She takes with her the address book and its playing card pages and does not hear you screaming at her to leave it behind.

. .

'He's a what?'

DD has just got back from badminton at the Otters Aquatic Club and he smells like you imagine an otter would.

'I don't know, men. An astrologer or something.'

DD sits down on the table where you used to put your feet and get shouted at. His dad was once posted as an ambassador to an Arab state where putting your feet up was a sign of disrespect. DD had certain ticks socialised into him. Like the inability to apologise and the eagerness to disagree.

'Not a witch doctor? Or a wizard? Or a Jedi?'

'Are you done?'

'I've been in and out of courts, trying to get Maali's photos back. And you've been visiting soothsayers?'

'Why courts? I thought Minister Cyril is your Appa's bum chum.'

'The cops say the box is evidence. Cyril Wijeratne's lawyer wants six weeks to review their claim. Six weeks!'

She pulls the address book out of her mess of a bag. She looks at him and waits for him to meet her gaze, which he never will do. Young Dilan was never big on eye contact, which is a sign of autism, though DD is no Rain Man.

'You think he's gone?'

'Don't ever say that,' he says. 'If he were dead, I would know.'

'How?'

'I would know.'

'Would you know if he's being tortured?'

'I can't think these things.'

'Why not?'

'Because thinking can't solve them. Neither can visiting astrologers.'

'He said stuff that only Maali would say.'

'Like what?'

DD always rubs his nose when he's hiding something. He was the worst poker player you ever met – and you've met some bad ones. He stops the rubbing and runs his pretty fingers through his sweaty hair.

She places your address book on DD's lap. You bought it at KVG's bookshop in the mall below Hotel Leo. He opens it and recognises few of the names. The page marked 'Jack of Hearts' is full of numbers and nicknames. He frowns at the list – Byron, Hudson, George, Lincoln, Brando – and guesses the worst.

'The Crow Man told me that this was hidden in his almirah. Under his teddy bear. How did he know?'

'Maali talked to everyone. Maybe he blabbed about it.'

'To a blind astrologer in a cave?'

'Maali hung out with all sorts. Who is this guy?'

'Says he helps politicians and cricketers and advertising agencies.'

'With what?'

'Charms and horoscopes. Curses. Evil eye stuff. Says he can talk to spirits. I'm aware how stupid this sounds.'

'Sounds pathetic.'

'My Aunty said I shouldn't wear short skirts, that I'd be cursed with huniyam or something. That evil eyes could charm me.'

'Have you been charmed?'

'He sells stuff like that thing around your neck.'

Unlike you, DD only has one thing around his neck. A small wooden cylinder with engravings in sanskrit. It came in a set of two, each of which had hung on the necks of DD's parents, until cancer took his Amma five years ago. Uncle Stanley had given them both to DD and told him to give it to the girl he would marry. Said it worked best when the blood of both man and woman were mixed and smeared on it. DD thought that gross and gave the other one in the pair to you on a trip to Yala. And then painted his room purple. That's when Uncle Stanley stopped visiting and started charging you rent. He didn't charge his son, until DD quit the law firm.

'What did this Crow Man look like?'

'Like that priest on *Kung Fu* that says "grasshopper".'

You let out a chuckle and no one hears you. DD never watched normal TV, especially not Buddhist westerns. He only rented videos of documentaries and musicals. The first film you saw with him was *Blade Runner* at the Liberty and he snored through most of it. The only show you ever watched together was Yorkshire Television's *Crown Court*.

'Never watched *Kung Fu*.'

'He sneezes a lot and lives in a garage filled with birdcages. He told me Maali was dead.'

'Where was this?'

'Kotahena.'

'Who did you go with?'

'His servant boy.'

DD goes silent and tightens his tie.

'You think I don't have enough to deal with? Haven't slept in three days. I can't be hunting for you in bloody Kotahena caves. You know how many kidnapping cases there are in this country?'

Jaki takes the book from DD. 'There are five numbers in this book with playing cards drawn on them.'

'Really?'

'One of them is yours.'

'What?'

'Yours, ours, the flat's. It just has our number and the Ten of Hearts.'

'And what were the others?'

She has bookmarked the pages by folding them like you would never do. She flips to each page and points at your drawings in red and black.

'The Queen of Spades goes to the CNTR offices in Hotel Leo, where that woman Elsa Mathangi works.'

'You phoned?'

'I phoned all the marked numbers. She wanted to know if we had the negatives.'

'Do we?'

'Um. Negative.'

DD notices the mess on the sofa. The reason why his absent mind had led him to sit on the coffee table which no one was allowed to put their feet on. It is the remains of the box under your bed. The broken cardboard and the unplayed records. The crooners Elvis, Shakin' Stevens, Freddie Mercury, exiled by him from your house, after cassettes replaced LPs and a-ha, Bronski Beat and the Pet Shop Boys replaced rock and roll.

'Why did you bring these?'

'Because they were his,' says Jaki. 'And I like Shakin' Stevens.'

DD scrutinises his nails before biting them.

'Maali told me about assignments for the Associated Press. Some English fellow. Joey or Jerry.'

'Jonny. Jonny Gilhooley. He must be the Ace.'

Bless you, Jaki. You're the only one of them who listened.

Jaki walks to the telephone and dials the number for Associated Press. The phone is picked up on first ring.

'Hello.'

'Can I speak to Jonny Gilhooley, please?'

'Speaking.'

She raises her eyebrows at DD.

'I'm calling about Maali Almeida.'

'What about him?'

'He's missing.'

You creep behind Jaki and listen to a voice that you have known too well.

'How much does he owe you?'

Jaki stares at DD, who has picked two records from the pile on the sofa. Your Amma's copy of Jim Reeves's *Twelve Songs of Christmas* and your own copy of Shakin' Stevens's *Give Me Your Heart Tonight*.

'A lot.'

DD frowns at her as she speaks.

'If it's less than twenty thousand, I can settle it for you.'

'I'm his girlfriend,' says Jaki. 'May I meet with you?'

There is laughter from the other side of the phone.

'Maali has a girlfriend? Of course he does.'

'Mr Jonny, there is a box of his photographs.'

There is a pause.

'Do you have this box?'

'Yes we do.'

Jaki lies like a pro, because she learned from the best.

'Can you come to the British Consulate, please?'

ACE OF DIAMONDS

DD and Jaki argue on the way there. It is an argument of infinite tedium, an argument between jealous cousins that has been replayed too many times. Like the pointless debates over who nations belong to, which gods are worth fearing and whether the poor should be helped or scorned. This argument is about you.

'What did he say about the Associated Press?' asks Jaki.

'That they paid on time. But never published anything,' says DD. 'Did he tell you he was with the JVP?'

'I don't believe that. Maali was a snob, forget that commie bullshit. He looked down on the peasants, just like you and Uncle Stanley do.'

The cheeky little brat, you think.

'And you are a woman of the people, I suppose,' says DD.

Not for the last time, you wish you could hug him.

'Why is the Associated Press at the British High Commission?'

Jaki reverses into the car park with one finger on the wheel and another pointing at DD's face. She guides the hatchback into a corner of the car park and she scolds him like she never ever scolded you.

'You should've talked to him,' she says. 'He listened to you.'

'He listened to no one.'

'He listened to you,' says Jaki.

'You just said you were his girlfriend.'

'No, DD,' she says. 'You were.'

DD raises his hand and Jaki does not flinch. He hit you many times. Slaps across the face that left marks for minutes after. You even deserved some of them. But the son of Stanley would never hit a girl.

'It's OK. No one knows. Just me.'

DD puts his hand down and stares at the rear view.

· ·

In the first month, you hardly spoke, though you did watch. How he slunk across the kitchen in sarong and T-shirt, holding black coffee and avoiding your eye. He was up early and worked late. You woke in the afternoons and began your day after dark. The after-dinner twilight was the only time your schedules overlapped.

In the second month, you began asking about his day and telling him about yours. You presumed lawyers rarely talked work because their work was complex and confidential. You find out it is only because it was mostly tedious, and rarely if ever like *Crown Court*, which played on ITN three nights a week. Though when Dilan Dharmendran told you about injunctions to stop forests being cleared to make way for factories, you pretended to find them fascinating.

By the third month, you had started drinking black tea at the dinner table and telling him that the war would escalate and the Tigers could not be defeated and that India may invade and that US phosphate mining companies and British arms dealers have been spotted in the war zone and he had taken to wearing boxer shorts and lingering for a second cup after dinner.

By the fourth month, Jaki had stopped doing the night owls show on SLBC and the three of you sat around the table, drinking sometimes more than tea or coffee. She told DD that she always thought he was boring, but that she was wrong. DD said he always thought she was weird and that he was right. Then he asked if you and Jaki were going out and Jaki looked at you and you blushed and said you were best friends.

By the fifth month, you were going on trips together. First to Galle, then to Kandy, then to Yala. You began renting videos from Nastars together. While Jaki watched Oscar winners *Platoon*, *Last Emperor* and *Rain Man*, you and DD devoured VHS tapes of *Falcon Crest* and *Crown Court*. That month, Jaki came to your room at night and asked if she could stay and you said no.

And then, in the sixth month, you went to his room and sat on his bed and touched his hair while he pretended to be asleep. You repeated it the next night but this time you stroked his skin. And, the next night, you massaged him and then he opened his eyes and said he could not do this because it was wrong and his family would be outraged. And, for a little while, that was that.

· ·

As instructed, they avoid the queues folded across the corners of the High Commission, where the gutters cast shadows over those seeking a visa to the UK. The hopeful migrants stand in shade and practise their half-truths. Jaki and DD follow a sign saying 'Cinema Room' and enter the glass door into a breeze of airconditioning.

The room has a giant TV screen and photographs of famous Brits, none taken by you. You have never been in this room, you cannot recognise its couches and breathable air. You cannot say the same for the burly man behind the writing desk.

'So, you're the wife?' he bellows with a chuckle.

'Not really,' says Jaki, even though he is facing DD.

'Fair enough,' says Jonny, drinking in the handsome boy with his eyes. 'Maali talked about this bonny lad a lot.' He darts his eyes back to the sullen girl. 'You, not so much.'

Jonny serves tea infused with ginger and royal jelly. The way he taught you to make it.

'He never spoke of you,' says DD, a coffee drinker with nothing but contempt for Ceylon's main export. 'How long have you known him?'

'Long enough,' says Jonny, pouring tea as if it were lager.

'He works for you?'

'Not exactly. But I wouldn't be worrying, son. He's gone AWOL before. He'll show up. Always does.'

'He told us every time he went anywhere,' says DD, his eyes shining. 'No word this time. No apology.'

'If you're expecting apologies from Maali Almeida, you'll be waiting a long time in a long line. I'm guessing you don't have the box.'

'It's in the car,' says Jaki.

'Not what I heard.'

'You heard what?'

'That one, Minister of Justice took it home. That's what I heard.'

'Who told you that?'

'You won't see that box again. You know where the negatives are?'

DD stares at the base of Jonny's sleeve just above the elbow. When he pours, the sleeve hikes up to reveal an Ace of Diamonds inked in red onto his pink skin.

'The box had five envelopes. One of them had an Ace of Diamonds on it.'

'I've had this tattoo since Uganda. What's your point?'

'One of those envelopes had photos that he took for you.'

'He didn't take photos for us. Just worked as a fixer.'

'Why tattoo the Ace of Diamonds?' asks Jaki.

'Always good to have an ace up your sleeve. And I was young and silly once. Just like you.'

'So why did Maali label an envelope with it?'

'Why did he wear the stupid bandanna? Who knows why Maali did what?'

'Maali said being a fixer was like being a coolie who spoke English,' says DD and switches to lawyer mode. Which meant he dialled up the accent and mimicked his father's pauses. 'Maali liked to exaggerate everything. You must know this. He took the work and cashed the cheques. Have you called any of the others?'

There is silence. Jaki rubs her forehead and DD fingers the ankh around his neck.

'I can't have been the only card in that box.'

'How do you know Maali?' asks DD.

'Met him at a party. You?'

'What party?'

'I think you know what party.'

'I don't,' says DD, though he does.

'So you have no idea what's in the envelope marked "Ace of Diamonds"?' asks Jaki taking a sip from her teacup. The sweetened tea is served in bone China, possibly stolen by his countrymen during the opium wars.

'He took his camera everywhere, so who knows? Maybe they were party photos. We have a few gatherings at the High Commission. Your father, Stanley, came to one.'

'Why hide them under a bed?'

'We all have things hidden under beds, laddie. Maali had more than most. I wouldn't be worried. I'll make inquiries. I'm sure he's fine. Does your dad favour federalism or the two-state proposal?'

'I don't understand your connection. Were you his friend?'

'Men like us are allies. You know this.'

'I don't go to those parties.'

'You should.'

Jaki gets up and examines the wall. She strolls past portraits of Lord Mountbatten, Sir Oliver Goonetilleke, Queen Elizabeth, Sir Richard Attenborough and the British High Commissioner. Next to the massive TV is a well-stocked bar, which Jaki runs her finger over. Next to that is a table filled with papers and bills.

'Would you like a stronger drink?'

She shakes her head and looks at the bills and reads the papers on top.

Jonny hurries over, scoops up the papers, stuffs them in a drawer and smiles like he has nothing to hide.

'Pardon the mess there.'

Jaki goes back to her seat and starts nibbling on her hair. DD takes a sip of tea and grimaces. Your boy loathed honey almost as much as he despised tea.

'You work for the High Commission or the Associated Press?'

'The former, it's Robert Sudworth who works for the Associated Press. He needed fixers. I hooked him up with Maali. That's all. The AP, Reuters, BBC, even Pravda, end up at parties here. When they ask me for someone who can get interviews with the army or the Tigers, I recommend Maali.'

'How long were you getting him these assignments?'

'A couple of years. I just set up the meetings.'

'Did you gamble with him?'

'I don't do casinos. Haven't been since Entebbe days. I equate gambling... with being an arsehole.'

'What do you equate card tattoos with?' says Jaki.

DD butts in before Jonny can respond. 'He was last seen talking to a middle-aged European at Pegasus.'

'Am I the only suddha in town? Don't be daft. Andy McGowan from *Newsweek* uses him a lot. Said he was the only fixer that was respected by both sides.'

'Because he spoke all three languages?'

'Maybe that. Maybe the red bandanna.'

DD narrows his eyes and Jaki widens hers. Not everyone had heard of the bandannas that the Red Cross handed out to reporters, medics and other non-combatants from the field. Though, as soon as hostages were found tied up with said bandannas during the Dollar Farm siege, red bandannas and medics and reporters all but disappeared from the war zone. They became as scarce as UN peacekeepers. But you kept wearing one, and bullets and death kept eluding you.

'Look, I'll call you if I hear anything. But I'm sure he'll turn up.'

The best thing about the Nikon 3ST that your Dada sent you from Missouri was that it didn't make a sound when clicking. You had taken more shots on these bullshit fixing missions than you did on photo assignments.

'When did you last see him?'

'Weeks ago. At a press gathering. He said he was quitting the war zone. I thought fair enough.'

Jonny should've played poker. He could lie with his eyes, his nose and his teeth.

'What do you know about CNTR?'

'Heard the name. Think it's some aid organisation. Which could mean a number of things.'

'So you know them?'

'Not really. CNTR could be raising funds for political groups. Or procuring weapons for militant ones. Or they could be genuinely helping the innocents. Hard to know who is what these days. Does your Papa Stanley know you're going around playing Detective Colombo?'

'Why did you offer to pay Maali's debts?'

'Not the first time. The AP pay him through me. I still have some backpay left.'

'Why through you?'

'We outsource clerical services to the international media. It allows journalists to protect their sources while maintaining a paper trail.'

'Do you know what's in those five envelopes?'

'I don't need to. I can guess. There's two wars going on. Which means a lot of ugly things get photographed. Maali's probably laying low now. I suggest you do the same.'

Two elderly gentlemen barge into the room without knocking. One looks drunk, the other looks mad. Jonny Gilhooley rises immediately. 'Ade, Jonny, match starting soon,' says the drunk one. 'Sorry for interrupting,' says the mad one, pulling the other from the doorway.

'We have to leave it there, folks,' says Jonny. 'Trust me, he's probably on a mission now. I'll let you know if I hear anything.'

On the car ride home, Jaki stares out the window at crows and checkpoints.

'There was a drink voucher on his table. One of the papers he cleared away.'

'What's that?'

'You get it with your chips. A leaflet giving you free drinks for the next hour. So it has the date and time on it.'

'Didn't like that guy. The politer an Englishman is, the bigger the liar.

'And who tattoos cards on their arm?'

'So, what about this leaflet?'

'It was from Pegasus Casino, dated Monday 11.22 p.m. Strange for someone who equated gambling with being an arsehole.'

RED BANDANNA

Jonny would boast that the red bandanna idea was his. He mentioned it to Gerta Müller at the Red Cross at an embassy cocktail party and she, demonstrating the stereotypical efficiency of her countrymen, had boxes of them available within the month. It was to be the equivalent of a white flag for non-combatants, a no-fire zone on the battlefield, a talisman to deflect slings and arrows like the mythical henaraja thailaya. Everyone seemed to overlook that it was a red flag and that most of those swinging guns in the war zone were bulls.

You liked how it went with your safari jacket and chains, though that was before JVP-ers began taking fashion tips from the Khmer Rouge.

'It was a good idea,' Jonny said, long after it had failed. 'It's a pity your yakos couldn't honour it.'

'Why have you lived here for twenty years if you detest the natives so much?' you once asked him.

'You know what they say about the land of the blind?'

'You sound like your colonial grandpas.'

'I lived in Newcastle upon Tyne for twenty-five years,' said Jonny. 'I detest the natives there, too. Nothing personal, laddie. All humans are scum.'

'Suddha came, sold things that didn't belong to him, got rich and buggered off.'

'How long? How long will they sing this song?' sang Jonny out of key.

Jonny and you never had anything more than a professional relationship. Though, admittedly, this exchange did take place while sitting in your underwear in his Jacuzzi. You were both being fondled by strapping brown lads. Ratne and Duminda were in their twenties and pretended to work as masons on Jonny's Bolgoda villa. For some reason, his big-screen TV played a cricket match.

'Do we have to watch this crap?'

Jonny was cultural attaché at the British High Commission, though he had his fingers in many pies, three of which were being pushed into Duminda's open mouth. He'd been in Lanka for over a decade and had built many glorious homes. He was busy tending to his catamite and took his time answering your question. 'Sorry, bonny lad, you don't like cricket, you can't fart in my hot tub.'

You have necked with DD's boss, had relations with his cousin, received fellatio from members of his soccer team, and banged a waiter in a toilet while you were on a date. But you have never ever thought of doing anything with Jonny Gilhooley.

'These assignments you send me on. These fixing jobs. I know they're not for the Associated Press.'

'Why do you care who signs your cheques?'

'Same reason Maggie Thatcher cares about our silly war.'

Jonny took a drag from a beedi cigar placed in his mouth by Duminda, who then drags on it before nuzzling smoke into Jonny's ear.

'What gave you that stupid idea. You don't get so mouthy when you're short of cash, do you, laddie? But, since we're talking turkey, I'll tell you the truth. We're here to promote democracy, freedom and human rights.'

You both laughed like two drag queens and so did the boys, despite not hearing the joke. You asked Ratne to reach for another beer and to not stop doing what he was doing with his other hand below the bubbling water. You shook your head at Jonny.

'Apparently, that's what the US are doing in Panama and Nicaragua and Chile.'

'We used to own them too. Here's Her Majesty's official position. Brittannia is sick of owning the world. We'd much prefer to just watch.'

'Like that preacher Jimmy Swaggart.'

'We pick the right side. Support the right team. And we're right most of the time. No one's right all the time.'

'Sounds like a slogan. "The New Brittannia. From Malvinas to Maldives. Right most of the time."'

There was a pause as you both got distracted by your companions. The boys departed to make lunch while you wallowed in hot water. Jonny watched the cricket while you watched him. 'Something bothering you, laddie?'

'I don't like being in danger. I need better money.'

'Fair enough,' said Jonny. 'I put in a request. Which was rejected because of your big, fat mouth.'

'What?'

'You're supposed to be a fixer for the AP. You take reporters where they want to go. Get them interviews. Make sure they're not killed. No one asked you to take pictures. Or brag that you're spying for the Queen.'

'Brag?'

'You told that boy of yours. Who told his dad. Who told his boss. Who called for a meeting with my boss.'

'Is Bob Sudworth really a journalist?'

'Not my place to say. Or yours.'

'The Brits just lost a big arms contract to the Chinese. Looks like the SL government has other options. Sad for you lot.'

'I work for intelligence. I don't get involved in hardware.'

'So what happens to all the unsold hardware?'

'I used to be a hippie, you know. I'm a pacifist, for fuck's sake.'

The boys returned carrying bathrobes and the news that lunch was served. Duminda was better endowed than Ratne, whose underwear bulge resembled a small boy or a big girl. Jonny donned the robe and copped a feel. Duminda performed his well-rehearsed smile.

'If you can keep the political commentary to yourself, maybe we can consider that raise,' said Jonny.

· ·

The rule imposed by the Sri Lankan government for all embedded journalists was that they did not lodge with or break bread with terrorists. This was not official AP policy and, in the fog of war, was subject to the discretion of the reporter and fixer.

Jonny introduced you to many journalists, all of whom had the same requests. Can we see the bodies? Can we get an interview with The Leader? The former was possible, the latter not at all. You explained to them that you cannot build rapport with any fighting force without sharing a cup of tea. And talking to the Supremo was as easy as an exclusive with Elvis.

It was in early '87, one of your first assignments. Your reporter was Andy McGowan, a chirpy lad with a broken heart, working for *Newsweek* as a stringer. Jonny had paid you a hefty advance, which you gloriously doubled at the Pegasus, before spectacularly quartering it at a poker game with other war correspondents.

It was your second visit to Vavuniya on the hunt for child soldiers. There were reports of teenagers being trained in suicide squads and orphans being taught to use T56s and you had taken Andy all across the north and found no evidence of either.

At the Vavuniya barracks you found Associated Press correspondent Robert Sudworth, furious that his fixer had ditched him when asked to explore the jungles of the Vanni. The commanding officer, Major Raja Udugampola, future head of the STF, refused to give them army protection in enemy territory. He was your former boss and was unlikely to grant you special favours, considering how you parted.

Unlike Andy the scruffy gonzo, Sudworth was always well turned out. Even in the field he wore designer camouflage and tailored slacks. He conquered McGowan with the usual charm offensive. 'Terribly sorry to say this, but the child soldier angle is a non-starter. I got some leads in Akkaraipattu, but the Tigers will not let you photograph or interview them. And no family with children will talk.'

Sudworth led the two of you to his borrowed Jeep and told you in hushed tones, 'There is another story, chaps. If we pool our resources, we can share the exclusive.' Bob Sudworth's resources included a bodyguard named Sid, a Scotsman who apparently spoke English, though you understood none of what came out of his mouth. Built like a tank, and appointed by KM Services, a private security firm for mercenaries, he wore camouflage and boots and carried an Uzi.

According to Sudworth, there was a village of civilians that were being forcibly combat-trained by the LTTE. The army had the location but weren't ready to send in force. You had no way of getting entry and told them so, and then Sudworth revealed that the budget that had room for a bodyguard also had a generous allocation for you.

After many disclaimers, you agreed to drive them there and were amazed at how easily you talked your way from the Nambukulam checkpoint to the Omanthai one. When you arrived at the village, it was clear why.

There were old men and young women. Uncles, grandmas, farmers, cowherds and schoolteachers, all loading rifles and firing at targets, all under the supervision of Colonel Gopallaswarmy aka Mahatiya, a founding Tiger cadre, from the Supremo's village, whose stock was rising within the chain of command. The tall moustachioed colonel was a leaner, hungrier version of the Supremo and agreed to interviews with Sudworth and McGowan and gave permission to photograph the villagers.

None of them admitted to being coerced into anything and none of them looked to be speaking under duress. 'We fear the army more than we fear them. The army burned our village,' said a boy barely out of school but too old to be of any use for the child soldier angle. 'We are training to protect ourselves from threats like these.'

Major Raja's staff saw the story as an example of civilian oppression under the LTTE. But the Tigers were spinning it as a tale of people power. This war will never end, you think as you watch the villagers fire their weapons. You were allowed to try out your Nikon without restriction, and told only 'Never shoot the Colonel', though you ended up doing just that.

McGowan and Sudworth, now Andy and Bob to you, called you 'the finest fixer east of Mexico', and promised a fat bonus to your fixer fee. And just then the army announced its arrival with a lobbed grenade. Bullets stabbed the air and maimed the trees and made holes in the ground. You and Bob and Andy scrambled to what looked like, but couldn't have been, a tea bush. You huddled beneath the rock at its base. Bodyguard Sid drew his Uzi and took bullets in his shooting arm and watched the gun sail into the dust and swore like a Scotsman before passing out.

They say it is like firecrackers, but that is only partly true. It is like firecrackers played through loudspeakers positioned right next to your eardrums. McGowan started to weep, Sudworth repeated a single cussword, and the dust started popping around you as if invisible rains were pelting the ground. And then the air was smoke and noise and shrieks. The three of you huddled under a flat rock, behind that flimsy bush, and prayed to gods you didn't believe in.

So you did what you needed to. You tied your red bandanna to a stick and wedged it into the bush, where it flew high like a flag of truce drenched in blood. For the forty-five minutes of that noisy and inconclusive gun battle, not a single bullet came your way.

• •

When the shooting stopped and the Sri Lankan army marched into the camp, the villagers had either fled or were dead. Bob and Andy carried the very unconscious and equally heavy body of Sid the Scot while you held your bandanna on a stick above your head like the leader of a socialist marching band. You held your arms up and shouted in Sinhala. 'We are international journalists! We have a wounded foreigner!'

The three of you walked slowly into the mist, ready to duck if the bullets started flying again. You were greeted by medics, who took care of your wounded and kept back the merely traumatised for questioning. One red bandanna and two press passes saw you and Andy through, but Robert was taken to the hut by the coconut grove for further questioning. He went without protest. Either the battlefield had turned him into a fearless warrior or had spooked him into silence. At the time you could not tell which; that stiff upper lip can hide all manner of secrets.

You were walking with Andy across the coconut grove when you spied a second visitor to the hut. It was a prisoner with the black sack over his head. As the door of the hut was shut, you noticed an open window and read the light and the angles correctly. Andy helped you halfway up the tree and that was all the elevation you needed. You were lining up your shot when a third character entered the hut. This was someone whom you recognised and you pasted yourself to the trunk in the hope that he did not spy you.

Your eyes found a table with documents on it and your zoom lens gave you the faces of three figures sitting around it. At the tail, Bob Sudworth. At the side with mask taken off, a sweaty and beaten Colonel 'Mahatiya' Gopallaswarmy, leader of the largest Tiger faction. And at the head, the commanding officer of the forces that had just overrun the village. Your former boss, Major Raja Udugampola.

. .

After that tour, Jonny took you for a drink at the Arts Centre Club and handed you an envelope. In it was a larger cheque than you'd been expecting and a photograph taken before the worst of the shooting at Omanthai. Jonny eyed the skinny boys fiddling with acoustic guitars on the stage and poured more beer from under the table. The Arts Centre was having legal trouble over their liquor licence, which it circumvented by asking patrons to bring their own while contributing to the legal fund and keeping all beverages out of sight.

'Bob was well-impressed, laddie. So was Andy. Looks like my red bandanna wasn't a bad idea.'

'I was pretty impressed by your mate Bob.'

'Look. You can take a break. Have a holiday. Stay away from the casino. And, when you're ready, we'll talk assignments.'

'Seventy Tamil civilians were killed in the Omanthai massacre. There were children bleeding in front of me. But I took this photo instead.'

'Big assignments. Big money. No more bleeding children.'

The photograph was nothing special. Just of a woman in a sari being ushered away in the early moments of the shooting by the Colonel. She faced the camera as if she spied you hiding in the trees. The moment you snapped, she was draping her sari over her head, though too late to mask her face, and how pretty it was, even in the swirling dust.

'That is Colonel Gopalla-whatever? Mahatiya.'

'And that is apparently his lover.'

'So, he is defying the Supremo's No-sex-please-we're-Tigers directive? Naughty fellow.'

'These are rumours spread by the army. I'm sure even the Supremo isn't celibate. All a ploy to stop suicide bombers from getting girlfriends.'

'Still, it's a valuable photo.'

'What did Bob have to say?'

'Considering that Mahatiya and Supremo Prabhakaran aren't getting on.'

'Bob should know all about that. He had a long chat with the Colonel.'

'Good for him. Got any other photos for sale?'

'Not for you.'

An old *Island* newspaper hid the drinks and you used the news section to keep the flies from the devilled pork. In it were stories of peace accords and speculation that the Indian Army may double its boots on Lankan soil.

'Our intelligence guys think that fixer is below your paygrade,' said Jonny. 'You have a good future. Don't ruin it.'

He was still looking at the boys at the bar, whom he knew he could not approach even in a place like this.

'So Bob never mentioned a chat with the Colonel?'

'I haven't spoken to Bob.'

'For a career liar, you're pretty bad at it, Jonny.'

'You need to stop messing with the JVP, by the way. There's nothing more pathetic than a middle-class commie.'

When Jonny changed the subject, it meant the discussion was over.

'I'm not unsympathetic, mind. We've all been there. May have cheered myself when the Cong fucked the Yankies. May even have wept for comrades slaughtered in Indonesia. And no doubt the fingers of capitalism will choke us all. But we gotta face the facts, laddie. The biggest killer of commies is commies. The only murderer more prolific than Stalin or Mao or Pol Pot is God herself.'

'That's a helluva speech,' you said, eyeing the waiter in the tight T-shirt.

'They say Colonel Gopalla-Mahatiya is starting a rival faction. Mutiny against the Supremo. Heaven forbid, laddie!'

'The Colonel's not dumb enough to take on Prabhakaran.'

'Looks like the government censor banned the LTTE villager story,' said Jonny, watching you closely.

'That's convenient for Bob. He can pose as a reporter without actually reporting.'

You returned his gaze. You watched each other silently as the band took another unscheduled break.

'You got something to say, Maali?'

'If I had a picture of Bob and Colonel Mutiny and Major Raja Udugampola having a confidential chit-chat. How much would that be worth?'

Jonny frowns and then shakes his head. 'But you couldn't have a photo, bonnie lad.'

'How would you know?'

'Because pictures like that get you killed. And you love life more than you do photos.'

'Will they send Sid the Scotsman after me? What a good use of your mercenary budget that was.'

'They won't need to send anyone. You'll have the Tigers and the army after you with grenades. Don't even joke about photos like that, Maali. You better be joking.'

'Of course,' you said and pocketed your cheque. 'All I brought back from the brink of death was that red bandanna. And this bleeding heart.'

SAY MY NAME

You want to ask the universe what everyone else wants to ask the universe. Why are we born, why do we die, why anything has to be. And all the universe has to say in reply is: I don't know, arsehole, stop asking. The Afterlife is as confusing as the Before Death, the In Between is as arbitrary as the Down There. So we make up stories because we're afraid of the dark.

The wind brings your name and you follow it through air and concrete and steel. You move on breezes through a Slave Island alley and you hear the whispers in every doorway. 'Almeida... Malinda...' Then the wind blows through busy Dehiwela streets and you hear more voices. 'JVP-er... activist... Almeida... Maali... missing...'

From Slave Island to Dehiwela in one breath, faster than a helicopter ride. At least death frees you from Galle Road traffic, Parliament Road drivers, and checkpoints on every street. You ride past the faces of oblivious people ambling through Colombo's shabby streets, the mortal brothers and sisters of the dearly departed and quickly forgotten. You are a leaf in a gale, blown by a force you can neither control nor resist.

Sri Lankan visionary Arthur C. Clarke said thirty ghosts stand behind everyone alive, the ratio by which the dead outnumber the living. You look around you and fear the great man's estimate might have been conservative.

Every person you see has a spirit crouching behind them. Some have guardians hovering above and swatting away the ghouls, the pretas, the rahu and the demons. Some have distinguished members of these latter groups standing before them, hissing idle thoughts in their faces. A few have devils squatting on their shoulders and filling their ears with bile.

Sir Arthur has spent three decades of his life on these haunted shores and is clearly a Sri Lankan. Austria convinced the world that Hitler was German and Mozart was theirs. Surely, after centuries of armed plunder, courtesy of the sea pirates from London, Amsterdam and Lisbon, may we Lankans at least help ourselves to one sci-fi visionary?

The rain spits out lightning and the thunder breaks wind. You've lost count how many times it has rained since your untimely demise. Either the monsoons have come early or the universe is shedding tears for you and your silly little life. Today, the tears fall thick as globs of ink, diving from angry clouds onto the heads of the meek.

· ·

'I saw the list of the missing,' says one raincoated European to another.

'Recognise any names?' asks his colleague, running a finger down a typed sheet shielded in polythene.

'Maali Almeida. He's listed there as JVP-er and activist. He wasn't either.'

The man in the raincoat is Andrew McGowan, war correspondent and sometime friend. His face is wet and red, though you cannot tell if it is from rain or tears.

You are right back at the start, on the banks of the Beira, where the rains have stopped and a crowd has gathered by the temple. This is unusual, as it is neither Poya nor a day of almsgiving. On the outskirts of the crowd are burly Europeans in light blue raincoats who appear to be forming a barricade. A truck arrives and seven policemen exit. Among them are your dear friends ASP Ranchagoda and Detective Cassim, who bring up the rear, seemingly there to observe the chaos rather than control it.

The cops and the raincoated Europeans face off like polecats and serpents. The crowd rumbles like the sky above them. You get your bearings and look around. The stench pollutes nostrils you no longer have. The endless rains have flooded the river and burst the Beira's banks. The road encircling the lake is littered with wrinkled plastic, shrivelled fish, rotten food and sodden paper. Everyone looks astonished – who knew fish could survive the filth of this lake?

The crowd looks at the police who are talking their way in and the Europeans who are talking them back out again. You are more interested in what the crowd has turned away from. At the edge of the river are more Europeans in raincoats; some are taking photographs, others holding umbrellas over those with cameras. And what they are photographing on the banks of the Beira are bones. Soggy bones, laid out on plastic with playing cards placed on each one. There is a full house of Aces and Jacks, a Diamond straight with a high Nine, and five single cards of no use to anyone.

The cards flutter before your eyes, Kings and Queens and Jacks in a mad swirl, like the opening titles of a Bond movie filmed during the Summer of Love. This time it feels like the nausea is coming up at you from the earth's core, entering through the soles of your feet and filling your belly and throat with clay. The cards rest on bones, spinal cords and ribcages and random limbs. Among them you count fifteen skulls, and you spy the one that once belonged to you. The only part of your body that sank before being returned to the fridge.

· ·

'Have you heard from Malinda?'

'Nothing.'

'The UN forensics team has claimed those skeletons,' says Stanley Dharmendran.

'Why is the UN here?' asks DD.

'They are in Colombo for a conference.'

'On what?'

'This is all nonsense. Done by the opposition. To stir things up for us.'

'Are we ordering more cuttlefish?'

You were rarely invited to Otters Aquatic Club with father and son. Perhaps because you were a frequent topic of discussion. The father thought of it as a pep talk, while the son went for the free bites. Over a plate of mustard pork, Stanley tells his son that a leaflet by CNTR titled 'Mothers of the Disappeared' was held aloft in parliament by a human rights activist for the Sri Lanka Freedom Party named PM Rajapaksa. 'We have morgues full of our innocent dead,' said the young MP from Beliatta. 'Let us at least identify them and give their families some peace.'

'He has a point,' says DD, stuffing his pretty face with devilled cholesterol. DD wasn't the best lover you ever had, but he was by far the comeliest belle, the perfect ten. When you fall in love, it is not with a face or a body but with the largest and most important of all organs: the skin. And DD's was smooth and black and unbruised and varnished. You wish you could rub your nose on it and taste it with your fingers. You try but all you get is a whiff of chlorine and sweat. It is hardly anything, but for now it is something. DD wraps a towel around his shoulders.

'It's easy to shout when you're in opposition,' says his dad. 'Let young Rajapaksa run a war and see what happens. If he had to deal with the JVP, what would he do?'

'Appa, we're just talking about identifying bodies.'

'We are talking. About letting foreign devils. Meddle in our affairs.'

'Didn't your Excellency the President invite the Indian Army in? Are they angels?'

'I voted against that, Dilan. You know this. Don't bite your nails, men. How old are you?'

The UN forensic team had been invited by Rajapaksa to train our local authorities on identifying bodies against the records of the missing. Meanwhile the CIA were rumoured to be training our torturers. The UN team had been staying at the Colombo Oberoi and running conferences for government servants. How exactly they got to the bones before the cops did will remain another unsolved mystery on this isle of secrets.

'They are asking for dental records and blood types. As if our betel-chewing fools go to dentists.'

DD looks around while continuing to munch on devilled squid.

'Very classy, Appa. That journalist by the pool didn't quite hear you.'

Stanley cranes his neck to see a man in a towel whacking an arrack and scribbling on a notepad.

'Just a waste of time and money.'

'Isn't everything?' DD sighs.

Stanley looks from his plate to his son's face.

'Stop speaking like that, Dilan. You sound like Maali.'

'How would you know what he sounds like? Have you ever talked to him?'

'He is a talented fellow. I hope he is safe somewhere. But we have to face facts, son.'

'Here's one. In 1989, the Beira was ranked by Greenpeace as the forty-sixth most polluted lake in the world.'

'Maali is a smart young man. But sometimes it's not good to be too smart.'

'Sri Lanka has lost twenty per cent of its forest cover since Independence. Sri Lanka has had the highest suicide rate in the world for the past ten years. None of this makes the headlines or the sports page.'

'If he was arrested, I'd be worried. The STF don't keep prisoners.'

'Then where is the body?'

Stanley stares at Dilan for a long time.

'Come on, Appa. That is ridiculous.'

'Minister Cyril Wijeratne has asked me to liaise with the UN forensics team.'

'To do what?'

'To assist with their investigation. To make sure they are following protocol.'

'Sri Lanka has protocols?'

'If he's not dead, maybe he doesn't want to be found.'

'And that would be just fine with you, no?'

'If you can't help me, then I will ask Jaki.'

Rarely, since DD's mum passed away, has the third seat at this table been occupied. Jaki has been sitting quietly, watching the swimmers and the waiters. She looks up at her Uncle Stanley and removes three items from her maroon handbag. Two are framed photos of X-rays of an ill-fated art project, the other a chain with a wooden capsule. 'OK,' she says as she places them on the table.

Stanley looks at his son and takes a breath. 'Dilan. I can't believe you gave him your Amma's chain. She wore that for twenty years.'

DD looks up and shakes his head. 'It's not him.'

'The blood smeared on it. Is that yours or his?'

The blood oath in Yala was his idea, some New Age brotherhood thing. Apparently his mother and father had done the same thing as part of a Hindu ritual. When DD mentioned it to Jaki and his dad, neither were very amused. So he never brought it up again.

'If the body parts aren't his, it's better to know,' says Jaki.

'Yes, it is,' says Stanley, and DD drops his own wooden chain with your blood in the untouched ashtray and storms off to the changing rooms.

..

At the morgue, the ghosts gather around the tables and grumble. The bones have been placed on long strips of cellophane, two box air-conditioners are brought in to cool the room, and the five men wear white coats and crouch over the bones and pick at them with silver utensils. Three government pathologists are also in the room, presumably to learn from the experts, whilst spying on them.

You look down on this from the high ceiling and watch the other spirits scattered like flies along the walls. The Kaffir slaves huddle in the corner, dead prostitutes float above their bones, a young boy with teeth marks in his side peers at the arsenal of silver tools, an Englishman in a crumpled white hat sits in the corner yawning. You recognise the two students. Their eyes are purple and their tongues hang.

'What are you all looking for?' sneers a familiar voice. Sena wears a tunic and cape made from material that is black but no longer a rubbish bag. 'You think you're going to get a proper burial? A posthumous knighthood?' he says, looking at the Englishman. 'You'll all get dumped in an incinerator. That is all.'

'But now they can carbon date and...' says the Agricultural student from Jaffna.

'Find what? That this boy was eaten by a crocodile fifty years ago? What's your name, son?'

'Vincent Salgado,' mutters the timid lad in britches.

'You think there'll be a Vincent Salgado memorial statue?' mocks Sena. He swaggers behind the men in white coats and rubs himself on their behinds. One by one, the forensic scientists place their hands under their coats and scratch.

'Maali hamu!? You're here too? What the hell. Have you listened to nothing I've said?'

You can't explain why you're here or what you hope to see, only that you were drawn here and you are not able to leave.

'What if they find your frozen skull in the Beira?'

'They'll toss it back in,' says Sena. 'The chances of them matching bones to records is...'

'Less than birthing conjoined twins, which is one in 200,000.'

Facts from the *Reader's Digest* might be the last thing the brain lets go of.

'Maybe we'll be on the news,' says one of the dead sailors.

'Where do you get news?' asks a dead prostitute.

'I peep in the windows at the flats down Navam Mawatha,' says the sailor, adjusting his cap. 'They get good reception.

Care to join me? They are showing *My Fair Lady* on the Rupavahini channel.'

The dead prostitute smiles and shakes her head.

'"UN offers forensic support to SL government",' says Sena. 'It will end up as a tiny article at the end of the paper. You think they'll admit that bodies were found in the Beira? Keep dreaming, fools.'

Your gaze falls on a lightbox at the side and the X-rays pasted to it. X-rays of two lungs filled with mucus and three wisdom teeth buried beneath a row of molars. It has been taken from a frame that cost more than the X-rays, kept to remind you of a short-lived art career, of another thing that you loved and never saw through.

..

'This is a special report from the Sri Lanka Broadcasting Corporation. The remains of fifteen unidentified bodies have washed up on the shores of the Beira Lake. A UN forensic team in conjunction with Sri Lanka government pathologists are attempting to identify the skeletal remains. A government spokesman claims that the bodies are from before 1948 and have no bearing on the current political climate.'

Jaki is given her first warning for delivering unapproved news reports. Her boss, a Mr Som Wardena, says he received a call from a government minister giving SLBC a 'severe reprimand' that such actions will not be tolerated.

The UN guys file the report, which the local guys leak to the Minister, who shares it with Minister for Youth Affairs Stanley Dharmendran, who discusses it with his son, who shows it to his flatmate. They both cry for an afternoon and then stop. For the next few days, Jaki scans the newspapers before deciding on the action that gets her fired.

'Two bodies from the fifteen have been identified. One belonging to Sena Pathirana, the Gampaha organiser for the Janatha Vimukthi Peramuna, and the other to Malinda

Almeida, a Colombo-based war photographer. Both are suspected to have been killed by government death squads. The UN claims that, this year alone, 874 unidentified bodies have been buried and 1,584 Sri Lankan citizens have been reported as missing. This is a special report from the Sri Lanka Broadcasting Corporation.'

She delivers this report deadpan and her voice does not falter when she reads your name. She is sacked on the spot and evicted from the SLBC by underpaid security guards. She takes a three-wheeler to Galle Face Court and lies on her bed looking at the revolving fan and flipping through your address book and crying.

'Thank you, my darling,' you whisper. 'Now go find the King and Queen.'

She does not hear you. She turns up the gloomy music and pops two of her happy pills.

'The negatives are with the King and Queen, little girl. It's now or never. Go find the records. You know where.'

You whisper, you hiss, you bellow, you shout – and she still does not hear.

. .

'You heard? They killed Maali Almeida.'

'Who? Government?'

'Could be LTTE. Who knows?'

'Why kill a photographer?"

'Tigers kill anyone who criticises. Especially half-Tamils.'

'I thought he was JVP.'

'Who says?'

'These days, who can say?"

Two journos at the Press Club who had worked with you but did not know you. Both were war correspondents who sat in Colombo offices and wrote copy for government press releases. You spit on them and watch your saliva evaporate before it touches their oily heads. The wind brings your name once more and you climb upon it and leave the hacks to their unverified reports.

'Damn shame. Almeida was thrown from a chopper into the Beira.'

'Who said?'

'My brother-in-law is in the army.'

'Your B-I-L is full of shit. No president would waste a helicopter on a JVP-er.'

'He wasn't JVP. He took photos of the Bheeshanaya. And I didn't say president. We all know who does the dirty work around here.'

'I saw Malinda do Hamlet in college. Like an omelette.'

'Bit of a left-hand batsman, apparently.'

'Bad scene, no?'

A circle of men at a watering hole who you have never met. They know nothing of you and less of what they speak. Though it is true you were terrible in *Hamlet*. You hop on another wind.

They say the only thing worse than being talked about is not being talked about. That may be true of Irish playwrights in jails but not of dead fixers in the East. The darkness falls and all you can hear is the din of your name being rolled on tongues and spat upon.

You are discussed at the Indian High Commission, where the ambassador holds an emergency meeting of RAW, a gathering of Indian spies, to find out if any of them had you on their payroll. Everyone, except for I.E. Kugarajah, shakes their head and the meeting is adjourned.

Around the casinos, more gamblers talk idle. The Pegasus uses chicken wire to fence off the balcony on the sixth floor and the bartender who used to fondle you in the stairwell is let go without notice. The ghosts at Hotel Leo remain as uninterested in you as the world is in them.

You never wished to be famous. Despite the absent father and the indifferent mother, that adolescent fantasy never entertained you. You never sought popularity, though out in the war zone whenever you donned that red bandanna that is precisely what you got. You tried to be no one's friend and ended up being everyone's. You wonder if the news has travelled to the north and east and if you will be transported there, should anyone mention your name. Everything in the afterlife seems to come with a radius and a barricade.

'You announced it on radio? Before we told his mother!' In his rage, DD has adopted his father's rhythms. 'Where's your brain?'

'There were nine names in the address book, on the Jack of Hearts page. All of them said wrong number. Some of them scolded me in filth when I mentioned Malinda.'

'We're going to tell her now.'

'They hated each other.'

'They won't release the body.'

'I heard it was just pieces.'

Jaki bites her lip and lets go of a sob.

'We will have a memorial service. And we will demand an inquiry. And we will do this properly.' There is nothing more sexy than DD reeling off a list of things that he would never get around to doing.

'I called the King of Clubs number again. No one picked up. Then there was a gruff voice. Asked if I was Special Task Force.'

'STF? Not CIA? Or KGB? Do you even know what you're doing?'

'I'm trying to find out how Maali's skull ended up in the Beira. No one else seems to care.'

• •

The girl is playing with fire, thinking it is candyfloss. They have arrived at your Amma's house and they find your mater sprawled on the sofa. She has just completed a long shift and her third cup of tea. When the news is broken, her hand starts to shake.

'That's life,' she says. 'I knew this would happen. Stupid boy. He never ever listened.'

'OK,' says Jaki.

'Don't say that, Aunty.' DD is playing with another bone carving around his neck. 'He was killed. Appa is doing the inquiry.'

'What for?' says your Amma, staring at an empty cup. 'They won't catch anyone. They can't bring him back.'

'We need to be sure that the body is his.'

'You know, he started lying very early on. He told fibs about the servants. When he wanted money, he'd come and say, "Dada says you're stingy." That was when he was eight.'

Your Amma does not offer them any tea, which is unusual for her. She always insists on getting the kettle put on, especially for visitors she loathes. She takes a gulp and smiles at the two of them.

'Which of you were close to him?'

Jaki and DD look at each other.

'She,' says DD.

'Not me,' says Jaki.

'Did he tell either of you that he tried to suicide?' says Lakshmi Almeida, raising that eyebrow, the way she did when you told her about Aunty Dalreen.

Your lover and your friend look at each other and look away.

'When his father left, he blamed me. He quit all the classes that Bertie sent him for. Fencing, badminton, Cub Scouts, rugger. I was to blame for everything that was wrong with everything. Then, over breakfast, he said, "Ammi, if the Beatles break up, I will kill myself."'

'Beatles?' asks DD.

'Thought he preferred the Stones,' says Jaki.

'It was a joke for him. "If the '71 uprising fails, I will kill myself" or "If the Liberty shows one more Jerry Lewis film, I will kill myself." Always looking for attention. Always looking to hurt me.'

'That's not true, Aunty. He loved you.' DD is a terrible actor and even worse at telling lies.

'He took my sleeping pills. But not enough to do the job. Just enough to make me look bad. Such a tiresome child.'

'We're all in shock, Aunty Lucky. No point talking these things now.'

'You never asked him why he did it?'

Jaki stares at the teapot and the unused cups beside it.

'I know why he did it. Because his father left him and forgot about us. And I was the only one around, so I was the thing he could punch.'

You lift the teapot and smash it on your Amma's head and hold a jagged shard to her throat and ask her to retract the lie. And then you are jolted from your reverie and stare at the untouched teapot and your Amma's unwrung neck and realise that from now on other people get to tell your story and there isn't a gosh darn thing you can do about it. So, you bounce off the walls and you yell.

'Did he talk about me? Say I was a bad mother?'

'Not that often,' lies Jaki, helping herself to a cup.

'Let me brew you a fresh pot,' says your Amma, rising.

'He told me you put gin in your tea,' says Jaki, taking a sip and wincing. 'Thought he was making up stories. Seems he wasn't.'

DD has his face in his hands. It is unclear if he is sobbing or snoozing. Eventually, he rises to his feet and keeps his eyes on the floor. 'Aunty, we just came to tell you. Will you be OK? I can make funeral arrangements.'

'I heard there's not much to bury,' says Amma, raising her eyebrow again.

'He wanted to be donated to science,' says Jaki, draining her glass. She gives a rare smile. 'That's what he wanted.'

Sweet girl, you think. The only one who remembers.

'I think cremation will be best for all. Not like he was religious or anything,' says Lucky.

I never asked for a gravestone, you think, and curse your Amma for every rainy day since your birth. She did not know that you took the pills on the day you realised that you liked boys and there was nothing she or him or anyone could do about it. Not everything is about you and your shitty marriage, mother dearest.

They have the obligatory conversation at the door.

'Remember when he went off to the Vanni for three months. You remember, Dilan?'

DD nods.

'He told me he never loved me and that everything was my fault.'

DD gives my mother a hug. Jaki just nods.

'He said a lot of nasty things that he didn't mean.'

'Oh, he meant it,' says your Amma.

When she closes the door, she goes to the couch and makes sure that Kamala and Omath are nowhere nearby. She stares out the window and lets water spill from her eyes. First a drop, then an eyeful, then a fountain. Your Amma who never cried in front of you or anyone else is weeping.

At first, you wish that you could appear before her, if only to embarrass her. Tell her the odds of surviving a plane crash and the odds of surviving an STF abduction are exactly the same: thirty-eight percent. But then, you decide to do the opposite. You decide right then, better late than never, a few days after your sudden death, to let her be.

• •

You know very little about this In Between place, though you have learned to harness winds. Not all sprits know how, which is why you find many of them confined to dingy rooms banging their heads against imagined walls.

If you catch the right wind, it can take you places. Though rarely to the doorstep of where you need to get.

'You heard about Maali?'

If the wind is a crowded bus, then hearing your name is a tuk-tuk that splutters from door to door. Something of a teleporter but nothing like *Star Trek* or *Blake's 7*. One moment you are on a tree waiting for wind and the next you are at the rumpus room at the High Commission where Jonny Gilhooley is watching cricket on a giant screen.

'Has he turned up?'

'You could say that. They found a head and some bones in the Beira.'

'Jesus.'

Jonny is speaking into a brick-like contraption, supposed to be the latest evolution of the phone, though you cannot imagine anyone carrying radiation-spewing boulders in their pockets willingly. Sharing the room with him are two old men who you recognise from before. They appear to be having an argument, which you are unable to follow.

'I know. It's terrible. We're all shocked.'

Jonny scratches at the tattoo on his thigh of a serpent eating its own tail. You move in closer to his earpiece. The voice on the other side has a clipped cadence that you cannot mistake, polished from years of barking at fixers in war zones.

'Jonny. This wasn't ours, right?'

'Don't be daft, Bob. Just be careful. Maybe take a holiday.'

'You think I'm a target?'

'Did anyone see you having your little chat with the Colonel and the Major?'

'Of course not.'

'Not even the other journos.'

'Andy McGowan? No way.'

Robert Sudworth, correspondent for the AP, who spent forty-five minutes with you flattened against a bush at the wrong end of a shooting range in Omanthai. Who had a penchant for village maidens and had not filed a single story since arriving in this isle a year ago.

'Not who I mean, Bob.'

THE SEVEN MOONS OF MAALI ALMEIDA

'You think Maali was targeted? By whom?'

And right then the trishaw arrives, piloted neither by Scotty of the *Enterprise* nor by Villa of the *Liberator*, and you are in a hotel room and there is a dusky young lass snoring under the sheets and Bob Sudworth in a towel looking dishevelled and hungover.

'Just be careful, Bob. That's all.'

'Is that a threat, Jonny?'

'Don't let your business interfere with mine.'

'My business is journalism, what's yours?'

You're not sure where this room is, but from the window in the mid-distance you see the red tower that is Hotel Leo. Sudworth is puffing on a Bristol and sipping Lion lager. The voice on the other end is Jonny's Asianised Geordie, and in the background you hear the two old men arguing in avian chirps.

'Bob, I'm not a child. You've been lunching with Israelis. And meeting with Tigers. And my guess is that you aren't filing stories on gunrunning.'

'You got something to say, Jonny? Maali was a mate.'

'Not saying he wasn't.'

'I'm just here to do business. That's all.'

'Thought you were a journalist.'

The line clicks and Robert Sudworth looks down at the beer on his table and the lady in his sheets and decides to refrain from touching either.

..

They are in a wood-panelled office with photographs of UNP stalwarts adorning the walls. DS, Dudley, Sir John, JR, a vintage collection of privileged arseholes with neither the imagination nor the compassion to lead this paradise to glory. You swirl around the room like a bad smell and settle on the mahogany table, wanting to punch them both, but settling for spewing curses that they cannot hear. On the table are files and envelopes and a shoebox that does not belong to anyone in the room with breath.

'This is about Malinda Almeida, I am presuming.'

'It is about photos belonging to CNTR,' says Elsa Mathangi.

'I saw those photos. You're lucky not to be jailed.'

'We just want what's ours, sir. You keep the rest.'

'Very generous. Who is publishing them?'

'We are not journalists.'

'Do we even know that these are from '83?'

'Where else could they be from?'

The popular mythos surrounding the riots of '83 is that they began at the Borella Kanatte, at a funeral for thirteen soldiers killed up north by Tigers, in what was then the biggest attack ever. That unlucky number thirteen seems a minor skirmish compared to the rivers of corpses that have flowed since. In truth, the riot originated in an office not unlike this one, with angry men in ties cyclostyling electoral forms for drunk men in sarongs.

'Looks like you have a big photo studio. How did you enlarge the faces and all?'

'Malinda took care of all that. Said he had a boy.'

'I'm not a Chinaman with a ponytail. Why would I release these to you?'

He opens the box and holds up the envelopes. Ace, King, Queen, Jack, Ten. Unsuited. A royal straight.

Elsa gets that look you have seen before. Where she is considering diplomacy and deciding against it.

'There has been no acknowledgement of July '83. Forgetting things does not erase them. If you bring even one killer to justice, you will win back the trust of the Tamils. You will never win this war without that.'

The Minister picks the envelope marked 'Queen of Spades' and turns it upside down. The photos drop before her. Each a closeup, done by Viran at the FujiKodak shop, for a generous fee and a complimentary suck. The dancing Devil, the man with the stick, the boy with the petrol can, the beast with the brown cleaver. Faces enlarged to be almost recognisable.

'If these are seen, this country will burn again. Is that what you people want?'

Elsa gathers them up, hoping that they won't be reclaimed. Black-and-white prints of people setting other people on fire fill the table. As Elsa collects them, the Minister picks out two. He sits back on his expensive chair and holds them up.

'And what are you planning for these?'

One is an enlargement of the other. The original showed a naked Tamil man being taunted by boys with sticks. In the background is a Benz, whose numberplate isn't visible, but the man in the back seat is. He peers out of an open window and surveys the violence. His expression is unreadable, and his mouth is firmly shut. The other photo is a blurry close-up of the same man. Minister Cyril Wijeratne holds it up and hisses.

'What are you planning with this one?'

'You admit it is you?' says Elsa, wisely choosing not to smile.

'Be very careful, miss. You're not the first accuse me of organising mobs. As if I am that powerful. The mobs were furious and sadly the Tamils had to suffer. That is all.'

'Innocent Tamils.'

'It was very sad.'

'So why didn't you stop it?'

'1983 was your people's fault, not mine,' says the Minister. 'If you wake a sleeping lion, it will maul you. Always remember that.'

'How did the mob know where the Tamil houses were?'

'You are not playing your cards very well, Mrs Mathangi.'

'Ms.'

'I intend on giving you these photos. Except for these two, of course.'

'Of course.'

'But I want the negatives. Where are they?'

'Maali's girlfriend and boyfriend might know.'

'Those are Stanley's children. I can't touch them.'

'One of them you can't touch.'

'If you get me the negatives, you can keep these others.'

'If I had the negatives, I wouldn't need them.'

'There is another favour you can do me.'

Elsa tries to read the Minister's smile and waits for the rupee to drop.

..

You float on the ceiling and watch Minister Cyril tell Elsa Mathangi about a British arms broker with Israeli hardware whom the government would like to talk to but can't under the terms of their new Chinese contract. He tells her that these arms can be given to Colonel Mahatiya, on the proviso that he uses them to wrest the Tiger leadership from the Supremo. But Mahitiya doesn't trust the army or the Brits. So the government needs an intermediary.

'Do not mention this to your partner Kugarajah. Our sources show that he has links to both the Tigers and the Indian secret service.'

'You think I don't know this?'

'In return you get all your photos, except for these, of course. And you won't be jailed. It is a dream offer for someone in your position. Best offer you will get.'

'What I'll get is killed. Either by you or by them.'

'We only kill bad people. And those who threaten the state are bad people, possibly the worst.'

'What about the people who died in '83?'

'You know 1983 was a long time ago. And there's little point in bringing it up now. Unless you want it to happen again.'

'What if I take the negatives back to Canada and tell the press that the SL government are arming terrorists?'

'But you are smarter than this. I need your decision before you leave this office.' The Minister could've used the word 'if', but didn't need to. Power is when you can issue threats without speaking them.

'If CNTR agree to this, we want India out. And we want Tamil civilians protected.'

'No CNTR. Just you. You seem to have forgotten about Almeida. We did not kill him. But we're not sure about you or your Kuga.'

'We are not in that type of business, sir.'

'You're not very upset to have lost a colleague.'

'I have lost many colleagues, sir. This we are used to.'

'So have I, my dear,' says the son of a great man and the uncle of a feather boa wearer. 'Don't ever forget that.'

'I'll try my best.' Elsa never played poker, though she would have been excellent at it.

'You have the weekend. That is all you get. I need the negatives and I need your presence at a meeting on Sunday.'

'May I take the photos now?'

You watch as the Minister picks up his phone and grunts out an order. And then as the armed men in black who aren't police or army come in to escort Elsa Mathangi from the room. One stays behind to clear the envelopes. Elsa drops her smile and shakes her head as she is pushed out of the room.

The Minister puts down the phone and nods. 'Forty-eight hours. Starting now. I want the negatives and your word, now. I'll keep the photos till then.'

. .

'If I get another call about Maali Almeida, I will send you – yes, you personally – to Jaffna to run errands for the Indians.'

He uses a kitchen knife to open a letter and almost nicks the edge of his finger.

'Bloody bastard. I bet that homo's ghost is here to ruin my day.'

If only he knew, you think. If only.

'Mendis, did you hear me?'

'Yes, sir,' comes the timid squeak from the stout corporal organising the files in the corner.

'You said there were visitors?'

'Yes, sir. Two cops.'

'Send them. Hold all the bloody calls, unless it is you-know-who.'

'Yes, sir.'

The stout man exits through the door by the filing cabinet. The room is oblong and messy with files and maps and tables with weapons on them. An Uzi, a Kalashnikov, a 38 Browning, some grenades and dumdum bullets sit in a glass cabinet with a key in its lock. The desk at the corner has multiple telephones on it and a name board saying 'Major Raja Udugampola'. You have sat at this desk before and asked for favours and received orders in return.

The stout man returns with two police officers. One is burly and quiet, the other is wiry and talkative. The Major keeps opening letters with knives and frowning at them.

'ASP Ranchagoda. Detective Cassim. I have chosen you because you come recommended. You boys have a lot of work.'

'Sir!'

They stand to attention and avoid the big man's gaze.

'How much garbage left at Leo?'

Cassim's hand itches to reach for the notebook on which that figure is written. But perhaps he recalls the story that Major Raja once broke a private's nose for fidgeting.

'Seventy-seven,' he shouts out.

'Don't lie. I thought it was forty-odd.'

'More came in last week, sir,' says Ranchagoda.

'I have asked for a curfew. The Minister will call now. You will supervise transport. At the Kanatte, the STF will take over. You have enough vehicles?'

'We have three lorries.'

'Cha! Not enough. I can get drivers. Will have to make a few trips. I am also hearing some very bad stories.'

'Sir?'

'That we are hiring criminals. There's talk of feeding bodies to cats? This better be bullshit.'

'Hard to find good garbage men, sir. No one you can trust. Our buggers aren't saints, but no murderers or drug dealers.' Ranchagoda speaks, while Cassim stares at the floor.

'That is good.'

'I don't know anything about cats, sir.'

'OK. Let's see. Get it done. Now get out.'

As the cops are leaving, one of the phones rings. You are startled out of a reverie, one which featured you exchanging envelopes at the reception outside. You were invited into this room on only two occasions. Once to be commended for your efforts and once to be told that your services were no longer required.

A light blinks beside the phone and the Major picks it up. 'Yes?'

'Could I speak with Major Raja Udugampola, please?'

'Who is this?'

'My friend has this number in his address book.'

'Who is your friend?'

'Malinda Almeida.'

Click.

'Mendis!'

He slams down the phone and waits for the corporal to enter the long corridor.

'You bloody baboon! I said no calls.'

'Sir, that was your private line.'

'But no one has this number.'

The light by the phone blinks again.

'OK, get out!'

He waits till the corporal has closed the door behind him. 'Yes.'

'How did you know Malinda?'

'Miss, this is the headquarters of the Sri Lankan army. This number is classified. I will have you traced and placed under detention.'

'Why did Maali have this number?'

'I am Major Raja Udugampola of the Sri Lankan army. I have given a press statement. Almeida was employed as an army photographer from 1984 till 1987. I have never met the arsehole personally. He has had no dealings with the army for the past three years. If you call again, I will massacre you.'

He slams down the phone and tidies his desk. He places his letters in a tray and stuffs the envelopes in the bin. The phone blinks again. The Major is about to swear and is glad that he does not.

The voice at the other end is loud enough to be heard all the way to the corridor.

'Ah, Raja. Don't say I don't give you support, ah?'

'Sir, I appreciate very much.'

'You have your curfew. From midnight to midnight. That better be enough.'

'Yes, sir. More than enough. Thank you, sir.'

'President asked me why.'

'What did sir say?'

'I told him.'

'And?'

'He said, "You sure twenty-four hours is enough?"'

They say that laughter is music, but that is just one of a thousand untruths that we suckle ourselves with. Some laughs are piquant, some are hideous, some can curdle the blood. The sound of Major Raja Udugampola and Minister Cyril Wijeratne cackling in unison is the ugliest music to ever hit your recently checked ears.

'And another thing.'

'Tell sir.'

'One more pickup.'

'You have the name, sir?'

'Elsa Mathangi. You will find her at...'

'I know, sir. The Hotel Leo.'

'Keep her under watch. Be ready to pick her up on my call.'

'What kind of guest, sir?'

'Give her the royal treatment.'

'Information or punishment?'

'Both.'

'Then I'll use The Mask.'

'Use whatever yaka you want. Don't fuck it up.'

FOURTH MOON

*'I'm an angel. I kill firstborns while their mamas watch.
I turn cities to salt. I even, when I feel like it, rip the souls
from little girls, and from now till kingdom come, the only
thing you can count on in your entire existence
is never understanding why.'*

Greg Widen, *The Prophecy*

CURFEW

On curfew days, nothing moves except for winds and spirits and the eyes of checkpoint guards. You have spent the night in a tree, staring at the half-moon and the clouds obscuring it. Wondering what every Bodhisattva and each of Arthur C.'s thirty ghosts have wondered before. Is it possible to make it all stop?

The first curfews you remember were the ones that followed the 1983 massacre. After that, curfews became as commonplace as Poya holidays. They would follow each burst of violence, like floods follow rains. Down south, up north and right here in the wild, wild west, the government would take people off the pavement, cars off the street and freedoms off the table. Jonny once said curfews were there for governments to maintain order, catch bad guys and 'do things they couldn't in broad daylight'.

Your tree gets crowded with suicides muttering. Suicides are the easiest to spot, after the pretas; their eyes are yellowy green, their necks are often broken, and they always chatter, though only to themselves. You let the wind carry you from checkpoint to checkpoint, past empty roads and barren bus stands. Cats patrol the side streets, crows guard the roofs and creatures without breath walk slower than most.

A lorry rumbles along the main road, a light-blue Ashok Leyland, the first vehicle to appear all morning on what is usually the busiest stretch of Galle Road. It does not slow down at the Bamba checkpoint and the guards do not raise a hand or an eyebrow. A few moments later, a green Toyota is stopped and the driver is pulled out of the vehicle and searched. The man points to the medical sticker on his windshield and is let go.

A second lorry, this one red and wood-panelled, gathers speed at the checkpoint and is waved past by the guards. You hop on its tail as it turns down Bullers Road. The ride is bumpy and the stench magnificent. A lack of nose hasn't excused you from the fragrances of frozen bodies decomposing.

You are not alone on the roof of this truck. There are other creatures without breath bobbing along with you. The wind rushes through them and makes streaks of their faces. Forgotten smiles and bewildered eyes flutter in the air as the lorry turns into the kanatte.

There are two other vehicles, both trucks, both with their backs open, both with men unloading cargo. The cargo is corpses, unwrapped and limber, some still frozen, others festering. The air thickens with flies buzzing delight at the banquet before them. The men doing the labour wear thick masks, mostly old sarongs wrapped over mouths and noses, as if they were highwaymen or assassins, which a sizeable bunch of them probably are.

You wish you had your camera, just as you wish you had somewhere to develop negatives and someone to show them to. Just like you wish you had more time and something to care about. Just like you wish you knew who killed you. There is no one in uniform, though some of the men move like soldiers, upright and quick, with little conversation or pause.

At the gate, two cops and two men, who are neither army nor police, check IDs and write them down. It is a lone example of order and organisation in this pandemonium of gurneys and wheelbarrows. Some wear gloves, others wear siri-siri bags. Some wear shoes, others wear slippers. There is no chatter except for groans as bodies are hoisted onto slabs and wheeled towards the towers of the crematorium. The groans come from the men lifting and the spirits watching.

The men in black shout the orders and check that the bodies are stacked straight. If a barrow tips over, it will stall every weaving Lankan queue behind it.

The truck that just arrived is unloading onto the car park, a second one has half its cargo on the barrows, and a third is filling up with empty gurneys back from the crematorium. Walking to the third truck are three men who, despite having half their faces covered, are recognisable from their slow swagger as being more bovine than human. Balal and Kottu lumber like buffaloes; Drivermalli trots on his fake boot.

At the edge of the chaos, Officers Ranchagoda and Cassim stand like traffic lights and attempt to regulate the chaos while succeeding in contributing towards it. On most of the corpses, its spirit squats like a succubus, staring down like a grieving child, trying to figure how to breathe itself back into its shell.

You look up at the giant chimney, spewing black smog towards the heavens, where the stars look away and the gods refuse to hear. You remember the many times you saw Colombo's air fill with this smoke. You are not among these piles of flesh; you can feel that in bones you no longer have. The barrows and gurneys are pushed towards the tower, carted towards the giant hole in the wall and emptied into the furnace. The inferno accepts the bodies with a hiss and a belch, while each spirit wails, only to be heard by those who have stopped listening.

Outside, you hear tyres screeching and a voice raised. You fly out of the crematorium to see Major Raja Udugampola waving his arms at the throng. The air is humid with whispers and is broken by the Major's sing-song yelp.

'What the hell are you donkeys trying to do?'

If you close your eyes, the Major's high-pitched inflections may seem comical, as if he were dubbing Bugs Bunny into Sinhala. It is only when you see his hunched orangutan frame that you realise that this voice could pound on your chest with both fists until your ribs cracked.

'We are two hours late, you lazy fucks! My men will unload. Bring the rest of the garbage. Now! Or I'll throw all of you into that fire!'

There is commotion as men in black who are neither army nor police growl at officers in plain clothes. Ranchagoda and Cassim shout at Balal and Kottu, who push Drivermalli, who curses the government while obeying its orders. The cops barge into the cabin with the driver, while the garbage men hose down the interior of the truck. They wash away patterns of red and brown and yellow and blue, a kaleidoscope made of dead people's insides.

'Where we going, sir?' asks Drivermalli as he makes the engine purr.

Ranchagoda smiles at him with his jagged teeth.

'Where do you think?'

Detective Cassim is silent and ASP Ranchagoda can bear it no longer.

'Your face looks like a pittu. No point thinking so much. These are all terrorists and thugs.'

'But they aren't.'

'As if you can tell?'

'They are young. I don't agree with this. I never have. Applied for my transfer last year. Still waiting.'

'The JVP threatened the army and police and their families. We are protecting our families. If you are old enough to kill, you are old enough to die.'

'And their families? Who protects them?'

'Should have looked after their kids better. Drivermalli, what's the hold-up?'

'Lanka will be destroyed. First by fire. Then by flood,' mutters Drivermalli as he treads lightly with his good foot.

'What you say?'

'Nothing.'

You sit on the hood of the truck as it rumbles into motion. You hear your name wafting on the wind delivered by a voice that you cannot place when shorn of its usual theatrics.

. .

'I will have Maali's body returned to the family,' says Stanley to his son.

'There is no body, Appa,' says DD, voice low, eyes shining.

'Who told you that?'

'The UN forensics.'

'You met them?'

'They met me.'

'Where?'

'At the Arts Centre Club.'

'You shouldn't go there.'

'Why?'

'Full of drug addicts and poofs. It will get raided soon.'

Your Dada and Stanley would've got on well. Like a house on fire, filled with the bodies of flaming faggots. You try to imagine them dressed like aunties, comparing horoscopes and picking wedding dresses for their sons.

'I'm quitting Earth Watch Lanka,' says DD.

'I think. That is wise,' his father says. 'You were very close. Some time off will clear your mind. When you're ready, you can always work with the firm.'

'I've taken a job with the UN.'

'I see. This is the Environmental Programme?'

'I'm setting up a local forensic unit for identifying bodies.'

'Is that with that Rajapaksa fellow?'

'This unit will be apolitical.'

'Nothing in this country is apolitical. I wish you would grow up, Dilan.'

Stanley leans forward and places his hands on his boy's shoulders. You can see he is seething, but DD cannot see that, and you could build cathedrals from the things that DD cannot see or know or understand. Father lets out a deep sigh. In profile they look identical enough to be twins.

'If we don't make this country better, who will?' says the younger.

'Do what you need to do, son,' mutters the elder. 'Do what you need to do.'

It is only when Jaki stumbles in from the kitchen that you realise that you are back at the flat at Galle Face Court. You wonder what is different about the room and notice the spaces on the wall where your photos used to hang.

She breaks the father–son moment like a JVP-er with a foghorn, like a goon with an electoral list. She holds up the address book and a sheet bearing the names of five playing cards.

'I've worked it out. I've got all the names.'

DD looks tired and burdened.

'What names? What are you saying?'

'The five envelopes that had playing cards drawn on them...'

'Yeah, yeah. And the same cards drawn in the address book next to numbers.'

'I know who the numbers belong to,' says Jaki.

You do not know whether to be cheerful about this or fearful for Jaki. And, by the looks on their faces, neither does father or son.

Jaki flips opens your address book to bookmarked pages. 'There's an Ace of Diamonds. That number goes to Jonny Gilhooley. The creep from the Embassy.' Jaki circles the name on the paper. 'Maali also mentioned some guy called Robert Sudworth from the AP.'

'I work with the AP. Never heard of a Sudworth,' says DD. 'You're thinking of that weirdo Andy McGowan.'

'Sudworth?' Stanley shakes his head. 'There is a rep for Lockheed Systems with that name.'

'Lockheed what?' asks DD.

'They sell weapons to most of the SAARC governments.'

'Next you'll say Maali was an arms dealer.'

'I doubt that,' says Stanley. 'Arms dealers can afford their rent.'

He looks at his son, who averts his eyes.

'Queen of Spades goes to Elsa Mathangi at CNTR,' says Jaki.

'Appa, did you do that check?' asks DD.

'I told you already. Emmanuel Kugarajah is linked with LTTE proxies like EROS. And with RAW, the Indian Secret Service. Arrested for assault in the UK, but charges were dropped. Elsa Mathangi was a fundraiser for the Tigers at Toronto University. CNTR is funded by the governments of Canada and Norway. But also by the US Fund for Peace.'

Stanley has either got his Youth Ministry to do some homework or is making up tales for his gullible son.

'There's a US Fund for Peace?' asks DD.

'Is their budget the same as the US Fund for War?' asks Jaki and no one smiles.

'If CNTR are a front for the LTTE or RAW, we can guess the rest.'

'Can we?' says DD.

'Neither are averse to silencing their own employees.'

There is a pause and then Jaki coughs. 'The Jack of Hearts is followed by these names. Byron, George, Hudson, Guinness, Lincoln, Brando, Wilde. Most said wrong number. A few hung up when I mentioned his name.'

Some men that you tasted gave you their numbers, which you wrote down and never called. When they asked for yours, you gave them a fake one, but only after they let you photograph them.

'Maybe other JVP-ers. Must've heard about the body,' says Stanley.

DD shakes his head and plays with his hair. 'Maali was friendly with everyone. We know this, Jaki. So what was King and Ten?'

'King of Clubs went direct to the office of a Major Raja Udugampola.'

'Are y'all mad?' Stanley's tie flaps in the breeze. 'Udugampola is head of operations for the STF. You called his direct line?'

'I tried the number.'

'Please tell me. You did not speak to him.' Stanley's hand is shaking.

'No,' says Jaki, overselling the lie.

Stanley squints at her and then buys the bluff.

'This is not a game, Jaki? Udugampola is a thug. He has CIA-trained torturers in his squad. You've heard of the Mask? If Malinda is involved with him, we better all lie low.'

'Are we getting Maali's boxes back?'

'Minister Cyril Wijeratne gave me his word.'

'OK,' says Jaki.

'What was in those boxes?'

'We all want to know. Uncle did you call him?'

'How many times to tell? You don't believe? I'll call him now.'

'OK,' says Jaki.

Stanley Dharmendran walks inside, picks up the phone and starts dialling without having to look the number up. The number contains many zeros which try the patience of Stanley's finger on the circular dial.

'So Johnny is Ace, STF is King, Elsa is Queen, Jacks are JVP. What's Ten?

'I told you before. The Ten of Hearts is next to our flat number.'

'So what does that mean?'

'Maybe it's pictures of us?' says Jaki. 'Or maybe just you.'

DD takes the book from Jaki and begins turning pages.

'Your name is here under J. It says Jaki. And in brackets it says Cousin Dilan. How old is this address book?'

You get a biting pain where your chest once was and it

makes your invisible arms ache. You think of all the pictures in the envelope titled 'The Perfect Ten'. And you realise that, for you, those pictures are the least worth stealing, and the most worth protecting.

Your Weakness

You're back at the Otters Aquatic Club, the first and last time you were invited to the weekly father–son chat. You were there as Jaki's date and never invited back. This was still in the first six months, when you and Jaki were hitting the clubs and casinos and behaving like a couple, except in the bedroom.

Stanley was being cordial and playing host with vigour, ordering imported beer and platefuls of cuttlefish. You had had your first and last badminton game as mixed doubles: DD and Jaki vs Stanley and you. After half a game, it was clear to everyone that Jaki was bad and, after a full game, it was evident that you were worse. But what you lacked in shuttle skill, you made up for in banter.

'DD. I think I've found your weakness.'

'What?'

'Badminton.'

Stanley said nothing as you kept missing shot after shot and costing game after game. Except at the end, when you were miraculously poised at game point, and lobbed the shuttle into the net, you heard him mutter, 'Bloody shit!' with more pent-up fury than all his angry smashes.

You began by discussing *North & South*, an American miniseries starring Patrick Swayze that the three of you were addicted to. Stanley's eyes glazed over with a fake smile. You were talking about how unrealistic the battle sequences were when he changed the subject.

'They once threw a grenade at my car. Just close to here. Down Bullers Lane.'

DD talked a lot about how his Appa had been on the LTTE's kill list right until the 1987 Peace Accord. To this day, they travel in separate vehicles, even when going to Otters.

'Malinda, your mother is Tamil?'

'Half-Burgher, half-Tamil.'

'And your father?'

'Passed away three years ago. He was Sinhala.'

'I'm sorry to hear that. So what are you?'

'A Sri Lankan.'

'That's what the young will say. I hope your generation can think like that. It is too late for us.'

'It's all tribal bullshit,' said Jaki. 'Race before country.'

'There is truth. In tribalism, my dear,' said Stanley. 'Sinhalese outnumber Tamils. But Tamils are cleverer than Sinhalese. We work harder. And we have to be better. And we have to conceal it, as well. Or the Sinhalaya gets jealous.'

'Are you still worried for your safety, Uncle?' You tried to look him in the eye but kept glancing at his son stripping down for a swim. The sweaty T-shirt and shorts were discarded for a blue Speedo.

'I keep my distance and lower my profile. I abstain from troublesome bills. I don't confront the Sinhalaya. I work with them. We all want peace in our life. Isn't that right, Malinda?'

And then Stanley gave you a lecture on Tamil traditional homelands and how Tamils had kingdoms in the north throughout medieval history and colonial rule. Jaki asked why the Sinhalese were so insecure and Stanley replied that it is the same reason Whites in America fear the Negro they once enslaved and DD does the dolphin for two lengths followed by the breaststroke.

'But race isn't fact. It's fiction,' said Jaki. 'It's man-made shit. Who can tell a Sinhalese and a Tamil apart?'

'That's not true,' said Stanley. 'It is a fact that Negroes run faster, that Chinese work harder, that Europeans invent things.' He then went off on a monologue on nature vs nurture, which somehow managed to mention that he swam and ran for Royal College in the '50s. He concluded that your race, your school and your family will dictate how the dice of life will roll for you.

DD arrived in a towel and ploughed into the cuttlefish, but not before he gave you a smile. He nodded as he always did to his father's lectures. You and Jaki did not.

When the cuttlefish was gone, Stanley signed the bill and for the first time since badminton looked you in the eye.

'We are educated Colombo Tamils. We must be careful and not attract attention. You understand, no?'

You think of the lottery of birth and how everything else is mythology, stories the ego tells itself to justify fortune or explain away injustice. You wonder if you should hold your tongue.

'Uncle, this country was inherited by arrack-swillers who sent their children to British schools. Mostly Sinhala – but not all. What they all were was Colombians. And being an English-speaking Colombian exempts us from the rest of this country's sufferings.'

'I didn't know there were Marxists left in this country,' says Stanley, giving you the fakest of smiles as he rises to leave. 'Tell me, Maali. How much does your photography pay you?'

'Appa!' DD looked embarrassed and flabbergasted.

'It's OK, DD,' you said. 'It's OK to ask that as long as you're prepared to answer it. How much do you make by not voting on troublesome bills?'

'Big topic. And I have to go. Another time maybe.'

Stanley looked annoyed for letting his mask slip in front of his son.

'No problem, uncle. If you're uncomfortable divulging, you shouldn't be asking. But I'm happy to tell you.'

'I'm not interested.' Stanley signs for the bill.

'I make what all the world's millionaires do not.'

Stanley raised an eyebrow. 'What is that?'

'Enough.'

You smiled and Stanley left and Jaki rolled her eyes, having heard that punchline before and not from your lips.

DD put his arm around your shoulder and gave you a side-hug. One that appeared brotherly but did not feel that way to you. 'I love seeing someone sticking it to Appa. Jaki, where did you find this guy?'

Jaki stubbed out her cigarette and shrugged. 'He found me.'

Her mouth smiled but her eyes did not.

· ·

Months later, you had an argument over the dinner table about his Appa and his failure to condemn the government shelling of civilians in Jaffna.

'Appa condemns all violence. He always has.'

'Does he ever try to stop it? Or, at least, question it?'

'He doesn't owe anyone anything. We can't change the world, Maali. We can only solve bits, here and there.'

'Spoken like a privileged arsehole.'

'Here we go. The birth lottery speech. It's easy to be righteous when your Dada left you guilt money from Missouri.'

'You can use your privilege to help others or to exclude them.'

'So, what do you want me to do?'

'Nothing. Just keep saving those trees.'

'Better than photographing corpses.'

'OK, you've convinced me. Let's go to San Francisco and make money and love and let this shit country burn to the ground.'

'It'll burn whether you photograph it or not.'

'No, I'm serious. Let's do it. I'm ready.'

'You're too much of a coward,' says DD. 'All big talk. You'd never do it.'

DD took his plate and dumped it in the sink along with the frying pan that he just ruined with too much heat and too little oil. Which meant he'd be sulking and won't do the dishes again tonight and they would stack high until Kamala came on Thursday.

'Do what?' said Jaki, standing at the door.

..

DD said he was coming out to his Appa and you told him what a terrible idea that would be and he accused you of being a self-hating faggot and said that he was going to quit his job and go do his master's in Tokyo.

And that's when you asked if you could borrow some money and he asked how much and you told him and he asked what for and you said to spend a month up north in a Vanni refugee camp and he asked what for and you told him another lie.

'Will this ever stop, Maali?'

'If you can't spare the cash, just say. I don't need lectures.'

'Is this for Associated Press? Or the army?'

'I can't say.'

'Then I can't give.'

'Fine. I'll borrow from someone who doesn't claim to love me.'

'Why don't you speak to Jaki?'

'She's more broke than I am.'

'About us.'

'What about us?'

'She needs to hear from you. She follows you like a puppy waiting to be petted. It's disgusting.'

You left promising to tell Jaki, which you didn't. He parted, saying he couldn't lend you the money, which of course he eventually did. You lost a small portion of it at the roulette table, used some of it to buy a blow job in Anuradhapura, and the rest you gave to a family fleeing the shelling in Vavuniya.

·· ·

You had the talk while driving to watch Jaki performing in some play by some famous Russian starring Radika Fernando, the lady who read the news. He told you that he had only dated girls and that you were dating his cousin and that none of this made sense and that his Appa would be horrified and he didn't need drama. You told him OK and then let your fingers snake into his lap all through the performance. Later, you told Jaki that she had great chemistry with her co-star and she said maybe she had a crush on her and you laughed and she said, 'Exactly, I knew you wouldn't care.'

·· ·

For one week since your return from the Vanni, the connecting door to his room was locked. You spent days in the casino, while Viran developed your rolls of film. The boy had been ordering new equipment through the FujiKodak shop and taking it home along with your prints.

There was a hum in your ear that no amount of smoke or winning streaks could dispel. And, when you closed your eyes, all you could see was children in bunkers holding onto each other, tiny heads tucked under tiny elbows, eyes wide and empty.

And then, he returned drunk from an office party and caught you on the couch watching videotaped episodes of *Crown Court* and dragged you to your bed even though Jaki may have been in her room and you never did things when Jaki was home and awake.

And, during that most furious and sweaty coupling, he got pissed off when you pulled a condom from your wallet and asked you if you had AIDS and you said no but you were going to get tested and he asked you if you had sex with anyone in the Vanni and you said no. Because a blow job isn't sex and it isn't sex if you don't see the other person's face and it doesn't count if you were thinking about him during it.

After you got to do the thing to him that he most enjoyed and you lay spent on his messy bed, he pulled you by the beard and brought his face, which still smelled of expensive booze, to yours, and said, 'If you do this with anyone else, I will kill you. Don't think I'm joking.'

You were startled by the front door opening and Jaki stumbling in. It appeared she had company, though she may have been talking to herself, which she sometimes did.

He looked at you and squinted his eyes and you stroked his ebony skin as if it was the coat of a prize pony.

'And if Jaki finds out about this, she will kill us both.' You kissed his mouth, which was lush even though it tasted of fermented grape.

You heard Jaki crashing into her room, chatting to a guest, imaginary or otherwise, and then her door closed and locked. Clearly she had better things to do than assassinate her flatmates in their bed.

BLACK MOON

The Minister's glasses tint in the sunlight as if to shield him from the sullied car park, the busy crematorium and the cemetery filled with angry spirits, many exiled there on orders given by the voice in his throat.

'Stanley, there is no proof that these photos were taken by Malinda Almeida. So how are they his property?'

Travel for you has become swifter than anything out of *Star Trek* or *Blake's 7*. The mention of your name seems to transport you across phone lines, and now you are in a plush Benz sitting next to the Right Deplorable Minister of Justice.

His Dead Bodyguard sits on the hood, scanning the scene for assassins. In the front seat is a driver and a goon; both are in black and wearing headgear.

The Minister has a phone in his car in a country where less than half the population can afford one in their house. He is speaking into this brick and you do not need to hear the other side of the chat.

'...I know, I know, men. But I am looking at this objectively. Purely from a standpoint of justice. You are too close to this, Dharmendran. One must be impartial. Put the country's interests first.'

'... Yes, Stanley, the UN still has these so-called bodies. Bloody nonsense men. We have demanded them back. We will get them and identify them properly.'

'... There are some disturbing photos in that box. My legal team is analysing. Don't want to be taken for a ride. Some are classified army property. I don't know if making them public will be good for the country.'

'...'83? Yes, I believe there are some from that year. I don't think bringing all that up is useful at this time. I know you agree.'

'... Look, Stanley, I have work. When I get the photos back, I will put a meeting with you and we will go over each one and you tell me what is to be done.'

'... We need your input Stanley. This may be a Sinhala country, but we look after everyone. That is the priority. All great nations have been ruled with iron fists. Britain, France, Japan, Germany, look at Singapore now.

'... I told you I am busy. I will tell you as soon as I reach a verdict. You have my word.'

'... You know, Stanley. This is Sri Lanka's worst time. My astrologer says it is a black moon. A rahu or apale time. The UN can come in and preach to us, but what are they doing about South Africa or Palestine or Chile? No one else can solve our problems, am I right?'

The Benz rolls through the cemetery car park and settles on a spot of shade not far from the giant chimney. The men in black exit and open both doors, which strikes you as odd. Does the Minister plan on exiting from both sides? The driver reaches in and grabs a box from the seat and the Minister exits left. You had not noticed what you were floating right next to.

'... I have some business, Stanley. Will call you as soon as there is word.'

A guard, who is neither army nor police, opens the boot and pulls out a gunny sack and you get that feeling of someone walking over your grave and defecating on it. Behind you is Sena, the Engineering student from Moratuwa, the Agricultural student from Jaffna, some dead Tigers, and a few others you don't recognise. It wasn't just your name that brought you here so quickly, it was the bones in the sack.

'This is how you dress for your funeral?' mocks Sena. He now has a longer cloak and spikes in his hair and serrated edges on his teeth. 'Let us join the mourners.'

The Minister is flanked by his two officers in black and a Demon in shadow. One officer with the gunny sack, the other with a disintegrating box marked with an ace high straight. Usually a winning hand, though maybe not this time.

That is when you lose it and start clawing at the Minister's face, at his throat, at the back of his neck. The Minister's Demon stands between you and his master, and shoves you away. You are flung over the Benz into the arms of Sena, his embrace cold and oddly comforting. The Minister walks past three parked trucks and men in sarongs hosing them down.

'I can help you kill your killers,' whispers Sena in your ear.

At the entrance of the crematorium is Ranchagoda and Cassim. They salute the Minister.

'Everything clean?' asks Cyril.

'Yes, sir,' says Cassim.

'Yes, sir. Almost,' says Rancha.

'Curfew will be over soon,' says Minister Cyril. 'Get it done.'

There is less smoke in the air and the smell now is not of burning flesh but of the barrels of chemicals deployed to mask it. All that remains of seventy-seven bodies are smouldering embers, a fading stench and a shadow that none of the living can see. The opening to the furnace has a gurney before it. A man in black places the sack upon it. Another places the box. He stacks the box and the sack and you watch them topple.

The Minister sighs as your bones and your photos tumble into the furnace. He then turns and walks to his car. The Minister's Demon gets on the hood and gives you a shrug and a salute.

THREE RATS

You don't know how long you are there staring at the smoke. And you are not the only one. Not by a lengthy stretch. Seventy-seven souls gaze down on the embers and ash that once housed their spirits; about as relaxing as sitting on a haansi chair and watching your house burn down. The wailing has died and for now even the bats and the crows are silent.

The whisper hits you between the ears as most whispers prefer to. Sena has his head to your shoulder and his voice to your lobe. 'I'm sorry for your loss.'

'Piss off.'

'They will get away with it. Because karma is bullshit.'

You feel a shiver run through you. His voice has a crackle to it as if it has been doubled at a higher pitch and channelled through warring frequencies.

'Am I in for another speech?'

'You know the problem with karma, boss?'

'Sena, I'm not in the mood.'

'The assumption is that everything is in its right place. So, we do nothing and let karma take its course. It's as pointless as saying "Inshallah".'

'Did they toast your corpse as well?'

'This apathy only serves the privileged. That cripple over there, he broke someone's legs last birth. Serves him right. Those peasants were wasteful in previous lives, so now they starve. That factory owner was once a Bodhisattva of generosity. So, he deserves all his houses. And, if I polish his Porsche, maybe his varam will rub off on me.

'Don't talk to me. I can't whisper to the living or lead anyone to my negatives or find my killer. You're just another big fucking talker.'

The scars and the bruises on Sena's body are beginning to look stylish, as if they've been touched up by a tattooist.

'Buddhism forces the poor to believe they belong where they are. The order is made to appear natural. It is self-serving bullshit that keeps the poor sick.'

'They burned my photos, Sena. What's left?'

You watch him float with an elegance he never had before. There is something else odd about him and it takes a moment to figure out and then you do. He no longer calls you 'sir'.

'All religion keeps the poor docile and the rich in their castles. Even American slaves knelt before a God that looked away from lynchings.'

'What's your point?' you say.

'My point, Mr Maali, is that karma does not balance things. Do good now, receive good later. Reap what you sow. Do unto others. All bullshit.'

'An atheist commie. How fascinating.'

'What else?'

'The Soviets, the Chinese and the Khmers were godless. Maybe not believing in gods gives you permission to become a demon.'

'As if believing in God or karma keeps you kind.'

'I agree, Comrade Pathirana. We are all savages, regardless of what we kneel before.'

'This is my point. The universe does have a self-correcting mechanism. But it's not God or Shiva or karma.'

He swoops down on the rumbling truck.

'It's us.'

. .

Sena expects you to follow, which, of course, you do. The truck has been hosed down but still smells of meat. Drivermalli is hunched over the wheel and has two ghouls perched on his shoulders hissing into his ear. He switches on the engine and Balal and Kottu climb into the cabin and lie on the tattered upholstery. They let out sighs and close their eyes and pat the fat around their bellies and the cash in their pockets.

'Ready to punish the men who killed us?'

'They burned everything. Everything I did. Everything I saw. All gone.'

'It takes more than photos to stop this train, putha. Leave your pity party, brother. Think of why you were Down There. What was your purpose? Was it just gambling and taking photos and squeezing cock?'

'I was there to witness. That is all. All those sunrises and all those massacres existed because I filmed them. Now, they are as dead as me.'

'You can whine. Or you can work.'

Seven float atop the truck, the two of you, the two students, one from Jaffna, one from Moratuwa, and three grotesques whom you try not to stare at, though of course you do. One has stab marks on its face and worms crawling out of them, one has four broken limbs and one has the grey pallor of a thing that's been drowned.

All are victims of the Bheeshanaya of the last twelve months, the purge that crushed the JVP. And all appear to be following Sena.

'What are you looking at, ponnaya?' says the thing with worms in its face.

You have had more homophobic abuse in the afterlife than you had in twenty years of playing with boys.

Sena stands up and delivers his talk.

'Comrades. Keep your blood cool. They tried to kill us but here we are. We are part of something vast. The force of our injustice will sweep this land. The In Between is the same as Down There. No different from The Light. There is no force that governs butterflies or Buddhas or what is fair. The universe is anarchy. It is trillions of atoms pushing at each other, trying to clear space.'

Rain falls on the curfew night, where nothing moves aside from winds and spirits and this lone truck. The crowded buildings and teeming roads are empty and silent. Sena looks up at the opening heavens and laughs.

'It seems the universe is with us, too! Are you ready, my warriors?'

The students nod, the grotesques nod and you give a shrug.

'While you were sleeping, Maali brother, we have been busy. Crow Uncle asks about you. Maybe it is time to wake up, no?'

'And do what?' you answer. 'Make more speeches?'

'It's not how we died. It is how we were made to live. Tonight we balance the scales.'

'I thought the scales never balance. Not even in the long run,' you say.

The warriors who were once Engineering students frown each time you open your mouth.

'Crow Uncle taught me tricks. But I have found a better teacher.'

'You have joined the Mahakali?'

'We ally with whoever can help us.'

What happens next happens quickly, like a gunshot or a heart attack. It is only when you are sitting in a mara tree much later that you are able to reassemble the moving parts. The students slink down on to the hood of the vehicle; the grotesques run alongside the truck and catch the eye of Drivermalli.

Sena places his face in front of yours. It is unclear if he is about to kiss your lips or devour your nose. 'Everyone's a pacifist. Everyone claims non-violence. Except when it comes to mosquitoes or rats or roaches. Or terrorists. Then it is kill or be killed. As if some lives mean more than others, which, of course, they do. Mosquitoes have killed half of humanity. I have no problem using DDT. And I will answer to any god that questions me.'

Sena dives into the driver's seat and snarls into Drivermalli's ear. His speech is vitriol peppered with swear words and it causes the driver's eyebrows to furrow. The truck gathers speed on the empty road that leads to Hotel Leo, where bodies are parked and secrets are buried. This vehicle will not make it that far.

The grotesques stand in the middle of the road and grasp the bones around their necks. They chant something that you cannot decipher, though you suspect it to be a mix of Pali, Sanskrit, Tamil and Demon.

Drivermalli squints at what he sees and then shakes his head. He utters words that pass from his ears to his mouth. 'I will answer to any god that questions me.'

He rubs his eyes and gapes at the grotesques poised in the middle of the street. He swerves, but of course the brakes don't catch, because an Engineering student is wrapped around the pads, so the truck goes hurtling into a bus stop next to an electric transformer, and you think you see people sitting there, but then the truck hits the transformer, which makes an almighty racket, the sound of the almighty being kicked in the shins.

Then it cracks and falls onto the bus stop and the queue standing beside it.

Drivermalli's face hits the steering wheel and the slumbering thugs fly to the ceiling and wake up coughing. Then something catches fire and explodes, and then there is screaming inside the truck. Sena and his band of angry men dance among the flames and chant curses and insults, while inside the truck three rats burn.

You look around and you see body parts that do not belong to the rats in the truck. How many were at the bus stop during a curfew? Three? Five? And then you see a mother and a child from the war zone, the old man with shrapnel and the dead dog. And they are telling you something that you can't hear. Asking for something that you can't give. And then the dog speaks and you are back in the present watching Sena and his wrecking crew do something even more perplexing.

Something curious for ones who have caused a crash and danced in its flames. They pull at the driver's door, which creaks open despite its hinges being crushed. Drivermalli crawls out of it whimpering, while the flames lick at his prosthetic limb. The spirits dab at them and chant at the burning truck. When Drivermalli passes out, the flames upon him are gone.

Crowds gather quickly wherever there is disaster, for the same reason you peek at your handkerchief after blowing your nose. People pour out of roadside shops, ignoring the curfew, and stand at a distance and shriek at the burning truck. A few bring out buckets of water to douse Drivermalli and pull him away from the carnage. There are people on the ground bleeding and screaming. Some do not move.

The ones who don't move have figures in white smocks standing behind them. Looks like Helpers arrive faster than ambulances in this town. The dead are led away with that look of confusion on their faces that you are more than familiar with.

Two figures crawl out of the burning truck and Sena and his ghouls pounce on them. Balal and Kottu are seized by the Engineering students and led towards the field next to the road. They do not struggle. They only stare at the burning truck and their smouldering bodies.

Sena and his gang chant as they lead the garbage men across the scraggy turf. There you see a standing figure with trains of hair and a chain of skulls. You are not close enough to see the faces etched in its skin, nor do you wish to be. Sena turns to you and motions for you to follow. His eyes are a mix of reds and blacks. The hum at the edge of the universe fills your already checked ears. You do not follow.

THE MASK

You do not know the name of the tree you are perched on, only that it has thick leaves that seem to catch winds and whispers. You watch smoke rising from distant rooftops and wonder if it is people or photographs that are burning out there.

Your name wafts in from the east and you try your best to ignore it. Everything you were and everything you did is now dust. No one will retrieve your negatives, except for the insects who will nibble on them until the blacks turn to white. Soon you will cease to hear your name and that will be the end of it all.

'Just take a minute, that's all I'm saying. This Malinda thing has got you panicked.'

'No. It's the Minister thing that has got me panicked, Kuga. I know you're not working for CNTR. That panics me.'

You leave the nameless tree and find yourself on the seventh-floor suite of Hotel Leo. The CNTR headquarters have been reduced to cardboard boxes and rubbish bags. The walls bear empty squares, the shapes of the photos that once hung there.

Kugarajah stands by the window smoking, while Elsa Mathangi loads a suitcase with files.

'And if they stop you in Customs?'

'I will say they are files from the Canadian Embassy where I work.'

'Can we discuss this?'

'Is there a van outside?'

Kuga parts the curtain and takes in the bird's-eye view of Slave Island. He breathes in a cigarette and shakes his head.

'It's still curfew. There are three vans down there. And one Jeep. I'm just saying. What if we go along for now? At least till we get the photos. If the government owes you favours, that's not a bad thing.'

'Use your head, men. The Minister will not give us the photos. And how do you think this will end? When the Tigers find out I'm fixing up Mahatiya with the government, they'll snap my neck.'

'The Tigers won't hurt you. I will guarantee that.'

'You will, will you?'

'I would never put you in danger.'

'Then why don't you volunteer to make deals with Colonel Mahatiya?'

Elsa surveys the mess as she zips the suitcase closed. You look at the boxes gagged with duct tape and wonder if they are bound for the Embassy or the incinerator.

'I'm no gambler like Malin. Maybe he's out there. Selling negatives to the Israelis.'

'He's gone.'

'You know who killed him?'

'Do you?'

'If he was killed for the photos, we're not safe.'

'OK, I'll book your flight. Canada or Norway or London?'

'I'll book my flight, thank you. You just need to get me out of here.'

You watch as the two lovers circle each other. Elsa wheels her bag to the door. You remember taking their cheque and then resigning. Though you still cannot recall why.

'You'll take care of the boxes?'

'They'll be sorted by morning. What does CNTR say?'

'I'm not calling anyone until I'm out of the country. I've told only you, who I don't even trust.'

'So that's it? You're giving up?'

'I came here to help the Tamil people. My corpse helps no one.'

Kuga walks up to her and raises his hand. Elsa flinches as he strokes the hair from her face.

'You never asked me to come with you.'

'Come with me, then.'

'I have one more job left to do.'

'That's why I don't ask.'

'What's your plan?'

'There's a busload of Germans leaving from the Hilton this afternoon. Can you get me on that bus?'

'They probably have eyes on both exits.'

'But not the service lift.'

Kuga smiles and picks up the phone. 'Tell the Minister you have a lead and you expect to have the negatives by Sunday night.'

'Can you get me on the bus?'

'Have I ever let you down?'

Elsa takes a deep breath, grabs the phone and does what she has to. On your last night she told you that moderates in this town either end up on planes or on concrete slabs.

The twenty-four-hour curfew has cleared the streets and freshened the air. It is cleansed of the stench of breath and the winds blow freely, bringing only the occasional whiff of smoke and dust. Opposite the hotel is a black Delica van with tinted windows, and in the back seat is ASP Ranchagoda, looking sleep-deprived and angry, his drooping eyes pointing to the entrance of the hotel.

A Jeep pulls up next to them and the windows go down. The pot-bellied man at the wheel wears tinted glasses and a surgical mask. Next to him sits Major Raja Udugampola, holding a walkie-talkie.

He looks at the cop, who sits up straighter and holds his face to attention. 'I want both entrances watched. Tell me when she leaves. Follow her and do not lose her. On my command, take her in. Is that clear?'

'Yes sir,' says Ranchagoda.

The Major puts the walkie-talkie to his mouth. 'There's been no movement. But we have eyes in place.' There is a crackle through the walkie-talkie. The Major furrows his brow and listens. 'There's always room at the Palace, sir.' There is more static and the Major eyeballs Ranchagoda. 'If not, we'll make room,' he says.

He does not reply to the final crackle. He puts down the walkie-talkie and speaks slowly to the ASP. 'You will bring me the girl, or the negatives. If you come back with both, I will pay you overtime. If you come back with one, I will be happy. If you come back with neither, I will not.'

'I have to do this alone, sir?'

'Scared? Aney, sweet. Don't worry, baba. My friend will sit with you and hold your hand.'

The man in the mask steps down from the Jeep and, even though his eyes and mouth aren't visible, it is clear that he is grinning.

The Palace

Major Raja Udugampola was a desk soldier; you saw him on the field only once. Akkaraipattu in '87. First, he ordered the earth movers to dig graves large enough to bury villages in, then he made soldiers dress the bodies in Tiger uniforms and pose them. Then, he made you and the Lake House hacks take the photos. Then, he confiscated your film.

None of the other photographers lasted more than two massacres. Most couldn't stomach the gore and many were averse to the high risk and average pay. But you were hooked.

Because, according to silly old you, the problem was that the folks in Colombo and London and Delhi didn't know the full extent of the horror. And maybe clever young you could produce the photo that turned policymakers against the war. Do for Lanka's civil war what naked napalm girl did for Vietnam.

The Major ordered all embedded journalists to call him if they ever got a whiff of where the Supremo was hiding. He shared a six-digit number and dangled a six-figure reward at anyone who led him to Prabhakaran, and this time the figure wasn't in rupees.

This was early in the war, when the army was stupid enough to believe that the Supremo could be caught and the war could be won. To Major Raja, journalists were more expendable than the bullets his bosses bought from the British. Which is another reason why so many quit.

The memory arrives in the form of cough. A whooping cough that hurts your brain and makes you roll forward. It singes the edges of nerves you no longer have and takes you back to a place that was both room and corridor. The walls were lined with filing cupboards and display cabinets. Uzi machine guns, Browning revolvers, dumdum bullets and boom-boom grenades, all preserved under glass in a military museum belonging to a major who never fired a weapon in anger or fear.

You stood at the desk looking down on the big man's balding head. You attempted to clear your throat and it brought forth a cough, one more violent than expected. Major Raja Udugampola, aka King Raja, looked at you in revulsion.

'Need to see a doctor?'

'No, sir. Just smoker's cough.'

'Is that what you call it? Not homo's cough?'

You stood still for a very long time while he watched you. There was a vacant seat before you, and he did not offer it, so you remained on your feet. On the table was a file bearing your name and photographs from frontlines taken by you – black and white, eighteen inches by five, matte finish. It was the shelling at VVT, where mortar landed flaming bodies onto coconut trees. It lies on a stack of photos and you remember each one. It was a season of monthly massacres. When both sides took turns slaughtering villages as payback for the last month's carnage. The Major only ordered photo shoots of Tiger atrocities. Kokilai, Kent Farm, Dollar Farm, Habarana, Anuradhapura. State-sponsored slaughter rarely required photography.

'This is good work. We have to document these things. What the Tigers do to innocent women, children and babies. Otherwise, Tamils will say these things didn't happen.'

A pause hangs between us.

'Such a shame about the other thing, no?'

'Sir?'

'Malinda Albert Kabalana,' he said, looking down at your file. 'We will not be renewing your contract after today.'

'My contract doesn't expire till 1990.'

'Correct. But your behaviour violates penal code 1883.'

'I'm not familiar with...'

'You're having unnatural relations with soldiers. This cannot be tolerated in wartime. Or any time. You have been warned before.'

Any relationship in the war zone is unnatural. Friendships are forced and brittle. Terror and boredom and loneliness can brew strange alliances and comfort can be found in a stranger's arms. You knew how to spot a beautiful boy who liked handsome men, whether they were in uniform or sarong or national dress. Whether they were smiling on a bus or arguing with their wives. You only played with the quiet ones, the village boys, the confused loners, the ones with no one to squeal to, or so you thought.

The Major stood up, did a slow march around the desk, and came to a halt by your side. He watched you for a while and you kept your eyes front. He rubbed his hand on your cheek and let his fingers brush your neck. 'Are you a sissy?'

'No, sir.'

His fingers brushed past the things around your neck, back when you wore more than three. The ankh, the Om, the dog tag, the capsules, the blood vial, all the way down to your belly and below to your crotch. He rubbed with the back of his fingers, not with force, though not all that lightly. As if looking for rolls of film hiding behind delicate flesh. His hands were calloused and his touch was tender. You stood at attention and remained stoically soft.

'You know it's not just one problem.'

You stood frozen as his fingers lingered on your shrivelling groin.

'There's a rumour that you are sick. Will I get AIDS from touching you?'

He pulled his hands from you, walked behind his desk, and picked his hat from a nail on the wall.

'Let's go.'

• •

The Jeep was driven by a young soldier with a prosthetic leg who did not look at you. Major Udugampola sat across from you, his knee trespassing the space between both of yours. If he leaned forward, he could smother your nuts with his kneecap. 'Don't fool yourself. We have better photographers than you,' he said. 'Fellows who are loyal. Fellows who stand by their people. Who don't have big mouths.'

'Sir, where are we going?'

'The boys call it Raja Gedara. Maybe after me. The King's House. Palace. Funny fellows. I did help with the design, of course. Shall I tell you why we're letting you go?'

'My contract says that I can freelance.'

'Only with permission. Did you obtain permission to take Robert Sudworth to see a Tiger Colonel?'

'I fix for the Associated Press. Robert Sudworth was one of theirs.'

'What about his bodyguard?'

'Bob Sudworth is paranoid.'

'A mercenary from the KM services. You took unauthorised combatants to the frontlines.'

'Their papers were stamped.'

'Not by me. You received permission to take the AP to the Vanni army camp. Not to take arms dealers for meals with the enemy.'

'Arms dealers?'

'I have met Sudworth once. In the Vanni, to be precise.'

'Is that so?'

'Is that so? You were there.'

'I was there?'

'After we attacked the camp. And took the Colonel prisoner. You don't remember that?'

'I was wounded in the gun fight. I don't remember anything.'

'What wounds?'

'I don't see what I'm not supposed to.'

'Aney. Sweet innocent boy.'

He leans forward and his knee brushes your crotch.

'It would help if I knew which side you were on.'

'Good journalists don't take sides.'

'True. What about homo photographers?'

'Sorry?'

'I have seven complaints of cadets being molested by you.'

You looked out of tinted windows at the emptying streets and wondered if a curfew had been announced. You cannot prove a thing, you thought. Only seven, you also thought. There was no molestation there, you both knew this. Molestation was what happened moments ago in the Major's office. You repeated the mantra that got you through thirty-four years.

'I am not a homosexual. I have a girlfriend.'

'Cut the crap. There have been complaints. If you travel with the army, you follow army rules. A young corporal in the Vijaya division's medical exam has come back HIV-positive. I can't have your types here.'

'I don't know any corporal.'

'Shut your mouth. I hired you. I will not bring sickness into the army.'

'I am not sick.'

'Is that why you use Red Cross condoms? I can see your cough. I can see the marks on your skin. This will not do.'

The Jeep took a right on Havelock Road and rumbled into a leafy avenue, where the houses were large, where the walls were high and where no rubbish collected on the street. The road turned twice and the driver cut into a bylane.

'There are more disturbing rumours, of course. Ones that I cannot prove. We are fighting a war on two fronts. I have no time to be chasing queers with cameras.'

At the foot of the cul-de-sac was an enormous gate, which opened by remote control and unveiled two guards with machine guns, both of whom saluted.

'The place is not fully operational yet. But it will be.'

The soldiers confiscated your camera and your wallet, but you were not afraid. Just like you were never afraid to step on to minefields and board boats with Tigers. You believed that no harm would reach you, because you were protected, not by angels, but by the laws of probability which stated that really bad things happened not very often, except when they did.

At first glance, it resembled a knock joint, a place you would take a middle-class conquest. You had a standard way of smuggling boys into knock joints and that was by making them wear the burka which you found on a clothesline of a burning village near Akkaraipattu. The only way to shuffle them past reception without receiving looks.

The building had its back to the gate and was being painted green by soldiers on scaffolding. The pathway led past parked trucks and abandoned wheelbarrows and came to an unfinished concrete staircase. There were three floors, each with seven rooms on them. The rooms all had large windows with tinted glazing, not a standard feature in a knock joint. You could see an identical set-up in each. Wooden table, bucket, rope, broomstick, PVC pipe, barbed wire, a tap in one wall and a plug point in the other.

'I brought you here to tell you only this.'

The Major walked behind you and unsheathed his baton. You had not noticed the things hanging from the soldier's belt until then.

'Many who are discharged from the army, who have seen what you have, get emboldened into becoming activists. Into switching sides. Not a good idea.'

You saw no ghosts in the empty rooms on the first floor, but you felt them. This was before you knew spirits existed. Having seen how easily a bullet can erase a soul on the battlefield, having watched breathing creatures turn to rotten meat before your eyes, you had no room for belief. That's until you visited the Palace and felt the tingling fear in the fetid air, and heard the whispers in the shadows.

The smell of shit and urine hit as soon as you climbed the stairs. The second floor rooms were identical to the first except they had people in them. One in each, all boys, all dark and all bruised. A few were seated and hugging their knees, some were staring back at the window and not seeing you pass.

'Those windows took half my budget,' said the Major tapping his baton on the side of his knee. 'They are sound-proof, one-way mirrors. Got them sent from Diego Garcia.'

The boy in the last cell looked out the window at you with his mouth open and eyes wide. It took you a moment to realise that he was screaming at the soundproof window. Diego

Garcia was a horseshoe isle south of Lanka, commandeered by the British after the Napoleonic Wars, who cleared it of two thousand natives and leased it to the US. By the '80s, it was a military base that exported more than just double glazing to Western allies in Asia.

'They are sending me trainers, to coach my interrogators. They even persuaded the government to give me more budget.'

The third floor was identical to the two below. Oblong rooms, tinted windows, minimal furniture, unbearable stench. But these rooms had more than one occupant.

In Room One, two men in masks were beating a boy with pipes. In Room Two, a boy was strapped to a bed and shrieking. In Room Three, two boys were hung upside down with bags on their heads. In Room Four, a man in a surgical mask and tinted glasses was leaning over a man in a chair.

'That is the Mask. That is who all the guests to the Palace meet first.'

In Room Five was a naked girl sobbing on her knees while a shirtless man circled her. Rooms Six and Seven had boys lying on the table and not moving.

Major Raja Udugampola grabbed you by the shoulders and pinned you to the far wall. Behind his shoulder was a window with bodies on tables.

'I am letting you go before you can embarrass me.'

You placed your hands on his crotch and rubbed. He slackened his grip and took a breath, then he pulled your hands off and pushed them to the wall.

'But if you do embarrass me, there are worse things that could happen to you than losing your job.'

He kissed you on the cheek, and then on the mouth. Then, he slapped you hard twice. Then he scratched his eyebrow, clenched his fist and punched you in the stomach. You felt the wind leave your gut and your eyes lose their sight as you braced for another blow, which did not arrive.

Then he let you go.

Chat with Dead Priest (1962)

You leave Galle Face Court and float back to the place you could never revisit. On many a dark night, long before the dark night took you, you used to wonder if you could go back there with a camera, sit on the mango tree behind the lane and take the shots that would win you a Pulitzer.

The Major didn't blindfold you, because he knew you would never return. You have no doubt that all twenty-one rooms of the Palace were fully occupied during the bheeshanaya of the past year. The slaughter of suspected anarchists was not as prolific as the Indonesian state butchering a million communists in '65, so no one bothered to count. Some say five thousand, some twenty thousand, some say a hundred thousand, some say not that much.

Besides, only Americans get Pulitzers. The Americans, whose CIA sponsored that Indonesian massacre, who have a naval base south of the Maldives, and have sent teams of interrogation trainers to this so-called Palace in this so-called paradise.

You never came back here, because you knew that no one left the Palace alive. You'd seen the corpses brought back and posed on slabs in police stations and army barracks. Slain 'suspects' useful for propaganda in the fight against insurgents, agitators, criminals and terrorists. Though most of them weren't. Occasionally you'd spot a journalist or a professor in a cell, a known face beaten out of recognition. And you'd take an extra shot and hide it in your box and clip the negative in your hiding place, a place where no one with a good set of ears would look.

From your perch on the mango tree, you see the lights flickering on the second floor and you hear the screeches and the whimpers and the rattle of electricity. The smell of bile floats with the breeze. The unwelcome stench of someone else's vomit, a rancid bouquet of force-fed food, and sweat scented with terror. More lights come on, followed by more screams. What could it be? Water to the nostrils, electricity to the groin, nails to the feet?

You never returned here, because you were scared of what you'd see and scared that you'd end up in a dungeon yourself. Now, after all the bad things have happened, you still can't make yourself float across the garden to where the flickering lights are.

'Come closer,' says the croak. 'You don't have to look if you don't want to.'

On the roof you see the shadow. It is large and shapeless and you see no eyes, not even red ones. Black fumes reach out from the roof, though there are no chimneys. They reach like tendrils that feed the black mass. You find yourself floating towards it, beckoned by the voice.

'It's all terribly, terribly wrong. I used to be a priest, you know.'

'Buddhist?' you ask. 'Or Catholic?'

'Does it matter? I have seen the world's dark heart. And I have not yet met my maker.'

'Why do you sit here?'

The creature takes shape and you see its black teeth and its black eyes and the outline of its crouching back.

'There is energy here. Come sit with me. There is no God to follow, no Devil to fear. Energy is all there is.'

'Do you live here?' you say, knowing this to be a less than accurate verb. You do not step on the roof.

'When I was a priest, non-believers would argue with me. Either God is willing to stop evil or he is not. Either God is able to stop evil or he is not.'

'I've heard this joke before.'

You suddenly miss Dr Ranee and wonder why you have not seen her in a while. Does she know you were with Sena, who just killed five civilians to punish a couple of rats? Is she drowning in more bewildered souls and unfilled forms and Ear Checks and arguments against The Light? Or has she dismissed you as yet another lost cause that began with decent intentions?

'Is there anything more horrific than this building upon whose roof we sit?' asks the Dead Priest.

'There are buildings like this where old men play with scared children in every room.'

'I have been to those rooms. I have fed on those screams.'

'You enjoy the screams?'

'Epicurus thought God was either impotent or malevolent. For if he is willing and able to stop evil, why doesn't he? But there is one possibility unexplored by the great Greek.' The shadow forms a large body and a larger head. The creature has the head of a beast or a misshapen Afro.

'That God is absent?'

'No.'

'That God is distracted?'

'Nehi! God is incompetent. He is willing to prevent evil. He is able to prevent it. But he's just badly organised.'

'You mean he navel-gazes like the rest of us.'

'I mean he's always late, and cannot prioritise.'

You feel a coldness that curdles the blood and scrambles the cells. It is something that has scared you forever that you've never been able to name.

'You feel it, do you not. Energy. That is all. The alpha and the omega. The universe cares not if it is positive or negative. Will you sit?'

You are emboldened by a wind that blows in from Mutwal, one that you can hop on if those tendrils reach for you. 'I was not tortured. I am not tormented. I might have been killed, but I'm not even sure of that. You cannot feed on me as you feed on those below.'

'Are you sure?'

The outline shifts and the thing no longer looks like a priest in a robe. It crouches like a hound and you see things hanging from its neck. 'I have watched you on that tree, Mr

Photographer. You know that there is no order to it. You have known it always.'

And, suddenly, the cold transforms into something familiar. Not something, perhaps more of an absence of thing, an emptiness that stretches to the horizon, a void that has known you forever. When your dear Dada departed, you ran through different scenarios every night while trying to sleep. Maybe he sensed you were queer, maybe he wished you were him, maybe you reminded him of her, maybe he hoped you'd be worth more. You relived every sullen word, every petulant glance, every slight, every put-down until your chest was hollow.

'You feel it, do you not? That is the energy.'

That hollowness and that loathing were not entirely unpleasant. Despair always begins as a snack that you nibble on when bored and then becomes a meal that you have thrice a day. 'Who do you blame for this mess? Was it the colonials who screwed us for centuries? Or the superpowers that are screwing us now?'

There is a terrible scream from down below and the roof spits out black shadows which the Dead Priest sucks up through what looks like a large straw.

'Who screwed us?'

'The Portuguese assumed the missionary position. The Dutch took us from behind. By the time the Brits came along, we were already on our knees, with our hands behind our backs and our mouths open.'

'I'm glad we were colonised by the British,' you say.

'Better than being slaughtered by the French,' says the Priest.

'Or enslaved by the Belgians.'

'Or gassed by the Germans.'

'Or raped by Spaniards.'

'Sometimes, when I think of the mess this country is in, I think it might be better to let the Chinese or the Japanese buy us over, let the Yanks and the Soviets own our thoughts or let the Indians take care of our Tamil problem, like we let the Dutch take care of our Portuguese problem.'

You are now sitting in the shadows and breathing in the void.

The Dead Priest sits across from you and whispers into the dark. 'This island has always been connected. We traded spices, gems and slaves with Rome and Persia long before history books were invented. Our people too have always been tradable. Look at today. The rich send their kids to London, the poor send their wives to Saudi. European paedophiles sun on our beaches, Canadian refugees fund our terror, Israeli tanks kill our young and Japanese salt poisons our food.'

It is then that you realise that there is somewhere you have to be and it is not here. And that, if you stay here any longer, you will forget why you arrived.

'The British sell us guns and the Americans train our torturers. What chance do any of us have?'

The Priest has grown muscular and crawls towards you as she speaks. Her voice doubles, trebles, and then multiplies. You recognise this walk and this growl. You pull away from the shadow and it blocks your exit.

'The Brits left us with an unpolished pearl and we have spent forty years filling this oyster with shit.'

It now has its face against yours and you are no longer sure if it is a he or a she. You feel the cold and the empty roaring through you. His eyes are made from a thousand other eyes and her voice is a thousand other voices. That hum at the edge of our hearing is not a she, or a him, or an it, or a they. It is cacophony.

'Here's the stinking truth, take a good whiff. We have fucked it up all by ourselves.'

The Mahakali's arms are around you and someone else's arms are around you and everyone's arms are around you.

'Say it once more. Louder and slower.'

Its teeth are as black as its eyes, and when its mouth grows wider you see its black tongue and the eyes peering from its throat.

'We have fucked it up. All by ourselves.'

FIFTH MOON

*Call unto Me, and I will answer thee,
and show thee great and mighty things,
which thou knowest not.*

Jeremiah 33:3

In Dreams, I Walk

Your descent into the maelstrom is interrupted by a woman with a clipboard. Around you the air has become flesh, around you are faces begging for death; the expressions flow from orgasm to pain. You are about to pass out when a sound jolts you.

'Excuse me! This one is on his fifth moon. He cannot be taken. Don't pretend you don't know this.'

Dr Ranee's voice is as shrill as an ice cream van and you respond to it like a toddler playing on a veranda. You leap from the grasp of the shadow and find yourself in the arms of the doctor, from fire back into frying pan.

'You cannot touch him till his seven moons. Those are rules. I know what you are doing and we are not scared. There are rules even you cannot break.'

You flee from the creature towards the mango tree. Dr Ranee pushes you towards a branch. You look back and the Mahakali has become shadow again. Serpents of shade and creepers of black reach from the building to feed the shape.

'Go piss on yourself.' It speaks like a dozen priests trying to harmonise at once. There is a cackle of laughter and then a hail of spit.

Dr Ranee scampers up the tree and drags you onto a wind and you are back to gliding over rooftops.

'I will come with force and drive you from this place.' Dr Ranee delivers her parting yelp as the wind takes you both. You wonder if she was this brazen with the LTTE. You wonder if they warned her before they struck her down.

'Your fifth moon, Malinda. Day after tomorrow, there is nothing I can do for you.'

'Why does my head hurt?'

'They will file you under "lost" and you will end up in that thing's gut. You don't have a head. The pain is your stupidity trying to escape.'

'I didn't know it was the Mahakali.'

'Yes, you did. This place is crawling with hell-beings. They feed off this torture. You know that Sena is working for it. Why do you think he is interested in you?'

'He said he'd teach me to whisper. He will if I join him.'

The wind pulls you higher than usual. The rooftops and the treetops inch away and your nausea succumbs to euphoria. You rise to the earth's ceiling and the city becomes a postcard. The air is cooler and fresher and the wind blows in from all sides. From this height, Colombo does not look like a mess. It sleeps in shadows decorated with trees and lights. Even the Beira Lake looks mildly picturesque.

'I can help you whisper.'

'You can?'

'I only offer it to souls who have committed to The Light. You're making me bend rules. I hate bending rules.'

'Thank you for getting me out of there.'

'I don't do it for thanks.'

You arrive at the edge of a cloud and your astonishment must appear comical, for she takes a break from scolding you to allow herself a chuckle.

You have flown over clouds in 747s before but this sight seems to have eluded you. It is the blue of a swimming pool, except the water is made of vapour and is warm and bottomless and you are buoyant enough to keep your head above it.

You look around at the sea of clouds that surround you, each with a turquoise pool rippling at its centre, invisible to the distant world Down There.

'This is where dreams are. I come here many times. To visit him and my girls.'

'Him? You mean God?'

She laughs. 'No, child. My husband. The father of my babies.'

'The professor?'

'He supported me though he didn't agree with me. He stopped all politics after I died. He's Down There. Looking after my girls. He's a lovely father. And I visit him in dreams and tell him whenever I can.'

You cannot draw your gaze away from the cloudy blue.

'We can visit people in dreams?'

'As long as you don't get lost,' she says.

'I can visit anyone?'

'As long as the sleeper grants permission.'

'And how do we...'

'Just hold my hand. Think of the person. And...'

She pulls you down and you plunge into a pool made of cloud.

..

You are in a bedroom that you recognise from the posters on the wall and from the smell of sadness, which you realise was lavender all along, and you are unsure how you missed that. Jaki is snoring. She wears a Joy Division T-shirt that comes down to her knees and has her arms sprawled out like a martyred Christ.

'Match her breath.' Dr Ranee's voice is in your ears, though you cannot see her in this gloomy room. You do as she says, even though it is a ludicrous request to put to one without lungs. You inhale and exhale to the rhythms of Jaki's nostrils. You get images of sloth bears, of strawberry fields, of coral gardens. And then it stops.

Jaki wakes and stumbles to the toilet you shared with her for seven monsoons. She is not quite sleepwalking but not quite awake. You hear the flush and then she goes through the wrong door and accidentally on purpose falls back asleep on your old bed. She hugs the pillows and breathes in the sheets.

The room is as you left it, empty and neat. She falls back into a rhythm of snores and you lie next to her.

You hear laughter and see a maze of strawberry bushes and you see DD chasing Jaki and you recognise the hotel and the garden from Nuwara Eliya. You are chasing them both with a camera and everyone falls in a heap at the centre of the maze. You are clicking them rolling on the floor and DD says pay attention to Jaki, stop ignoring Jaki, and you say you are not and then you realise that you came to speak to her and have not done so yet.

'Jaki, my lovely. Jaki, my sweet. Everything you need is hidden...'

'Do not be literal, men. It will be forgotten.' Dr Ranee's voice is back in your ear. 'Speak indirectly. In pictures, not words.'

You shared a bed with Jaki for a whole month before she noticed you missing in the morning. After a while she stopped trying to kiss you, and after a while you stopped hugging back. You never had the talk and she never asked, and after a while your excuses got flimsier. Then, you moved into the spare room, and then, things were easier.

Jaki is on a beach in Unawatuna watching you give DD a massage. DD glares at you. 'Go massage Jaki. Or she'll put salt in my ice cream again.'

Whose dream is this, you wonder. Are you my DD or a DD that Jaki dreamed up? And why are the freaks on this beach staring at me?

'People in dreams are never who they seem,' says Dr Ranee. 'Especially people in other people's dreams.'

You give Jaki a massage and whisper in her ear.

Dr Ranee reminds you. 'Pictures are good. Words are not. Sing a song, if you like.'

You wonder who is whispering in Dr Ranee's ears and who is whispering in their ears and how much of our thoughts are other people's whispers.

'The King and Queen. Find the King and Queen. Who no one listens to. You know where they are.'

You are in a bedroom again, and from the smell and the mess you know whose it is.

'I can't be queer. Look how messy I am. Queers are neat.'

'Don't use that word, kolla. Makes you sound stupid,' You are both unclothed and under the sheets and he has his back to you and you are breathing in his hair and your hands travel his skin. 'I am not a queer, you are not a faggot, we are not ponnayas. We are beautiful men who like handsome boys.'

'Have you told Jaki?' he asks.

'I will,' you say.

'I hate this damn country. All we talk about is other people.'

'What would you rather talk about?'

'Hong Kong.'

First, it was Hong Kong. Then it was Tokyo. When he became more comfortable with being a boy who liked beautiful men, it became San Francisco.

You are in Yala and Jaki is snoring in a tent with two other girls, and you and DD are hiding in the treehouse being naughty.

'Colombo is oblivious about what happens up north. You know why?'

'Because people are OK if bad things happen to people who aren't them.'

You nibble his earlobe and grunt. 'Help Jaki find the King and Queen.' You convinced him that he'd be happier accepting who he was, even if he had to stay in the closet. You convinced him to move from corporate to environmental law. When you came back from Mannar with your film confiscated, your pay docked, and a twisted ankle, he gave you a sports massage and said, 'One day, you'll feel nostalgia for today. You'll look back on this shitty day and think those were the good times.'

He wasn't often right, but he got that spot on. You are back in the pool and others are swimming. Dr Ranee is in an embrace with a tall man with silver hair.

'The dreams are ending. Have you said all you need to?'

You realise you have not said a word and you dive back in. This time, the pool deepens and swirls and you are swept up in a river of photographs. You land on the banks where bodies lie, some asleep, some being sniffed at by cats. You crawl to a red carpet leading to a marquee where a woman sits on a throne and people in funny outfits sit on stools while a band plays Jim Reeves.

The court is covered in frescoes, done in the style of the cave paintings of Sigiriya. But these are not of topless women, not famous frescoes of concubines posing al fresco. These are of journalists with their hands tied, activists with their shirts torn, newsreaders with broken noses. Famous men in custody, whose bodies were never found. Photos you took for the King, who kept the negatives and never paid you for them. Major Raja Udugampola shared a misconception with your other employees, Elsa the Queen and Jonny the Ace. None of them knew that your Nikon used rolls of thirty-six and not thirty-two. Which meant you got to keep four photos from each reel, and cut out the negatives, and they never knew otherwise.

The woman on the throne is Lakshmi Almeida Kabalana, your dear Amma. She has something on her lap which looks like a fluffy animal but is actually a teapot. You look around at the members of the court. Your eyes rest on three European tourists in Hawaiian shirts. You look down at your jacket only to find it transformed into a robe of colours. In your hand is a jester's staff.

'Most people in dreams are ghosts like you,' says Dr Ranee's voice right on cue. 'Some get lost in the dreamscape, weaving in and out of other people's sleep.'

When you approach the throne your mother bursts into sobs, like she never did when you were alive. The thing on her lap is neither fluffy nor an animal nor a teapot. It is a bundle of letters.

'I thought you threw them.'

'I did.' She sniffs some snot into an embroidered hanky. The regal outfit suits her, much better than the housecoats she used to mope about in. 'I didn't even open them.'

'You didn't think I needed them?'

'He knew you needed him. But he left. And then God took him. And then God took you.'

'I never met him. I lied to you. All I got were three phone calls and a letter.'

You had told her falsely that you met Bertie Kabalana, his second wife Dalreen, their two girls who were your pen pals, and had Thanksgiving dinner in Missouri. That he told you how tiresome she was and you all had a cackle about it over turkey and cranberry sauce. It was a story crafted to wound. Because telling her that he died while you were on a plane and his grieving family had no words for you would've set your mother on another holy rant about God's will.

Your father had apparently written to you twice a year since he left in '73. You found one in 1984, under some teabags in the bin. Your mother later admitted that she was careless; she usually dumped them at the travel agency she worked at.

'All I got was you' – the bundle of letters has vanished from her lap – 'to remind me of that selfish bastard.' Your mother never swore, except when speaking of your father.

'Was that my fault?'

'*He* left. Not me.' There are rumbles in the court as the Queen raises her voice. 'You weren't easy, but I never gave up. He can't get to leave and then play the hero with a birthday card.'

You sat by the phone on the fourteenth, fifteenth and sixteenth birthdays waiting for a call from Missouri. On your seventeenth, you were too busy being kissed by a hunk in a suit to care.

'He doesn't get to see you turning into him,' shouts your mother. And then the court erupts and you hear a whisper.

'Tell the truth Amma. You had a baby to save a marriage. Everything else is myth.'

'Dreams are ending. Return to surface.' And then you are at the edge of the cloud pool and Dr Ranee is saying goodbye to two teenage girls and a silver-haired man. There is a song in the air and it is sung by Jim Reeves and it is called 'It's Now or Never'. And you know that it is a song best sung by the King and Queen and then you are in the bedroom you began in. 'Always good manners to leave the dreamscape the same way that you enter. It is an act of respect for those who follow and for those who dream.'

Jaki wakes up from your bed in a flash. She is humming 'It's Now or Never' but not the Elvis version or the Jim Reeves version but the Freddie Mercury version used on the B-side of that famous song and then she is pulling a box from under your bed and pulling out the records and then she pulls out *His Hand in Mine* by Elvis and *Hot Space* by Queen, both of which are terrible albums by great artists.

She opens the gatefold sleeves and finds a note scribbled in your handwriting and confetti falls in large dark squares. The negatives rain into her lap, black with sharp edges, some featuring ghostly white figures striking strange poses. You give her a hug that she does not feel and you whisper one last command in her ear. Jakiyo. I am sorry for everything. Please make a thousand copies and paste them all over Colombo.

What yakas Want

Dr Ranee hovers at the edge of the dreamscape. She ties her hair in a bun and tries to hide her glistening eyes. You watch the spirits flit in and out of other people's slumber. They are of every shape, size and eye colour.

'Happy now? Whispering all done? Let's go to the River of Births. It is still before your seventh moon.'

'I have two more moons.'

'You have one and a half.'

'I can't. Not yet. Jaki needs to find Viran. I need to find my killer. I need to keep my friends away from the monsters.'

'There are always things to do. Most are pointless.'

'Jaki heard me, I think.'

'Are you sure you were killed?'

'The Crow Man said so. So did your ear readers.'

'Yes, but are *you* sure?'

'If I knew, I'd tell you.'

'The Crow Man is a crook. The pretas aren't always right.'

'Clearly. They said I have killed others.'

'*May* have killed. That's what they said.'

'Is the Mahakali the biggest demon of them all? Does the Mahakali have a boss?'

The good doctor shakes her head and shakes her head and shakes her head some more. 'Do you know nothing of the country that has fed and clothed you?'

Whatever Dr Ranee is these days, she's also a teacher without a classroom. Such beings are easily distracted into giving lessons. 'There isn't one Satan that we have to destroy. There are hundreds of devils and thousands of yakas roaming every road and every street.'

She is right. It is not Good vs Evil out here. It is varying degrees of bad, squabbling with conglomerates of the wicked.

'For every bloody ill in this country there is a yaka.' She says the Black Prince causes miscarriages and delivers menstrual cramps. The Mohini seduces lone drivers at night, the Riri yaka spreads cancers. The monk with the trident is technically a ghost but his rage has turned him into a ghoul.

'Ghost, ghoul, preta, devil, yaka, demon. Did I get the hierarchy right?'

'There is no hierarchy to this chaos, child. Even pretas are up to no good.'

She says that pretas come in many shades. Mala pretas steal flavour from your food, gevala pretas take the solid from your shit, most of them are adept at reading ears and appetites.

It grows tiresome to listen to, but at least she is not revisiting the subject of your dwindling moons.

She drones on about all the demons swirling about this In Between. 'I have lost more souls to yakas than I can count.'

'And what do yakas want?'

She says yakas are obsessed with pleasures of the flesh. When food goes bad, it is because yakas devour the nutrients. When sex loses passion, it is because yakas steal the pleasure. They stand around watching the living, and the foolish invite them in.

'Yakas can do a great many things, except enter The Light or be born human,' says the good doctor. 'They can cause mischief, do harm, spread wickedness. But only if you invite them. And never before seven moons. Not even the Mahakali can touch you, unless you let them.'

She says the Naga yakas have beautiful faces and cobra heads and cannot forget about 1983. She says the Kota yaka rides a cat, wears pearls and carries a battle-axe. The Bahirava yaka is born of the screams of Sita and only rises when the gods fight or when the sun bleeds.

'But you are right. The Mahakali is the most fearsome of them all. I cannot protect you from it after your seventh moon.'

'I just need one more moon to get my photos out.'

Enough now. Come. Meddling with things Down There will help neither you nor them.'

'Sena says...'

'If you're going to quote Sena, then go. Don't waste my time. You have seen what The Mahakali can do.'

Dr Ranee's eyes are mostly white but you do spot a few specks of yellow and green.

'You have two more sunsets. Please avoid all things with black eyes.'

'Sena's eyes aren't black.'

'Not yet. No one is born a devil.'

'That can't be true.'

She says that yakas are made, not born, and each has a story that they no longer tell. The Cannibal Uncle was a Pettah bomb blast victim. The Feral Child was made to kill his uncles for the Tigers. The Sea Demon had been ragged to death at university. The Atheist Ghoul was a provincial councillor carved up by the JVP. Black Sari Lady lost five children to the war.

She says yakas are terrible gamblers and, like most casino rats, end up in sewers of debt, which they pay off by running errands. 'Your Sena is in debt to the Mahakali. Demons get ghosts to deliver them souls. It's not that complicated.'

She stops talking and shakes her head. She has fired all her arrows and none have hit their mark. She tears a page from her clipboard and crumples it.

'Thanks for helping me. Again. I promise, Dr Ranee. I will come to your Light before my seventh moon.'

'You won't.'

'Where do I come?'

'The River of Births. Take the weakest wind from the Beira. Follow the canals to the three kumbuk trees.'

'I promise.'

'Two promises are worth less than one.'

'I loved a boy who said things like that.'

'Did you keep the promises?'

'Not a single one.'

'Was he angry?'

'I never noticed.'

'Did he hurt you?'

You look through your camera and see no answers. You scratch your head and look down at your one sandal.

'I'm sure I deserved it. Goodbye, doctor.'

There is a wind blowing in from the ocean and you hop its footboard.

'I have a promise to keep.'

She looks up as the wind takes you. She looks sad and disappointed, but not surprised.

FujiKodak shop

The negatives are sealed in plastic casing and sellotaped to Queen's *Hot Space* and Elvis's *His Hand in Mine*. You knew these were the least likely to be pulled from the collection by anyone with a functioning set of ears. Of course, not everyone who uncovered snips of negatives taped to two bad albums would know what to do with them. So, you taped a note on the inner sleeve, just for clarity.

> PLEASE HANDLE CAREFULLY.
> IF FOUND, RETURN TO MALINDA ALMEIDA
> FLAT 4/11 GALLE FACE COURT, COLOMBO 2.
> IF MALINDA IS UNAVAILABLE,
> VISIT THE FUJIKODAK SHOP,
> 39 THIMBIRIGASYAYA ROAD
> AND HAND OVER TO VIRAN

Jaki clasps the records in her arms and runs over to DD's room.

'No, you stupid mutt,' you shout, but of course she does not hear.

DD is asleep in his Calvin Kleins. He has put on some flab around his waist, and has a morning chubby at the front of his pants, caused, you hope, by his dream of you.

'Aiyo, don't wake him!' you shout.

Jaki shakes her cousin by the shoulder until he splutters awake.

'Who... what?'

'Who the hell is Viran?' she asks.

.·.

The Delica van follows the Lancer at a not-so-subtle distance. Jaki eyes it while they circle the Thummulla roundabout. She does it thrice and the Jeep keeps pace. She goes back to Thimbirigasyaya and the Jeep follows. Then she does another U-turn.

'What's going on?' asks DD in the passenger seat. Ebony skin over square jaw, hair spiky and neat, even at this ungodly hour.

'They're not in uniform. Bad sign.' She keeps her eyes on the road and her tongue between her lips.

DD turns around for a look. 'It's just a van, Jaki. Let them pass.'

Jaki slows down to a chorus of horns in the traffic behind and the van does not overtake. Without warning or indication, Jaki cuts into the maze that is Longdon Place.

'They're not interested in passing us.'

'It's just a stupid van. Did you sleep enough? Shall I drive?'

'OK,' says Jaki as she floors the pedal and takes sharp turns through the labyrinth. Of the three of you, she was the most skilful driver and, therefore, the most reckless. She enters the bellybutton of Thimbirigasyaya and exits through Bambalapitiya's nostrils. Cars and trishaws change lane without indicating and flee from her path with whining horns.

The road is filling with fumes and fumers and brake lights that don't work. The van is nowhere in sight. As the car passes checkpoints, DD holds a cigarette to his mouth and does not light it. Which means he still has not technically lost the bet he made months ago.

Miraculously, they find a park in front of the FujiKodak shop. They see no signs of the Delica van.

The inside of the shop is filled with photographs of colourful Asians cracking impossible smiles. There is a cabinet of cameras and a display of film rolls. Stickers and posters in Fujifilm's green and white. Smaller stickers and posters in Kodak's yellow and red. Behind the counter, two women stand, one receiving film, the other dispensing envelopes. It is surprisingly organised and the customers appear to know how to queue. The line is three people deep and DD strides to the front like only an entitled brat can and demands, 'Where is Viran?'

The lady motions to the doorway behind her. Jaki and DD pass a studio filled with lights and screens to where a short boy in spectacles is hunched over a contact sheet.

'Viran?'

'Yes?'

'Malinda told us to come.'

The boy speaks to Jaki while his eyes dart to DD.

'He is gone?'

'It seems so.'

The boy shakes his head and looks at the floor.

'Abroad or arrested?'

DD delivers his line with a sigh.

'They say he's dead. But no one has seen a body.'

Viran's face falls. He cleans his glasses with his shirt.

'Then maybe he's just hiding?'

'You're friends with Maali?'

'I've known him for years. He developed his film here.'

Jaki puts the records on the table. The Queen album sleeve is in tatters and the King has sellotape around his mouth.

'It says you know what to do with these.'

'You came alone?'

'Just us.'

'No one following?'

'Of course not.'

'Are you sure?'

'There was a van behind us. But we lost it.'

'Then, let's hurry. You have to go to the Arts Centre Club. And talk to Mr Clarantha. This is what Maali wanted for the first set of copies.'

'First set?'

'He asked me to make two sets. One for Mr Clarantha. One for someone else.'

'Someone else?'

You met Viran down at the New Olympia cinema at a 10 a.m. screening of *Escape to Athena* starring Roger Moore,

Telly Savalas and Stefanie Powers, watched by straight couples fornicating and men fondling men. He was five feet two but had seven inches where it mattered. He also had an interest in old cameras and a job at FujiKodak and a dark room in Kelaniya with some serious kit that he'd inherited from his uncle. He was delicate and talented, smelled like soap and talcum, and was uninterested in politics. Until he saw your JVP photos for the Associated Press.

You told him that if a beautiful boy and a girl with big hair walked in one day carrying Elvis and Queen records and asked for him, he was to take the negatives home and develop them to eight-by-ten prints with low light and extra contrast.

. .

The second set of photos was for Tracy Kabalana, your father's youngest daughter, who once promised to safeguard your photos when she arrived with your father on one of his rare visits to the homeland. She would now be reaching voting age and you are unsure if she'd remember this, considering you literally broke her father's heart.

It began with a few AP photographers getting roughed up outside the Press Club, then Andy McGowan had his film confiscated, and then the journalist Richard de Zoysa was abducted and killed. You made the arrangements after a bender at the casino followed by a narrow shave with the army. You briefed Viran while he played with you by the rail tracks and reminded Clarantha of the promise made at your after-party. Uncle Clarantha was one of those rare souls who honoured drunken promises.

You catch a wind that leads you to Colpetty Junction. You float past the roof of a black Delica and land on the silver Lancer. In this city, as in most, wind moves faster than traffic. Jaki grips the wheel while DD quizzes her.

'Did he tell you about this?'

'At one of our after-parties with Uncle Clarantha. He told us what to do with his photos if he ever went into exile. You don't remember?'

'I was drunk. You were asleep.'

'So you do remember.'

The bar isn't open. The chairs are upside down on the tables and the cleaners are dragging their mops across the parquet. Clarantha is smoking a cigarette at the bar and reading the newspapers. He is a pudgy theatre queen who had three heart attacks in his forties. There was a rumour that he contracted the big disease with the little name. You never asked him, but too many late-night chats on mortality made you wonder.

'Hi Jaki. DD,' says Clarantha folding his paper. 'Sorry, we're closed.'

'Viran at FujiKodak told us to come.'

Clarantha pauses and puts the paper down. 'I don't want to hear that. Jesus. Where's Maali?'

'We haven't seen the body,' says DD. 'We don't know.'

'Then he maybe escaped,' says Uncle Clarantha.

'No,' says Jaki. She stares at him and shakes her head and watches his face fall.

There are two ghosts hovering around the jukebox, a vintage machine donated by a veteran Sri Lankan crooner who had brought it down from Las Vegas. There had been talk of selling it to buy the Arts Centre back from the trust that owned the theatre. The two ghosts hit the buttons with their fists and get only a few flickers of electricity.

'It's a dangerous time to be doing this,' says Clarantha.

'We understand,' says DD.

'I wanted to write plays that changed the world,' says Clarantha. 'Instead, I made musicals.'

'Musicals can change the world,' says Jaki.

'Shut up, Jaki,' says DD.

'I made a promise. I will keep it,' says Clarantha. 'How soon can that Viran fellow get the photos?'

'Tomorrow.'

'That's bullshit. How?'

'He has his own set-up, apparently. That's what he said.'

'He can deliver all the photos overnight?'

'That's what he said.'

'I only have twenty frames. Why the hurry? How many photos?'

'About fifty.'

'This is absurd! I'll need more hands. Does your office have helpers?'

'Let me ask.'

The ghosts look European and somewhat familiar. They are both wearing Hawaiian shirts and beach shorts. The chubbier one takes a run up and punches the jukebox. There is a vibration, the sound of a latch falling and then out comes Elvis's 'It's Now or Never'.

DD looks surprised, Jaki looks spooked, but Clarantha just shrugs. 'It does that all the time. We have a ghost called Iris.' He chuckles. 'Might be her.'

Jaki listens to the King croon and thinks thoughts that can only be of you.

'You're sure he hasn't fled the country?' asks Clarantha.

'Who knows?' says DD. 'Nothing surprises me about Maali.'

'OK,' says Jaki as she gets up, grabs her bag, and leaves the room.

• •

Jaki walks out of the Arts Centre Club, past the Lionel Wendt gallery and onto the street. Before entering her car, she scans the kerb for Delica vans and the pavement for men who are neither army nor police.

She starts up her Lancer and lets it slide down Guildford Crescent. Her car gathers speed and then takes the wrong turn. This means she is not heading home to Galle Face and you know exactly where this road leads and you begrudgingly approve.

When she parks on the street outside Hotel Leo, she checks for anyone following her, as do you. She then walks inside past the sleeping security guard and takes the lift to the sixth floor.

You overshoot your float by a floor and end up peeping into the window of the suite of the seventh. You see bare walls, empty boxes, an open door, and no Kuga or Elsa or framed photos taken by Nikon and developed by Viran. The room has not been ransacked like your flat in Galle Face Court, but the curtains have been ripped and tables overturned by someone in a not very good mood.

You float back to the Pegasus and watch Jaki at the blackjack table settling in for the night, ordering gins and smoking complimentary cigarettes that you wish you could taste. You try whispering to her, but neither of you are dreaming any more. You try and guess her thoughts as she plays the odds and counts the cards, like you taught her to, but badly.

You drift towards the poker table, where the Karachi Kid is playing high stakes with the Israelis. Young, pudgy, with a shaven head and baseball cap, the Karachi Kid was generous with his chips, which he used to bail you out with when you'd played too many hands. He kept a running tab and reminded you of it every time you sat at the table.

'Is there a camera in here?' he asks, looking at the ceiling. And then at the walls.

'Why would there be a camera?' says Yael Menachem. 'Unless you have one in that stupid hat.'

Yael Menachem is portly and loud; his business associate Golan Yoram is stocky and reserved. Also at the table are two Chinese men who pretend not to speak English. Some say they are relatives of Rohan Chang, the casino boss, there to spy on the high rollers. You played poker with them on your last night with breath, though you cannot recall if you won or lost.

'Let's go outside,' says the Karachi Kid. 'Smells of soy sauce here.'

The Chinese at the table are too busy out-betting each other to take offence. The Israelis and the Pakistani take their drinks out to the terrace. 'We saw the latest list,' says Golan Yoram, lighting his cigarette.

'And?'

'Just deposit a seventy percent advance and we can get everything.'

'Everything?'

'You want scud missile, we can get, brother.'

Menachem darts a look at the waiter, who places an ashtray on the table. He whispers his next question. 'Have you done business with Colonel Mahatiya before?'

'Anyone who has held a gun in this country has done business with me, my friend,' says the Karachi Kid, sipping his orange juice. 'You can take that to the bank.'

'Interesting,' says Menachem. 'We are in the movie business. This is all new to us.'

'You're being modest.'

'Yes. And I am never modest. And I don't like your prices. We will need eighty percent up front.'

'Man, I loved your Ninja film.'

'Which one? *Enter the Ninja* or *Ninja 3: The Domination*?'

'*Ninja USA*?'

'That's not mine,' said Menachem.

'Actually, I think it was *Enter the Ninja*. Superb, ah. Great action.'

'That film was a piece of shit. But it made money, right?'

'It did OK,' says Yoram.

The Karachi Kid hands over a sheet, which Yoram scrutinises before shaking his head. 'These prices cannot do. Where you get these prices?'

'These are market prices.'

'These are Hezbollah and Hamas prices. You will get broken Russian shit for these prices. You will get crap from Nicaragua for these prices. You raise your budget or no can do, sorry.'

'My client will need references, of course.'

'You can have this as my reference,' said Menachem holding up his middle finger.

'May I ask you. With all respect. Have you done business in this market before?'

'Of course.'

'Government?'

'Maybe.'

'Tigers?'

'Perhaps.'

'JVP?'

'Never.'

'What about our gambling buddy who went missing?'

'Who?'

'You know who.'

'He was a hippie and a fag. Hippies and fags die. Nothing to do with us.'

'Glad to hear,' says the Karachi Kid.

CHAT WITH DEAD SUICIDES (1986, 1979, 1712)

You float to the rooftop of Hotel Leo, where the night has grown old and the casino stays open. The night is restless with stalling cars and growling strays and gamblers at the bar telling themselves that tonight is the night they beat the house. You are ever the cliché – in death as in life. Hanging around the place you died is all ghosts ever do. It's as obvious as milling around a grave or loitering at your old home. And just as pointless.

Jaki is sitting at a table by herself, being served orange juice by the waiter who looked like an ox, the one you tasted on your last night with breath. She thinks she is alone and does not see you or the noose of suicides populating the roof and gazing at the moon.

The roof of Hotel Leo is peaceful at 3 a.m., except for the suicides hanging off its ledges. The first is a drag queen, a middle-aged man dressed in a Kandyan sari with bangles and chains and dollops of make-up.

'I did it because I was sad. That's what most of us are, you see. But I also did it because I was Buddhist. I thought reincarnation was cheaper than paying for a sex change.'

'Why haven't you gone into The Light?'

'I've been In Between all my life,' said the she who was a he. 'Maybe this is where I belong.'

The sari catwalks along the ledge, squats at the edge and gazes down on the spectacular fall into the car park or the rubbish dump, depending on the whims of the wind. The roof is crowded with spirits, mostly from not here, and mostly suicides, as evidenced from their yellow green eyes and incessant muttering.

You recognise a few from those moons ago when Sena and Dr Ranee were arguing about your worthless soul.

A girl in a tie with fetid skin and a hunched figure that looks like it has stewed in the ocean since the days of King Buvenekabahu are having a discussion nearby. You float through the dank air and eavesdrop. It is the thing you are most skilled at these days.

Like any gathering of crashing bores talking shop, these suicides are talking about suicide.

'Why is Sri Lanka number one in suicides?' asks the girl, peering through thick glasses. Are we that much more sadder or violent than the rest of the world?'

'Who the fuck cares?' says the hunched figure, as a lady in pigtails does her high jump over the edge.

'It's because we have just the right amount of education to understand that the world is cruel,' says the schoolgirl. 'And just enough corruption and inequality to feel powerless against it.'

'And we have easy access to weedkiller,' says the hunchback.

. .

You float around and do more eavesdropping. You meet five Tiger child soldiers who were brought to Colombo for rehabilitation and interrogation. They found a black datura plant in the prison grounds and made tea for five. They love the afterlife ('no one shouting orders at us'), and they jump off the ledge with the glee of toddlers.

It is difficult to doubt Sri Lanka's prolific suicide rate, judging by the rabble on this roof: the young, the old, the middle-aged, the male, the female, and all that is in between; the jilted lovers, the bankrupt farmers, the refugees of botched revolutions, the casualties of rape, the students who failed the grade, and more than a few closeted homos. They all float to the edge and take the plunge.

A closeted homo floats over to chat with you, but you are not interested in boys who are not beautiful, especially since you are no longer a handsome man. You catch the hunched figure glaring and you float over. 'I hanged myself at the Colombo port when the Portuguese burned my ship. I drowned myself in the Diyawanna Oya when I lost my land. If you have no money, life is not worth living. I would kill myself again if I could. Just to be done with all this.'

'Why don't any of these ones go to The Light?'

He looks affronted and hoiks a gob of betel over the ledge. You watch it disappear into the air.

'Why don't you?'

'I didn't kill myself.'

'You sure?'

'I tried when I was fourteen. Failed and never tried again.'

'Even suicide requires perseverance.'

'Apparently, The Light will cleanse you of your sins and let you have a fresh start.'

'Are you a Helper? If so, fuck off.'

You look at the stranger whose face you can barely see, whose story you can barely understand, and you ask him the question you have been unable to cough up since you died.

'If I helped people who wanted to die, am I a murderer?'

'How do you know they wanted to die?'

'I saw their suffering. I knew.'

'For most creatures that walk this earth, it is better never to have lived.'

'So, if I helped ease some pain, The Light should reward me, right?'

The hunched figure stares at you and laughs. 'If you want comfort, you came to the wrong place, fool.' And with that he hurls himself from the edge, roars with laughter and never hits the ground.

..

You are not surprised that Jaki is no longer sitting alone. You are surprised that she has been joined by a woman and that you recognise the woman as Radika Fernando, the newsreader. Their drinks escalate to gin and rum, and by the time the sun comes up, they are holding hands and smoking on the ledge.

Down six floors you see the Delica van parked and you see a man with a surgical mask berating a cop in the back. The Mask's slacks and shirts are ironed and creased unlike the cop's crumpled uniforms. The man evidently did not sleep in a van last night.

'What do you mean "gone"?'

'The CNTR offices are empty; there is no one there. Everything cleaned out,' says ASP Ranchagoda. The circles around his eyes make him look like a bullfrog.

'But we have had guards watching this place for two days. Have you searched the building?'

The walkie-talkie crackles and the Mask swears and holds it to his ear. There is a splutter of words and static. 'You fucking idiots. Elsa Mathangi boarded a flight to Toronto last night. She got there on a bus with German tourists.'

'How the hell?' says Ranchagoda. 'We didn't see her leave.'

'Solve that mystery in your own time. I need a solution now. The Major wants the negatives.'

ASP Ranchagoda looks up at the balcony and stares at the rising sun. Silhouetted against it, he sees two women smoking.

'I might have an idea.' says Ranchagoda.

The Mask follows his gaze and nods.

'We need ideas. What have you got?'

Ranchagoda opens the glove compartment to reveal a gunny sack and a small bottle.

'Not sure the Major or the Minister would approve your idea. But I might.'

You look up at the balcony, where Radika Fernando is leaning on the edge and playing with Jaki's hair. She kisses her goodbye and leaves, though the way she does both feels more like an au revoir.

You focus on the seventh floor, where you sat in that now empty seat and told Elsa you were done. You focus on the tinted windows of the casino where you played your last hand and cashed in all your chips.

POCKET JACKS

You and Jaki used to call the blackjack table the BJ table, just for kicks, even though neither you nor she had ever given or received one while seated there. If you just play the percentages at blackjack and count the run of cards, you can make a tidy gain over time. The Pegasus Casino only had two card packs in the shoe, which made it easier to count even for your tiny brain.

The casino is arranged in a semicircle around the buffet at the entrance, like a horseshoe that sucks up luck. The roulette wheels on either end of the 'U' are the noisiest, the black jack and baccarat tables are the most crowded, and the poker tables at the bend in the 'U' are the dimmest lit.

You had formulas for beating the house at cards, you had methods for surviving the bullets in war zones and you had techniques for smelling bullshit. At blackjack, you only had to beat the dealer, whose behaviour you could predict. In the war zone, you had to know who was dropping the bombs and where not to step. With bullshitters you have to figure what they need from you.

You got a run of picture cards and the dealer kept going bust and you saw that you had two hours before your first meeting and three before your second. You thought of the note on pink paper that you left on DD's badminton racket:

Come to the Leo Bar at 11 p.m. tonight.
I will have news. Love, Maal.

On your last tour up north, you told yourself and whoever was listening that, if you survived the shelling, you would leave. You would cash in your chips, pledge yourself to DD and follow him wherever he needed to go. The only thing worth less than two promises is three.

It felt good to be rid of Elsa and Kuga. They had given you a fat cheque on the promise of the negatives. A promise you had every intention of keeping. Soon, you would be rid of them all, or so you hoped.

You took your fat cheque to the blackjack dealer, and then you took your winnings and sidled up to your favourite table, right there at the turn of the horseshoe. The high-stakes poker where the rich kids, the pimps, the gunrunners and the economic hitmen came to steal from each other.

'You owe me money, my hippie friend,' said the Karachi Kid, sitting on a stack of forty large. He wore sunglasses and drank vodka, even though you were supposed to do neither at this table. He passed you a drink knowing you would refuse. 'But that is OK. Today, let us play.'

It was a six-hand game. Next to the Pakistani were two Chinese men – one short, one hefty – and next to them a Drunken Lankan Uncle, flanked by two Maldivian women. At the foot of the table was Yael Menachem, the clear chip leader with a stack that was sixty deep.

The two arms dealers at the table made no acknowledgement of knowing each other. Big China and Little China were mostly silent, except between hands, when they traded jokes in Mandarin and laughed without sharing the punchline. The Israeli was the most talkative at the table and the most skilled.

Everyone seemed to be stealing from the Drunken Lankan Uncle, who was holding bad hands and getting drawn into impossible showdowns. He went all in on a pair of Aces and watched the Karachi Kid make a straight. He stumbled off to the buffet, hoping the Maldivian ladies would follow, which they don't.

'Knew you had a straight draw,' said the Israeli to the Karachi Kid. 'You play tight when you're fishing and loose when you're bluffing.'

The Pakistani just stared ahead and chewed gum.

Things got loud when Little China raised on the flop and Yael Menachem threw in half his stack. When he saw that Little China raised with nothing and caught a full house, the Israeli threw a tantrum.

'Who are these people? Are these poker players? Who raises with Jack Three?'

He swore at the dealer and walked off with his chips. Big China and Little China followed him with steely eyes and shared another joke in Mandarin.

You and the Karachi Kid had been playing silent and aggressive. You got some hands, but everyone folded whenever you raised. You had under half an hour to Meeting One and decided to make the play.

The Karachi Kid knocked back his vodka and moved his entire stack into the middle. 'Let us see who pays whom tonight. These gooks have small dicks. They will fold. Even if they have an Ace.'

There was muttering in Mandarin and, this time no joke, they both glared at the Pakistani. One took the bait, the other folded. With everyone's stack in the middle, the action moved to you. In movies, a crowd would've gathered at the table, women of easy virtue would drape themselves on the highest roller, security guards will utter safe words into walkie-talkies and drunks will stumble by to 'ooh' and 'aah'. But this showdown took place in dim light with just the dealer and hell below as witness.

You never prayed when you gambled or when you stepped onto a battlefield or when you tasted flesh or when you told someone you loved them. You calculated the odds, laid out the options and then made the play.

The chances of being born with extra toes is one in a thousand, the odds that the pilot is drunk is one in 117, and according to some, the chances of getting away with murder are three to one.

You expected the worst. Guessed where the bombs may come from. Made the boy wear a condom. Asked the laws of probability to swing your way, which isn't the same as pleading to an invisible God. Or is it?

Jaki loved it when you did the maths. Even though she failed the subject twice in London, right after she told her mother about her stepfather.

You pretended she was there.

'Oh Jakio. Even a Two of Hearts will beat your Jacks. On a pot this high, I would fold.'

There were three Hearts on the table and two Jacks in your hand. You pushed your stack into the middle.

When the Nine of Clubs showed up at the river, no one was cheering. Karachi threw down a King high straight, Little China giggled and Big China showed everyone the Ace of Hearts and the finger. He said something in Mandarin that was unlikely to be 'Well played, mate', and looked at you.

You put your pocket Jacks next to the pair of Nines and Jack of Hearts and shrugged. An unnoticed full house will beat an obvious flush every day of the week and twice on Sundays. You wished you had a one-liner to leave the table with, but all you had was your Artful Dodger grin. The chips in the middle reached the crooks of both your elbows, as you hugged them and brought them home. Big China placed his hands on his scalp, and stared at the three Jacks and the two Nines.

'I guess tonight, Mr Karachi, I finally get to erase my tab.'

· ·

You took the Karachi Kid to the bar, where he told you his name was Donald Duck and that he ran a construction company. You asked him how much you owed him and he pulled a notebook from his jeans. He had written you down as 'Pegasus Hippie' and you paid the amount on the page and let him keep the change. 'Drinks on me!'

You paid all three waiters and added a tip, and you paid the pit boss for the chip extension and the bottle you broke at the bar after a losing streak. You then found the strapping young bartender, who was built like an ox and had a face like one, and passed him the thousand you owed.

'I won something downstairs. You keep this.'

'No problem. Aiye, I had forgotten.' He spoke with a lisp, which was the only stereotypically queer thing about him.

'I haven't forgotten you. What time is your fag break? Haha.'

'Any time, aiye.'

'I have a meeting now. After that, shall we meet?'

'Why not?'

This would be the last, you told yourself. The final fag before you went cold turkey. You got change for the payphone and made two calls. The first to your beloved. The call he told the police he never received.

'Hallo.' DD sounded sleepy.

'You got my note?'

'Just finished badminton.'

'I put it on your racket.'

'OK.'

'So, you're coming?'

'Where?'

'Hotel Leo bar. At 11 p.m.?'

'Maali, I'm tired. I have early meetings.'

'This is important. I have big news.'

'Jesus, Maali. We don't talk for weeks. And now you want to party.'

'No party. I've missed you.'

'I'm tired, Maal. Let's talk tomorrow.'

Click.

You dialled again and it rang and rang until it went to the engaged tone. You didn't plan to make a second call, but your fingers dialled the number your Dada made you memorise when you were five, and you knew that it would be answered, despite the lateness of the hour.

'Yes?'

'Amma, it's Malinda.'

'What's happened?'

'Nothing. I think it's time we talked. I've been thinking about things. Shall I come for lunch?'

'I'm very busy, Malinda.'

'Dinner, then?'

'If you're coming to fight, I don't have the time.'

'No fight, Amma. Just need to talk. Dinner?'

'No, lunch is fine. I'll get Kamala to cook.'

She ended calls as she usually did, without goodbyes or warning, usually before you could say something cruel.

You felt two thick fingers pinching your bottom.

'Who you calling, nancy boy?'

Jonny Gilhooley wore slacks and a blazer; Bob Sudworth wore a T-shirt and shorts.

'Good to see you, sport,' said Bob.

There was a reason you couldn't remember meeting a foreigner on your last night at the Leo. Because, in actual fact, there were two.

. .

Neither were pleased when you said you wanted to quit. The bar had grown crowded, and you and Bob took turns going to the sixth floor terrace for smokes.

You wrapped the money in paper napkins and placed it before the bottle of cheap gin. 'That's the advance for the next job. I'm returning it.'

'Someone beat the slot machines today,' says Jonny with raised eyebrow. 'And what's your big plan, laddie?'

'Me and DD are moving to San Francisco. I'm done with this shithole.'

Jonny laughs.

'By all means, visit the Bay Area. But why take your wife?'

'Should I take you, Joniya?'

'My travelling days are done, laddie.'

'So, then go back to where you came from.'

'I'm saving this country from itself.'

'By selling weapons to Tigers?'

You look at Bob Sudworth when you say this and he looks down at his drink.

'You can talk. You work for CNTR. Guess who pays their bills?'

'I just quit. I've been told I'm good at quitting.'

'What happened on your last tour?'

'What happened is everyone pays me to be a fixer. And asks me to be a spy.'

'We feel shit about what happened,' says Bob.

'Who's "we"?'

Bob shook his head and went off for a smoke. Jonny looked around the bar of tired gamblers just to make sure that no one was interested in him or his politics. At the table by the bar, the pit boss put down a reserved sign, and sat and waited. His eye fell on you and he nodded.

'Bob works for the Associated Press. I work for the British High Commission. You work for CNTR. The Major works for Cyril. We live in the house that JR built.'

'You sell weapons to a government who sells them to terrorists to use on Indians. Now, you want to arm a splinter group. How do you think this all ends?'

'What happened out there, Maali?'

'The same thing that always happens. I realised who you are. And what all this is. And concluded that I am done.'

Bob came back from his cigarette and Jonny left for the toilet. The money stayed on the table.

'I understand. You've had enough. You gotta go, you go. I'll miss you, Maali.'

'No, you won't,' you said.

'Who else could get me interviews with Major Udugampola *and* Colonel Gopallaswarmy?'

'How many articles have you filed since we started, Bob? I haven't seen one.'

'There are seven scheduled. All are getting legal clearance.'

'I'm not getting you another interview with Mahatiya. I'm not taking photos of his bunker for you. If I'm caught, you think a red bandanna will save me?'

'I'm sorry you got caught in the shelling. No one planned for that. At least we got you out of there.'

'You left me to wave at your helicopter. I had to take the bus.'

'Which we paid for.'

'Bravo.'

'Look...'

'Forget the shelling. I'm just sick of photographing dead people.'

Bob took a deep breath and was about to impart some wisdom. Something that would have eased your soul and soothed his conscience. The malli at the bar looked at you and pointed to his watch. Jonny came in from the shitter and grabbed the money and did not offer to pay the bill.

'Fuck him, Bob,' he said. 'Let's go.'

And they did.

. .

It was your last assignment in Jaffna. And everyone assured you it would be safe and it proved to be anything but. After it was over, they sent you home in a bus. The thirteen-hour ride gave you plenty of time to think, but all you did was replay one scene on infinite loop.

It was an hour after the last shell had dropped and the air was still smoky and smelly. You stumbled through dust and you saw the wailing. You could not hear it, because your ears were abuzz with the low hum at the end of the world, the frequency that spirits swirled at, the white noise of a thousand screams. But, all around you, you saw the wailing. People had stopped running and were rooted to the spot and staring at the heavens and roaring. There was a woman holding a dead child, there was an old man peppered with shrapnel, and a stray dog shuddering beneath a broken palmyra. The celestial finger released the mute button and the screams were unleashed on your ears. There were no medics or aid workers or soldiers or freedom fighters or insurgents or separatists to help. There were only poor villagers and one poor fixer. When the woman holding the dead child saw you, she stopped screaming and stared deep in between your eyes and pointed to the things around your neck. The ankh with DD's blood vial, the chain with the Panchayudha, and the twine with Tiger cyanide capsules. You told yourself you took them from Major Udugampola's weapons stash, in case you ended up captured, and it didn't matter by whom. The government could set you up as a traitor; the LTTE, as a spy. You would swallow these before they could ask you things that you had no answers to. The capsules were meant to be out of sight, hidden behind the other things around your neck, but they were one of many things the shelling had dislodged. Her voice came out in gasps and she pointed at the pills around your neck and you looked at her dead boy slung like a gunny sack and you handed her two and you watched her stuff them between her lips and you walked away and you went to the shuddering man with wood sticking out of him and you forced two in his mouth and then you squatted by the dog that was braying and stroked its quivering body and placed two under its tongue and closed its jaws.

. .

On your final night you didn't plan on going to sleep. Jaki was doing her late show and you wanted to pick her up in the morning like you always did. To watch the sunrise and drown in coffee till you passed out. Only this time you would tell her nothing but the truth.

You and the bartender went to the sixth floor terrace and had a cigarette and he stroked your crotch while you told him how you won big for the first time in years. He kissed your neck and told you that in life you only needed to win big once to make all the losses disappear. He wore Y-fronts under his denims and you slipped your fingers between its folds and fondled his eager flesh.

You glanced at your watch and saw that it was 11.10 p.m. and that, if DD were coming, he would've come by now. And that, since this was the last time, you had better finish joyfully. But even as his tongue flicked at your flesh you felt your interest waning. Maybe this was a sign that your roving days were over. You pulled the boy up from his knees and zipped up and lit another Gold Leaf, and then from the shadows you saw a figure emerge. You recognise the stride, and know the gait well. The body of a swimmer, the glide of a dancer.

He held the pink paper on which you wrote your note. He saw the bartender scurry across the terrace and his head turned and, instead of coming to your arms and letting you tell him that you had quit everything and were coming with him, he charged towards the bartender and the moon peeped out from the clouds and you saw the look on his face.

SIXTH MOON

*We are what we pretend to be,
so we must be careful about
what we pretend to be.*

Kurt Vonnegut, *Mother Night*

The Pangolin

Your thoughts are interrupted by an insitent tug, as you catch your name floating on the air. It is a low murmur carried by wind, a groan from the lips of a forlorn lover. There were many reasons you put your best photos in boxes. To prevent them being stolen or destroyed or, worse, criticised. But now they are to be seen. And you are excited and terrified.

'You can't be gone, Maali. I won't believe it.'

A 'Closed' sign hangs from the Arts Centre door. Downstairs at the Lionel Wendt gallery, five men are stuffing eight-by-ten shots into cardboard frames. Four men, to be precise, the fifth is only looking at photos and shaking his head and uttering your name in vain. The men work silently and at speed. Viran checks a list in your handwriting, then passes the photo to Clarantha, who places it on the frame and gives it to the two helpers from DD's office. One hammers nails, while the other hangs it.

DD is sitting behind the framing desk and sifting through the piles of discards, the shots that didn't quite make it to your list. He is wearing a long-sleeved starched shirt, which means he spent the night at his father's. You outlawed those laundered shirts from his almirah.

He is looking at wildlife photographs from Yala and Wilpattu, where he was present at the taking. They are from the envelope marked 'The Perfect Ten', the only envelope out of the five not to contain ugliness.

The storks at sunset, the elephants at dawn, the leopard in the tree, the snake in the grass, the obligatory peacock shot. And then there were the dozen photos of the pangolin that wandered into your camp at sunrise when you were stroking

DD awake while Jaki snored. Pangolins are nocturnal creatures and curl into balls when confronted with a housefly but this guy was up past his bedtime and nibbling at the jackfruit that Jaki was supposed to have put away.

You have close-ups of this strange creature, an evolutionary hybrid that makes the duck-billed platypus look commonplace. A mammal with scales, with the tail of a monkey, the claws of a bear and the snout of an anteater. Part dinosaur, part house cat. If we must have an animal as a national symbol, why not a pangolin, something original that we can own. Like many Sri Lankans, pangolins have big tongues, thick hides and small brains. They pick on ants, rats and anything smaller than them. They hide in terror when faced with bullies and get up to mischief when the lights are out. They are hundreds of thousands of years old and are plodding towards extinction.

DD thumbs through shots of forests that humans are yet to defile, bathed in the thick rays of a tired sun. He blinks back tears at the one of him, you and Jaki at the buffalo lake, the staged portrait of the three of you on Ussangoda's red soil hill. And then there are the ones of just you and him, shirts off lying by the brook, smiling with your eyes, and striking ludicrous poses. DD cries without sound, face contorted, lips curled; he shivers into his palms. Viran and Clarantha look up and then look back down at their work.

He told you in Yala that he'd been accepted to the University of San Francisco and was thinking of going. His monthly song. He'd often talk of running away from here, saying Sri Lanka was a dangerous place to be young and Tamil, but for the first time he spoke of running towards something. 'In San Fran, we can be who we are. Not who we're forced to be.'

'No one's forcing anyone. I am who I am. So are you. You don't have to run away from home.'

'I'm never free here. I can get chucked in jail for nothing. Appa or no Appa. If I stay, I'll get married and join the firm and be someone else. I'm only here because of you.'

He told of a life of art and bagels and kissing on the streets and dancing in public and not having to hide and, as stars cast spotlights through trees, you almost believed him. A week later, you took a two-month assignment with Bob Sudworth in Jaffna, which you couldn't turn down, though that's exactly what DD did to the University of San Francisco.

It was the same silly dance. DD would tell you he'd got a gig and you'd be impressed. He'd ask you to go with him and you'd say no because here you are doing what no one else is and there you'd be nobody. He would say he is going anyway and you'd say go, will you, and he would not. And this would happen over and over again, until one day it didn't.

Your mind floods with photographs and echoes of DD saying you loved your Nikon more than him and you saying that maybe he was right.

· ·

Clarantha and Viran are placing cardboard frames onto hooks and putting up the best of your wildlife photos. As per your list, they have omitted your shots of DD and Jaki, of the wildflower monsoons of 1988. You and DD had sat under a jacaranda tree, kissed in the rain, and agreed to stay together for one more year. He would save Lanka's natural beauty and you would expose its man-made ugliness. Expose the war and hasten its end. Monsoons and full moons make all creatures stupid, especially silly boys in love.

DD thumbs through photos of military hardware. The ones that filled the envelopes titled 'The King'. Most of your best work for Raja Udugampola was never published.

Captured Tiger grenades, rocket launchers, rifles and boots packed into crates with Hebrew and Arabic stamps on them. Scared little boys in uniform huddling at the frontlines. The bodies at Valvettithurai piled onto a pyre, the mass cremation that made you stop eating pork because the smoky stench of roasting human wasn't dissimilar to chops on grills.

Viran delivered beautiful black-and-white prints of captured terrorists tied to logs, the wreckage of the helicopter of a moderate Tamil politician, the mangled hull of Air Lanka Flight 512 from Gatwick, taken before the bodies of the German, British, French and Japanese tourists were removed from the wreckage.

And then there was the last assignment for King Raja. That he had not seen you since 1987 was an untruth. Soldiers have no problem bending the truth; they do it to themselves all the time. He had called you three months ago to the Palace to photograph the JVP leader Rohana Wijeweera, alive and in custody. Sri Lanka's ugly Che Guevara had smiled with you and chatted with the guards. Minus the beard and the beret, he looked like a music teacher. Three days later, you were called back to photograph his mutilated corpse.

There were photos from snipped off negatives that King didn't know you had. Father Jerome Balthazar, Anglican priest and human rights activist from Mannar, bound and gagged and dead in custody, though the authorities claimed he had taken a boat to India. D. B. Pillai, Radio Ceylon journalist, shot in custody and dumped on the beach, for the crime of reporting accurate casualties in his weekly broadcast. The burning car filled with young Tamil corpses, taken for Major Raja Udugampola's private files, but kept for yours.

All these now hang from the walls of the Wendt like you always hoped they would. Your plan was to orchestrate this from exile; instead, you have staged it from beyond the grave. Bravo.

'Where are you going after this, putha?' Clarantha asks Viran. He is rubbing Viran's back and twinkling his eyes. Viran arches his spine and smiles and clips the group shot of the Kokkilai massacre survivors on a peg by the window.

'Where to go, Uncle?'

'I am flying to Bangkok with my wife tomorrow morning. You need to disappear, as well. All of you!' he says to the two helpers.

'Where do we go, sir?'

'Go home. Take a holiday. I will send your pay.'

DD holds up the photograph of cyanide capsules collected from the necks of captured Tigers. They are attached to chains of string and sit on a plate in the morgue like red beans on a bed of string hoppers. You remember grabbing a handful and stuffing them into your safari jacket, though at the time you weren't sure for what.

. .

The photos you took for CNTR are now framed and on walls. Almost all of them are up and you feel vindicated and nervous. The ones that feature the barbarism of India up north in '89, the cruelty of Tamils out east in '87 and the savagery of Sinhalese down south in '83. Even the most grotesque of images – and there are plenty – have something that prevents you from looking away. Viran has fiddled with the exposure and done his own cropping and you would not complain even if you could. His craft elevates your banal snapping into something quite unintended.

There is one last printed reel and, to your horror, you see the boys sticking them in frames. These were not meant for your exhibition. This was for private viewing only. Viran knows this, but that's the trouble with artists: they only hear what they want to. When DD picks up the uppermost prints, you sense what is to follow. You look around for other ghosts who may aid you in preventing this catastrophe. But those who have drifted in from the theatre pay as much attention to you as the young do the old. While DD thumbs through the photos, all you can do is brace for impact.

They are of different men, some clothed, some with their shirts off, and a few who wear nothing. If the ghost of Lionel Wendt were here, he would peek over DD's shoulder and nod his approval. You knew a few of them by name, the rest by nickname.

Lord Byron from Kotahena with long hair and oily face was picked up while jacking on a bus and snapped with shirt off in a public toilet.

Boy George at Viharamahadevi Park, photographed under a tree, wore make-up and hummed Amaradeva while receiving pleasure.

DD breathes hard because he recognises the looks in the faces of these boys. The wild-eyed, dishevelled post-coital comedown. The look he rarely let you see.

Abraham Lincoln, by railway tracks, tried to punch you and take your camera.

The bartender at Hotel Leo taken at dawn in a room on the fourth floor, rented by the hour.

DD recognises two of the models, even though their faces are masked by the only prop you carried in your satchel along with your condoms, playing cards, film and red bandanna: a mini Devil mask. The last two photographs that went into the Jack of Hearts collection were the only two you could identify by name. Viran the FujiKodak boy lying in your bed at Galle Face Court on the week that DD was in Geneva with Stanley. Devil mask placed between legs. Jonny Gilhooley with shirt off in a Jacuzzi, showing off his Chinese tattoos. Devil mask covering eyes.

DD storms over to Viran, pushes him to the wall and slaps him hard. DD's open palm cracks like a bullwhip and Viran's glasses go flying and his eyes fill with tears as four pink fingermarks appear on his cheek.

DD grabs him by the neck and everyone gasps and Viran's eyes fill with terror while DD's eyes turn black. He slaps him twice, pushes down on his Adam's apple and watches Viran gasp for breath. He raises his fist and then the black drains from DD's eyes and he drops the photographs and the boy and storms out. He still glides like a dancer even when angry.

You fill up with that feeling you had when Aunty Dalreen told you that Dada had died while you were shouting at him.

Clarantha's gaze falls on the bare torsos peeping out from fallen photographs. He picks up the scattered shots and gazes at them with longing and perhaps a tinge of envy. Rock Hudson, in Anuradhapura, picked up in a supermarket and buggered by a temple fence. Captain Marlon Brando who entered you in a Mullaitivu army camp. You snapped him and his modest member while he slept.

He looks at Viran and shakes his head slowly and disdainfully like only a closeted queen can. 'These are beautiful.'

'Those are not for exhibition. Those are for private viewing.'

'I'm sick and tired of private viewing. Let's put them up. Maali will understand.'

You do not follow DD to see if he is OK. In death, as in life. You listen to his footsteps on the gravel outside and then to the sound of Stanley's Nissan breaking the speed limit.

. .

'What about these ones? Are you sure these are on the list?' asks Clarantha holding up six pictures.

'Yes, they are. I've checked three times,' says Viran. His voice is muffled by the swelling on his cheek; his jaw is stiff from stifling yawns. It is half an hour to gallery opening and the last pictures are about to come up.

The two helpers put a handwritten sign at the entrance. Below is a badly photocopied shot of a leopard killing a peacock.

'LAW OF THE JUNGLE. PHOTOGRAPHY BY MA'

Clarantha has finished making his seven phone calls. Whenever he has a show opening, he calls seven of Colombo's biggest gossips and between them the word spreads to the hundreds who will crowd the gallery's doorway.

He holds up the six photos. Two have been enlarged to the point of blurriness, two have a tree obstructing the view and two are crystal clear.

The enlarged ones feature Minister Cyril at the '83 riots. The jungle ones show grainy pics of three men sitting around a wooden table in a small thatched hut. One of them in uniform, one in a crumpled suit, the other in a bloodstained shirt. The clear ones show dead journalists whom the government deny arresting. It is only when he hangs up the last one that Clarantha recognises the face from the photo.

'Maali, you stupid bloody fool.' He sighs.

You give the man a hug and whisper 'Thank you' in his ear. The gallery is filled with the finest shots you ever took. You have borne witness. You have done all you can. Soon everyone will see them. Soon everyone will know.

Clarantha holds Viran's left hand and squeezes his right buttock. 'Now, you go outstation and wait for two weeks. There will be a big fuss and better if we are not there to answer questions. You understand?'

Viran leans into Clarantha and plants a soft kiss on the old man's ear. He was a gifted photo developer and a shameless tart.

'Take me to Bangkok with you. Leave your wife.'

'Darling, I've been pondering that one for forty years.'

They leave through the front door, while you sit in the gallery, surrounded by your life's work, and wait. You gaze at walls decorated with shots of pangolins and pogroms. They say the truth will set you free, though in Sri Lanka the truth can land you in a cage. And you have no more use for truth or cages or killers or lovers with perfect skin. All you have left are your images of ghosts. That may well be enough.

CHAT WITH DEAD DOGS (1988)

There are still a few hours of darkness left before your show opens, though a couple of ghostly canines arrive at the entrance for a sneak preview. Both are well-fed paraya dogs and neither seem interested in your life's work. By the way light passes through them it is clear that both pooches are dead and lost. You take a photo of them that is framed by the entrance.

'Excuse me, sir. Do you know where the River of Births is?' asks the one with wolf ears.

You are startled. 'Sorry, didn't know you could talk.'

'We didn't know apes could hear,' says the one with the dangling breasts. 'So condescending,' she says to her companion.

You remember what Dr Ranee told you. 'Find the weakest wind along the canals. And it will take you to the river. Look for three kumbuk trees.'

'Thanks,' says the lady-dog. 'Can you be any vaguer?'

'Calm down, Binky,' says the wolf-dog.

'I told you not to call me that.'

'Sorry, I didn't know animals became ghosts,' you say.

The wolf-dog shakes his head and the lady-dog glares at you and gives you three sharp barks before leaving the gallery.

You hear her parting words. 'If I am ever reborn human, I will swallow my umbilical.'

The wolf-dog barks his approval. Outside the Lionel Wendt gallery is a nameless tree with peeling branches and on it sits a Dead Leopard. You know it is dead because you can see through it and because its eyes are white. It looks straight at you and shakes its head.

Its voice is elegant and gruff ,though its lips don't seem to move. 'I was caught in a trap laid by a conservationist to catch a poacher. The grief-stricken conservationist brought my body to the Colombo university and then tried to kill himself. I was astonished. For the first time I realised. Some humans actually have souls.'

The Dead Dogs bray with laughter and the Dead Leopard slinks away down the nameless tree.

CHAT WITH DEAD TOURISTS (1987)

The three that stumble down the stairs all wear Hawaiian shirts – one in red, one yellow, the other blue. Red and Blue you remember from the Arts Centre Club jukebox. The one in yellow is a middle-aged lady who wears the shortest shorts.

They carry backpacks and cameras and flutter around looking at your photos.

They all look European. The two from the jukebox are stocky and pink, the blue one is swarthy and built like a rugby forward. They make appreciative murmurs followed by grunts of disgust as they pass your photos from the frontlines, the best of your propaganda pics taken for King Raja and Jonny the Ace. Checkpoints, battlefields, bomb blasts. They stop at the wreckage of the Air Lanka Flight 512 from Gatwick and gasp together. Then they start chattering.

'Look! Look, it is Frieda. You see?'

'Rubbish!'

'Eh, look. Frieda. It is you.'

'That is not very funny to me, Leon.'

You float to the picture they scrutinise and hover over their heads. The photo shows the plane's tail separated from its fuselage and bodies strewn across the tarmac. You compare the frozen faces with the shimmering ones before you. That was back when King Raja paged you whenever there was an attack. You happened to be in Negombo that morning, waking next to a brown boy who looked like Glenn Medeiros. Which allowed you to be first on the scene and to take that photo before they cleared the bodies.

'These is your work?' asks the one in the yellow shirt. She has the sing-song lilt of a German and a ready smile.

You nod and shrug and the other two raise their eyebrows.

'We make plan to fly to Maldives at 7.00 a.m. Flight got delayed. Bomb was timed to explode in the air.' The ogre in the blue floral shirt is from the land of 'Liberté, egalité, fraternité'.

'So they boarded us foreigners first. Typical Air Lanka, late as bloody usual. Saves the lives of the locals who turned up late. Those lucky bastards got to relax in the terminal with the duty-free booze,' says the red-shirted one in fluent cockney. 'While us poor mugs, who showed up on time, got to sit on the tarmac for three hours, with a bomb.'

They all nod solemnly.

The twenty-one who perished in the Air Lanka bombing were mostly foreign nationals who took with them what was left of Lanka's tourist industry. No one claimed credit for the attack. All fingers pointed to the LTTE attempting to sabotage talks between the government and rival Tamil group. Though it could have been any of them trying to scapegoat the Tigers. Such mysteries will remain as long as all we have are the likes of Ranchagoda and Cassim to investigate.

'Where are the rest of you?'

'Who?'

'The rest of the twenty-one.'

'Most of these jokers went home with their corpses. Some pissed off to The Light. We decided to stay,' says the Brit.

'Why?'

'You know how much I pay for this holiday?' says the Frenchie. 'How much I save up? My wife go home with her corpse. I say bye-bye.'

'This island ist wunderbar,' says the German, perusing your wildlife photos. 'Such good value. So much to see!'

'How do you get around?' you ask. 'Your bodies never left the airport.'

'Who needs airports? Or bodies?' says the Geezer. 'We ride the monsoon, mate. We tour your country through dreams.'

'Sri Lanka, c'est magnifique,' says Monsieur.

That's where you'd seen them before. They were munching strawberries in Nuwara Eliya while you were chasing Jaki through the labyrinth. They were lying on Unawatuna beach while you massaged DD's shoulders. They were in DD's wet dream of Yala, tramping through the jungle without a guide.

You ask for a photo and they oblige with glee. Then they walk around the exhibition, shaking their heads, muttering.

'You have lovely country. Why you photographing this shit?' asks the Fräulein.

'How long do you plan touring other people's dreams?'

'Come on, mate. We only just got here,' says the Geezer.

'And people's dreams of places are much nicer than the actual places,' says the Fräulein. 'This is proven fact.'

'One of those Helper jokers reckoned that The Light returns after ninety moons. We got time,' says Cockney. You decide against telling them that the Air Lanka bomb was a thousand moons ago.

They stare with fascination at your pangolin photos but breeze past the ones featuring nubile men with blurry faces. They stall at the last exhibit, placed behind a pillar as per your request. 'I don't understand. Who is these?' says the Frenchman.

They are the six photos that Clarantha had wondered about. The pearls of your collection. All composed in the heat of battle, the sharp focus made up for the clumsy angles. Two show faces from the '83 riots, two show deaths in custody. And two show men, with no good reason to seek the other's company, entering and exiting a hut in the Vanni. The lens zooms through the mob to capture a Minister's bored expression. It softens around the postures of the lifeless priest and dead journo. It weaves through trees and window grills to spotlight documents on a table. The results may not be pretty, but they don't lie.

'Not your best work, mate,' says the Geezer in red. 'Hmm. This has no interest,' mutters the Monsieur in blue.

You notice more spirits drifting in from the stairwell, some even use the front entrance.

'Herr photographer,' says the Fräulein in yellow shirt. 'Are these the photos that got you killed?'

You look down at your camera. The Nikon is cracked and dented and stained with mud and blood. You hold it to your right eye and you try to remember.

SLAYING MONSTERS

The kanatte is unusually quiet that afternoon: no funeral processions, no snakes, no wandering streams of restless dead. The devils appear to be having siestas and even the winds are silent.

'Bloody hell. Where you been? How many times am I supposed to say your name?' Sena squats at the foot of the mara tree, sharpening twigs with his claws.

'Are those arrows?'

'No. Just things I use to stab if I need.'

'Will you?'

'You've been dead for six moons, no?' he asks.

'Haven't counted.'

'Have you remembered what you need to?'

'My photos are being exhibited. There's that.'

'Are you ready to be of service?'

'To whom?'

'Are you ready to do something useful?'

'What's the use of that?'

Sena laughs and rolls his head back and you notice how muscles ripple under his darkened skin. How his scars have turned to ink and how the patterns on his flesh are pleasing to look at. His teeth glint and his eyes shine in a mix of crimson and ebony. The laughter echoes through the trees and bounces off the silent graves, which at that very moment stop being silent.

'You can hang out with the suicides at Hotel Leo and sulk. Or you can be useful.'

The earth mumbles like it's forgotten the words, a low hum in a key between B-flat and B, at a frequency you would struggle to whistle at. The mumble becomes a rumble and smoke rises from the field of graves and you see the faces and you see the eyes. It is hard to know how many sets there are. There could be twenty, or twenty times that. The ones you see come in reds and blacks and yellows and greens. Some have scars that glisten like Sena's and all of them hold spears of varying length. It appears your favourite Dead Anarchist has finally raised that army.

While you have been bouncing around the In Between, Sena Pathirana has been recruiting. His crew is mostly Dead JVP-ers, Dead Tigers and Dead Innocents Suspected of Being Either. You recognise the students from Moratuwa and Jaffna, whose bodies were buried in water and incinerated along with your own. They do not appear to recognise you.

There are Slain Journalists, Defiled Beauty Queens, Tortured Revolutionaries, Murdered Housewives. There are Colonial Slaves, Victims of Bombs, Beggars Killed by Drunks and Child Soldiers you recognise from rooftops.

As expected, the crew bicker and complain and curse, but when Sena gives an order they become silent and obedient. They fly about on winds with a precision and speed not unbecoming of soldiers. At Nugegoda the unit scatters to pre-assigned posts. You are made to shadow Sena as he floats to a boarding house in Kotahena.

'Where we going?'

It's a decrepit housing block four storeys high. You enter through a stairwell that smells of urine and glide through a door of damp plywood. A prosthetic leg is leaning against a wall next to a metal plate on the floor with rice and dhal that smells of fermented onions. Squirrels are nibbling the rice and scattering it across the floor. The room is smaller than the Palace cells. It contains a mattress, a tiny television and newspapers scattered on the floor and smells of sweat and tears.

On the mattress sits Drivermalli, in a sarong, his stump on a pillow and his good leg curled below. There is a bandage on his arm and burn marks on his shaved scalp. He drinks from a plastic bottle of Portello. The syrupy liquid has gone flat and has stained the plastic in blood purple. On the TV is a Bollywood dance with the actress dressed like a Hindu goddess with skulls around her neck. The only neat thing in this room is an army uniform draped over an ironing board. Below it is a khaki jacket with casings of TNT in the lining.

'Ade my squirrel princes!' shouts Drivermalli. 'Looks like the devils are back.'

One squirrel lifts its head, while the others continue their nibbling. They were evidently as used to Drivermalli's rantings as they were to his stale food.

'How many of you this time? Last time I counted three.'

Drivermalli looks up directly at where you and Sena are floating. Sena crawls onto the mattress and hisses in his ear. 'We are here for you. We will find you peace.'

Drivermalli's face contorts and he begins to shiver. 'Please get away from me.'

Sena pulls back to the window ledge and whispers to you. 'Best not to do too much talking. Can freak them out. Plus I can only do four whispers a day, so best not to waste them.'

There is a knock on the door and a low voice says, 'Thambi.'

'It's open,' calls out Drivermalli. His eyes dart from the TV to the window to the squirrels to the ironing board and the jacket with wires.

'I know you are here,' whispers Drivermalli, eyes darting around his room. 'And I want you to leave.'

A dark man with hairy muscles and a thick moustache walks into the room. He shoos the squirrels, who scamper through the grilled window. He drags a chair from next to the ironing board.

'Talking to yourself again, Thambi?' says Kugarajah.

· ·

Kugarajah has three photographs. One of a slaughtered village, one of bodies by the Malabe roadside and one of an assassinated provincial councillor. All taken by you.

'You are doing a great thing, Thambi. Cyril Wijeratne's death squad has killed thousands like this. You are being a true hero.'

'That's what they all say.'

'You're hearing voices again? Did you take those pills I gave you?'

'I can't see them,' says Drivermalli, grabbing his crutch and hoisting himself to his foot. 'But I hear them. They are here now. At least two of them.'

You flutter to the ceiling and Drivermalli raises his head and shudders in the breeze that you leave.

'How is your arm?'

'Sometimes I forget that it hurts. Portello helps. Those pills don't.'

'Is there anyone you want me to give a message to, Thambi? Family?'

'My family is ash.'

'Anything you want? Chinese food? Russian woman?'

'You'd give me a woman?'

'It's against the rules. But, for you, I will. What do you need?'

Drivermalli fastens his prosthetic leg on and looks down at the jacket. 'I want it to stop,' he says.

'What time is the meeting?' asks Kugarajah.

'Today evening.'

'Shall we run over the plan?'

..

Sena does not answer your questions, but insists that you follow him through deepest, darkest Dehiwela, past the zoo and the hospital to a leafy cul-de-sac where the houses have flower gardens and the kids play cricket on the empty road. He shadows a balding man who serves as both wicketkeeper and umpire.

'I have looked long and hard for this piece of shit. Watch the pain we will give him.'

'This cricket uncle?'

'He is the next monster we will slay.'

You look at the man delivering a tennis ball over his head and watch the youngster belt it into a coconut tree. The only thing monstrous about the man is his comb-over and his protruding belly. The family have a leisurely rice-and-curry lunch served by a smiling wife with hair down to her waist. Five spirits enter the house and disperse to different rooms. They check the light fittings, the roofing, the curries on the table, and then eavesdrop on the table banter.

The man changes his shirt and walks to the bus stop. He jokes with the boy at the cigarette kade and takes the number

134 bus into Colombo. His gives his seat to an old lady and does not attempt frottage with any of the schoolgirls who board at Kirulapone. Sena and his troops ride the roof of the bus and for a moment you are worried.

'This bus is full of people. If you crash it, all will die.'

Sena's army laughs.

'Calm down, hamu. We aren't doing any more car crashes. Too messy. We are more professional now.'

'Where are Balal and Kottu?'

'With the Mahakali.'

'Don't they get seven moons?'

'Helpers don't lift fingers for scum like that.'

'How many others died when you crashed their car?'

'Not that many. We are slaying monsters. No one wants innocents to die. But we sacrifice a few to save many. That's how wars work.'

'Now you sound like an army guy.'

'You sound like a child.'

The man gets down at Havelock Town and lights a cigarette as he walks. When he turns into that long lane of high-wall houses, you can guess where he is heading. He passes a lit Bristol to the guard at the entrance of the Palace and walks in through the back door. It has been two moons since your last visit. And the rooms are as quiet as the grave never is. No sounds this time of machinery or screaming. On the rooftop, you see shadow and wonder if the Mahakali resides there still, knowing there is no reason for it to ever leave.

Sena's army floats above the parapet and peers at the windows. The windows are large and open, unusual for prison cells. Through them you see sprawled figures, most of them emaciated, some motionless, some shuddering. It is hard to know what age they are, impossible to determine their race. Despite all speeches made to the contrary, the naked bodies of Sinhalese, Tamils, Muslims and Burghers are indistinguishable. We all look the same when held to the flame.

On a floor below, the mild-mannered father of three from Dehiwela has changed into a stained shirt. He puts on a surgical mask, picks up a PVC pipe and enters a cell where a boy hangs from a rope. He pushes his tinted glasses along the bridge of his nose, lifts the pipe and brings it down hard onto the hanging boy's feet. The boy has no voice left to scream with. He gasps and stops moving.

'That is the gaathakaya. The Mask. The regime's most prolific torturer. Hundreds have died at his fingers. Soon, he will die at ours.'

You watch the Mask walk up the stairs to a room where a shuddering boy has just awoken. You do not wish to see what happens next. Many in the platoon share your revulsion and float away from the wall. Sena leads everyone to the mango tree and speaks in a hiss. 'Comrades. This place distresses you. Some of you have died here. Some have friends trapped here. The Mahakali sits on the roof feeding off this rot.'

'Comrade Sena. I am only on my second moon. No one will tell me. Who is this Mahakali?' calls out a Ragged Student. 'Who is she?'

'The beast who walks,' says a Colonial Slave with a back full of lashes. 'The demon of a thousand faces.'

'The keeper of the skulls,' says a Tortured Revolutionary with a broken neck.

'The dark heart of Lanka,' says a Slain Checkpoint Guard with a hole in his head.

'Don't give me fairy-tale crap,' says Sena, his teeth reflecting the moonlight. 'The Mahakali is the In-Between's most powerful being. She soothes those who suffer, absorbs their pain. And the Mahakali has agreed to help us with our Mission. We call it Mission Kuveni, after the discarded mother of Lanka.'

There is the banging of spears on the parapet wall and grunts of approval amongst the platoon. There is a rumble in the shadows near the water tank on the top floor and all fall silent.

'Do not fear, comrades. I am going to present our terms. Whoever likes can join.'

The entire platoon exercises its right not to join and Sena floats to the top floor and drifts towards the rumble and the shadow. You turn to the Dead Child Soldier, not caring if your question is sniggered at.

'Thambi, I am only on my sixth moon. What is this Mission Kuveni?'

..

'It's a pakka plan, boss. Comrade Sena's plan.'

'Bullshit,' says a Slain Journalist. 'One of the Dead Tigers came up with the plot.'

'The plan has been there for about seventy moons, Uncle,' says the Child Soldier. 'It started when...'

The boy tells the story of a young Tiger cadre from VVT who arrived in Colombo on the back of a truck disguised in an SL army uniform. The boy had recently lost his parents and two brothers in an army air raid over Vavuniya. He took a job as a driver for Rohan Chang, manager of Pegasus Casino at Hotel Leo, who outsourced staff to Major Raja Udugampola for off-the-book errands.

The cadre's name was Kulaweerasingham Weerakumaran though his fake ID said Kularatne Weerakumara. It is easy to Sinhalise a Tamil name, by amputating the consonant at the end. None of that mattered, as his colleagues and bosses called him Drivermalli. The boy spoke accentless Sinhalese and worked long hours. His fake leg endeared him to all who tolerated his occasional pacifist rants. The undercover Tiger found himself in a garage full of government-owned vehicles.

'Even if the country is in debt, even if wars escalate, even if floods drown harvests and droughts kill seeds, even if GDP plummets and inflation gallops, there is always budget to provide each and every Minister with three luxury cars,' says the Slain Journalist.

Weerakumara drove vans for Hotel Leo, trucks for Major Udugampola and a flotilla of Mercedes Benz salons to transport Minister Cyril Wijeratne and his retinue.

Since the fatal car crash at the bus stand, he has been given sick leave to recover from second-degree burns and will report to work next week. He is to be relieved from driving duties and sent to work in car maintenance.

Sena comes down from the shadow of the Mahakali to murmurs from his crew. He bows to them all and says, 'It is done,' and there are cheers.

..

The Palace is eerie, even in the harsh afternoon sun. Black curtains mask the soundproof windows and the corridors fill with shadow and quiet. The smell is that of a public toilet, of human waste, industrial chemicals and slime. But it is the silence that chills, even on a hot balmy day.

Sena hand-picks the crew for today's mission and takes them to the mara tree outside the Palace for a final briefing. 'This is where I died. And when they killed me, all I remembered was the pain. And then I sat in this very tree. For how many moons, I do not know. It was the pain I felt of being bullied by school, by society, by the law, by my country. The pain of knowing there is always something stronger than you. And it is always against you.'

The spirit crew murmurs and wind blows across the branches.

'In wars, they send pawns to kill pawns. In this war, the pawns get to take out the bishops, the rooks and the king. Major Raja meets Minister Cyril today. Next meeting is in a few hours. The Mask will be present. It is perfect. No collateral victims. Just cops.'

'For once!' you exclaim and the ghouls turn their heads.

'If anyone has issues with our plan, they can fuck off. Because of bleeding hearts like Maali Almeida, this war will go on forever.'

'Nothing goes on forever. It's the one thing the Buddha got right,' you say to the Dead Child Soldier who is not listening.

'We don't need cowards and champagne socialists. We have Dead Tigers who can whisper in ears. We have JVP Martyrs who can speak in dreams. We have Dead Engineers who can channel electricity. Drivermalli has received the jacket. He will use it tomorrow.'

You think of dead lakes overflowing with corpses, of police stations where the rich lock up the poor, of palaces where those who follow orders torture those who refuse to. You think of distraught lovers, abandoned friends and absent parents. Of lapsed treaties and photographs that are seen and forgotten, regardless of the walls they hang on. How the world will go on without you and will forget you were even here. You think of the mother, the old man and the dog, of the things you did, or failed to do, for the ones you loved. You think about evil causes and about worthy ones. That the chances of violence ending violence are one in nothing, one in nada, one in squat.

You drift down to the Palace roof, avoiding the Mahakali's lair. Sena watches you go and carries on speechifying. You hear voices that you recognise from the floor below. You have not been on this floor before. Not during Major Raja's guided tours, nor on your visits after death. The walls look a little cleaner and the floor does not smell as dank. In the corridor is Detective Cassim, ASP Ranchagoda and the Mask, his glasses tinted brown and his mask a surgical blue. Detective Cassim has his palms on his forehead, rocks back and forth as if praying. But that is not what he is doing at all – in fact, the opposite. He is cursing.

'I tell you this is not legal!' snaps Cassim. 'I cannot witness this. It is against my religion to harm innocents.'

'Go to the mosque if you want to pray. This is definitely not the place for that. The Mask stares into the open window and takes off his glasses to clean them. His eyes are clear and sharp, as if he had a good night's sleep before his cricket match and family lunch.

Cassim storms down the corridor and almost walks through you.

'Let him go,' says ASP Ranchagoda. 'Let him write his report, then calm down, then tear it up. That's his usual scene.'

'He won't write any reports about this,' says the Mask, putting his glasses back on.

You peer into the room. There is a bed, a single lightbulb, some PVC pipes and ropes hanging from the ceiling. And, curled up like a squirrel on the floor, with a gunny sack barely fitting over her bushy curls, is not a Tiger separatist, a JVP Marxist, a Tamil moderate or a British gunrunner. It is your best friend, Jaki, the other great love of your life.

SEVENTH MOON

‘God's gift,' the warden said, 'His violence... God loves violence. You understand that, don't you?... Why else would there be so much of it? It's in us. It comes out of us. It is what we do more naturally than we breathe. There is no moral order at all. There is only this — can my violence conquer yours?'

Dennis Lehane, *Shutter Island*

'I will not have time to question her now,' says the Mask. 'You may have to use more sedation.'

You get up close and see that Jaki is breathing. Her chest rises slowly and falls quickly. Her breath carries the smell of sedation, like nail polish mixed with syrups. You scream at the walls and the men outside. You cry out to Whoever, who sends only silence and absence.

'I will question her after the meeting,' says the Mask. 'If she knows where the negatives are, we may release her. But stay out of sight.'

'Why?'

'Don't tell me she saw you?' asks the Mask.

'No,' says Ranchagoda. 'I grabbed her from behind. Was wearing sunglasses.'

'Sha! Master of Disguise! Let's hope you're telling the truth. If she has seen us, she cannot be released.'

Cassim has returned as swiftly as he left.

'This is Stanley Dharmendran's niece. The Minister will have our guts,' he hisses.

'We lost the Elsa woman,' says Ranchagoda. 'We need the negatives. This little girl knows where they are.'

'*You* lost the Elsa woman,' snarls Cassim. 'I had nothing to do with it.'

You plead in Ranchagoda's ears. 'Let her go. I will take you to the negatives. Please, please, please let her go.' He hears nothing.

The Mask walks up to Cassim and puts his hands on his shoulder. They are roughly the same height, but the Mask appears a head taller.

'There is no I, me or you, Detective Cassim. There is only we. You are part of the squad now.'

'Then I will go upstairs and type my resignation.'

The Mask squeezes his shoulder blades and Cassim hunches in pain.

'You will type what I tell you to type. Then you will stay here and make sure no one steps on this floor. Is that clear?'

'Yes, sir.'

'I have a meeting with the boss and the big boss. Ranchagoda, I need you there. Cassim, give her more juice if she stirs. And stay guard.'

They both light up cigarettes in the corridor. Ranchagoda looks back at his partner and shrugs.

Cassim slumps into a chair and stares through the window at the girl with the sack over her head. He rubs his shoulders and his sweaty neck. You whisper in his ear with everything you have.

'She is innocent. Please please release her. You don't agree with this, Detective Cassim. You never have. This is against your religion.'

He pauses for a moment, looks around, then puts his face in his hands and lets out a groan. It is loud enough to wake the dead, but Jaki does not stir. His colleagues watch him with amusement, and blow smoke in his direction.

You call out to Dr Ranee. To the angels of silence and absence. You ask them to take you to The Light, that you will sign any ola book they put before you. You pray like you have never prayed. To the Crow Man's sorcery, to the gods you loathe, to the magic of electricity and to the hand that rolls the dice. And in answer, you receive the quiet hum at the edge of the universe, followed by that great silence.

You weigh up your options and realise you have only one.

You go seeking Sena, knowing exactly where he is to be found.

．．

The spirits are gone from the mara tree, though Sena floats over a branch, sharpening his spear. He is chanting what could be a mantra or a Tamil rap song. You charge towards him with every wind you can muster.

'I will join your damn army. Your Mission Kuveni or whatever.'

'Another bus missed, Mr Maali. My crew are all in their places, ready to pounce. Today the death squad will fry.'

'The Minister has a demon protecting him. I could tell him what you have planned. He's got enough muscle to wrestle the Mahakali.'

Sena stops his sharpening and glares.

'You wouldn't fucking dare.'

'My friend is in the Palace. I need to whisper in ears. You will help me.'

'Only the Crow Man can grant those powers.'

'Then you will take me to him.'

．．

The strongest wind leads you to the Crow Man's cave. It gets there swiftly, and when it does you find yourself weeping. Memories pour from you like snot until all that is left is the fear. Being kidnapped in Sri Lanka is the first step to being disappeared. It's less risky to dispose of a body than to release a suspect who may speak out, especially one connected to power. They will not let Jaki go, even if she tells them what they want to hear.

The breeze drags you to the ceiling of the Crow Man's cave and you gaze down through the birdcages like a gargoyle atop a cathedral. The squawks of budgies and sparrows add to the voices that stalk your ears like flies. You look down on the Crow

Man's shaven skull and the table before him. You spy a familiar wooden ankh on a stool. And then you hear a familiar voice.

'I need protection. For my son. He is in more danger than before.'

'Do not leave the house today,' says the Crow Man. 'There are unholy things in the air. Something big is going to happen.'

'Last time you said this, nothing small even happened.'

'Have I not protected you, sir? I have given my maximum. But your son's rahu time is very, very bad. I advise you to send him abroad.'

'There are plans. Like that,' says the customer, handing over a wad of thousand-rupee notes.

'Is he still associating with bad friends?'

'No more,' says Stanley, picking up a packet full of chains and charms. 'He no longer associates with bad friends.'

. .

You see the Sparrowboy seated in the corner, in the shadows cast by candles, lettering shapes onto sheets of paper. Pali, Sanskrit and Tamil set down in ink by juvenile hand. You glide past the birdcages towards his stool, creating a wind that flickers the wicks and scatters the shadows. The Crow Man sniffs at the air and frowns.

'Jaki is in the Palace. Tell Stanley. Hurry!' you shout. 'Tell him now.' It feels as if your voice is reverberating.

The Sparrowboy stops his writing and gazes in your direction. His eyes cloud.

'There are unwelcome spirits in this room,' says the Crow Man, looking at neither Stanley nor you. 'Please be gone.'

You dart at the Crow Man and snarl. Your one sandal scatters the money on the table. It is the first time your wind has moved an object but you do not stop to celebrate.

'You're a fucking fraud. I did your errands. My red bandanna is on your shrine. Why can't I whisper?'

'Whispering comes to those who deserve it. Evidently, you do not.'

'Excuse me. Are you speaking. To me?'

Stanley's tie flutters in the breeze. He holds a bottle of ointment, snake oil sold to a snake, and looks up at the blind man.

The Crow Man fills his palm with coloured dust taken from a wooden tray. Mystical powders in brick orange, sun yellow and drag queen purple. When he blows them in your direction, you realise from the fragrance of curry and the stench of violet that turmeric and lavender has been mixed with chilli. The dust smarts your eyes and pushes you to the corner near the Sparrowboy.

'Sorry, sir. Just clearing the air. Let us begin.'

You shout again, giving it all you have and more. The body you once had and the soul you never believed in. 'Jaki is in the Palace. Tell Stanley now!'

'I feel there is a presence around my son,' says Stanley to Crow Man. 'I feel it around me at times.'

'What kind of presence?' asks the blind man in robes, as he casts breadcrumbs to the parrots. Behind him, the Sparrowboy lights the lamps of each shrine and then goes back to his corner and his transcribing of letters you cannot read.

'It is like a wind. An ugly chill. I get shivers whenever I am around my son.'

'Is there someone who would mean harm to your son?'

'Yes.'

'Are they alive?'

'Not any more.'

The Crow Man stares at you with his sightless eyes. 'Do you have something that belonged to this person?'

Stanley hands over a pink paper with writing on it and twine with crumpled cyanide capsules hanging from its neck.

. .

'Teach me to whisper. Or I will burn down your shrine!' You float behind the Sparrowboy, rubbing chilli from your eyes.

'Those who aim to destroy. Only destroy themselves,' says the Crow Man, a showman playing a conjuror, shrouding parlour tricks in metaphysics.

The Crow Man pours out a concoction from his grinding pestle to a small glass bottle, previously designed to hold a quarter of arrack. It looks like kola kenda, the green medicinal porridge with the consistency of vomit that your mother used to inflict on you each morning for seven years.

'Rub that oil where your son sleeps. Serve this to him every night.'

The Crow Man looks to where you are and shakes his head.

'Do you feel its presence here?'

'I think I do,' says Stanley, wrapping the bottle in newspaper and slipping it in his pocket, next to the snake oil ointment.

The Crow Man places your pink note and your cyanide capsules inside a brass lamp. He lights a ball of camphor and throws it in. He chants in a monotone which reminds you of the goth bands Jaki used to play in her gloomy room. The flame spits out smoke, which makes you cough even though you have no lungs.

The Crow Man calls to the Sparrowboy, who is absorbed in scribbling at his desk. He points to a stick with a lamp hooked at its end. The boy takes hold of it and waves the smouldering poison around the room. You see Stanley place more thousand-rupee notes on the betel leaf, light green on dark green. And then a sandbag of smoke slugs you in the gut and you are thrown from the cave.

You are left in the gutter, coughing and spluttering, reminded of Kilinochchi and the shelling and the three corpses with cyanide on their tongues. You look at the things around your neck. The ankh with DD's blood, the gold Panchayudha and the Nikon that does not work. You cannot find the cyanide capsules.

'Jaki is at the Palace! Help her!' You shout once more to Whoever and No One, the wailings of a newborn in a cot. Stanley exits the tunnel by the cave into the Kotahena slum, hurrying past the shrine where hundreds kneel every moon. He fails to notice a red bandanna draped on a rotting pineapple amidst the fading flowers and putrid piles of fruit.

At the head of the shrine, looking down on candles and lamps, is a painting, a crude drawing on cheap paper, laminated and framed, its border dotted with letters in Pali, Sanskrit and Tamil, printed by familiar hand. The painting is of a beast made of shadow. With the head of a bear and the body of a large woman. Its hair is serpents and its eyes are black from corner to corner. It bares its fangs and belches mist. You feel your insides hollow.

The figure wears a necklace of skulls and a belt of severed fingers. The belly is bare, hanging over the girdle of flesh. Human faces are etched in the skin of the souls trapped within.

Once again you find you have fallen to your knees with no idea how you got there.

THREE WHISPERS

'If you want to whisper, you only have to ask.'

The voice comes from the shrine, but the voice is not singular, it is a colony of ants singing out of tune. A beast climbs out of the crude painting, serpent hair followed by skull necklace. It perches on its haunches, towering above you, bathing you in its shadow. Its body is covered in letters tattooed in familiar scripts that you cannot read.

The letters turn into faces, which speak to you in unison.

'If you wish to whisper, bow before this shrine. And after your seventh moon all you are shall be mine. Decide quick. You have no time.'

You look at the faces in the skin. It is hard to know which are human and which are beast, and you recognise only two. Balal and Kottu stare at you with fish eyes, both wedged in the Mahakali's fleshy thigh.

THE SEVEN MOONS OF MAALI ALMEIDA

'I will grant you three whispers. You may use them as you please. And you will join today's mission. And you won't try to leave.'

The heads all speak in a voice that sounds like Jaki's. And you know that moons are rising and clocks are ticking. And you know The Light will only bring you more questions without answer. And you know that some lives are worth more than others, each one a poker chip in a different colour. Your life is a plastic ten-rupee chip from Pegasus, and Jaki's is a gold-plated casino plaque from Vegas.

You bow your head and breathe in the shadow.

'Do it now.'

'Are you willing to forfeit all your moons, Mr Photographer?'

'Take them. Do it quick.'

'Are you willing to forsake The Light?'

'I will forsake whatever. For fuck's sake. Do it now.'

You feel chains where your bones once were, interlocking manacles running up your spine. It is a slow sensation that creeps up to your neck and then disappears.

'It is done,' say the voices.

The young artist behind the crude sketch in the shrine leaves the tunnel, just as Stanley is getting into his state-sponsored BMW. At the wheel is DD, who looks as unattainable as he did when he first made you coffee and talked about native forests.

Stanley places a bottle of green, a vial of ointment and a jar of ash on his lap. You watch him rub some ash on his son's forehead. You watch him place a thing around DD's neck and tie it. He tells DD to start the car.

The BMW rolls forward and then stops with a lurch as the brakes catch. Blocking the path, and leaning on the bonnet, stands the Sparrowboy. He is glaring at them and holding up a note. 'What the hell,' says DD, winding down the window. The boy scurries around and leans across him and waves the paper in Stanley's face.

Stanley takes and unfurls it. It is in English lettering with Sanskrit curves. Seven words whispered into the boy's ear before being etched in pen.

'Jaki is in the Palace. Save her.'

He darts a look at Sparrowboy, who mouths the word 'friend'.

'What's the Palace?' asks DD, reading over his father's shoulder, in a voice that feels distant and bored. 'A club?'

Stanley's eyes are blazing; his brown skin grows crimson.

'It's not a bloody club. Drive. Thimbirigasyaya Road.'

'Roads are all closed. We should get home before curfew.'

'Where's Jaki?'

'She went out last night. Must be sleeping.'

'Did. You. See her?'

'No.

'Drive.'

You watch the car driving towards closed roads filled with traffic. You have a pair of Fives and there are black Kings on the table. You wonder if all Stanley's influence will be enough to get past that Palace gate. Will it be enough to reach Jaki's cell and spring the lock?

You have gambled everything on this chance to save the friend you let down the most. You savour one last moment of freedom and then turn to face the Mahakali.

. .

Do not be afraid of demons; it is the living we should fear. Human horrors trump anything that Hollywood or the afterlife can conjure. Always remember this when you encounter a wild animal or a stray spirit. They are not as dangerous as you.

Ghosts are afraid of other ghosts. And of you. And of the infinite nothing. It's why they do misguided things. But that's not the only reason.

They do things because they can no longer taste or speak or hump. They rage against those who stole their lives, those who replaced them, and those who no longer speak their names. Because they know what you know and what every you-that-isn't-you knows. In the end, there will be no one left to tell your story. No one to answer your questions. None to hear your prayers.

Somewhere, Dr Ranee is shaking her head and tearing up your file. Somewhere, men in offices are ordering air raids on children in huts. You ride the back of the Mahakali as it leaps from rooftop to roof towards the Palace. Its skin is scaly and the serpents in its hair hiss in the wind. The sunlight is reaching golden hour and even the stalled traffic below looks beautiful. You see Stanley's state-sponsored BMW edging between a bus and a truck and urge it on its way. What will your final cards be, now that all your chips are in the middle?

The Mahakali's back is tattooed with letters and faces. As you near the Palace, the faces begin speaking to you. All at the same time, but this time, not in unison. Most of these souls are petrified and have been trapped here for longer than they know. Not all of them are human.

At first the static sounds like ants with miniature microphones crawling over a carcass, then like pebbles in plastic boxes shaken by horrid children. Then, like Portuguese, Dutch and Sinhalese spoken at the same time, and then it is words voiced at different speeds, tongues tripping over each other, screams masked by sighs, surrenders turning into curses.

...if you protect my granddaughter, I will give you my soul.

...only the rich have keys to this city. Not scum like me.

...through many a birth I wandered, seeking but not finding the builder of this house.

Each voice hissing into the ether, shouting at the visvaya bellowing into used frequencies. The airwaves are jammed with spirits cursing and pleading. The confused, the jealous, the angry and the afraid, some making mischief, some seeking mercy.

>...*let's go over together he said, and then he let me jump.*
>
>...*it won't work. We're already dead.*
>
>...*they said crying stops the dead from leaving. So I did not shed a tear.*

The Mahakali enters a winding lane hidden in residential Colombo, replete with verdant trees and unexpected cul-de-sacs. The creature slows down to navigate this surburban labyrinth. The gardens below you grow larger, the walls get taller and the lanes remain empty of people.

You see the Minister's Benz parked next to a four-storey building that looks like it once housed a governor from an empire that no longer exists. Your captor passes the car park and glides two lanes down to a familiar building with guards at the gates. It leaps to the roof of the Palace and the faces on its skin contort in agony and let out shrieks. The beast glances back at you and smiles. It looks like a beautiful woman dressed to kill.

'Use your whispers now. Then come to the car park over there. We will need you later. Please don't try to run. Runners never get very far.'

. .

Cassim sits slumped at his desk, head in hands, report typed and curling over the ribbon. From the groans escaping the soundproof windows below, it appears that activity at the Palace has resumed.

On the table is Jaki's maroon handbag, which is open and looks as messy as it usually does, making it impossible to ascertain if it has been rummaged through. Though it clearly has.

You float over Cassim's shoulder and read the report. It states that Jacqueline Vairavanathan, aged twenty-five, of Galle Face Court, Colombo 3, leaked classified state information on national radio, was a close associate of suspected JVP terrorist Malinda Almeida, and was found in possession of narcotics.

You look at the canister on the table with two happy pills left in it and Jaki's yellow laminated national ID card propped next to it. Cassim bites his lip and stares into space. You curl beside him and spit words into his ear.

'They will kill her and blame it on the man who typed the report. They will kill her and leave you with this bucket of shit. Get her to the gate now.'

He stands up with a start and looks around the room. He checks if the radio is on and then listens hard at the silence. You don't stop to pause, in case you lose this whisper.

'They will say you took bribes. That you are a rogue cop. But you are better than all this. Stanley is on his way now. If you save her, he will give reward. You will get that transfer. Because you don't agree with death squads. You never have.'

Cassim gets up and paces the room. You do not know what he is thinking. Who knows what one must sell to the Mahakali to access another's thoughts? In the corner is a rucksack and in it a bottle of clear liquid and some bandages. Below that is a box of surgical masks, a cap, a white shirt and black trousers. Standard issue for men who were neither army nor police.

Detective Cassim folds a bandage and douses it in liquid. You smell nail polish and treacle as he folds it in his pocket. Then he changes his mind. Throws the bandage back in the rucksack and walks towards Jaki's cell.

..

When he gets there, he gasps. Jaki is awake and trying to get the gunny sack off her head, which is difficult with hands tied behind back. She jerks her body, rolls forward and grunts.

Cassim unlocks the door and tiptoes into the room. Jaki hears the sound and cowers to the wall.

'Who is that? Where is this?'

'Please, do not take off your hood. If you see us, they will not let you leave.'

'Who's they?'

'Do you have the negatives?'

'What?'

'Maali Almeida's negatives. The things in that box that started this whole bloody mess.'

'I don't,' says Jaki, playing blind man's bluff. 'Believe me, I don't. I sold them to Elsa Mathangi. She will have them. Please can I call my uncle?'

'Don't take off your blindfold.'

'I am Stanley Dhar—'

'I know who you are.'

'Can I have some water?'

Cassim exits the room and locks the door. You float to Jaki, wrap your arms around her and feed her what you can in frantic whispers and gasps.

'You've been arrested, Jaki. Stay calm, be brave and you will be saved. Uncle Stanley is coming for you. Tell Detective Cassim this...'

The Detective returns with a teacup and a plastic bottle of water. He warns her before he takes off the sack.

'Drink your water. Do not look at my face. I want to help you. But I do not trust you.'

She looks down with squinted eyes as he removes her hood and unties her hands. She keeps her eyes closed and does not attempt to take in the space or glimpse her captor. She holds the cup with numb hands and tries not to spill.

He watches her drink.

'If you give me the negatives, I will release you now.'

Jaki finishes sipping and looks at the ground. She is groggy and garbled and mistakes your whispers for her own thoughts. Later she will have no recollection of what was said or to whom.

'I know you are the one who searched our apartment. I know you are not to blame for this.'

You whisper and she speaks. Your words, from her ears to her mouth. She does not question what she says.

Cassim is silent.

'Uncle Stanley will reward you. Uncle Stanley can get you transferred tonight. Release me and you can be released. I promise you.'

Cassim leans back and folds his arms. 'How do you know about my transfer?'

'I know you are a good detective. I know you are better than this. And I know you will do the right thing.' You run out of breath, even though you have none. You feel as if you have sprinted up eight floors and jumped off the top.

'Minister Dharmendran can deliver this?'

'He can and he will. Please, Detective. If we stay, both of us are lost. Both of us. Help me. And we will help you.'

Fatigued and frazzled, you retire to the corner and watch. If these are your two whispers, then what will you do with your third?

Cassim lets her finish two more cups and then pulls her to her feet. Her legs buckle and she holds onto his shoulder as he drags her down the corridor. He places her on the seat in the office and pulls his report from the typewriter. He crumples it into his pocket and sticks a fresh sheet in the ribbon. He starts typing with fury.

Detective Cassim extracts the sheet and then signs in ink. He gets up and hands her a box of surgical masks and the uniform.

'Wear the mask, the cap and this uniform. I will stamp your release forms. Don't let the guards see your face. Be quick!'

He goes to the office to stamp the letter and puts it in an envelope. When he returns, Jaki is dressed and ready, with her clothes stuffed in her bag. The black trousers fit well, though the white shirt hangs baggy off her stooping shoulders.

By the time they reach security, Jaki can stand up straight. The guard squints at Cassim's forged letter from the Minister.

'Quick, quick, men. We have an appointment. Minister Cyril has signed this. You want to check with him?'

The guard shakes his head and folds the paper and looks away as Cassim leads Jaki out of the Palace.

A BMW speeds down the quiet lane and skids to a halt. Stanley clambers out in a cloud of dust in time to take hold of Jaki as she sinks from Cassim's shoulder. He glares at the cop as he hands the keys to DD.

'Has she been hurt?'

'No, sir.'

'How long was she here?'

'A few hours, sir.'

'Is her name on any list?'

'No, sir.

'Sure?'

'Yes, sir.'

'Dilan! Take her to our house. Don't open the door for anyone.' Stanley looks at Cassim.'You go with them. Stay at my house until I get back.'

DD looks confused, but helps haul Jaki onto the back seat, where she slumps down and begins to sob. Long sobs with long pauses in between.

'Take her now.'

'Where are you going?'

Stanley lowers his voice and questions the Detective. 'Who is in the office?'

'Sir, the Minister and the Major are having a meeting.'

'The other building, top floor, yes?'

'I think so.'

'You go with these two,' says Stanley. 'Get them home safe.

And you tell no one. Anything about this. Do I have your word?'

'Yes, sir.'

Stanley stuffs whatever notes the Crow Man didn't get into Cassim's hand.

'If you talk. I will have your badge.'

'No, no, sir. I don't want money. Please, sir.'

'Take this and go,' snaps Stanley.

'Sir, about the transfer.'

'What?'

'The madam said... Doesn't matter. We can talk later.'

'What?'

'Nothing, sir.'

Stanley stomps off towards the four-storeyed house, two lanes away, with a state-sponsored Benz in its state-sponsored car park.

· ·

Detective Cassim gets in the passenger seat, much to the horror of DD.

'What the hell's this? Where's Appa going?'

Jaki wipes her eyes with her sleeve and shakes her head.

'I had a creepy dream. Then I woke up with a bag on my head,' says Jaki. 'Is the exhibition happening?'

'I don't care,' says DD.

'He has a meeting,' says Detective Cassim. 'Drive now. Forget you ever saw this place. Or me.'

DD does a U-turn at the end of the cul-de-sac and drives back towards roads with traffic lights, where screams are less easily ignored. He takes Jaki and the policeman back to his father's house, away from the flat at Galle Face Court where you shared your dreams, your fears and your shorts, away from this dungeon that hides on a dead-end road. The BMW takes the bend and vanishes down the lane and you wish DD and Jaki and Cassim Aces and Hearts and Sixes.

'Go safely, my dears,' you whisper. 'May every roulette wheel be kind.'

And then the trees freeze and the breezes cease. The voice creeps between your ears and the stench of rotting souls blocks your nose. The universe breathes through you and appears to have forgotten to brush its teeth.

'Are you done, Mr Photographer?'

You look back at the Mahakali and the faces pulsing through its skin like infected veins. It motions for you to climb its back and you realise that disobedience is no longer an option, civil or otherwise. You nod. 'I think so.'

'Then your service has begun. Come. Serve.'

You climb the spine of the beast and watch Stanley tread up the road, like a marathon runner who forgot to pace himself.

* * *

You watch from the sky as Stanley passes the curl in the road and heads towards an office building behind tall walls.

It is four floors high and unremarkable in its architecture. Concrete boxes, painted grey and stacked skyward. The windows that aren't tinted are veiled in venetian blinds.

When the Mahakali comes to a stop, you leap off its back and watch it melt into shadows cast by this ugly building.

At the base is the face of a polecat. It gives you the same disgusted look that all dead animals give you. 'What are you looking at, ugly?'

'I get it. Animals have souls. You dream, you do things for pleasure, you feel happy and sad. You understand pain and grief and love and family and friendship. Humans don't acknowledge this, because it makes it easier to carve up the ones we find tasty. Which isn't you, but that's neither here nor there. I am profoundly sorry.'

The polecat looks surprised or hungry or annoyed or, you don't know, it's a polecat.

'Screw your apology,' it says before vanishing into the Mahakali's flesh.

There are good reasons humans can't converse with animals, except after death. Because animals wouldn't stop complaining. And that would make them harder to slaughter. The same may be said for dissidents and insurgents and separatists and photographers of wars. The less they are heard, the easier they are forgotten.

The sun is descending over Colombo and there is not a cloud in sight.

Soon your final moon will be reaching for the sky.

. .

Balal and Kottu look at you from the Mahakali's leg.

'Forgive us for what we did,' says Kottu.

'What did you do?'

'Unholy things,' says Kottu.

'But only because we had to,' adds Balal.

'Great apology,' you say, as the Mahakali slides off the wind and perches on a mara tree.

'We are garbage men,' says Balal. 'We don't make the garbage. We just clean it up.'

'What's it like in there?' you ask.

'In where?' says Kottu.

'You will find out soon,' says Balal.

'Do you want your money back?' asks Kottu.

'What money?' you ask.

The security detail is not as extensive as the Palace around the corner, and of course none of the guards see the Mahakali and the souls it carries as it leaps through the doors and bounds up the stairs. You are taken along with it, as powerless as most humans are in the face of catastrophe. There is no one to stop the Mahakali, as it glides across these corridors of power in the direction of a bomb.

Mission Kuveni

The beast seems to know its way around this building. It walks up to the first floor, then glides out the window, up the side of the building to the third floor and then takes the stairs to the fourth, where a secretary sits outside a large room. She is a full-figured lady with photos of three full-figured teenagers on her desk who each bear her face.

The sign in the lobby reads 'Department of Justice Administrative Branch'. The first floor is cubicles of women in saris, pecking at typewriters, and the fourth has men in ties carrying files. The legend outside the lift allocates a floor to Accounting, Finance, Records and Personnel.

There are buildings like this around the island, though most centre around the capital. Buildings that make losses while they report profits. This must be where they allocate budgets for torturers, organise pension plans for abductors and approve home loans for assassins. You remember one thing your Dada said that didn't make you cringe, though it is unclear why it was shared with a ten-year-old.

'You know why the battle of good vs evil is so one-sided, Malin? Because evil is better organised, better equipped and better paid. It is not monsters or yakas or demons we should fear. Organised collectives of evil doers who think they are performing the work of the righteous. That is what should make us shudder.'

In the waiting room stands Drivermalli, perched on his prosthetic, leaning on a column. He is sweating and breathing unevenly. You think of the people pushing paper in the floors below, of Stanley trying to push past security at the entrance, and wonder if one day they will invent a bomb that knew whom to spare. The one good thing you can say about a bomb is that it isn't racist or sexist or concerned about class.

You follow Drivermalli down a hallway with misted glass doors, into a large room with a huge windows. What you see in there is both impressive and terrifying.

..

The events that led to the loss of twenty-three lives on the fouth and fifth floors of the Department of Justice Administrative Branch is later attributed to bad luck and evil charms, with the Crow Man claiming partial credit. It was actually the work of Sena's crew of the dead, playing with winds and altering fates. Though you yourself could claim a hand in saving at least one life on this, your final moon.

Humans believe they make their own thoughts and possess their own will. This is yet another placebo that we swallow after birth. Thoughts are whispers that come from without as well as within. They can no more be controlled than the wind. Whispers will blow across your mind at all times and you will succumb to more of them than you think.

Ghosts are invisible to those with breath, invisible like guilt or gravity or electricity or thoughts. Thousands of unseen hands direct the course of every life. And those being directed call it God or karma or dumb luck or other less than accurate names.

In the large room on the fifth floor, Sena has stationed his army with a precision our military never had. The Mahakali perches by the corner window, the producer of this film set and the director of this film.

The Acid-scarred Woman whispers in the ears of Ranchagoda and muddles his thoughts and ensures he forgets to pat down Drivermalli before he enters the room.

A bomb victim checks the circuitry of the vest to make sure that current flows through its wires. The Defiled Beauty Queen arrives first and distracts the Dead Bodyguard, the Minister's Demon, with a dance that she practised for a pageant before her tragic end.

The Dead Mother is tasked with triggering Drivermalli to detonate the bomb at the right moment. Sena has a system of checks and balances that is as meticulous and as organised as everything in Sri Lanka is not. Nothing to be left to probability.

Today this platoon of Dead Anarchists, Dead Separatists, Dead Innocents and Dead They-Can't-Remember-What will destroy a death squad in one fell swoop. And you will watch from the Mahakali's shoulder.

..

'I didn't know you could see the Beira Lake from up here,' says the Minister, gazing through the window at the temple afloat on green waters. 'Looks like a dream.'

'As long as you can't smell it,' remarks the Major. Next to him, on the Minister's sofa, is a balding man who smiles awkwardly and keeps his arms folded. He is introduced as the STF's finest interrogator and you recognise him even without his mask.

The Minister's Demon lies back on a shelf of unread law books and watches as the Defiled Beauty Queen enacts dance moves from both the Kotte and disco eras. She looks him in the eye and arches her back. Her shoulders roll and her wrists twirl, while her breasts perk and her hips glide in arcs. Evidently, her shrine at the Crow Man's has earned her wealth and she has invested it in eyes and choreography. Her lips blow kisses while her body flutters its lids.

'I want you to sit in on today's meetings, Major.'

'Yes, of course, sir.'

'It is a strange time, Major. We are inviting Indians to invade us. We are doing deals with Tamil terrorists. We are killing our own Sinhalese. This is the worst it has ever been.'

'It will get worse, sir.'

'You are also getting charms from the Crow Man?'

The Major blushes and pulls at the orange bracelet hidden under his sleeve. Another tug and it snaps off his wrist.

'My wife gave. I don't believe in this nonsense.' He drops it in the ashtray.

The Minister pulls back his white sleeve to reveal a similar bracelet. The Major fishes the discarded wristband back from the ashes and puts it in his pocket.

'Don't be so cocky. Men who do our kind of work need protection from all sides. Ado, where are these guards?'

He does not know that both of today's guards are stricken with food poisoning and are chained to a toilet bowl by rivulets of diarrhoea. His secretary rushes in. The girl has just been transferred from the Ministry of Fisheries and, judging by the politeness of Minister Cyril, it seems he has not yet begun to paw her.

She opens the door and announces. 'Sir, your 5 p.m. is here.'

In walks Drivermalli, tall, dark, nervous and flanked by an anxious ASP Ranchagoda. They both have the good sense to look solemn and avoid all eyes.

'Officer, stand outside until those bloody guards show up. Drivermalli, stand over there, please.'

The cop exits and Drivermalli stands upright, his boots shined, his camouflage hanging loosely on his lanky frame.

The Dead Mother slips behind the boy and blends into the curtains. The Minister's Demon looks at Drivermalli and then turns back to the dancer. He has watched his master berate a soldier on many occasions and is more interested in the fusion of Kathakali and electric boogie from the late Miss Kataragama 1970.

The Minister and the Major look to the third man in the room, the man with neither hair nor mask. They wait for him to do what he was brought for. The interrogator walks to Drivermalli's ear and spits words. 'Why did you leave the hospital?'

'I felt better, sir.'

'You don't look better,' says the bald man staring at the boy's singed scalp and scarred cheeks.

'How did you manage to escape the fire, when the other two died?'

The Minister looks at the Major, who shrugs. The interrogator pulls at the flesh behind Drivermalli's ear. It is no more than a pinch but it draws blood.

'I don't remember, sir,' says Drivermalli. 'Please, that is hurting.'

'You've got fat, no?' The interrogator lifts a hand and every spirit in the room braces itself, for the punch in the stomach that doesn't come, except for Drivermalli. 'How come?'

The interrogator bends down to scratch at his knee and spies a trail of ants crawling up his leg. He swears and dabs at his shin. He does not see the Dead JVP-er he once tortured guiding insects to his feet.

The Minister takes over the interview. 'How did you crash that van into the transformer?'

'I can't remember, sir.'

'You were drinking?'

'I don't drink, sir. Only thambili.'

'Do it now!' hisses Sena.

'Do it now!' whispers the Dead Mother into Drivermalli's ear.

The switch is located in Drivermalli's pocket and his hand hovers around it but does not make the move. He is sweating even though the room has three working fans.

'Is something the matter, son?' The Minister gets to his feet and walks over.

'Do it now!' hisses the Scarred Woman perched on the sofa. The interrogator, having just expelled the last of the ants, feels an icy breeze hit his heart. He frowns at the fan.

'Do it now!' says the Dead Mother into the ear of Drivermalli. His lips are quivering, as though he's about to burst into tears. Yet his hand remains still.

You look across the room and see the Minister's Demon snoring by the bookshelf while the Defiled Beauty Queen strokes the hairs between his pointed ears. The Minister, the Major, the interrogator and the driver are all in the same room. You wonder if all coincidences are as meticulously scripted as this one. You think of Dr Ranee and her theory of Lankan death squads and the pictures she used without asking. Who claimed that Sri Lanka was the first democracy to produce the modern death squad, building on models developed by Latin American dictatorships. One of many unverified claims made in her book, hidden amidst sentences that unwittingly justified the things she condemned: *An organised hierarchy to manage factory-level violence may not be an act of savagery, but an act of rational men in the face of barbarism.*

'Do it!' whispers the Mahakali and every soul in its belly and every spirit in the room goes quiet.

'Sir, I have been hearing voices,' confesses Drivermalli.

'Do it!' hisses Sena and the Scarred Lady and the Defiled Beauty Queen. The Dead JVP-ers are injecting itches all over the interrogator.

..

A feeling that's been bubbling inside of you since entering this ugly building now curdles at the base of your broken neck and floods your senses. Your final moon has seen a lover betrayed, a best friend dangled over an abyss, and will now end with a bang that takes the bad guys with it. So why do your eyes smart and why your ears fill up with static?

You pick up your camera and look around the room and see the faces of the living. The cop, the thug, the soldier, the politician. You watch the spirits poised to turn the room to powder. And you see the Mahakali standing on the ledge at the window, surveying the spectacle with glee.

'Stop this!' you shout. 'Stop this now!'

'What are you doing, Mr Maali?' Sena emerges from behind the curtain. He casts a glance at the Minister's Demon, who is now snoring in rhythm to the Beauty Queen's song.

'There are people downstairs. Office workers. Three floors of them. There is the secretary with a picture of three children on her table. There is my friend's father downstairs. Who is a pompous idiot, but has no part in this. And then there's this deluded fool,' you say, pointing at Drivermalli. 'How many will die today? Did you count?'

Sena charges at you and pushes you to the wall. 'We are about to end this war, and you are worried about civil servants? They stamp the paper that keeps these monsters in power. Fuck. Them.'

'You said no innocents would die.'

'There is no one innocent in this building. Not even your boy's daddy. If they work for the system, they deserve their fate.'

'Sir, I am hearing voices,' confesses Drivermalli, though no one hears him.

At 5 p.m., every government office evacuates as part of a daily drill to beat the rush hour, regardless of what is on their table and what needs doing. Even the ones without suicide bombers on their top floor will shut their shops at five on the dot.

The more you stall, the less the casualties. Sometimes it's not the bet you lay, but how long you take to lay it.

You and Sena trade barbs, while Drivermalli mutters to himself in words you cannot decipher.

You feel a fist in your spine and a knife at your throat.

'Enough baila, Mr Maali. The Mahakali says you have one whisper left. You better deliver. Now.'

'I used up my three already.'

'Mahakali says only two were heard. Use your whisper now.'

'What about the secretaries and accountants downstairs? How different is this from the LTTE bombing civilians? Or the government butchering JVP? What will this nonsense achieve?'

Sena pushes you in front of Drivermalli and the spirits in the room chant, 'Do it now!'

..

You look Drivermalli in the scars on his face. Will this be the last thing you do before the Mahakali swallows all that is left of you? You ponder photography and journalism and the whole goddamn mess. In the end, was any of it really worth doing?

The answer may likely be no, and yet you decide, at the eleventh hour of your seventh moon, to use whatever's left of your voice. 'Drivermalli. I have travelled with you and seen who you are. I have been where you have. You know me.'

Drivermalli looks up for a moment and then looks down at his feet.

'You see me not, but I know you hear. These men deserve to die. But does the woman outside who just made you tea? Do all those people downstairs? Do you?'

'What are you doing?' Sena looks horrified. A few of his followers try to lance you with their spears. In the corner behind the snoring demon, the Mahakali breathes in shadow. The faces on its skin have turned into crosses and arrowheads.

'We send pawns to kill kings. But bad kings get replaced by worse kings, and more pawns get sent to die.' You address your comments to every creature in the room.

Drivermalli is sweating and shuddering. He tries to ignore the voices swirling around him and the kilos of wire bearing weight on his good leg. He recites a line fed to him by IE Kugarajah, memorised while he fed his squirrels.

'All enemy combatants are complicit. All deserve death.'

'These are not combatants, malli. Boys like you blow themselves up. And what changes? Is your life worth sacrificing, even for this scum? Is hers? Are theirs?'

Sena spits venom in your face. He pulls you by the neck and carries you towards the Mahakali. 'That was your last chance, Mr Maali. The Mahakali will have you for a thousand moons.'

. .

But his curses are drowned out by the commotion at the door. The cheap plywood swings on its hinges and the spirits in the room jump.

'Chantal!' snaps the Minister. 'You don't knock?'

But it is not Cyril Wijeratne's secretary who enters the room. It is Stanley Dharmendran.

The afternoon light silhouettes him in the doorway. His puffed shoulders and measured stride remind you of his son. Until he starts to speak.

'Minister. I need a word. Now.'

'We are busy, Dharmendran...'

'My sister's daughter. Was taken to the Palace. I demand an explanation.'

The Minister and the Major look shocked and glare at the Mask. The Mask shakes his head and looks to ASP Ranchagoda in the corridor.

The attention of the squad and the spirits scatter from the boy with the bomb, who sweats and shivers alone.

''We have to question everybody, Dharmendran,' says the Minister. 'Can't exempt those with connections.'

'So you. Bring her. To the Palace?'

'I am sorry Dharmendran, but this is not the time...'

Sena tightens his grip. You push at him and bite his wrist. The knife hits the ground. You aim with your bare foot and kick it like you did when you played rugger for five minutes. Unlike then, this time your aim is true and your target is hit. The knife goes flying and its blunt handle hits the Minister's Demon in the belly. He groans and wakes with a growl.

The spirits gasp and Sena yells and the Mahakali floats by the window, eyes blazing and faces awake. Drivermalli speaks for everyone in the room to hear. 'The answer to your question is... I do not know. I have thought long and there are no answers. There is only this. There is only now.'

The room holds its breath. The Minster's demon leaps to where his master sits in slow motion. Drivermalli repeats his line and finishes his thought.

'All enemy combatants are complicit. All deserve death. Perhaps my worthless life will finally be worth something. Otherwise, what was the point?'

And with that, he puts both his hands in his pockets.

A Thousand Moons

All the most powerful forces are invisible. Love, electricity, wind. And the waves following a bomb blast. First the blast wave, where the air is compressed to breaking point and pockets of wind push outwards, travelling faster than sound and smashing everything in the way. This wave snaps the Major in three and dashes the interrogator against the wall, granting them both the instant death denied to their many victims.

Then come the shock waves. These are supersonic and carry more energy than the sound of the blast, which is still yet to arrive. These pierce Ranchagoda and impale him on the door.

The building feels its ground shake and its walls crack. The stairwells fill with panicked civil servants pushing each other out of the building. The drivers and guards in the car park hear the blast and look up at smoke bursting from the fifth floor window.

The waves turn the room's furniture into flying clubs and daggers which bludgeon Stanley's cowering body. Drivermalli's skull lands on the floor in the bathroom while the rest of him is sprayed on the walls. And then the room catches fire and blast winds pull at the windows. They shift fans from ceilings and concrete from walls.

In the floor below, paperweights and filing trays become grenades and mortar shells, as foundations rumble and the air fills with smoke and roars of terror. You watch the car park fill with frantic people. The first to exit are howling and holding their bags, the second are caked in dust and blood, the third have to be carried by others.

The blast winds scatter the spirits, who are thrown from the room into the corridor. They dust themselves off, break into cheers and dance on the flames. The Dead Tigers shake hands with the Slain JVP-ers. They squat by the lift and watch the smoke escaping the office and they wait.

Inside the room, the fire creeps towards the windows and leaves the bathroom and kitchen unsinged. Coughing in the tub with a fractured elbow is Minister Cyril Wijeratne. All he remembers is leaping into the bathroom when the driver started speaking. He tells himself that he saw something in Drivermalli's eyes, but deep down in a place that itches he knows that he was pushed into the bathroom by a force that was not human.

The Minister's Demon sits on the tub and slaps his master awake. He looks at you and smiles as Sena emerges from the smoke.

'You woke that bastard up, Maali.' Sena grabs you by the hair and drags you from the room.

The Minister crawls from the bathroom. 'You are the reason that scum still breathes.'

The spirits cheer Sena's entrance. Sena raises his fist and nods. 'We got three and lost one,' he proclaims with a smile and pulls tighter on your hair.

You spy a foot wearing a high heel buried under rubble that used to be a wall. You see a tie with Stanley's shattered body attached to it.

'You got a lot more than three, you prick,' you spit back.

'Mr Photographer is mine,' says a voice from the smoke. The Mahakali emerges, a bull on two legs. It is pointing at you. 'You better not run. Runners never get far.'

Sena pulls you by your hair and walks you toward the beast. You try to break free but you are as feeble as you were when you had breath. A lover not a fighter.

'Sorry, Maali,' says Sena. 'Maybe I'll see you in a thousand moons. Maybe never. Whichever takes longer.'

The Mahakali grabs you with a clawed fist and pulls you towards the faces on its skin. You howl. but your cries are drowned by the wails.

They come from the fire and crawl from the smoke. Major Raja Udugampola, the Mask, the ASP and Stanley

Dharmendran. Their bodies are bloodied and tattered and their feet do not touch the ground.

The spirits descend on them and there is a struggle and then the Minister's Demon breaks through the scrum and jumps on the Mahakali, who lets you out of its grasp. The Minister's Demon blows you a kiss and says, 'I owed you one. Now I owe you none.'

It pushes the Mahakali's head of snakes into a wall. 'Thank you for protecting my watch. Now we are even. Run, you fool!'

The Mahakali reaches for the Minister's Demon's throat. The Dead Bodyguard buries a punch in the beast's gut. The faces scream in different keys.

'You are no Mahakali. You think I don't recognise you without your robes? Talduwe Somarama! You got past me once. Never again!' And the demon's fist collides with the Mahakali face.

The wind sails in from the flames down the emergency staircase and out the third floor windows. You jump it and pass the Minister sprawled on the stairs. You see bodies on the third and fourth floor not moving. There are not many of them, but there are enough.

..

The wind carries you down to the streets, where you spy ghosts by the roadside, some you have spoken to and some you have avoided.

You float over the fading rooftops and see your seventh moon hiding behind a cloud, waiting for the sun to disappear. You fly through tangled electricity cables that weave past old churches, shabby balconies, trees that whisper and half-built skyscrapers. You hear the shrill screech of the Mahakali behind you, bouncing from roof to street.

Sena rides a swifter wind and snarls curses at your heels. You keep running, colliding with ghosts blown across your pathway.

As you approach the canals, you spy the Dead Atheist saluting you and the Snake Lady laughing with her mob. You see the Dead Dogs howling from the bus stand, the Dead Suicides jumping off roofs and the drag queen waving at you mid-jump. You ride on towards the muddy waters and you wait for the weakest wind.

You hope the Mahakali has not followed you here, but you feel whispers and expect it to materialise from behind each tree you pass. You hop the weakest wind and let it carry you gently along the canal, scrutinising the overhanging branches for spears and fangs.

The sky clears itself of clouds and the sun breaks out in orange acne. You are glad that it has not yet set. Your seventh moon is peeping from the clouds and about to raise its head. And there, by the bank, you see a kumbuk tree, and you see Dr Ranee, He-Man and Moses, all in priest garb waving to you. They point to a second kumbuk and then to the cross stream next to a third.

From behind this steps out the Mahakali. Its eyes are blazing and its fingers exhaling smoke. It appears to have devoured the blast and its victims, and seems ready for dessert.

'Jump in the water!' shouts He-Man in his squeaky steroid voice. 'It can't follow you there.'

The Mahakali leaps from the tree and you dive into the whirlpool, and the last thing you feel is a claw being dragged across your spine.

As you fall towards the water, you see the many eyes looking up at you, eyes that once belonged to you and, for now at least, they are all white. The water is the white of frosty bulbs. And, as you hit the surface, you hear the breaking of glass. You no longer care if your photos are seen or not. Because Jaki and DD still have breath and, even though that won't make up for this whole damn mess, it is something. And, without a doubt, that is the kindest thing you can say about life. It's not nothing.

The River of Births

This river is as wide as the pool at Otters but there are no diving boards at its end. It stretches along endlessly, like roads through Australian deserts or American cornfields, which you have seen in *National Geographic* and never got around to visiting. You watch the river stretch through coconut groves and paddy fields and disappear over a hill in the distance. You think of other things you will never get to do.

As per Dr Ranee's directions, the weakest wind from the Beira has delivered you here, and the demons are no longer in sight. The river is not deep; you can feel the bottom with your toes. It is sludgy and booby-trapped with rocks. The sun has now set and the moon is in the sky. The water is as warm as the air is cool. You are not alone at this river; all around you are swimmers braving the currents and hugging the banks.

You pass each swimmer, noticing their eyes and their chatter, how they all talk at once, some to each other, some to themselves, and you find yourself muttering in languages you didn't know you knew. 'You are not the you that you think you are.' 'You are everything you have thought and done and been and seen.'

The other swimmers are looking at you and through you, and at each other and through each other. They have your face, though some have messier hair and some are women and some have no gender.

You swim towards the horizon, you pass a Tamil plantation worker arguing with a Kandyan nobleman, you drift past a Dutch schoolteacher chatting with an Arab sailor. Similar faces, identical ears.

So this is it? This is The Light? This is the place where demons cannot follow? You let the waters wash over you and you sink beneath the surface. You do not have to hold your breath and you do not have breath to hold you.

You sink to the bottom and there it is. The thing that had eluded you all these moons. The last thing you did, the last thing done to you, the thing you forgot to recall. The truth you avoided seeing, the answer you feared the most.

You breathe in the clean water, wipe the mud from your lens, and remember the last breath you took as Malinda Almeida Kabalana.

YOUR PRICE

When the figure emerged from the shadow of that rooftop, you realised how much Stanley Dharmendran resembled his son. The sloping gait, the symmetrical skull, the dark skin, the white teeth, the bounce in the step, the swivel in the hip. He said something short and sharp to the bartender, the ox-boy who you had just been touching. And then he turned to you.

From the shadows, two men brought a plastic table and then two Formica chairs. You recognised these men. They were not waiters or bar staff; they were employed by casinos to beat those who beat the house and collect from those the house had beaten.

Stanley motioned for you to sit, and you had a choice between facing Colombo or facing the staircase and the thugs in the shadows. You chose to face the threat and sat with your back to the view. Stanley leaned back and you saw in his hand a pink note with your handwriting on it.

Come to the Leo Bar at 11 p.m. tonight.

I will have news.

Love, Maal.

You had left it on DD's badminton racket and, while it was possible that DD had read it and given it to his Appa, the odds are six to seven to one that Appa found it first.

'Would you like something to drink, Malinda?'

'I'm actually meeting DD at 11 p.m.'

'He was in bed when I left. I don't think he'll be coming.'

'He didn't get my note?'

'You left it on the wrong racket.'

'But I spoke with him.'

'Did you? Jesus, Maali. We don't talk for weeks. And now you want to party.' Stanley elongated his vowels, so his accent resembled the British public school poshness that DD kept trying to shed in public. Father and son shared the same walk, the same skin and the same toffee voice.

'So what did you want to tell my son?'

'None of your business, Uncle Stanley.'

'Fair enough. This won't take long,' said Stanley. 'I just came to ask you one thing.'

You noticed that the bar downstairs had gone quiet and that no one was likely to trespass on this terrace, unless they were looking for an illicit smooch.

'I'm waiting for the punchline, Uncle.'

'In the note you say you have news. I am not interested in your news. I just want to know one thing. What is your price?'

'Price?'

'How much will it take for you to be gone from Dilan's life?'

'Maybe a million dollars,' you say with a smirk. 'Or the amount they paid you to join the Cabinet. Whichever's larger.'

Stanley doesn't appear offended.

'There must be a realistic figure.'

'If DD wants to kick me out of his life, he can tell me himself. I'm hardly around, anyway.'

'Where have you been?'

'I've been up north reporting on the IPKF.'

'For whom?'

'None of your business, Uncle Stanley.'

'Dilan thinks it's the army, but apparently you haven't worked there for years.'

'They called me to cover Wijeweera's capture.'

'They say you were sacked for being HIV-positive.'

'That's untrue.'

'Have you checked?'

'I'm positive. That I don't have AIDS.'

An old punchline, delivered with Stanley's cadence.

'Dilan is a good boy. A brilliant boy. But he is distracted. I think it is best for him to focus. Don't you?'

'So, he should join your firm and hide money for rich thieves?'

Uncle Stanley lights a cigarette and passes you the pack. Of course he would smoke Benson and Hedges, a brand that tasted of imperialism, despite being made in the same factory as Gold Leaf and Bristol. You take one and light it and watch the tip flare like a filament and then fade to soot. He watches you struggle with the matches but does not offer his lighter. DD boasted that his Appa had given up a two-pack habit after their mother croaked and how you could too if you listened to him.

'I thought you gave up.'

'Dilan didn't smoke till he met you. He used to blame me for his mother's cancer. We've had rough times but we're OK now. He is what I have. You must understand this.'

You puffed and wondered how you could extricate yourself from this chat. A bathroom break, perhaps.

'You were doing an unnatural act with that waiter, no? Have you tried that with my son?'

Stanley is leaning forward and smoking his Benson through a cupped hand.

'Why is it unnatural?'

'This is my son, you pig. I didn't send him to Cambridge to come home and get AIDS from a queer.'

The bodyguards in the corner are also smoking. They take a step forward when Stanley raises his voice and then step back when his hand goes up.

'You raised a pampered fool who knows nothing of this land or its people. I opened his eyes.'

'It is easy for a Malinda Kabalana to preach. You mix a young Tamil boy in your politics and you know what happens.'

'I would never put DD in danger.'

'That's why you invited him to Jaffna?'

'I would have looked after him,' you say.

'You wrote the word "Love" on this note. This is not natural.'

'Marriage is not natural. Cutlery isn't. Nor is religion. It's all man-made shit.'

'What would you know of love?'

'I care for him more than you do.'

'Then. You will take this money. And you will go.'

You looked at the sack on the table and the rupee notes on it.

'You caught me on a good night. Tonight finds me debt-free. I have quit all my clients. And I'm ready to go wherever DD wants. San Francisco, Tokyo, Timbuktu. I'm done with this shithole. And he'll be safer abroad.'

Stanley smoked silently and watched your face. You imagine a chessboard between you, his bishop versus your knight, both of you scheming to turn your pawn into a queen. But all that is on the table is an almost empty pack of Bensons, and a wad of cash that costs too much.

'Will you let him do his doctorate?'

'Whatever he wants.'

'And what will you do?'

'Photograph weddings and bar mitzvahs. Maybe get back into insurance. Whatever.'

'And the gambling habit?'

'I'm done.'

It didn't feel like a lie when you said it this time.

'Will you keep doing unnatural acts with bartenders?'

You paused and you considered and you took a breath.

'No, sir. I will be true to DD. And no one else.'

Stanley stubbed out the last cigarette and smiled. 'That's all I needed to hear, putha.' He raises his hand again and two shadows emerge from the dark.

You had seen them around the casinos many times before you knew who they were. In the years since 1983, Balal Ajith had shaved his beard and Kottu Nihal had acquired a belly, so you did not recognise them from the photos you enlarged at the behest of the Dark Queen and the Handsome Jack. The beast with the cleaver and the man lighting the fire.

How strange for the lone Tamil Cabinet Minister to be working with two thugs from '83, you thought, as they grabbed you and held you down. A stack of notes fell from your jeans and Kottu pocketed it, while Balal pulled on the things around your neck. You felt the chains cutting into your nape and you knew what each one felt like. The black string of the Panchayudha was coarse, the silver chain of the ankh was cool, and the twine of the cyanide capsules drew blood. As you felt your skin being garrotted, you thought that if they wanted to throttle you they should be pulling from the other end.

'I had all your chains cursed by a holy man. That's when I saw these capsules. Why should you wear a capsule around your neck if you are not a terrorist? Why garland yourself in poison unless you are ready to die?'

You could explain to Stanley that you did it in case you were captured, you did it in case someone else needed it, you did it to remind yourself that we are all a phone call away from a fade to black. But Stanley slapped you and punched your nose and squeezed the liquid into your mouth. You tried to spit but he locked your jaws with his paws. You bit down on his finger and he screamed and pulled at the Nikon 3ST around your neck and then brought it down on your face. Your eye exploded and your head snapped back and you caught a glimpse of Kottu and Balal. They both looked as astonished as you.

The camera smashed into your face two more times. Then you received the kick to your stomach that made you heave and gasp and swallow.

'Dilan is all I have. The rest can go to hell. You understand, no?'

You could not breathe, and you needed to breathe so you could vomit, and there was a chisel in your head and a hammer in your chest and needles in your gut. And you no longer wondered who the 'you' was, and who the person saying the 'you' was. Because both were you, and you were neither.

'You will clean up?' asked Stanley, wiping his hands with table napkins.

'Of course, sir,' said Balal.

'Don't mention to the Major, please.'

'Sir, we did not expect this,' said Kottu. 'We only came to kidnap. How to take this body downstairs like this?'

'I didn't expect this either,' said Stanley. 'He gave me no choice.'

Balal nods and Kottu shakes his head.

'Sir, it will be a higher cost to take out this garbage.'

'You can take the money on the table.'

'In vain, sir. If you had told we would have taken him to a better place.'

'Goodnight.'

You heard the tread of his polished shoes on the dusty terrace, dragging his feet like his beautiful son. You were blinded and shivering. You waited for your life to flash before you but all you saw was shadow and cloud. All you heard was the voice of the father telling you to put your best foot forward and the mother telling you to stop sulking and the silly boy asking you to speak to his father and the sad girl saying OK. You opened your eyes and you were floating above the terrace and you could see through every floor.

Your vision X-rayed through Hotel Leo's walls, as if death had turned you into Superman. You saw the gamblers on the fifth floor and the pimps on the fourth and the whores having teas in the mall below and Elsa and Kuga arguing like cousin-brother and sister in the suite on the eighth. And then, on the sixth, you saw two thugs lifting a coiled tyre and hurling it off the edge. Like the tyres that they burned people on, except this tyre uncoiled and revealed itself to be a body. You flew down with it and thought of excuses and reasons and all the people who would never hear them.

As the body banged against the side of the building, it left blotches of crimson and obsidian, of scarlet and ebony, and you felt a thousand screams gushing past you. And you felt something that wasn't quite comforting but wasn't all that unpleasant. Something that was invisible and true, the semblance of a microscopic point in this gargantuan waste of space.

You saw DD's face and how different it was from his father's and you saw him on a plane landing somewhere sunny and you pictured him purifying poisoned wells and you daydreamed of him smiling. You imagined him lending his life to some pointless cause just like you had and it made you happy. We must all find pointless causes to live for, or why bother with breath?

Because, on reflection, once you have seen your own face and recognised the colour of your eyes, tasted the air and smelled the soil, drunk from the purest fountains and the dirtiest wells, that is the kindest thing you can say about life. It's not nothing.

..

When your body hit the tarmac, it made no sound, or at least none that could be heard over the din of the city and the hum at the end of the earth. You felt your self split into the you and the I, and then into the many yous and the infinite Is that you have been before and will be again. You woke to an endless waiting room. You looked around and it was a dream and, for once, you knew it was a dream and you were happy to wait it out. All things passed, especially dreams.

You woke with the answer to the question that everyone asks. The answer was 'Yes'. The answer was 'Just Like There But Worse'. That's all the insight you had, so you decided to go back to sleep.

THE LIGHT

'The bees knew it first.
Then the ice. Then the trees.
Then all the world's mothers.'

Tess Clare via Twitter

Five Drinks

The water does not hurt your eyes. In fact, it soothes them like a warm towel dipped in lemongrass and cinnamon and served at those hotels down south which you frequented with rich men. The water is not blue or green or blue-green, but white. The same white that a Ladybird book once told you was made from every colour in the spectrum. Though, when you went to art class and mixed every paint you could find, all you got was black.

The water swirls in currents and pulls you to its depths, past shoals of eel, schools of fish and rocks coated in algae. The stones form curious shapes under the water, revealing crevices that hide sources of light. Raindrops pierce the surface above you and send bubbles sinking to the bottom of the pool. You dive deeper and find yourself at the mouth of a cave, shielded by rolling water and jagged rock.

The walls and ceilings and floors are scrambled-egg-yellow and the light widens your eyes. You move forward because it is the only direction. Walls to your sides, a babbling brook at your feet and light ahead. The walls and ceilings become mirrors, each curve reflecting light onto the other. And, if you walk slowly enough and tilt at the right angle, you can catch your reflection. Your eyes go from green to blue to brown. But your ears, they do not change.

'You made it just in time, Maal,' says Dr Ranee. 'Everything has to be last-minute with you, no?' She is seated at a thin table with crockery on it, as if it were a banquet for one.

'The Light is just mirrors? Not heaven or God or your mother's birth canal?'

'I didn't think you'd make it, putha,' she says. 'It's good that you're here.'

'Now what?'

'You have to drink.'

'I'm not thirsty.'

'Sit.'

You take a seat at the table. There are only cups, each of different size and colour. There are five of them. A teacup with golden liquid, a mug with purple fluid, a shot glass with amber liquor, a king coconut with a straw in it, and a bowl of gotukola porridge, that panacea for colds and coughs, bruises and bugbites, inflicted by many Lankan Ammas on helpless toddlers.

She smiles at you and, for once, she does not raise a clipboard or an eyebrow. 'The tea is if you wish to forget everything. The Portello is if you wish to remember. The arrack is if you'd like to forgive the world. This I recommend. The thambili is if you'd like to be forgiven. The kola kenda is if you'd like to go where you most belong.'

'And I suppose taking a sip from each is out of the question?'

'You suppose correctly.'

'So, this is it? What if I'm a coffee drinker?'

'You're not.'

'What if I feel like a Portello but I want to be forgiven?'

'If you wanted to do pros and cons, you shouldn't have waited till your seventh moon.'

'I was a pro. My life was a con.'

'No time for dumb jokes, either.'

'So, how do I choose?'

'I think you know.'

You look around at the reflecting mirrors and at the woman in the white robes. You walk to her and you hug her like you never hugged your mother.

'I hope your children live long lives. And I hope you and your husband are twinned for eternity.' You don't know why you say it, only that you mean it.

'That is very kind, Maal. Now drink.'

You take off your sandal and place it on the floor. You take off the ankh, the Panchayudha and the crumpled capsules in twine and place them on the table. You wipe your camera with your bandanna, which you place next to your chains. Then you put your camera down.

It was never a contest. You have no more time for intoxication and you have no thirst left to slake or sweet tooth to indulge. Fresh kola kenda is indistinguishable from kola kenda gone bad. Old joke. You reach for the slimy green porridge and pour it down your gullet. You close your nose and you hold your breath and wait for it to take you to the place you need to be.

QUESTIONS

You wake in the presence of the one true God. You recognise her, though you forget her name.

You do not wake and you know not that you do not wake. The sweetest thing about oblivion is it cannot be felt.

You wake in your mother's birth canal and swim towards the light and when you reach it you scream with disappointment.

You wake naked next to DD and cannot remember what day it is.

None of the above.

You are at a white desk and you are standing, though your feet do not bear the weight of your body or your soul. On the table is a telephone with a circular dial and a ledger book. You are wearing a white smock and an Om around your neck, and before you are a throng of people and they are all shouting and you cannot hear them.

You cover your ears and blink your eyes and the sound whooshes at you like an unexpected wind. They are all spitting questions at you, ones that you have no answers for.

'I can't be here. How do I get out?'

'I need to see my babas. Where are they?'

'Not saying it's your fault, but mistakes happen, no? Can you send me back?'

You blink again and the sound goes off. You look around and you know this place. It is filled to infinity with screaming souls and fools in white who cannot help them. And now it appears that one of those fools is you.

The phone rings. The voice is a familiar one, though you cannot put a name to it. 'Open the book. If you need answers, open the book.' Click.

Before you is a ledger book with the design of a bo leaf on the cover. You open it. There are just four small words, handwritten on ruled paper in a hand that you recognise as your own. The words distil the wisdom of millennia, insight from when the universe was first audited.

The words read: *One at a time.*

You look at the faces of the throng, you spy old people and teenagers, people in saris and hospital smocks, people with shadows under their eyes and wails on their lips. And then a face you know. You blink at him and you hear only his voice while the rest of the crowd scream on mute.

'I come here every Poya,' says the Dead Atheist. 'Just to see if you guys have anything new to offer.'

'Name?'

He places his decapitated head on the counter, tilts it upwards, fixes you with his marble eyes, and sneers at you with his hook nose.

'Spare me the routine.'

'How may I help?'

'My children are teenagers now. They have grown obnoxious. I no longer enjoy watching them.'

'So you want to enter The Light now?'

'What's on the other side? I ask every Poya and none of you pricks can tell me.'

He was the first ghost to talk to you seven moons ago. And it seems the moons have not been kind.

'They say it's different for everyone.'

'I've heard this one.'

'But, basically, it is a casino,' you say. 'You get to pick a drink or a card or...'

'Or a virgin? Have I told you my theory of virgins?'

'You basically get to choose where you go next.'

'And you chose this.'

'It chose me.'

'Smells like bullshit.'

'Sorry you feel that way.'

'Is that what your book tells you to say?'

'Yes.'

'So, do I get compensated for being shot by the JVP?'

You look at the man and the ledger book in front of you and decide not to open another page. 'You get to spin the wheel. Because that is what the game is. Lankan roulette. The JVP who killed you are dead. You can spend the next thousand moons cursing them. Or you can take a spin. What will you choose?'

He frowns and scratches his head, like a sceptic trying to explain away a miracle. 'Screw you,' he says and walks away.

..

In that first moon, after a shaky start, you send eight souls into The Light and thirteen away for Ear Checks. Moses and He-Man are your line managers and they nod in unison, though offer little in the way of instruction or praise. Everyone who comes to you is dead and damaged and reminds you of the women and children from the border villages who squatted and screamed while their homes burned. For the most part, you follow the ledger book, though at times you depart from the script.

Like when the lady in an engineer's helmet asks why she had to die in an LTTE bomb blast, when she protected hundreds of Tamil labourers from the '83 pogroms. Why, despite a lifetime of wearing hard hats she had to die of a head injury. You open the book and it says:

Karma evens out over lifetimes. If the wronged reach
The Light, they are sent Somewhere Better.

Somewhere Better is a euphemism that the book coughs up a lot. Moses tells you it is to avoid theological arguments with those religiously inclined, which, after death, are surprisingly few. You told the engineer and her headgear that she can complain about it if she wishes or she can go into The Light. But the result will remain the same. 'It's how it works. You receive outrageous fortune long after you have forgotten your tragedy. And vice versa. The only thing you need to be is patient.'

She shakes your hand and smiles. 'Should I keep my helmet on?'

'I carried a camera around my neck for seven moons. It only weighed me down.'

'And what if something falls on my head?' she says.

'Something will always fall on your head,' you say.

'I've worked on construction sites in Kandy,' she says. 'You don't need to tell me that.'

'And did you blame gravity or the hills when that happened?'

'If it's all the same to you,' she says, 'I think I'll keep my hat.'

..

Dr Ranee congratulates you on your numbers. She invites He-Man and Moses to celebrate at the edge of Galle Face Green, just across the road from where you used to live. You celebrate with a sunrise and a cool breeze. Up Here as it is Down There. And you shrug off any praise.

'Was just dumb luck. I'm not recruiting anyone. I haven't drunk the kola kenda.'

'Not true,' says the good doc.

'Is this a joke that I ended up here?'

'Is it a joke that you end up anywhere?' says Moses.

'No such thing as ending up,' says He-Man. 'You are now. And you won't be soon.'

'I thought we were off duty,' you say. 'Enough with the sermons.'

'We are pleased at your progress,' says Dr Ranee.

'Can I go back and choose a different drink?' you ask.

'If you want,' says Doc. 'Like going to a casino and asking for the same hand.'

Drivermalli comes to your counter looking like a prosthetic man. His head is disconnected from his body, as are his limbs from his torso. He doesn't know who you are. Why would he? He submits his ola leaf and you send him to Level Forty-Two. He comes back more traumatised than before and you send him through the yellow door just like the ledger book tells you.

He shakes his head and walks to the edge of the corridor, where a familiar figure dressed in black garbage nods and grins. Sena is flanked by ghouls in cloaks and, when Drivermalli reaches them, they welcome him like a lost brother, which Drivermalli most certainly is. You alert security, but by the time He-Man gets there Sena and the ghouls have left, taking Drivermalli as their newest recruit. This could be your problem if you make it. So you don't.

· ·

The Dead Lovers from Galle Face Court come holding hands and they look at you and smile. The boy recognises you.

'You lived at our place, no?'

'A long time ago.'

He turns to her and nods at you. 'Remember, Dolly. This one used to screw that dark boy.'

She wears pink chiffon today and looks like she's been crying.

'We had a big fight,' she says. 'We think it's time to separate. I guess after fifty years, the honeymoon is over.'

'That's sad,' you say.

'We are tired of watching couples under umbrellas. All they do is lie to each other while they grope,' she says.

'So, will we be punished for being suicides?' asks he.

You open the ledger book and read what it says:

The universe does not care what you do with your meat suit

You repeat this to them.

'Really?'

'There's no shortage of meat,' you say.

'So, even we can go into The Light?' they ask.

'If that's your choice.'

'But is anything better than a sunset at Galle Face viewed from the top floor?' asks he.

You think of Niagara Falls and Paris and Tokyo and San Francisco and all the other places you never took DD to. You don't know the answer, but pretend that you do. You shake your head and watch them smile.

..

DD packs for Hong Kong after his father's death. He turns up at the funeral with a white boy in spectacles and you wonder about things not worth wondering about. But, strangely, you feel something that feels a lot like pride. If you were put on this earth to help this beautiful boy out of the closet, then it can't have all been a waste.

Lucky Almeida joins the Mothers' Front and campaigns for mothers whose children have been disappeared. You visit her in dreams and tell her that it is OK and that you don't blame her and that you are sorry for it all.

Jaki moves in with newsreader Radika Fernando and has amazing sex and never calls out for you once.

Lanka disintegrates. War continues and the people comfort themselves that the current lot weren't as bad as the last lot, even though in many ways they are worse.

The government denies that the blast that killed twenty-three took place at a government office. The Minister, who survives with injuries, says the building belonged to an Asian Fisheries company where he was called to discuss marine exports. He thanks his doctor, his well-wishers and his astrologer.

The Mahatiya faction is discovered by the Supremo and his wrath is brutal. Two platoons of traitors are tied up in caves down by Vakarai and beaten until the tide rolled in to drown them. The LTTE go after all associates of Colonel Gopallaswarmy. Among them, a Colombo-based organisation called CNTR, whose offices at Hotel Leo are bombed, despite there being no one there.

··

You tell Dr Ranee that you would like to be reborn, but not just yet. You are savouring some rest between what was and what will be. You are resting in peace though you have no grave. You say you will stay till your mother passes over, and she thinks this a good idea.

You settle into a routine that you enjoy and even look forward to. Even on the sad days, when you have to process young children or those leaving lovers behind, you come to realise that every death is significant, even when every life appears not to be.

You have stopped calling out for your father, because you know he is nowhere near and never will be. And even if he did hear and even if he did come, he would not recognise you, because you were not even a supporting actor in his life, merely an extra. See you later, Dada. We never even got to say hello.

When he finally appears, he looks dishevelled and confused. But, you feel no rage towards him, only sorrow. He was a man protecting a child he never knew. Fighting for a country that doesn't exist.

He is dressed in the suit from his funeral, his eyes green and yellow and his face is dusty and sad, Stanley Dharmendran seems stunned to see you. Then he looks you in the eye and bows his head. 'I'm truly sorry,' he says. 'I did it because—'

'It doesn't matter,' you say.

'Thank God Dilan is OK.'

'That is true. Thank Whoever.'

'Can I speak to him?'

'That will take deals with your old friend the Crow Man. Which I personally don't advise. I can sign you up for a Dream Walking course at Level 36. Though results can be variable.'

'He has a new foreign friend. They are performing intercourse.'

'Thanks for the update.'

'What if they go to San Francisco? That place is full of AIDS.'

'Uncle Stanley, there is nothing you can do about things Down There. The sooner you accept that, the better.

'So then what?'

'Meaning?'

'What now?'

'Now is where I forgive you.'

'But I don't know where I am.'

'Then. Uncle Stanley.' You do the signature pause. 'You came. To the right place.'

Where Did Lionel Go?

So what about your photos? Did they shake up the world? Did they burst the Colombo bubble?

They stay on those walls for weeks after the bomb, but you can't bring yourself to go to the Lionel Wendt. You stay clear of places where the likelihood of bumping into Sena or the Mahakali is high. Dr Ranee assures you that no demon can touch you, now that you are wearing the white robes, but you are not fully assured.

When you finally venture there alone, you are unsurprised to find the gallery empty. Your photographs have attracted more spirits, though very few humans. Perhaps because it is monsoon season and humid as hell or because people had better things to look at than black-and-white prints of dead bodies. Ghouls and pretas and poltergeists come to you to chat, but you are done talking about pictures.

On the sixth day, Kugarajah arrives and helps himself to the 1983 photos, the IPKF killings and ten photos of dead Tamil villagers. He startles the Dead Tourists who are mesmerised by that pangolin taken at sunset.

'Mate! He's stealing your stuff,' the Britisher yells at the security guard. The guard, an old man in a brown uniform, ambles up to Kugarajah as he makes for the exit nearest the sign saying *Law of the Jungle. Photography by MA.*

'I am the owner of these photos,' says Kugarajah as he barges past him. The old man in the brown uniform shrugs and goes back to yawning on his stool.

You are afraid that the dead from the photos will find you and berate you for your unflattering portrayals. But most of the bodies in your shots perished a long way from this gallery. If you were them, you'd let the universe devour you, so you could finally drink of that blessed oblivion and be done with this lottery.

..

A few days later, Radika and Jaki come in while DD stays in the car with his bespectacled white boy. He tells them that he wants nothing to do with your photos or your death and Radika pretends to look concerned.

'Why don't you take a break from work? See if you want to stay in Lanka or not. If you need to talk...'

'Stick to newsreading,' says DD and drives off.

You try to follow, but the Crow Man's curse repels you. The air pushes you away and the wind refuses to carry you.

Radika walks around the exhibition with Jaki, shaking her head as she looks at the framed atrocities. 'What was this damn fool thinking?'

'He thought photographs were the best way to end the war.'

'Are you going to make a report about your abduction?'

'To whom?'

'We will report those cops.'

'I don't remember any cops. Just the one who helped me escape.'

'Why don't we go away this weekend? I don't think coming here's a good idea.'

'Maali wanted the Colombo bubble to see the real Sri Lanka.'

Radika looks around the empty gallery. She sees not the clamour of ghosts, only the spaces between them.

'Looks like Colombo isn't one bit interested.'

Jaki takes a seat by the door and asks Radika to leave. That afternoon, a few visitors trickle in. A parade of students, a collective of artists, a tutorial of professors and a van of journalists. Many of them are shocked and awed and you feel equal parts hubris and indignation when some of them take photographs of your photos. By evening, word has spread and there is a stream of visitors. You recognise a few from the theatre scene, a few from the music scene, and others from the teledrama scene. Some more famous than others. Some not very impressed.

Jonny Gilhooley arrives with Bob Sudworth. They shake their heads and say very little. Jonny removes the two photos showing the meeting of the Major, the Colonel and Sudworth. He also helps himself to a few of the nude pictures that Clarantha had put up after DD left, despite your instructions. Byron, Hudson and Boy George. Another theft that barely disturbs the security guard's nap.

Your acquaintances from the press come and begin sharing stories. Jeyaraj, from the *Observer*, says you were a fool, while Athas, from *The Times*, says you were a genius. This is the closest to a eulogy that you will ever get.

Jonny goes up to Jaki at the door and whispers in her ear. You float close enough to eavesdrop. 'Get out of here now, sweetheart. They will burn this gallery to the ground.'

'OK,' says Jaki and does not move. Perhaps she feels emboldened by dating the ex of a Minister's nephew. Most likely, she has not calculated the odds and therefore does not care. She sits there all evening, as the place begins to throng and people are asking each other who this MA is, and then a high-pitched voice pierces the air as if through a foghorn, even though Minister Cyril Wijeratne does not hold one.

The Minister has a bandaged leg and an arm in a cast. He sits in a wheelchair, propelled by Detective Cassim. The Detective looks like he has worked overtime since the blast. He sees Jaki seated in the corner and catches her eye. Jaki stares at him as if wanting to say 'Sorry but I've forgotten whatever I promised you and Stanley is dead'. What she would like to say is 'Thank you for saving me', but she's unsure how to convey that with a gesture, and then Cassim averts his eyes and pushes the Minister forward.

The Minister grunts, his feeble frame shuddering. 'Ladies and gentlemen, due to dangerous intelligence reports, a curfew will be declared at 9 p.m. today. I advise that you make your way home as swiftly as you can.'

There is chatter and there are shouts and then there is panic as a bottleneck forms at the entrance and the Colombo 7 bubble begins to burst, jostling like a Colombo 10 bazaar. They do not see the Minister's Demon walking beside the wheelchair. He gives you a wink and a nod.

The men who are neither army nor police position themselves at the exits as the Minister makes Cassim wheel him around the exhibition. He pauses at a photo, points to it, and then Cassim dutifully takes it down. You watch in silence as photos of dead journalists, kidnapped activists and beaten priests are erased from your walls, along with exploded planes, dead villagers and rabid mobs.

After the Minister leaves, with a lapful of frames, so do the spirits. You do not know if this is out of respect for you or out of boredom. You end up alone before walls filled with gaps. You hear the Dead Tourists bang the jukebox in the Arts Centre upstairs, and on comes a song your Dada used to love, that you ended up loathing. 'The Gambler' by that great philosopher Kenneth Ray Rogers.

The photos that remain came from only one of your five envelopes. They show sunsets and sunrises, hills of tea and crystal beaches, pangolins and peacocks, elephants with their young, and a beautiful boy and a wonderful girl running through strawberry fields. It is the envelope titled the Perfect Ten, and it pleases you like your own work rarely ever does.

And even though the photos are black and white, they gleam incandescent like all the colours of a royal flush. This island is a beautiful place, despite being filled with fools and savages. And if these photos of yours are the only ones that outlive you, maybe that's an ace that you can keep.

CHAT WITH DEAD LEOPARD

'The only God worth knowing is electricity,' says the Dead Leopard, standing upright at the counter, paws on your ledger book. 'It is true sorcery worth kneeling before.'

'What do you know of electricity?' you say, watching the queue behind him lurch back as if a fart had poisoned the air. 'And how are you speaking without moving those... are those lips?'

You have had many visits over the moons you have been at this counter, but never a member of the animal kingdom. You point to the ledger book and the beast shuffles to the left, removing its paws. You pick up the book and open it and read seven words:

Animals have souls.
Every living thing does.

The leopard studies you with its eyes and you are startled. Its eyes are not green or yellow, as on most dead beasts you have encountered. They are not brown or blue like those of the *sapiens*. They are white. 'When the cabins in Block Three at Yala got electricity, I was impressed. I spent night after night hiding outside them, marvelling at the fluorescent lamps. If barbarian monkeys could create something like this, imagine what I could do.'

'How can I help?'

'I want to be reborn as *Homo sapiens*. And you will assist.'

'That's not my job.'

'I need tools to create. The human meat suit comes well equipped.'

'Not sure I can help you.'

'Then let me meet the Creator. I will plead my case.'

'I don't believe in Creators.'

'Don't be silly. Even slaughterhouse pigs believe in a Creator.'

'I don't believe anyone is watching over anything.'

The leopard snorts and licks its paw.

'Why should a Creator watch over you? Wasn't creating you enough?'

It is not often you are stumped by a feline. This jungle cat appears to have a larger soul than most of the former *Homo sapiens* who have darkened your counter.

'I guess every creature thinks itself the centre of the universe.'

'I don't. Because we're not. We are microcosms,' says the leopard. 'An ant colony contains the universe. Though it is not its centre.'

'Big word to describe a tiny thing,' you say, and the animal blushes like a kitten.

'I've spent a lot of time staring at insects.'

'They do say insects control more of this planet than humans.'

You flip the page of your ledger book and stare at the words:

Do not get drawn into conversations you wish to exit.

'Insects have genius. No doubt. There are thousands of species on both land and water far more intelligent than humans.'

'Look, I have a busy shift.'

'But none have invented lightbulbs yet.'

The leopard proves difficult to dismiss. You flip the pages of your ledger, but find nothing of use.

'You want to invent lightbulbs?'

'I have prowled your cities and observed how you live. It is both disgusting and remarkable.'

'What's wrong with being a leopard? You're the king of the jungle over here.'

'Not when the jungle keeps disappearing.'

'You sound like a boy I once knew.'

'I tried to survive without killing. Lasted a month. What to do? I'm a savage beast. Only humans can practise compassion properly. Only humans can live without being cruel.'

'Aren't most herbivores kind?'

'Rabbits don't have a choice. Humans do. I want a taste of that.'

'There's not much to taste.'

'Everybody is just trying not to get eaten. I need a break from the food chain.'

'Have you had... your ears checked?'

'Of course.'

'There is no animal more savage than a human.'

'Of that, I have no doubt. But most evil can be cleansed from within.'

'When you're a human, you won't remember being a leopard.'

'How did you get this job, if you have no clue how things work? Nothing is forgotten. We just don't remember where we put it.'

'Maybe we should swap places,' you say.

'That is precisely what I am suggesting.'

'Most *sapiens* are disappointed with themselves. Be careful what you...'

'Yes, yes. I've heard this. But you can create light with some wires and a switch. I'll take my chances.'

'Not sure if you get to choose.'

'Oh, that is one thing I am certain of. We all get to choose. If you can't bring me back as a human, bring me back as a leopard with the smarts of a queen bee, the soul of a blue whale and the opposable thumbs of a savage monkey, cos opposable thumbs are essential when screwing bulbs.'

Confused, you open the ledger book and read what it tells you to do.

. .

You go moons without thinking of DD and the boys who fondled you. You lose track of the country's wars as they morph into conflicts unrecognisable from their causes. You hear that Drivermalli has joined Sena, who has taken his army up north and was last seen trying to assassinate an Indian prime minister. And then, while perched on your favourite mara tree in your favourite cemetery, you hear your name floating on the wind like a crumpled leaf.

'Malinda Almeida. He was my best friend.'

You catch the breeze and let it throw you into the air. You are unsurprised to find yourself in Galle Face Court on that famous terrace.

Jaki is in shorts and has cropped her hair and speaks into a phone that doesn't have a wire. 'Did you ever meet him?'

The voice on the other end sounds American and confused. 'I'm sorry. What is this about?'

'You are Tracy Kabalana?'

'How did you get my number?'

'Did you receive a parcel of photos from Sri Lanka last year?'

'My dad was Sri Lankan. He passed away years ago. I never knew my half-brother. Mom never spoke his name. I haven't opened the parcel.'

'I'd be happy to buy the photographs from you. All of them.'

'I don't know where it is. It might have been thrown away.'

'He spoke fondly of you, Tracy.' Jaki lies like a poker player, though that doesn't make what she said untrue.

'I'm sorry, lady. I can't deal with this right now. I gotta go.' Click.

Jaki swears and lies back on the beanbag. Radika Fernando runs fingers through her cropped hair and shakes her head.

'Has she got them?'

'The girl is all of fifteen. What was Maali thinking?'

'He once told me that you were stupidly in love with him,' says Radika. Her newsreader voice is nowhere in sight.

'When?'

'That night at your flat. When we first kissed. He told me to set you up with a nice Tamil boy.'

'So you did the opposite,' says Jaki, stroking the fingers at her scalp.

Radika picks up two photo frames and places them on Jaki's lap.

'Are we ready to pack these?'

'Why?'

'How many times to tell, Jaki? You want me to move in or not?'

'Can I keep one?'

'No.'

'Why?'

'Because I want you to see me, not him.'

Both photos had been lifted from the exhibition at the Lionel Wendt. One was of you and Jaki in a tree house overlooking the great rock near Kurunegala, which Queen Kuveni threw herself from, leaving only her curse. The other was a shot of four bodies, taken from the top floor of a broken building. A woman and her baby, an old man with glasses, and a pariah dog. Each is surrounded by shrapnel, though that is not what killed them.

Jaki nods and lets Radika put both photos in a box, which she carries away. Jaki sighs and closes her eyes and does not hear you say goodbye.

· ·

Dr Ranee is not at the River of Births when you lead the leopard there. You take the weakest wind but you cannot find the three kumbuk trees. The river is empty and still, and there is no one floating on it.

The leopard growls and claws at the tree by the waters. 'I've met sloth bears smarter than you.'

'I'm helping you. So maybe ease on the insults.'

'I believe it is I who am helping you.'

'Whatever you say.'

'I met an elephant in Udawalawe who predicted the coming of the next Buddha.'

'When is that?'

'Not for 200,000 moons.'

'Superb prediction.'

'I met shadow creatures who live in mirrors and watch you watching yourself.'

'Sounds like fun.'

'I've met a pacifist eagle who refused to hunt mice and let her chicks starve.'

'Most cold-blooded killers I've met say they hate killing. It's usually another slice of bullshit.'

'I've watched your kind. Both as beast and as ghost. I can't understand why humans destroy when they can create. Such a waste.'

'There it is. One, two... three kumbuk trees. If you jump in front of the third, the river will take you.'

'Where?'

'Where you need to be.'

'I need to be human.'

'Drink from the right bowl and maybe you will be.'

The leopard inches closer to the bank and dips a paw in the waters.

'That's damn cold. Why don't you jump with me?'

'I don't want to be reborn.'

'Why not?'

'I may come back a leopard.'

'None taken. You really want to spend eternity behind a counter?'

'It's not bad. You meet some odd characters.'

'Jump with me.'

'Are you Dr Ranee in disguise?'

'Who?'

And then you tell him about Ranee and Sena and Stanley and DD and about boxes under beds. The leopard sits on a branch and listens till the moon is high in the sky.

It arches its limbs and this is how you would photograph it if you still had a broken Nikon around your broken neck. But you don't, so you blink, and imagine that you do.

The leopard nods its head and shakes its tail and jumps into the water. And right then, with the moon in the sky, you realise you have nothing left to tell and no one left to tell it to. You recognise this as a simple fact and are neither dismayed nor gladdened.

So, you jump.

And when you jump you know three things.

That the brightness of The Light will force you to open your eyes wider. That you will choose the same drink and it will take you somewhere new. And that, when you get there, you will have forgotten all of the above.

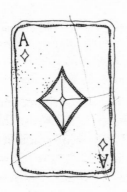